Lara Adrian lives with her husband in coastal New England, surrounded by centuries-old graveyards, hip urban comforts, and the endless inspiration of the broody Atlantic Ocean.

'Evocative, enticing, erotic . . . Enter Lara Adrian's vampire world and be enchanted.'

J. R. Ward, *New York Times* bestselling author

'A thrilling blend of dark passion and heart-pounding action. Lara Adrian always delivers a keeper!

Gena Showalter, *New York Times* bestselling author

ASHES
OF
MIDNIGHT

LARA ADRIAN

ROBINSON

Constable & Robinson Ltd
3 The Lanchesters
162 Fulham Palace Road
LondonW6 9ER
www.constablerobinson.com

First published in the US by Bantam Dell,
1745 Broadway, New York, NY 10019

This edition published by Robinson,
an imprint of Constable & Robinson Ltd, 2009

A copy of the British Library Cataloguing in Publication
Data is available from the British Library.

ISBN: 978-1-84901-105-1

Printed and bound in the EU.

To the phoenix that lives in all of us:
strong, glorious, indestructible.

ACKNOWLEDGMENTS

With gratitude and appreciation to my editor, Shauna Summers, and everyone on the publishing team at Bantam Dell, and to my agent, Karen Solem. It truly is a joy working with you all!

Big hugs to Zazoo, Picky, Gem, Jules, Pebbles, Sly, Rangi, Mandy, and the rest of the amazing crew at the Midnight Breed fan forum for all your friendship, love, and support (not to mention the gorgeous eye candy!). You blow me away with everything you do!

A debt of thanks to my writer friends Kayla Gray, Patricia Rasey, Elizabeth Boyle, Larissa Ione, Jaci Burton, and Stephanie Tyler for understanding when I need to unplug from the world for often weeks at a time, yet still stand by, ready to pick up right where we left off or jump in with a quick read. You are the best!

Last, but never least, thanks and all my love to my husband for giving me the kind of happily-ever-after that many would say could only exist in fiction. Here's to the next twenty years.

⇥ CHAPTER ONE ⇤

BERLIN, GERMANY

The vampire had no idea that death awaited him in the darkness.

His senses were overloaded with need, his hands and arms full of a half-dressed redhead who pawed at him with barely restrained lust. Too fevered to notice they weren't alone in his Darkhaven bedchamber, he willed open the carved double doors and guided his eager, panting prey inside. The woman teetered on a pair of tall heels, laughing as she twisted away from him and wagged a finger in front of her face.

'Hans, you fed me too mush champagne,' she slurred, stumbling into the dark room. 'My head's all woozy.'

'It will pass.' The German vampire's words were sluggish, too, though not from the alcohol that had inebriated his unsuspecting American companion. His fangs were no doubt filling his mouth, saliva flooding over his tongue in anticipation of feeding.

He tracked her with deliberate movements as he closed the doors behind him and prowled toward her. His eyes glowed like embers, transforming from their natural color to something otherworldly. Although the woman seemed oblivious to the change coming over him, the vampire held his head low as he approached her, careful to conceal the telling heat of his

⇥ 1 ⇤

bloodthirsty gaze. Except for that shuttered amber glow and the dim twinkle of stars outside the tall windows overlooking the Darkhaven estate's private grounds, there was no light in the room. Then again, being one of the Breed, he could see well enough without it.

So could the one who came to kill him.

Enveloped in shadows across the large chamber, a dark gaze watched as the vampire grabbed his blood Host from behind and got down to business. The first pungent copper whiff of the human's pierced vein made the observer's fangs erupt from his gums in reflexive response. He hungered, too, more urgently than he wanted to admit, but he had come here for a greater purpose than to serve his own base needs.

He had come for vengeance.

For justice.

It was that overriding mission that held Andreas Reichen's feet firmly to the floor as the other vampire drank greedily, blindly, across the room. He waited, patient only because he knew this male's death would bring him one step closer to fulfilling the vow he'd made some twelve weeks ago . . . the night his world had disintegrated into a pile of ash and rubble.

Reichen's restraint was held on a threadbare leash. Inside he churned with the heat of his anger. His bones felt like hot iron rods beneath his skin. His blood raced through his body, liquid fire that seared him from scalp to heels. Every muscle and cell within him screamed for retribution – screamed it with a fury that bordered on nuclear meltdown.

Not here, he warned himself. *Not that.*

The price would be steep if he gave in to the full measure of his rage, and by God, this son of a bitch wasn't worth it.

Reichen held that explosive part of himself at bay, but the effort came a fraction of a second too late. The fire in him was already swelling, burning through the fragile tethers of his self-control . . .

The other vampire suddenly lifted his head from where he'd been feeding at the woman's neck. He drew in a sharp breath through his nose, then grunted, animalistic . . . alarmed. 'Someone is here.'

'What'd you say?' she murmured, still drowsy from his bite as he sealed her wound with his tongue then shoved her away from him. She staggered forward, huffing a couple of choice curses under her breath. The instant her sluggish gaze lit on Reichen, a scream ripped from her throat. 'Oh, my God!'

Feeling his eyes smoldering with the amber fire of his rage, his fangs tearing through his gums in readiness of the fight to come, Reichen took a single step out of the shadows.

The woman screamed again, hysteria rising in her wild, panicked eyes. She looked to her companion for protection, but the vampire had no further use of her. With a callous sweep of his hand, he knocked her out of his way and stalked forward. The blow sent her careening to the floor.

'Hans!' she cried. 'Oh, God – what's going on?'

Hissing, the vampire faced his unexpected intruder and crouched into an attack stance. Reichen had only a moment to cast a quick glance at the confused, terrified human.

'Get out of here.' He sent a mental command that unlocked the bedchamber's doors and swung them open. 'Leave, female. Now!'

As she scrambled up from the polished marble beneath her and escaped the room, the Darkhaven vampire leapt into the air in a single, fluid arc of motion. Before his feet could touch down, Reichen launched himself at the bastard.

Their bodies collided, the explosion of Reichen's forward momentum propelling both of them across the width of the chamber. Fangs huge and gnashing, fierce amber eyes locked on each other in the deadliest kind of malice, together they crashed like a wrecking ball into the far wall.

Bones cracked with the impact, but it wasn't enough for

Reichen.

Not nearly enough.

He threw the struggling, furious Breed male to the floor and pinned him there, one knee crushing his throat.

'Ignorant fool!' roared the vampire, arrogant despite his pain. 'Have you any idea who I am?'

'I know who you are – Enforcement Agent Hans Friedrich Waldemar.' Reichen bared his teeth and fangs in a profanity of a smile as he glared down at him. 'Don't tell me you have already forgotten who I am.'

No, he hadn't forgotten. Recognition flickered behind the pain and fear in Waldemar's slitted pupils. 'Son of a bitch . . . Andreas Reichen.'

'That's right.' Reichen held the bastard in a gaze so deadly furious it must have burned to hold it. 'What's the matter, Agent Waldemar? You seem surprised to see me.'

'I – I don't understand. The attack on the Darkhaven this past summer . . .' The vampire sucked in a choked breath. 'I'd heard no one survived.'

'Almost no one,' Reichen corrected tightly.

And now Waldemar knew why he'd been paid this unexpected visit. There was no mistaking the bleak awareness in the other male's gaze. Or the stark fear. When he spoke now, his voice shook a bit. 'I had nothing to do with it, Andreas. You must believe me –'

Reichen snorted. 'That's what the others said, too.'

Waldemar started to squirm, but Reichen pressed down harder with his knee planted heavily against the vampire's throat. Waldemar wheezed, trying to raise his hands as the weight began to crush his air channel. 'Please . . . just tell me what you want from me.'

'Justice.'

With neither satisfaction nor remorse, Reichen grabbed Waldemar's head in his hands and gave a fierce yank. His neck snapped, then the Breed male's head fell back to the floor with a heavy *thunk*.

Reichen exhaled a deep sigh that did little to purge his anguish, or the grief he felt at being alive and alone. The sole survivor. The last of his family line.

As he stood and prepared to leave this latest death behind him, a glint of polished glass on one of the room's several mahogany bookcases caught his eye. He stalked over to it, his feet moving automatically, sharpened gaze fixed on the face of his enemy that stared out from within the silver-framed photograph. He grabbed the picture and stared down at it, his fingers hot where they pressed into the metal of the frame. Reichen's eyes burned the longer he looked at that hated face, a growl curling low in his throat, raw with visceral, still-smoldering rage.

Wilhelm Roth stood among a small group of Breed males wearing ceremonial Enforcement Agency garb. All of them were decked out in black tuxedos and starched white shirts, their chests festooned with bright silk sashes and gleaming pendant medallions, gilded rapiers sheathed at their sides. Reichen snorted at the self-importance – the power-hungry arrogance – etched in those smug, smiling faces.

Now they were dead men . . . all but one.

He'd saved Roth for last, having meticulously worked his way up the chain of command. First the Agency death squad members who'd ambushed his Darkhaven home and opened fire on every living being inside – even the females, even the infants asleep in their cribs. Next he'd targeted the handful of Enforcement Agency cronies who had made no secret of their allegiance to the powerful Darkhaven leader responsible for ordering the slaughter.

One by one over the past several weeks, the guilty had met their end. The vampire lying dead and broken on the floor was the last known member of Wilhelm Roth's corrupt inner circle in Germany.

Which left Roth himself.

The bastard was going to burn for what he'd done.

But first he would suffer.

Reichen's gaze drifted back to the framed photograph in his hands and froze there. On first glance, he hadn't noticed the woman. All of his focus – all his fury – had been centered solely on Roth. Now that he had found her, he couldn't tear his eyes away from her.

Claire.

She stood off to the side of the group of Breed males, petite yet regal in a sleeveless ghost-gray gown that made her light brown skin look as smooth and lush as satin. Her soft black hair was swept up in a careful chignon, not a single strand out of place.

Time had not aged her so much as a year from when he'd known her – not that it would, when she was kept youthful and strong by the blood bond she shared with her chosen mate these thirty-some years. She was looking at Wilhelm Roth and his criminal friends, smiling with a perfectly schooled, perfectly unreadable expression.

A perfectly proper mate to the vampire who had proven to be Reichen's most treacherous adversary.

Claire.

After all this time.

My Claire, he thought grimly.

No, not his.

Once, perhaps. Long ago, and for merely a few months at that. A brief handful of time.

Ancient history.

Reichen stared at her image behind the silver-framed glass, surprised at how easily his fury for Wilhelm Roth could bleed over to the vampire's Breedmate. Sweet, lovely Claire . . . in bed with his most hated enemy. Was she aware of Roth's corruption? Did she condone it?

It hardly mattered.

He had a mission to fulfill. Justice to claim. A deadly, final vengeance to serve.

And nothing would stand in his way . . . not even her.

Reichen's gaze bore down on the photograph, fury smoldering in the amber light that reflected back at him from the surface of the glass. His fingers burned where his skin met the metal of the frame. He tried to cool the acid tempest swirling in his gut, but it was too late to hope for even a small measure of calm. With a snarl, he tossed the photograph to the floor and turned away from it. He stalked to one of the tall windows and willed open the pane, knowing he couldn't trust his touch now that his rage was so close to ruling him.

Reichen stepped onto the sill in a crouch, hearing the hot spit and sizzle of melting silver and cracking glass as the framed photograph burst into flames behind him.

Then he leapt into the thick autumn night to finish what Wilhelm Roth had started.

≼ CHAPTER TWO ≽

Claire Roth's lips pursed in contemplation as she stared down at the architect's model spread out on the table in her library. 'What do you think about moving the bench away from the strolling path and closer to the koi pond, just on the other side of the cottage roses?'

'An excellent idea,' said a bright female voice over the speakerphone situated nearby. The young woman was calling from one of the region's Darkhavens. Having seen some of her work elsewhere within the vampire community, Claire had been working with her for the past week, privately consulting on the design of a small garden park. 'Have you decided about the material for the walkways, Frau Roth? I believe initially you'd mentioned cobblestones or crushed rock –'

'Would it be possible to keep the paths natural instead?' she asked as she moved along the side of the table, perusing the rest of the scale model. 'I'm thinking soft earthen walkways trimmed with something simple yet inviting. Forget-me-nots, perhaps?'

'Of course. That sounds lovely.'

'Good,' Claire said, smiling as she considered the change. 'Thank you, Martina. You've done a wonderful job. Really, I couldn't be more pleased with how you've taken my jumble of rough ideas and turned them into something so much more than I imagined.'

The young Breedmate's voice brightened on the other end of the line. 'The park is going to be beautiful, Frau Roth. It's obvious how much time and care you've put into your vision of what you'd like it to be.'

Claire quietly registered the compliment, feeling less pride than relief. She wanted this slice of empty land to be turned into something beautiful. She wanted it to be perfect. Every planting, every carefully placed sculpture, bench, and strolling path was intended to be a place of total peace and tranquillity. A sanctuary meant to inspire the mind, heart, and soul. She wasn't one to pick up the torch for a cause – well, not in a very long time, at any rate – but she had to admit this project had become something close to an obsession for her.

'I just need it to be right,' she murmured, blinking past a sudden misting of her eyes. She'd been overly emotional lately, and was grateful that there was no one in the library to see her weakness.

'Don't worry,' Martina's cheerful voice soothed. 'I'm certain he's going to love it.'

Claire swallowed, caught off guard. 'W-what?'

'Herr Roth,' the young Breedmate replied. An awkward silence stretched out for long moments. 'I, um . . . I'm sorry if I'm prying. You'd asked me to keep the park and its design a secret, so I suppose I assumed that you meant it to be a gift for him.'

A gift for Wilhelm? Claire had to work to contain her bemused reaction to the idea. She hadn't even seen her mate for half a year. He came to the country only because his blood compelled him to. Claire had grown to dread those visits, expected as his mate to feed him from her veins and to take his blood in exchange. Wilhelm hardly pretended to feel differently about their coolly obligatory arrangement. They had discreetly lived apart nearly all of the three decades of their pairing – he in his Darkhaven mansion in the city, she and a handful of security staff here in the country manor a couple of hours away.

No, the garden park was not a gift for her chronically absent mate. In fact, she was sure he'd be furious if he found out that she'd undertaken the project on her own. Fortunately for her, Wilhelm Roth hadn't taken an interest in anything she thought or felt or did for quite some time now. He was more than content to leave her to pursue her assorted philanthropic and social activities; his business with the Enforcement Agency was all that mattered to him, particularly of late. That was his obsession, and in a quiet corner of her heart, Claire was glad for her solitude. Especially these past difficult weeks.

Martina let out a small sigh over the speaker. 'Please, Frau Roth . . . forgive me if I've overstepped my bounds in any way.'

'Not at all,' Claire assured her. Before she had to offer Martina either a pleasant lie about her motivations for the park's construction or explain her estrangement from the Breed male she saw infrequently at best, a hard rap sounded on the library door. 'My thanks again for the lovely design, Martina. Let me know if you have any other questions before we proceed with the project.'

'Of course. Good night, Frau Roth.'

Claire ended the call, then stepped out of the room. She closed the door behind her, still feeling protective of her secret undertaking and seeing no reason to invite questions from Wilhelm's loyal hounds. But now that she was standing alone with one of the half-dozen Enforcement Agents assigned to look out for her and the property she occupied, she realized that her little side project was the least of the security detail's concern. The guard seemed agitated, uncharacteristically twitchy.

'Yes. What is it?'

'I need you to come with me, Frau Roth.'

'What for?' She could see now that the big male was visibly rattled. Considering he was Breed, in addition to being armed to his fangs with firearms and combat gear, rattling someone like him was no small thing. Something was terribly wrong.

The comm device clipped to his black bulletproof vest was crackling with intermittent static and snippets of urgent conversation among the other agents posted at the country house. 'We're evacuating the premises immediately. This way, if you would.'

'Evacuating? Why? What's going on?'

'I'm afraid there is no time to waste.' More static sounded over his comm. More voices issuing clipped orders in the background. 'We're readying a vehicle for you now. Please. You must come with me.'

He started to reach for her arm, but Claire stepped out of his range. 'I don't understand. Why do I have to leave? I demand that you tell me what's going on.'

'We had a situation at the Darkhaven in Hamburg a short while ago –'

'A situation?'

The guard didn't elaborate, simply spoke right over her. 'As a precaution, we're clearing out of here and taking you to another location. A safe house in Mecklenburg.'

'Wait a minute – I have no idea what you're talking about. What situation in Hamburg? Why do I need to be moved to a safe house? What exactly does any of this mean?'

The guard gave her an impatient look as he barked his position into his comm device. 'Yes, I'm with her now. Bring the vehicles around to the front and prepare to roll out. We're on the way to meet you.'

He made another grab for her and Claire's patience snapped. 'Goddamn it, talk to me! What the hell is going on? And where is Wilhelm? Get him on the phone. I want to talk to him before I let you haul me out of my own home with hardly an explanation.'

'Director Roth has been out of the country since July,' the

agent told her, his schooled expression seeming to suggest that he didn't notice her embarrassment over the fact that a basic security detail could know more about her mate's whereabouts than she did. He cleared his throat. 'We're attempting to contact the director now to brief him on the attack –'

'Attack,' Claire replied, awkwardness forgotten as her skin went cold and tight. 'Good lord. Was someone attacked at the Darkhaven? Has someone been injured?'

The guard stared at her for what seemed like endless minutes before he finally hissed a curse and blurted out the details in a toneless spill of words. 'The Darkhaven in Hamburg was breached less than an hour ago. We just received the call from one of the guards who managed to escape. The *only* guard who escaped,' he amended. 'It was a complete annihilation. Everyone present at the mansion tonight is dead.'

'Oh, God,' Claire whispered, leaning back against the closed library doors for support. 'I don't understand . . . Who could do something like that?'

The guard shook his head. 'We don't have a clear count of how many attackers were involved in the strike, but the surviving agent said the assault was like nothing he'd ever seen before – fire everywhere, as though hell itself had blown down the gates and swept through the place. There's nothing left but cinders.'

Claire stood there, stricken and voiceless, trying to process everything she was hearing. It was impossible . . . unbelievable. It just didn't make sense. God, so much of what had been happening lately made no good sense at all.

So much random violence.

So much senseless death.

So much pain and loss . . .

'We can't delay,' the guard was saying now. 'We have to get you evacuated before this location comes under attack, as well.'

'You really believe that whoever did this will come out here? Why?'

This time the guard didn't pause to tell her anything more. His fingers clamped down hard around her arm and he started walking – quickly. The message in his brisk stride was plain enough: Claire could hurry to keep up with him, or he would drag her out of there. Either way, she was leaving the premises and doing so under heavily armed, grim-faced security.

There was no stopping for a coat or her purse. She fled with the guard, out of the house and into the chill of the late October evening. The cold autumn breeze bled through the fibers of her wine cashmere sweater and her gray wool pants as she ran alongside the guard to the paved drive, the soles of her suede loafers scuffing in her effort to keep up with the longer-legged gait of the agent dragging her along by the arm.

Claire was shown to the open back door of a Mercedes that idled in the center of a vanguard of four other vehicles.

'Get in,' the guard instructed her, and gently but urgently guided her inside ahead of him.

As he slid in next to her on the leather seat and closed the door, Claire tried to rub away the bone-deep chill that seemed to emanate from within her body rather than without. Everything was happening so fast. She was still trying to come to grips with the terrible news of the attack on the Darkhaven in Hamburg, let alone register the idea that not a few minutes ago her biggest worry was the proper placement of a garden bench or flower bed. Now the handful of Wilhelm's relatives and personal guards who'd resided at the Darkhaven were dead and she was being removed from her home in the middle of the night, fleeing from an unknown, unfathomable evil.

Why?

The question wailed in her mind. It was the same thing she'd been asking herself some three months ago, when another Darkhaven had fallen to tragedy – a tragedy that also had left behind only ash and smoke in its wake. But that had been an accident, according to the investigating Enforcement Agents. A freak explosion so fierce and total that it likely killed all of the Darkhaven's residents instantly.

And still the question haunted her, as painfully as it had when she first heard the awful news . . .

Why?

'We are in and rolling,' said the guard seated behind the wheel, radioing to the other vehicles. He stepped on the accelerator, and, like a fast-moving snake, the fleet of black sedans began to speed as one down the lengthy, forest-lined driveway.

Claire sat back, trying not to feel the anxiety that hung in the stale air of the car. The woods around them seemed darker than usual, so strangely quiet. Overhead, the thin moonlight was blotted out by the densely needled tops of the towering pines. The vanguard cleared the first bend in the nearly mile-long private drive. They sped up on the straightaway, all of the cars lurching into a higher gear as they gunned it for the main road.

There was no warning of the assault that hit the lead car in that next instant.

From out of the pitch-dark forest came a blinding ball of orange fire. It smashed into the first Mercedes in the line, exploding the car on impact. Claire screamed, feeling the sonic vibration of the blast all the way into the soles of her feet.

'What the fuck is that?' shouted the guard next to her in the backseat. 'Jesus Christ, hit the damn brakes!'

Red taillights went bright in front of them, and it was all their driver could do to avoid crashing into the back of the other sedan as it skidded to a stop. Like a toy train suddenly gone off its track, the caravan of vehicles bunched up, their line skewed and broken.

And up ahead, the first car was engulfed in flames that shot high into the black sky.

Just then another fireball launched out of the cover of the forest. It flew in a speeding, comet-bright arc, projecting straight toward the halted cars. Yet another orb of flames came quickly in its wake, both of the airborne threats awesome in their terrible, burning beauty.

The guard seated beside Claire leaned forward, his fingers clawing into the headrest of the seat in front of him. 'Back up – fast, damn it!' he yelled at the shell-shocked driver. 'Throw this thing into reverse and get us the hell out of here!'

Tires squealing, the Mercedes jerked into a violent backward retreat. As the car spun around on the narrow track of pavement, its bumper crunching into the vehicle behind them in the driver's panic, Claire watched the guards in the two remaining cars out front throw open their doors and try to make an escape on foot. One of them leapt to safety in the woods.

The other proved only seconds too slow. The first fireball crashed down into the hood of his car, obliterating man and metal both in a sickening roar of twisting, flying debris.

Claire screamed, turning her face away from the carnage just as the second fireball rained down onto the empty car ahead of them on the road. The thundering explosion shook the earth and chewed a deep, smoking crater into the ground.

The guard next to her made the sign of the cross on his chest, then punched the back of the driver's seat with a nasty curse. 'Go, you moron! Hit the fucking gas! Get us out of here!'

Too late.

From out of nowhere – from out of the sky itself, it seemed – came a rolling, fiery sphere of heat. The fireball soared down past the windshield of the vehicle, the glow of it so intense it filled the interior of the Mercedes with blinding white-hot light. Whatever it was, it felt charged with the power of ten suns, as electric as a bolt of lightning, concentrated into an orb the size of a bowling ball. All the hair on Claire's arms and at the back of her neck rose up as the thing smashed into the ground mere feet from the hood of the car.

Another fireball hit behind them, knocking Claire and her two companions forward in their seats. The driver's head hit the steering wheel with a sickening *crack*. The airbag detonated with the impact, setting off the car's security system. Amid the bleating alarm and the puff of chemical smoke from the deployed airbag, Claire also smelled the trace scent of blood. She wiped her forehead and swallowed hard when her fingers came away stained crimson.

Shit.

It was never a good idea to bleed in front of vampires, even vampires disciplined by Enforcement Agency training and dedicated to the service of her very powerful, very unforgiving mate. Not that she really expected to live long enough tonight to worry about the potential blood thirsts of her guards. It didn't seem likely that she or any of them would survive these next few moments.

'Run,' growled the one in back with her. He had a gun in each hand. His pupils were contracted to vertical slits in the center of their amber irises as he glared at the door handle beside her. The panel swung open with the force of his Breed mind. 'Run as far as you can. It's your only hope.'

Claire scrambled out and hit the ground in a clumsy stagger. Her legs were weak, shaking. Her head was ringing, her heart hammering in her chest. She heard the guard roar as he got out of the vehicle on the other side and stood to face whatever assault was coming.

Claire drifted toward the tall black shadows of the woods as the chaos continued all around her. A couple of guards raced past her, weapons drawn, as though any of them could stand against the hell that had arrived here tonight. She couldn't imagine what kind of army had opened up such a brutal offensive strike. Claire shot a terrified look over her shoulder as she made her way to the edge of the forest.

Whoever the attacking forces were, they were coming closer now. The unearthly glow of the forest behind her was growing brighter, marking their progress. Her steps slowed as the orange light reached through the trees like rays of scorching sunshine in the midst of coldest darkness. She stared, transfixed, unable to look away from the approach of what was probably going to be her death.

A silhouette began to take shape.

Not an army, but a single man.

A man whose entire being was alive with flames.

For one instant – one jarring, delusional instant – Claire thought she recognized the broad cut of his shoulders, the fluid swagger of his stride. Impossible, of course. Still, a glimmer of familiarity kindled in the back of her mind. Could she know him somehow?

But this was no man – certainly none that she knew, now or ever. This creature was something out of a nightmare.

He was death incarnate.

The *crack* of a gun firing jolted Claire's attention to the gathered group of Enforcement Agents nearby. Another bullet rang out, then another and another, until the air was filled with the sound. For all the good it did.

The man of flame kept walking, unfazed. The bullets popped like firecrackers as they neared him, exploding harmlessly the instant they met the wall of heat that surrounded his body.

When the last shell was finally spent, he paused.

He lifted his hands in front of him, though not in surrender. With little more than a second's warning, he turned loose a volley of fire on the defending guards. Claire couldn't bite back her scream of horror as the flames engulfed them, incinerating them on the spot.

She knew the instant the man noticed her. She felt the heat of his eyes pierce her from across the distance, every nerve ending in her body going taut with fear.

'Oh, God,' she whispered, stumbling backward a few paces.

The man of flames took a step in her direction, all of his terrible fury now rooted entirely on her.

Claire bolted, not daring to look back again as she plunged into the woods and ran for all she was worth.

✦ CHAPTER THREE ✦

He walked unfazed through the smoldering ash and ruin on the pavement. His boots crunched over broken glass and wrenched metal, past puddles of spilled, flaming oil and the smoking remains of the Breed males who'd fired on him with their paltry weapons.

Their bullets hadn't stopped him.

Nothing could, not when he was like this.

The ground sizzled under the heavy soles of his boots – not from annihilated debris, but from the heat that was still running through his limbs, an electrical crackle that traveled every inch of his body in pulsing waves of lethal, pure living energy.

He'd let his fury get out of control tonight; he knew that. He'd understood well enough how important it was to contain the fire inside of him, but his hatred of Wilhelm Roth had made him careless – first in the city, then here. His thirst to complete his vengeance had pushed him over a steep ledge and now he was falling, falling . . .

Failing, when justice was so near his grasp.

Roth hadn't been at his Hamburg Darkhaven. Nor had he been among the dead who'd tried to flee these grounds tonight. His vision flooded red with heat, Reichen cast a ruthless eye over the wreckage. He could see no sign of the bastard.

But Roth's mate was here.

She would know where to find him. And if her lips refused to give him up, her blood would tell soon enough.

Claire.

Her name flickered like a shorting-out circuit in his mind, dimly, darkly, only to be devoured by the rage that owned him. Right now, to him, she wasn't anyone he'd known, once or ever. She was no one he'd ever held in his arms. No one he'd ever loved.

Right now, like this, his fury knew only that she was the female who belonged to Wilhelm Roth.

And that made her as much Reichen's enemy as Roth himself.

He stalked toward the edge of the woods where he'd watched the Breedmate run. Vaguely he registered the scent of melting pine pitch and singeing leaves as he passed into the thick stand of trees. Low-hanging branches curled out of his way, bent from his path by the heat rolling off him with each stride.

He knew precisely where the female had fled. He could hear the rapid panting of her breath as he walked deeper into the forest. She was afraid, the scent of her terror a crisp note that the drifting smoke didn't quite conceal.

Up ahead now, her footsteps went silent. She'd found someplace to hide from him – or so she thought. Reichen's boots chewed up an unerring path toward her. Bloodred, laser-sharp, his focus locked on a huge ball of crumbling earth and the exposed, twisted dead roots of a fallen tree. Roth's Breedmate crouched behind it.

Reichen heard the pound of her heartbeat kick even faster as he neared and the current traveling his body began to cook the ancient root ball, steam rising from deep inside the dark clump. It would be just moments before the whole thing ignited. His heat was too strong now and roiling outward in pulsing waves. He wouldn't be able to stop the coming explosion, even if he tried.

'Come out, female.' His voice sounded rusty and foreign to

him. Tasted as dry as ashes in his throat. 'You don't have much time left. Come out of there while you still can.'

She didn't obey him. Some distant part of him wasn't exactly surprised by her stubborn resistance – he might even go so far as to say that he'd expected it. But another part of him, the part that was lit up with pyrokinetic fury and deadly short on patience, let loose with a ground-shuddering roar.

The warning, such as it was, proved effective.

He caught a flash of movement – heard the quick rush of footsteps flying over leaf-strewn ground – in the instant before the tree root detonated. Sparks shot out in all directions, sending streamers of orange light high overhead. Reichen saw Roth's woman bolting deeper into the woods as smoldering debris rained down around the crater that now gouged the earth where she'd been hiding.

On a black curse, he went after her. She was running fast, but he was faster. There was nowhere for her to go. It didn't take her long to figure that out for herself. Her steps slowed, then stopped altogether. Reichen paused where he stood, some ten paces away from her. Leaves crackled and withered above his head, all around him branches scorching from his heat.

Her hands flexed and fisted at her sides, her feet shifting as she seemed to weigh her chances of escape and quickly dismiss them. 'If you're going to kill me now, then do it.'

Her voice was quiet, but without the slightest falter. The velvet sound of it awakened scattered memories that shot through his mind in a barrage of images: He and this woman, naked in bed together, caught in a tangle of sheets, laughing, kissing. Her deep brown gaze dancing in golden candlelight as he fed her sugared raspberries on a midnight picnic by the lake. Her arms wrapped around his waist, her cheek resting against his bare chest as she confessed that she had fallen in love with him.

Claire . . .

It took long moments for him to shake loose of that

remembered past. He forced himself to think of a more recent one, the one that he could still taste in the bitter tang of the smoke that hung in the forest air. The one that was soaked in the blood of too many innocent lives.

'I haven't come for your death, Claire Roth.'

She went very still at the mention of her name. Reichen stared at the rigidly held spine ahead of him, the delicate shoulders squared and unshaking, defiant, as his enemy's mate slowly pivoted to face him. Her large, dark eyes held his gaze across the distance. He saw a note of recognition there, but it was swallowed up by disbelief. She mutely shook her head, staring at him as if he were a ghost or, rather, some kind of monster. He knew he was, especially after tonight, but seeing it in another's eyes – in *her* eyes – made the anger in him surge a bit wilder.

'Tell me where he is,' Reichen demanded.

She didn't seem to hear him. She stared for what seemed like forever, taking him in with that keen, inquisitive gaze. Finally, she gave a slow shake of her head.

'I don't understand how this can be,' she murmured. She took a step forward, only to back off a second later as blackened leaves and pine needles fell from their branches around him and turned to white ash at his feet. 'My God . . . Andreas. Is this a dream? I mean, I must be dreaming, right? This isn't real. It can't be . . .'

The words came haltingly, sounding weak, choked in her throat. Despite the intense heat pouring off him, she lifted her hand as if she meant to reach out for him. 'I thought you were dead, Andreas. All these three months since the fire destroyed your Darkhaven . . . I believed that you were dead.'

Reichen snarled at the threat of her touch. On a startled gasp, Claire snatched her arm back. She rubbed the fingers that would have incinerated on contact with him, no doubt feeling some measure of that truth on her unprotected skin.

Her confusion was clear. As was her horror. 'Good lord, what's happened to you?'

Of course she wouldn't know. He had been different when she knew him. Christ, everything had been different then. The heat that lived in him now had been cold and dormant, lurking deep beneath even his own awareness – until the hellish power of it had been beaten and tortured out of him for the first time some thirty years ago.

It had taken all he had and all that he was to snuff the accursed power and hold it down inside him. It had been so long since the heat had risen in him, he'd actually been fool enough to believe he'd driven the heat back for good. But it was still there, banked but smoldering. Waiting for the slightest chance to ignite while he strove to deny its very existence.

He had lived a lie for the past three decades, only to have it erupt in his face.

Now he would never be the same. Now Wilhelm Roth's treachery had reawakened that monstrous side of him. Now grief and anger had invited the terrible ability back into his life, and the fires were always burning inside him.

They were beginning to rule him.

To destroy him.

And because of the ruthless actions of her mate, Claire was seeing that hideous truth with her own eyes.

No, he would never be the same again.

And he would not rest until he had his vengeance.

Through the flames, Claire's eyes searched his, part in worry, part in pity. 'I don't understand what's going on, Andre. Why are you like this? Tell me what's happened to you.'

He hated the concern in her voice. He didn't want to hear it, not from Roth's mate.

'Please, talk to me, Andre.'

Andre. Only she had called him that. After her, he'd not permitted anyone to become that familiar – that intimate –

with him. After her, there had been many things he'd not dared permit, of himself or others.

The sound of his name on her lips now was a pain he hadn't anticipated. Reichen bared his teeth and fangs in a sneer meant to cower her, but she wouldn't relent with her demand for answers.

'Who, Andre . . . who has done this to you?'

He let the fire of his rage wash over him, his voice as rough as gravel in his throat. 'The bastard who sent his death squad into my home to slaughter my kin in cold blood. Wilhelm Roth.'

'Impossible,' Claire heard herself say, although whether she meant the awful charge against Wilhelm or the fact that Andreas Reichen was very much alive – alive and unfathomably lethal – not even she was certain. 'You need help, Andre. Whatever has happened to you to make you like this . . . no matter what you've done tonight . . . you need help.'

He scoffed, dark and dangerous. It was an animalistic sound, matched by the feral look in his eyes. His rage was obvious, a force so immense his body didn't seem able to contain it. Claire's gaze swept over him, over the pulsing currents of heat that ringed his limbs and torso and distorted his facial features to something monstrous and inhuman.

God in heaven.

This hellish heat *was* his rage.

'Oh, Andre,' she whispered, her heart tightening despite the confusion of emotions tumbling through her. 'I know how you must be hurting. I hurt for you, too, when I learned what happened at your Darkhaven.'

'Fifteen lives,' he snarled. 'All dead. Even the children.'

Pained to think of it, Claire closed her eyes. 'I know, Andre. I heard, of course. Everyone in the region was stricken when the news of it reached us from Berlin. It was an awful, unimaginable tragedy –'

'It was a fucking bloodbath,' he barked, the sharp, raw scrape of his voice cutting her off. 'Fifteen innocent lives wiped out at Wilhelm Roth's command. All of them murdered, shot like dogs on his orders.'

'No, Andre.' Claire shook her head, confused. Appalled that he could think such a thing. 'There was an explosion. The Enforcement Agency investigators concluded there had been a rupture in the estate's gas main. They ruled it an accident, Andreas. I don't know where you got the idea that Wilhelm —'

'Enough,' he growled. 'You can't protect your mate with lies. Nothing can protect him from the justice he deserves. I *will* avenge them.'

Claire swallowed hard. She wasn't so naive that she believed Wilhelm Roth's honor to be without a blemish or three. He was a cold male, distant but not cruel. He was a ruthless politician who'd never made a secret of his driving ambitions. But a murderer? Someone who could be capable of the kind of death Andreas accused him of? No, she couldn't reconcile that.

As difficult as it was to consider, Claire wondered if it was Andreas, not Wilhelm, who was the true monster here. She need only look past his broad shoulders to see the smoke and fire still rising from the carnage he'd left on the road. And there was yet more death and destruction in Hamburg, at the Darkhaven where Wilhelm Roth and his smattering of kin and staff had lived.

Death and destruction not so unlike the kind that had visited Andreas's own Darkhaven three months ago. The fire in Berlin had been immense. The annihilation had been merciless, complete. Nothing had been left of the mansion or its inhabitants when the smoke had finally cleared. The flames had consumed them all.

Oh, God . . .

Claire stared at Andreas, a sickness swelling to ugly life in her heart as the heat rolling off his body warped the air around him. Maybe there was an explanation for what had happened at his Darkhaven. Maybe he had snapped somehow. Had something occurred to send him over the edge, to bring out this terrifying side of him?

'Andre, listen to me.' She took a step closer to him, her hands held out before her in a gesture of peace, of calm. 'I don't know what's happened to you, but I want to help you if I can.'

He growled a nasty curse. The heat coursing over him seemed to intensify, putting a sharp electrical tang in the air.

Claire went on, hoping she might be able to break through whatever madness it was that gripped him. 'Talk to me, please. Tell me how to help you and let's sort this out together. I'm willing if you are.'

Although she'd forced a fearlessness into her voice, she couldn't help jumping a little as a crackle of illumination – as intense as white-hot lightning – began to arc off his body. He grunted through his teeth and fangs. His already thinned pupils narrowed to the barest vertical slits of black in the center of his fiery amber eyes. He was Breed, a predator by nature, but the vampire in him had never scared Claire. It was this other side of him – the side she'd never known he had, let alone seen firsthand – that made her blood run cold in her veins.

Uncertain now, horrified by all that had occurred tonight and wary of this stranger she no longer knew, Claire took another step toward him. 'Please, you must know that you can trust me. Will you let me help you, Andre?'

'Goddamn it, stop calling me that!'

At his bellow, a tree to the immediate right of her burst into flames. Claire threw a nervous glance at the fire suddenly climbing the trunk of the tall pine. Heat blasted toward her from the instant conflagration, hitting her face as though she were caught in a furnace.

Had he intended that as a warning, or a threat?

Was he able to control this part of him at all?

She wasn't certain he could. Claire inched away from the flames, keeping her eyes on Andreas, who followed her with a narrowed, searing gaze. She searched those eyes for reason – for some small thread of sanity – but all she saw staring back at her was rage. And pain. Dear God, so much pain in those eyes now.

'Tell me where he is, Claire.'

She gave a weak shake of her head. 'I don't know.'

'Tell me.'

She shook her head again as her feet carried her a few more paces away from this creature who had once been her friend . . . her lover. At one time, she had thought Andreas Reichen to be her everything. Now she was certain she was looking at her death. Hers and Wilhelm's both. 'I haven't seen Wilhelm in quite a while. He doesn't inform me of his business or his travels. But he's not here, and I don't know where he is. It's the truth, Andre.'

Another roar flew out of him as his name slipped past her lips. Nearby, another tree went up in flames like a Roman candle. Then another, and another. Heat exploded on either side of her, fire rolling high into the night sky. Claire couldn't hold back her scream. Nor could she curb the survival instinct that kicked her legs into motion as the forest around her began to burn.

She ran in the only direction she could, away from Andreas. Her sense of bearings was lost in the chaos of her terror, not that she actually expected she would escape. She ran, waiting to feel the scorch of hellish fire on her skin, certain that Andreas's fury would not permit her to live.

But still she ran.

She was breathless by the time she reached the edge of the woods. Breathless and shaking, her feet stumbling over the grass and rough ground. She lifted her head and nearly burst into relieved tears to see the manor house looming up ahead of her.

Behind her was darkness and the glow of flames in the distance. A jolt of adrenaline surged into her bloodstream, and Claire raced across the open lawn to the front door of the fortresslike estate.

The place was unlocked, left open in the guards' haste to evacuate earlier. Claire flew inside and slammed the door behind her, throwing all of the bolts and locks home. She ran for high ground, grabbing a cordless phone along the way and fleeing up the stairs to the third floor, praying that the sanctuary she'd just found wouldn't turn out to be her tomb. She was halfway through dialing Wilhelm's secretary before she realized the phone had no dial tone. It was dead, nothing but endless broken static on the line.

'Damn it!'

Claire threw the phone down as she drifted to the large, shuttered windows on the far wall. She had some inkling of what she'd see on the other side of the glass, but it still robbed her of breath when she opened the shutters and peered out over the estate's expansive grounds.

Black smoke plumed from the long drive and from within the forest. Orange fire twisted up over the treetops, licking at the starlit sky. And in the center of the woods, a brighter light glowed – throbbing white heat, blindingly intense.

Andreas. He was the source of all that eerie light.

Would he come for her now? If he did, she had nowhere left to run.

But the light from his body didn't move. Neither did Claire. Her feet stayed rooted to the floor near the window as she watched that unearthly pulse, unable to look away.

She watched, until hours passed and the fires on the road and in the forest began to die down.

She watched . . . as night crept steadily toward dawn and the glow of Andreas's fury continued to burn.

⇥ CHAPTER FOUR ⇤

She didn't know what woke her.

With a start, Claire lifted her head from where her brow had been pressed against the cool glass of the window. She didn't know how long she'd dozed – long enough that the faint pink blush of dawn had marched all the way over the horizon, bringing with it a drizzle-laden shroud of fog that blanketed the forest and the ground below.

Oh, God . . . *morning.*

Daylight growing brighter by the minute.

And no sign of Andreas's light anywhere.

Claire's breath misted the glass as she peered down from the window at the lifeless stretch of grass, pavement, and pines outside. Had he left while she'd slept? Was he gone now?

Was he dead?

After what she'd witnessed him do last night, she wasn't sure why the thought should put such a knot of dread in her breast. But before Claire could tell herself that she should be damned grateful just to have survived the night herself, she was already on the stairs, descending swiftly through the heart of the manor house. She freed the locks on the front door and eased it open, pulling one of the guards' coats off a stand in the foyer and wrapping it around her shoulders to ward off the wet chill as she stepped outside.

The striking quiet hit her first. No sound at all other than the intermittent patter of a light rain. It was so peaceful and still, she might have been tempted to think last night had just been a horrible dream. But then the pungent stink of extinguished fires carried across the grounds.

It had all been real, worse than the stuff of nightmares. Her nose burned with the acrid reminder of the violence she'd witnessed.

Claire drifted across the grass, bypassing the long drive to avoid the carnage of her vanguard. She didn't want to see what the fires had done to the Breed males who'd been killed last night, nor did she want to know how quickly the rising sun would consume whatever might remain of them. It was that thought – the understanding of what prolonged ultraviolet exposure did to the hypersensitive skin of the Breed – that pushed Claire deeper into the forest.

Toward the place where she'd last known Andreas to be.

It was difficult to tell where the fog ended and the trailing smoke from burnt trees and scorched ground began. Everything seemed cloaked in heavy gray mist. Her skin dampening with each step she took, Claire watched her feet move through the low-lying fog, following a blackened trail that led some long distance into the woods. The quiet reached out to her as she moved past singed bramble that clawed at her like skeletal fingers of the dead. The stench of old smoke and burnt vegetation grew stronger here, catching in the back of her throat.

And yet another sharp odor – not that of cold, extinguished flames, or even the electrical tang that had been rolling off Andreas's body last night. But there was something else in the air. Fresh, rising heat. The sickly sweet olfactory assault of burning flesh.

Oh, no.

She took a few anxious steps, faltering a bit as the earth dropped sharply, about a foot below her. The hole where the old tree root had been, she dimly registered. The hole that became a crater when Andreas blew her hiding place to bits in his rage.

It was at this spot in the woods that he'd lingered last night. He hadn't followed her at all. And he hadn't left before the sun began to rise.

He was still here.

Claire cautiously approached the large, dark shape huddled ahead of her on the fog-threaded ground. He wasn't moving, hardly breathing. The fire that had been burning around him and within him was gone now. His clothes were scorched and torn. His skin sizzled under the hazy rays of the sun, already forming blisters everywhere that he was exposed.

He didn't look so dangerous like this. He wasn't the monster she'd met out here in the dark; he was just a man now. A man made deathly vulnerable by the part of him that was something more than human.

Like this, it wasn't difficult at all to remember that she had once loved him like no other. It surprised her how easily the pain of their abrupt parting came back to her, as well.

Those days were long past, but no matter what she felt for him then or now, she could not let him suffer. She would not abandon him to the sun, no matter what he'd done or what he'd become in the long time since they had been together.

'Andre,' Claire whispered, her voice breaking the closer she got to him and saw the severity of his burns. 'Oh, God, Andreas . . . can you hear me?'

He groaned something inaudible, but unpleasant. When she crouched down and put her hand out to touch his shoulder, he bared his fangs and snarled like an animal caught in a trap.

'You have to get up.' Claire took off the oversize trench coat and held it up for him to see. 'I'm going to cover you with this to shield you from the sun. But you can't stay out here or you're going to die. You have to get up and come with me. Will you do that?'

He didn't answer, but he also didn't lash out at her when she gently placed the coat over his exposed skin.

'Can you stand up?'

He glared, his lip still curled back off his teeth. Something was very wrong with him, despite the fact that he was no longer livid with fire. His elliptical pupils hadn't dilated back to normal yet, and his irises were still bright amber instead of the absorbing hazel color she knew them to be.

All of the Breed transformed in this manner when they hungered or in times of elevated emotional responses, but this seemed different somehow. More severe. Claire couldn't see many of his *dermaglyphs* – the intricate skin markings present on every member of the Breed – but the ones that were visible on his arms and through the torn patches of his clothing didn't look right. Their colors were pulsing rapidly, changing and mutating, as though some part of him were short-circuiting from the inside.

'Stand up,' she said, more forcefully this time. 'I need you to walk, Andreas.'

To her surprise, he began to obey her. Slowly he dragged himself up off the ground. Claire offered him her hand when his knees buckled at first, but then he was on his feet, towering over her even though his spine was bent and his head was dropped low on his chest. Claire tugged the collar of the trench coat up over the back of his neck and skull to protect his head from any more UV damage.

'This way,' she told him. 'You can hold on to me if you need to.'

She noticed he didn't even try to take her up on that. With a pained grunt, he lurched into motion beside her. They progressed at a snail's pace, trudging in silence out of the woods and back across the lawn to the manor house. By the time they reached the front entrance, Andreas's feet were dragging beneath him like lead weights.

Claire tried to assist him up the few steps to the door, but he brushed her off as though her touch would burn him even worse than the sun's rays beating down through the dissipating haze. Instead she went ahead and opened the door, holding it for him as he climbed the steps and all but collapsed in the foyer. He went down on one knee, then staggered back up with a groan.

'Goddamn it,' he snarled, his breath sawing between his parched lips. He looked up at her, his face sweat-soaked and raw with UV burns. 'Where to now?'

Claire pointed to the other end of the foyer. 'You might be most comfortable downstairs in the cellar. Wilhelm had a private room installed down there when the house was originally built, but it's never used . . .'

He started moving even before she finished speaking. Claire followed him, sticking close in case he had trouble on the old stone staircase that led beneath the main floor. She heard his relieved sigh as the cool darkness enveloped him. He didn't need artificial light to see, but Claire's eyes took longer to adjust to the pitch-black surroundings. She flicked the switch and watched as Andreas staggered off the last step and sank down onto the cold stone floor.

He didn't move to Wilhelm's plush personal suite, just peeled off the trench coat and flung it aside, then let himself crumple in a broken sprawl. Claire said nothing as she eased down to sit on the third step from the bottom. She watched him in silence for a while, unsure what to make of him.

'Why did you do it?' His rough voice scraped out of the shadows, but his gaze was fierce with unearthly amber light. 'Why did you help me?'

Claire found it hard to hold that hot, scathing look. 'Because you needed help.'

He scoffed, a coarse, mocking sound. 'You were never stupid, Claire. Bad time to start.'

The slam stung, but she only shrugged. 'And you were never someone who would think nothing of killing dozens of people in the space of a few hours.'

He blinked, those amber irises shuttered for a long while. Did he know what he had done last night? Had any of it registered with him when he was in that state?

He blew out a low curse, then turned his face away from her. 'Andre,' Claire murmured softly. 'Whatever is wrong with you, I'm sure there are people who can help. But you don't have to think about any of that right now. All you need to do is rest, let yourself heal. You're safe here.'

'Nobody's safe now,' he muttered under his breath. He rolled back to face her, pinning her with the twin lasers of his transformed eyes. 'Especially not you, Claire.'

She stared at him for some long moments, unsure how to respond. She couldn't pretend she wasn't afraid. Even battered by UV light, he was still very dangerous. Still a lethal predator, armed with a terrible power she'd had no idea he possessed.

It staggered her that she could have believed she'd known him so well in the four months they'd been inseparable, yet she had been oblivious to the side of him she saw last night. Then again, she'd also thought he loved her, only to be blindsided when he simply vanished from her life without a word of explanation.

Now he was back – finally, after three decades, she was looking at him once more – though nothing like she'd imagined it might be to reunite with him. Now she didn't know who he was anymore . . . or *what* he was.

'Get some rest,' she finally managed to say.

Claire stood up and began the climb back up from the cellar, well aware that Andreas's eyes followed her the whole time. She flicked the light switch, plunging the place back into darkness before she closed the cellar door and leaned her spine against it.

Her hands were trembling, her heart banging around in her rib cage.

Dear God. She hoped she hadn't just made a terrible mistake.

One thing she knew for certain was that she had to find Wilhelm, and find him fast.

Wilhelm Roth was getting a blow job behind the wheel of a Jaguar XKR coupe doing 120 mph on an open stretch of highway when he noticed that his Breedmate had walked into the dream unannounced. She came up out of the median and paused on the side of the moonlit stretch of road about a quarter mile ahead of him.

For a second, Roth kept his foot heavy on the accelerator, thinking he would just fly past her like she wasn't there – give her a reminder of how he detested her unique talent and had long ago forbade her to use it on him. But as the Jag roared up the fast lane and Claire's face came into the light of his high beams, he realized she was upset about something. Visibly stricken. Not at all typical of the otherwise calm, cool, and collected female.

She lifted her hand to shield her eyes from the glare of the headlights, and Roth took the opportunity to vanish his dreamtime plaything. The naked blonde he'd conjured from the cheap porno film that was running as he'd dozed off disappeared with just a thought; the fierce erection he was sporting from the fly of his unzipped Armani trousers wouldn't go away quite that easily. Not that Claire would question him about it if she noticed. She'd learned her place years ago, and after all, it wasn't as if he could be held accountable for where his mind went when he was sleeping.

Precisely the reason he'd given her for barring her from dreamwalking around him.

That and the fact that it simply pissed him off to have his privacy invaded in any form.

Annoyed, Roth tucked himself back into his pants as he brought the car to a smooth halt right in front of his anxious Breedmate. She didn't wait for him to address her, didn't apologize for the interruption.

'Wilhelm, something terrible has happened.' She gripped the edge of the driver's side door, her dark eyes intense with worry. 'There's been an attack at the country house.'

Roth felt his jaw go tense with anger more than surprise. 'An attack? When?'

'Last night. A few hours ago.'

And he was just hearing about this now? Through her, and not his guards?

Roth scowled. 'Tell me what happened.'

'It was awful,' she said, closing her eyes as though the memory pained her. 'There were fires everywhere . . . explosions in the woods near the house and on the road. So much smoke and ash. We tried to leave, but we were too late.'

His anger spiked. 'Where are you now?'

'At home . . . well, at my home. I'm still at the country house.'

'All right.' Roth nodded vaguely. 'What about the men on watch there? Why is it they've left you to tell me all of this when they're the ones who owe me the explanation?'

'They're dead, Wilhelm.' Her voice faltered, dropping to a whisper. 'Everyone else who was here tonight is dead.'

Roth bit off a ripe curse. 'Very well. Stay put. I'll contact the Hamburg Darkhaven and arrange for an envoy to pick you up and bring you back into the city.'

Claire was shaking her head before he had a chance to complete the thought. 'Wilhelm . . . haven't you heard? The Hamburg Darkhaven. It's gone.'

'What?'

'The Darkhaven came under attack first. There's nothing left of it. No survivors, other than one Enforcement Agent who escaped the fires to warn us that we were likely in danger, as well.'

Roth absorbed this news in grim silence. He didn't have a lot of kin – no sons of his own to want to oust him from power, no brothers of any generation who'd managed to live as long as he had. The Darkhaven community he shepherded in Hamburg consisted only of a few nephews, who'd never been good for much; various household staff; plus a small garrison of guards on loan from the Agency. He hardly knew any of them, in truth, and frankly, he had more important things to consider than wasting any time mourning the loss.

'I'm sorry, Wilhelm,' Claire was saying now, sentiment he dismissed with a curt wave of his hand.

He supposed he had to know something like this was going to happen. He did know, in fact. He'd known from the moment he'd been informed of the first Enforcement Agency death at the Berlin office several weeks past – the up-close-and-personal killing of an agent who reported directly to him on covert, often unofficial, operations. When the second violent murder within his private contingent occurred, then the third and fourth, it left little question that someone was out for blood.

The only trouble with that theory being the fact that the someone in question was dead. At least that had been the report coming out of the Agency. At the time, Roth hadn't had the opportunity or the inclination to doubt the intel; more important business had already called him away to Montreal. That business was still his chief priority, but this assault on his personal holdings could not go unmet.

'I will take care of the matter,' he told Claire. 'And you needn't worry, I'll call in a few favors to find you temporary shelter in the region until I am able to return.'

'Where exactly are you, Wilhelm? One of your guards told me you're not in Germany.' She looked around at the dream landscape, her gaze clearly taking note of the jags of steep granite that flanked some of the stretch of rural highway his mind had manufactured. 'Are you in New England?'

Too clever, his Yankee-born Breedmate. And far too inquisitive now for her own good. Roth neither confirmed nor denied his whereabouts. 'Stay put, Claire. You'll be fine.'

'Wilhelm,' she said slowly. 'Aren't you even a little bit curious about who attacked us last night? I would think you'd want to know who's responsible . . . and why.'

Roth stared at her.

'Andreas Reichen,' she said, watching him much too closely for his reaction.

He was careful to give her nothing, not so much as a blink of his eyes or a kick of his pulse. He frowned after a moment, feigning confusion. 'You speak of a ghost, Claire. Andreas Reichen perished with the rest of his kin this past summer when his Darkhaven burned to the ground.'

In fact, Roth thought with private disappointment, the arrogant son of a bitch should have been dead long before then.

Claire shook her head. 'He's alive. He's . . . changed, Wilhelm. He has a terrible rage inside him – a power I can barely comprehend. The fires and explosions here and in Hamburg? He made them. They came out of him. I saw it with my own eyes.'

Roth listened, both incredulous and concerned.

'Wilhelm, he says he intends to kill you.'

He scoffed. 'The bastard will never get close enough to try.'

'He's here, Wilhelm.' Claire's gaze was imploring. 'He is here, in the house with me, passed out in the cellar. I don't know what to do.'

Roth's furious curse was punctuated by an electronic bleating that pierced the fabric of his dream. His surroundings warped and vibrated. The ribbon of dark pavement and the perfect starlit sky above trembled, the vision of Claire starting to fade out with the sound waves that were rousing him from sleep.

'My mobile is ringing,' he said, ready to be done with her

anyway. As he spoke, the Jaguar he'd been sitting in vaporized, leaving him standing on the strip of moonlit pavement beside her. 'I have to take this call now –'.

Claire's filmy image reached for him. 'What about Andreas?'

He ground his molars together at the apparent easy familiarity she still seemed to feel toward the other male, even after decades of separation. 'Keep the son of a bitch contained at the house while I make arrangements to deal with him.'

'You want me to stay here with him?' She stared, uncertain. 'For how long?'

'As long as it takes. I'll send another Agency detail to remove him at sunset.'

'Remove him into Agency custody, you mean? You won't let your men hurt him, will you?'

Her apparent concern was thoroughly pissing him off. 'My men are professionals, Claire. They know how to handle a situation like this. You needn't worry about the details.'

The jangle of his ringing phone came again, pulling him further away from her, back to consciousness.

'What about me, Wilhelm?' Claire murmured. 'How am I supposed to keep Andreas here until your men arrive?'

'Do whatever you must,' Roth replied flatly. 'You know him better than most, after all. Intimately, if memory serves. I'm sure you'll think of some way to detain him.'

He didn't wait for her to say anything more. The phone rang again and Roth's eyes snapped open, severing his thready connection to Claire.

He grabbed the mobile from the table next to his bed. 'Yes.'

'Herr Roth,' said a nervous Breed male on the other end of the line. 'This is Agent Krieger from the Berlin office, sir. There's been a murder here last night – Agent Waldemar's body was just discovered in his residence. His neck was broken. And . . . there's more, sir. It seems there was an incident at your Darkhaven in Hamburg, as well.'

Roth scoffed, full of sarcasm. 'You don't say.'

'Sir?'

'Assemble a combat team and send them to my country house as soon as the sun sets. The unit on-site has been attacked and eliminated. Now my Breedmate is there without any cover. She's alone, and she's holding Andreas Reichen for you.'

'Reichen?' asked the agent. 'I don't understand, sir. Wasn't he killed in that freak accident at his Darkhaven some time ago?'

Roth's fingers tightened on the thin case of the mobile phone. 'Apparently the bastard is very much alive . . . for the moment. Instruct the team that I want him taken out on sight. Make him dead, agent.'

'Yes, sir.'

⊰ CHAPTER FIVE ⊱

Reichen stood over her in silence, his hands braced on the arms of a moss green wingback chair in one of the estate's receiving rooms, where Claire had fallen asleep. For a moment, when he'd first come to alone in the pitch-dark cellar, he hadn't the first clue where he was or how he'd gotten there. Nor could he immediately recall why it was that most of his body was recovering from UV burns. It was like that for him sometimes, after the pyrokinetic energy faded. Hard to remember details. Hard to make sense of his surroundings.

Hard to know anything except the fierce blood thirst that overtook him once his inner fire had a chance to cool.

He had been disoriented when he first regained consciousness in the cellar, but then he'd breathed in the softest trace scent of vanilla and warm spices.

Claire.

Her blood scent had drawn him out of the dark and up the flight of stone steps, into the room where she dozed now. He breathed her in as he loomed over her, tempted to close his eyes and savor the memory of what had been, but instead he barely blinked. He watched the quick, darting movement of her eyes beneath her closed lids.

She was dreaming.

Reichen wondered how long she'd been sleeping, or where her dreams had carried her that her pulse would be beating as rapidly as a skittish hare's. His thirsting gaze drifted down from the delicate beauty of her face to the smooth golden brown skin of her throat. Ticking frantically at the right side of her neck, her artery beat beside a small scarlet-colored birthmark. Reichen's fangs were already filling his mouth, but now they throbbed, his eyes rooted on that tender patch of flesh with its diminutive teardrop-and-crescent-moon symbol riding so close to Claire's pulse.

Jesus, he was parched.

His belly was tight and empty, his limbs heavy and fatigued. He licked his lips, hardly able to keep himself from leaning in a bit closer, until the light beat of her pulse was banging in his own veins as loud and demanding as a drum.

God, he thirsted . . . so deeply that the need was primal, animal, urging him to sweep in and take his fill like the predator he truly was.

That it was Claire beneath him was the only thing that made him pause. How long had he wondered what she would taste like? How many times had he come this close – hell, even closer than this – to pressing his fangs into her buttery soft skin and drinking from her vein? He'd wanted that more than anything at one time. But it was the one thing he'd never done, not even in their most fevered moments together.

As much as he'd hungered to taste her, to bond her to him through blood, he had never taken his need for Claire that far. She was a Breedmate. Unlike the larger percentage of *Homo sapiens* females walking the planet, she was one of a small number bearing unusual blood and DNA properties.

Claire and those like her, born with the crimson stamp somewhere on their bodies, were also uniquely gifted with extraordinary psychic abilities. And, unlike other human women, they had the ability to form an unbreakable bond with members of the Breed and bear their young. When a Breedmate offered her blood to one of Reichen's kind, it was a precious gift – the most sacred of all. It forged a bond that could be severed only by death.

Reichen couldn't lie to himself and pretend that he'd never been tempted. But he'd hardly been the kind to settle down, especially then. For all his libertine ways, and as laughable as it seemed to him now, his honor had prevented him from taking something from Claire that could never be called back. One sip of her blood meant she would live in him for as long as he drew breath. He would be bound to her always, drawn to her always, regardless of any vow she'd made to another male.

Even through the smoke and fog of his recovering mind, he could still recall how hard it had been to exercise control where his hunger for Claire was concerned. But he'd been careful. As hard as it was, he'd been a pillar of restraint, right to the end.

If he'd known then that she was going to waste so little time giving herself to Wilhelm Roth . . . ?

Reichen growled just thinking on it.

His fury wasn't so cooled that he didn't entertain the idea of slaking his thirst on her right there and then. He leaned in, unable to tear his hungering eyes away from the rhythmic beat of her pulse. Her scent beckoned him as much as the rush of her blood beneath her skin.

She was even more beautiful than he remembered. This close, she robbed him of breath. Made him ache to touch her.

Jesus Christ, she made him burn far worse than sunlight or fury.

It stunned him to realize that he wanted her still, after all this time. After all her mate had done to destroy him. He wanted Claire for his own . . . still.

Reichen drew in a rough breath of air, his lips peeling back off his fangs. He wanted her, and, by God, he would take her.

'No,' he growled to himself. 'Damn it, no.'

Claire's eyes snapped open and went wide. She gasped, drawing back as far as she could get from him with the chair blocking her escape. Her dark brown eyes searched his face, too intelligent to misunderstand what had nearly happened.

Reichen mentally yanked himself to heel, despite the hunger that was still making his gums throb with the urge to feed. 'Pleasant dreams, Frau Roth?'

'Not at all,' she answered, staring hard at him. 'After what happened here last night, I'm sure I'll be having nightmares for a long time to come.'

A pang of shame jabbed him, but he ignored it. He had to keep his eye on the ball. 'You didn't happen to pay a dreamtime visit to your mate just now, did you?'

Claire didn't so much as blink. He could see the recollection in her steady gaze, the realization that although many years had passed since they last saw each other, Reichen had not forgotten her special psychic ability. Her cheeks darkened a bit, and he wondered if she was thinking of all the times she had dreamwalked into some of his most erotic REM fantasies during those intense, passionate few months in which they'd fallen in love.

He had not forgotten a single moment they'd shared, awake or joined in dreams, and he had damn sure tried.

'Wilhelm doesn't like it when I intrude on his dreams,' she murmured.

'That's not really a denial,' Reichen replied. He kept his hands braced on the arms of the chair, trapping her there while he continued his interrogation. 'Where is he, Claire?'

'I told you, I don't know.'

'But you do have some idea,' he said, trying not to be distracted by his hunger or his sudden, growing awareness of just how close their bodies were to each other. He could feel her heat mingling with his own, making his healing, irradiated skin feel as though it were being touched by flame. 'Make no mistake, I will find him. The others weren't able to run, nor will he.'

She looked wary, repelled. 'What . . . others?'

'His faithful hounds, the ones who carried out his orders with no regard for innocent lives. I've put them all down, one by one. Not him, not yet. I've saved him for last because I wanted him to know that I was coming. I wanted him to understand that he was going to have to pay for what he did.'

Claire swallowed, gave a small shake of her head. 'What you said last night – that Wilhelm is responsible for what happened to your Darkhaven . . . you are mistaken, Andreas. You have to be mistaken.'

'What I said is the truth.'

'It can't be –'

'Why not?' he snapped. 'Because that will mean you're mated not only to a known thug but a cold-blooded murderer, as well?'

Her slender dark brows came together in an expression somewhere between pity and contempt. 'This coming from someone whose own hands are stained with more than a dozen lives?'

Reichen reeled back, bristling at the reminder. He took a few steps away from her, then pivoted to begin a tense pace out of the room. He didn't know where he was going. He didn't damn well care. He knew he couldn't leave the house while it was daylight outside, and right now it felt like a cage.

Claire drifted out behind him, her footsteps all but silent on the polished marble floor of the hall. 'Andreas, I know you must be terribly hurt and confused after everything you've been through. We can try to sort all of this out later. Right now you need some peace and quiet while your body is healing from the UV burns. You need rest –'

'What I need right now is blood,' he snarled, swiveling a hard, amber-eyed look on her. 'Since you're so reluctant to surrender Roth to me, I don't suppose you'd be willing to let me take my fill of you either.'

She blanched, appalled, just as he wanted her to be.

Reichen continued his impatient prowl of the hallway, noting the assorted photographs and framed art on the walls. With his anger stoked, he looked for images of Claire and Roth, the adoring couple, eager for more kindling for the fury that still burned in his gut. There were only a handful of photos of them together, often among a group of Darkhaven or Enforcement Agency members, or in front of ribbon-cutting ceremonies taking place at various evening events. Claire's smile was perfect in each one: pleasant without being overly excited, polite without being overly cool.

Reichen didn't know that smile. It seemed as polished and brittle as the glass that overlaid it.

'Where does Roth conduct his business here?' he asked her, turning away from frozen, perfect Claire to look at the woman who stood behind him now, well out of arm's reach. 'If he has computers here, or any type of files, I want to see them.'

'You won't find anything like that here,' she said, simply stated fact. 'Wilhelm does all of his personal business from the Hamburg Darkhaven and an office he keeps in the city . . . as far as I know. We've never discussed his business affairs.'

Reichen grunted, unsurprised. He was already moving past another room off the hallway, glancing in at the casually sophisticated furnishings of a living room, then passing by an intimate ballroom that seemed a cavern of mirrored walls, polished parquet flooring, and a creamy, elegantly carved ceiling. In back was an ebony grand piano, its multiple reflections gleaming in all the surrounding polished glass.

'Good to see some things haven't changed,' he muttered. Claire glanced into the ballroom but looked confused. 'The piano,' he said. 'You have a gift for music, as I recall.'

Her frown faltered slightly as she stared at him. 'Oh, I don't . . . I haven't played in a long time. I suppose I got busy with other, more important things. Music isn't really a part of my life anymore.'

'No, I guess not,' he said, aware of how caustic it sounded.

'Is there anything left of you that I would remember, Claire?'

A long silence spread between them. Reichen expected her to walk away, or maybe run away, out the front door and into the daylight where he couldn't follow. But she stood her ground, pierced him with her deep brown eyes. Tenacious as ever. 'How dare you. I didn't ask you to storm into my life and tear it apart, but here you are. I don't have to explain anything to you, or justify where life has taken me.'

No, she didn't, and he knew he was being unfair here. Having those answers wasn't going to bring him any closer to Wilhelm Roth, either. Not that any of those arguments meant a damn thing when Claire was just an arm's length away from him and seething with an anger he'd seldom seen in her but rightly deserved.

'We both moved on, didn't we, Andre?'

'You certainly did.'

'What did you expect me to do? You were the one who left, remember?'

He thought about the abrupt way he'd left things with her: unfinished, unexplained. He thought about his reasons, ironically none of which mattered anymore. Certainly not after what had happened last night. 'I couldn't stay.'

'You couldn't even tell me why? One day we were together and the next you were gone without a word.'

'I had things to work out,' he said.

God, he hated that he was still able to feel the punch of uncontainable fear – of shock and overwhelming self-revulsion – that had forced him to run away from everything and everyone he knew and loved. After what happened to him the last time he saw Claire, he'd had no choice but to leave her. He hadn't wanted to harm her, and he couldn't trust himself to be near her, or near anyone, until he'd managed to control the horrific power that had been awakened in him for the first time all those years ago. By that time, he had already lost her to Roth.

He gave her a negligent shrug. 'I did come back, Claire.'

'More than a year later,' she replied curtly. 'Or so I heard, after friends in the Darkhavens told me you had finally turned up, back in Berlin again.' She shook her head, regret shining in her gaze. 'I didn't think you would ever come back.'

'So you didn't wait.'

'Did you give me any reason to?'

'No,' he said, letting the word slide slowly off his tongue.

There was more he wanted to say, things he probably owed her to say, but it was all pointless talk now. Claire was right. They'd both moved on. They'd both lived very separate lives, and despite the fact that those lives were converging now, in violence and bloodshed, nothing he could say would change a thing about the past or what might have been. He was here for one reason: to avenge the wrong that Wilhelm Roth had delivered on him.

Reichen started walking again.

Claire trailed him, hanging back now as though she didn't want to get too close. 'What are you doing?'

'I told you. Looking for any intel on your mate's whereabouts.'

'And I told you – you won't find anything of his here. This is my home, not his.'

Reichen heard the peculiar comment but he was already moving on. He saw a room filled with floor-to-ceiling bookcases and headed for that open door.

'Andreas,' Claire said from behind him. 'Please, stop this. The library is my space. It's private. You won't find anything important in –'

'Then you won't mind if I have a look,' he said, more intent than ever since she was practically insisting that he stay out.

What was she hiding in there? He strode past towering shelf after shelf packed with books, past the small sofa and the end table where a ginger-jar lamp still glowed from the night before. Farther into the room, he saw a dark walnut desk in a mild state of disarray, as if the work had been abandoned in haste.

And beyond the desk, spread out on a wide worktable, was some kind of architect's scale model. Reichen guessed it to be some kind of Darkhaven project – something that would probably result in another photograph of Claire and her perfect smile, posing as the perfect mate next to Roth and a number of his cronies. But as he neared the model, the hairs at the back of his neck began to rise.

He knew this piece of land.

He knew the shape of it, the look of it . . . the feel of it.

It was his.

The lakefront wedge of property on the model was the site of his Darkhaven. Or, rather, it had been, before Roth's treachery and Reichen's own despair had left it in ruined rubble.

'What the hell is this?'

Claire came up beside him, her expression anxious. 'Andreas, everyone thought you were dead. There were no heirs alive to claim the property. It was going to be auctioned among the rest of the Berlin vampire community –'

'This was my land.' His voice took on an odd shake. 'This was my home.'

'I know,' she said quickly. 'I know, and I couldn't let it be sold. When some of us in the region held the memorial service for you and your family a few weeks ago and I learned no one had come forward to claim the land, I purchased the property myself. No one knew. I wanted to put something special on it. I hoped it could be a kind of sanctuary in remembrance of the lives that were lost.'

Reichen stared at the model of the tranquil park with its reflection pools and walking trails and meticulously plotted flower beds. The design was lovely. Perfect.

Claire had done this . . . *for him.*

He was astonished. Struck speechless.

'It probably wasn't my place to do it,' she said. 'I'm sorry. I just couldn't stand the thought of your home – and your kin's lives – being forgotten or sold off to the highest bidder. It didn't seem right. Then again, what I did probably doesn't seem right to you, either.'

Reichen stood there, silent, unmoving. To say he was shocked by Claire's act of compassion was understatement in the extreme. He was moved – more deeply than he had been in more years than he cared to remember. He stared at the architect's model, seeing all the detail, all the care and thought that had been put into the design.

For him, and for the memory of his kin.

He slowly turned to Claire, knowing his face must have been as rigid as stone by the way she took a step back.

Good, he thought. *Good. Keep her away.*

Because all he wanted to do in that moment was drag her hard into his arms and kiss her until neither one of them could breathe.

But she was Roth's mate.

His enemy's mate.

And he was still dangerous, still too near the razor's edge of hunger. If he touched Claire now, he didn't trust himself to stop there. If he'd been honorable at one time in his life, the fire that had been reawakened inside him three months ago had all but devoured that part of him. He was a threat to Claire, in far more ways than one.

'I need to be alone,' he muttered, a throaty snarl of sound.

He meant that; he couldn't be around her right now. He didn't want to think about the brief but indelible past he'd had with her, or how swiftly his body – his weak-willed heart, as well – still responded to the mere presence of her.

He didn't want to look at her now, as she was moving closer to him, her expression tender and caring, her hand held out as if she wanted to touch him. Something he craved in that moment with every selfish fiber of his being.

His pulse hammered hard in his veins. His mouth was wet with hunger for her, his sex going tight and heavy with desire.

Only a single pace separated her from him now. He stopped breathing as she lifted her hand up and gently placed it against his chest. 'Andreas, I'm sorry. I didn't mean any harm –'

'Get out, Claire.' He drew in a breath that hissed through his teeth and fangs. 'Now, goddamn it!'

She startled at his thunderous bark of anger, jumping back from him as though he might strike her. She blinked up at him for a long moment, her lips parted but unspeaking. Then she fled the room without a word. When he was certain she was gone, Reichen drifted over to the library doors and shut them tight. He told himself he was relieved that she was gone. If she valued her well-being at all, she'd leave the house and run as far away from him as she could get.

He only prayed he'd be strong enough to resist going after her between now and sundown, when he would have a chance to go out and slake his blood thirst on someone else . . . anyone else but her.

⇥ CHAPTER SIX ⇤

BOSTON, MASSACHUSETTS

Lucan Thorne pressed his mouth against the warm, soft skin just behind his Breedmate's left ear. Standing with her in the living room of their private quarters within the subterranean compound that belonged to the Order, he found it hard to let Gabrielle out of his arms. Instead, he held her, willfully neglecting his duties as the leader of the band of Breed warriors for another moment to enjoy the pleasure of feeling her close. He let his tongue play over the little crimson birthmark that hid on the tender patch of creamy flesh behind her ear, the very spot his fangs had pierced a short while ago as he and Gabrielle had made love.

'If you keep it up,' she murmured, 'we're going to be in here all night.'

He grunted, smiling as he continued to nuzzle her neck. 'Not a half-bad idea. And you should know that keeping it up is never a problem when I'm around you.'

'You're terrible, you know that?'

He caught her earlobe between his teeth and gave it a little nip. 'That's not what you said twenty minutes ago under the shower with me. Or before then, in our bed, when you had your long, beautiful thighs wrapped around my bare, bucking ass. Then you didn't think I was so terrible. You were too busy coming and screaming my name, telling me to never stop.' He didn't even try to conceal his masculine pride. Not that he needed to, when his arousal was definitely obvious in both the emerging of his fangs and the hard rise in his dark jeans. Beneath his gray T-shirt, he could feel his *dermaglyphs* pulsing in response to his desire for her. 'Correct me if I'm wrong, or did you say at one point that I was a god? An *amazing fucking god*, was, I believe, your exact opinion.'

'Arrogant bastard,' she scoffed, but he could hear the humor in her tone.

Her soft laughter melted into an inhaled, tremulous hiss as he grazed the tips of his sharp canines down along the curve of her shoulder. He splayed one hand into her thick auburn hair and she tilted her head to give him better access to her neck, her fingernails scoring into his shoulders as his free hand delved beneath her loose knit shirt and the waistband of her yoga pants. She shivered as he trailed his mouth and tongue along the delicate line of her throat, mewled a sweet little cry as his fingers dipped into the velvety cleft of her sex. She was still wet, still hot and gloriously responsive to his touch.

'Lucan,' she gasped. 'Oh, my God . . . *my God* . . .'

'Yeah, that's better,' he growled, catching her mouth in a deep kiss as he brought her to a swift, shuddering climax.

When she was recovered, Gabrielle lifted a wry but sated look at him. 'Does your ego know any bounds, vampire?'

He smirked, cocking a dark brow. 'Probably not.'

With a roll of her eyes, she grabbed his hand to lead him out of their quarters. He could have stayed there all night and not tired of loving her, of pleasuring her. But nightfall belonged to the Order, and to the crucial work that demanded all hands on deck – even the females of the compound, who were proving to be invaluable partners in a battle against an evil few could imagine. An evil that seemed intent on nothing less than all-out war.

At least the evil now had a name: Dragos. In the past several months, the Order had uncovered a lot about the second-generation vampire and the operation he'd been running for decades – centuries, in fact – while hiding behind multiple aliases and shadowy, covert alliances within the general population of the Breed. But there was much they didn't know, as well. Suspicions too grim to leave unanswered. It was the Order's current mission to uncover Dragos's alliances, locate his base of operations, and cripple his efforts before he could gain any more critical ground.

They'd had some recent success there, the latest being the disruption of a gathering outside Montreal, where Dragos and a number of his associates had convened this past summer. The Order had not yet been able to discover the purpose of the gathering, but the unexpected arrival of several warriors to the place where the group had been meeting had forced Dragos and his coconspirators to scatter.

The disruption of that gathering had also netted the Order a very unexpected ally – two, if the Gen One assassin who'd been bred and raised to serve Dragos and had since come on board with the Order could be trusted. Lucan still wasn't entirely sold on the vampire called Hunter. The male was as cold as a machine, secretive and aloof. Not that his unusual upbringing, denied any comforts and raised in total seclusion from another living soul except for the Minion assigned at birth as his handler, could hardly be expected to produce an easygoing team player. Hunter had given no outward cause to mistrust him, but he still seemed to Lucan a lone wolf of dubious origin, and one whose loyalty had not yet been tested.

But the other new ally to come out of the developments in Montreal was an unquestionable boon to the Order. Her name was Renata, and she had come to the Order as the Breedmate of Nikolai. As Lucan and Gabrielle walked past the weapons room on their way to the tech lab at the other end of the compound's labyrinth of corridors, he saw Niko and Renata inside, competing to obliterate twin targets at the end of the range. Leave it to a gearhead like Niko to pair up with a female who knew her way around automatic weaponry. But the couple's shared interests went much deeper than metal and explosives; they were also guardians to an orphaned young Breedmate named Mira, whom they'd rescued from a dangerous situation in Montreal and taken under their wing as their own child.

With Niko and Renata at the range was Tegan, one of the longest-standing members of the Order, and the warrior's Breedmate, Elise. When Tegan saw Lucan and Gabrielle walking past, he said something close to Elise's ear, kissed her, then came outside to the corridor.

He gave Gabrielle a nod of greeting, but when his gem-green gaze lit back on Lucan, he was all grim business. 'You talk to Gideon yet tonight?'

Lucan shook his head. 'We were just on our way to the tech lab now to see him. Why do I get the feeling this is not going to be a good night?'

'Bad news out of Germany,' Tegan said, raking a hand through his tawny hair. 'No doubt you recall the explosion that took out Andreas Reichen's Darkhaven?'

'Yeah.' Lucan recalled, all right. The Order lost one of its best civilian allies – a true friend – the night that Reichen and his family were killed in the freak blast that leveled his estate. The loss had hit the warriors pretty hard, and not just for the fact that Reichen had been an instrumental partner in the Order's current efforts to take out Dragos. He was a good man, an honorable male who should have lived to see the peace that his efforts with the Order were helping to ensure.

Tegan's tone was as grave as his expression. 'Gideon got a report out of Hamburg today. Seems another Darkhaven over there went up in flames last night. Complete annihilation.'

'Good lord,' Gabrielle whispered, clutching Lucan's hand a bit tighter. 'Were there any survivors?'

'Just one,' Tegan said. 'An Enforcement Agent doing security detail there who managed to escape and report the attack. He died a few hours later.'

'You said 'attack'?' Lucan frowned, not liking the sound of that at all. 'What exactly do we know about this?'

'Not much right now. Gideon's still gathering intel, but the Agency is keeping a lot of it close to their chest. The Darkhaven that went down last night belonged to one of their directors. Second-generation civilian named Wilhelm Roth. Apparently, the director and his Breedmate were both out of town at the time, lucky for them.'

Lucan didn't know Roth, but then he and the rest of the Order weren't exactly on friendly terms with most of the Enforcement Agency, either here in the States or abroad. The Order tended to think the Agency was a lot of pompous blowhards more interested in their own personal gain than public safety, and the Agency tended to think the Order was a gang of dangerous vigilantes with no regard for the law.

Partly true, Lucan had to acknowledge. Neither he nor any of his brethren had any use for the kind of circle-jerk politics and head-in-the-sand policies that were the Agency's notion of the law. As a result, they generally disregarded them in favor of actually taking action and getting shit done. If that didn't sit well with folks like Wilhelm Roth and the rest of the Enforcement Agency, they were more than welcome to kiss the Order's ass and step out of the way.

'Let's see what Gideon's got,' Lucan said, already heading with Gabrielle toward the tech lab down the corridor.

Tegan fell in at an easy gait beside them, and Lucan couldn't help thinking back to a time not that long ago when he and his fellow warrior – both of them Gen Ones with many centuries of life between them – had spent more time at each other's throats than walking side by side as equals. Now, as the two of them strode into the tech lab with Gabrielle, the other warriors gathered in what served as the Order's conference room all looked up from what they were doing, as if the air had somehow gotten thicker with the arrival of the two eldest, most powerful members of the group.

The three most recent additions to the Order's ranks – Kade, Brock, and Chase – were dressed in basic black patrol gear, from their lug-soled Docs and dark denim, to their black shirts, leather jackets, and arsenal of semiautomatics and blades that rode at their hips. The trio of unmated males had taken on a lot of the grunt assignments, a night of hunting trouble on Boston's back alleys topped off by hunting of a different sort at some of the city's after-hours clubs.

As for the other, mated warriors, they did their share of heavy lifting for the Order, as well, but looking at them now – Rio seated beside his Breedmate, Dylan, and Dante, unable to keep from stroking the six-month swell of his Breedmate Tess's pregnant belly while he casually shot the shit with Chase and the others – it was clear that things were changing here at the compound. *Evolving,* Lucan thought, as Gabrielle let go of his hand to walk over and sit on the floor beside little Mira and Savannah, who was mated to the resident genius, Gideon. Lucan's heart went a bit tight as he watched his Breedmate smile and fall into an easy chatter with the child and Savannah, who'd been passing a squeaky rubber ball between them, playing a game of keep-away with an ugly little terrier mutt that belonged to Dante and Tess.

The whole scene was unnerving as hell.

Somehow, in the past year and a half, the compound had begun to feel less like a military stronghold and more like a home. That gave Lucan more than a little concern. Homes could be made vulnerable, especially in times of war. He thought about the two Darkhavens in Germany that had been standing strong one day and were rubble the next. It was hard to shake the coldness that settled in his gut when he considered how easily lives – and loved ones – could cease to exist.

'I can see by the look on your face that Tegan brought you up to speed on some of the news out of Hamburg,' Gideon said, spinning away from his fleet of computer workstations and regarding Lucan soberly over the rims of his pale blue glasses. 'Do you want to hear the really fucked up part of all this?'

'Why not,' Lucan drawled.

'I've been doing a little remote digging in the Agency records in Germany. Turns out they're having some problems keeping their guys alive over there.' At Lucan's questioning look, Gideon went on. 'Over the past several weeks, nine Enforcement Agents between the Berlin and Hamburg offices have been murdered.'

Tegan joined the conversation now, coming over to look at the data on Gideon's monitors. 'You talking assassinations?'

Lucan had been thinking the same thing, instantly wondering if the others like Hunter, trained Gen One killers who'd recently been ordered by Dragos to track down and assassinate the eldest members of the vampire race, had somehow now turned their sights on individuals within the Enforcement Agency.

'It's not like any of the stuff we've been seeing among the civilian populations,' Gideon said. 'Those killings are careful – shit, they're practically works of art they're so efficient.' He swung back around and typed something that brought up a morgue image of a bruised, bloodied Breed male who was missing part of his skull. 'These Agency killings are brutal, very personal. One entire field unit was taken out man by man, and there've been some high-ranking agents – I'm talking director-level folks – who've been cut down, as well. Someone over there is trying to make a very loud statement. If you ask me, it reeks of payback.'

⫷ CHAPTER SEVEN ⫸

A ndreas hadn't come out of the library all day.
Claire sat in the foyer outside the closed doors, having quietly taken up her post on a small upholstered bench a few minutes after he'd driven her from the room with his bellowed demand that she go. Her back ached from the uncomfortable seating and she was exhausted, having not dared to sleep for more than a few minutes at a time.

She didn't know what he was doing in there. She didn't even know if he was all right. There had been no answer when she knocked on the doors a couple of hours ago to check on him. Now she sat on the little bench with her feet drawn up on the cushion and her arms locked around her knees, staring at the silent room as if a wild, rabid animal waited inside.

It was nearly sundown. It wouldn't be long before the Enforcement Agency detail that Wilhelm was going to arrange for showed up to remove Andreas.

Claire knew she'd done the right thing in going to Wilhelm for help. She'd done the only thing she could, not only for her own imminent safety and that of her mate, but also for Andreas. The stark fear she'd felt for him last night had since muted into a wary kind of sympathy. He was so broken now. So raw with fury.

She only hoped he would have the sense to go quietly with

the Enforcement Agents when they arrived. If he put up a struggle . . . well, she couldn't even let her mind go there.

The latch on the library doors gave a soft *click*. Claire looked up, let her legs unfold and her feet settle on the foyer floor as Andreas came out of the room. He seemed much improved physically and even though he sent a dark glower in her direction, he appeared calmer, more rested than when she'd left him in there. Maybe there was hope that he could be reasoned with after all.

'You're still here,' he remarked, plainly displeased. 'I'd have thought you'd be hours away by now.'

'No,' Claire murmured.

Andreas scoffed. 'Roth must know of a number of Agency safe houses in the area where he could have sent you. I'm surprised you didn't bolt for one of them the first chance you got.'

Claire didn't tell him that Wilhelm had ordered her to stay at the country house. It had bothered her then, but now, being forced to hold Andreas's piercing gaze, she felt more than an inkling of shame to think that her mate would willingly keep her in harm's way. Of course, she had never presented herself as a hapless, helpless female, and Wilhelm wouldn't have expected her to remain in Andreas's company unless he trusted she could handle the situation.

That rationalization felt a bit hollow when she recalled the caustic way he'd told her to do whatever she must to detain Andreas for the long hours until the agents were able to get there. *You know him better than most. I'm sure you'll think of something.*

'It must be near dusk.' Andreas's deep voice ran up her skin like a charge. 'How long do you suppose it will take Roth to get here?'

Claire blinked, then shook her head. 'I don't know what you mean.'

His answering smile was cold, unconvinced. 'Are you really

going to sit there and pretend that you didn't seek him out for help and to warn him about me?' When she would have attempted to deny it, his mouth went a little tighter. 'Just so you know, Claire, I hope you did go to him. I hope you told him to come as fast as he could, because I'm damned well ready to end this.'

Her blood chilled. 'Are you really so eager to die, Andre?'

He scoffed. 'I'm not the one you need to worry about.'

Amber sparks lit up his irises, and she could see the points of his sharp white fangs as he spoke, potent reminders that although his anger seemed to have banked, it wouldn't take much for it to ignite again. It might be safer to try to lie to him, but she felt she owed him some honesty regardless of the risks. 'All right. I did go to Wilhelm. I dreamwalked to him while you were in the cellar, just as you guessed. But your misguided need for vengeance will have to wait because he's not coming.'

'You told him I was here?'

'Yes.' Claire stood up as Andreas took a step closer to her on the bench. 'He's my mate. I had to warn him.'

'You told him about the fires? About his Darkhaven in Hamburg?' At her nod, his eyes narrowed on her. He inched nearer, crowding her between his big body and the upholstered bench pressed tightly against the back of her legs. 'Does he know that you are left alone with me, at my mercy?'

Claire swallowed. 'He knows all of that.'

And still he's not coming.

Although Andreas didn't speak the words, they were written clearly enough on his face. Claire glanced away from him because it was suddenly too hard to hold his knowing stare. To her utter shock, she felt his fingers light gently beneath her chin. When she followed that guiding touch, lifting her eyes back up to him, there was nothing the least bit gentle in his expression.

'Does he have any idea how dangerous it is for you to be alone with me like this, Claire?'

He searched her face, his warm breath skating across her brow. He stood so close to her, she could feel his heartbeat pounding, the strong, steady drum of it doing something crazy to her own pulse, as well.

An unbidden yearning kicked up inside her, hot and twisting. It took all her strength of will not to turn her cheek into his palm and nuzzle against the warm curve of his fingers against her skin.

This was wrong.

This was insane.

Oh, God . . . this was something she hadn't known for such a long time.

Which only proved that Andreas was right. Being alone with him like this was very, very dangerous.

'If you were mine,' he murmured low under his breath, 'I would walk through the fires of hell itself to keep you away from a man like me.'

Claire stared into his amber-flecked eyes, unsure what to say to him. Unsure what to think. All she knew was the feeling that was suddenly ablaze inside her – a kindling sense of longing and regret that shook her to her core.

It was regret that won out.

Scowling suddenly, Andreas broke her gaze. He glanced over his shoulder, head cocked slightly to the side, listening. Claire heard nothing, but then she didn't possess the preternaturally keen hearing of the Breed. Nor did she have to hear in order to understand what was going on outside the manor house.

'Enforcement Agents,' she whispered. 'Wilhelm said he would arrange for a unit to come in at sundown to work everything out with you.'

Andreas backed off her with a dark chuckle. 'A death squad.'

'No,' she said. *Dear God, she hoped not.* 'Nothing's going to happen to you. I won't let it. Andre –'

He wasn't listening to her now. In fluid motion, he loped to the stairwell and started climbing the steps two at a time. 'Get out of the house, Claire. Do it now.'

Like hell she would. She hissed a curse and ran after him instead.

He ducked into a second-floor bedroom at the front of the house, heading straight for the window. He tore off the UV-blocking shutters and peered through the mangled metal at the grounds below, swearing something nasty. Claire came up behind him just in time to see the black shapes of several armed agents scrambling in stealth formation toward the house.

Andreas wheeled around, the tips of his fangs gleaming behind his upper lip. Accusation glinted hard in his eyes. 'Do they look like they've come to negotiate with me?'

Claire didn't have a chance to answer.

Downstairs, there was a crash of breaking glass, followed by the heavy pound of boots hitting polished marble. The agents were pouring inside.

'What will you do?' she asked him in a tight whisper, feeling the energy in the room begin to heat up already. It was Andreas generating the strange crackle in the air. His fury was growing, bringing with it the terrible power of his pyrokinesis. 'Andre, listen to me . . . you can't continue like this. Please. I'm begging you –'

His face was fierce, eyes blazing. 'Wilhelm Roth is the one who should be begging me. Not you.'

The thunder of footsteps continued on the first floor as the agents split up to search the house. Someone called for Claire, advising her to make her position known to the invading unit.

'Go on,' Andreas said. 'Let them take you to safety outside.'

She knew she should. God help her, she knew with every scrap of logic in her mind that the smartest, most reasonable thing for her to do would be to let Wilhelm's men escort her out of the house while they tried to convince Andreas to give himself up peacefully.

Her mind knew all of that.

It was her heart that hesitated.

'Goddamn it, Claire.' Andreas stalked over to her and seized her arms in a bruising grasp. He gave her a brisk shake. 'What the hell is wrong with you?'

A shattering clap of sound exploded from behind her. Heat arrowed past her right ear, blowing strands of her loose hair into her face. She felt the sudden impact of the bullet as it missed her by a scant inch and slammed into the upper left side of Andreas's chest.

'Nooo!' she screamed, horrified.

He staggered back on his heels, but the shot didn't take him down. The mingled scents of gunpowder and blood filled Claire's head.

They'd shot him.

Oh, Christ . . . no.

Blocking Andreas with her own body, she spun around to face the Enforcement Agent who stood in the open doorway of the bedroom. His huge black rifle was still aimed at Andreas, his finger hovering dangerously at the trigger.

'Are you all right, Frau Roth?'

For a long moment, she had no breath to speak. Her heart was jackhammering in her chest, her knees almost jelly beneath her. The agent spoke to her, but his focus was centered wholly on Andreas, who loomed behind her, throwing off heat like a furnace.

'It's okay,' said the agent. 'I've got him covered. He won't hurt you anymore.'

The agent stepped farther into the room, cautious progress that brought him to within arm's length of Claire. His weapon remained locked on target. As he neared, Andreas let loose with a feral-sounding growl. The heat that Claire felt coming off him before was getting stronger now, making the fine hairs at the back of her neck stand on end.

'Please,' she finally managed to croak. 'You don't have any idea what you're doing. Put down your weapon.'

The agent's eyes darted to her for only a fraction of a second, as though to gauge her sanity – or lack thereof. 'You need to step aside, Frau Roth. I have specific orders here. I mean to carry them out.'

Specific orders to kill Andreas on the spot.

The realization sank into her consciousness like poison. They *were* a death squad, just as Andreas knew they would be. Wilhelm had called for his death. Not only that, but he would have his men kill Andre in cold blood, right in front of her.

The agent's voice was lethally cold now, and in the narrowing distance outside the bedroom, more agents were making a swift climb up the stairs.

'Step aside, Frau Roth. I'm afraid I can't ask you again.'

The rifle came closer, a very convincing threat. She had no intention of cooperating with the agent, but in that next instant she sensed, rather than saw, Andreas's arm come up and around her to reach for the weapon with blinding speed. Heat traveled all along her side with the movement, sending out an electrical current that vibrated deep in her bones.

Andreas locked his fist around the gun's barrel. His arm was glowing with heat that radiated down to his fingers in rings of pulsing white-hot light. The energy leapt from him and onto the rifle in bright undulations.

Instantly, the agent's eyes went wide. His head lolled back on his shoulders and his body went into a violent spasm that made his teeth clatter. Claire smelled burning skin and hair. Sickened, she looked away as the Breed male dropped to the floor and convulsed from the sudden dose of lethal power. Before he was dead, another agent came racing into the room, his weapon at the ready.

'Claire, stay back!' Andreas roared at her.

At that same instant, he threw off more heat and light,

expelling it like a cannonball that materialized out of the palm of his hand. He threw the orb of fire at the newly arrived agent, killing him on the spot. Flames erupted all around. Fire crept up the far wall and onto the ceiling.

Andreas shot a fierce look over his bleeding shoulder to where Claire stood behind him, awestruck by the terrible power he possessed. 'Come on. We have to get out of here.'

She followed him out of the burning room and onto the second-floor landing. Two more agents were scrambling up the stairs to head them off. He stopped them halfway there, unleashing twin fireballs that exploded like bombs, tearing a hole in the silk-papered wall and taking a large bite out of the curving wooden staircase.

As they navigated to the ground level, Claire stayed close to him – but not too close, mindful of the searing energy that rode every inch of his body. When she got so much as a foot away from Andreas, his heat was overwhelming. The incinerating glow that had covered him in the woods last night was back again. If she touched him now, even accidentally, she knew it would kill her.

But as an inferno of his making surged hotter upstairs and in the foyer, and as Andreas dispatched the rest of the death squad that had come to kill him on what could only have been Wilhelm's explicit orders, Claire knew that this lethal being – this man she had possibly never fully understood – was her best chance of surviving the next few minutes.

So she ran when he told her to run. She stuck as close as she dared. It wasn't until they both were out of the manor house, feet flying over the cool, moonlit autumn grass outside, that Claire allowed herself to drop to her knees and let the tears fall.

She pivoted around, choking on the crisp night air and her own strangling confusion of emotions. Her house was ablaze. More lives were lost. She wanted to scream, but in the deepest corner of her heart, all she knew was a selfish, swamping relief that Andreas was still breathing.

She swiveled her head to look at him. The large, bright shape of him wobbled through her welling tears. How many times in the past few months had she wished that he were still alive? How many tears had she secretly shed for him and his perished kin?

No matter what Andreas said, she could not allow herself to believe for one second that Wilhelm had had anything to do with the destruction of Andreas's Darkhaven. She hoped with every shred of her being that his accusations were wrong.

But now, after what happened here tonight, she couldn't dislodge the sharp pebble of doubt that had embedded itself under her skin. And she knew she wouldn't be able to rest until she knew of Wilhelm's guilt or innocence for a fact.

She needed answers. Now more than ever, she needed to understand just what kind of man Wilhelm Roth truly was.

'Are you all right?' Andreas asked as she wiped her wet eyes and got to her feet.

Claire nodded, but inside she felt numb, a growing sense of sickness roiling in the pit of her stomach. 'He would have had you killed tonight,' she murmured. 'I didn't know, Andreas. I swear to you, I didn't know.'

He stared at her in silence, watching her through the pulsating glow of fire that still traveled his body. He was bleeding and wounded, monstrous with heat, all because of Wilhelm. And because of her. She regretted contacting Wilhelm now, regardless of any obligation she might have to him as his Breedmate. She had practically signed Andreas's death warrant herself.

'They will send more agents before long,' she said. 'When this unit doesn't report in to Wilhelm, he will only send in more to find you.'

'Yes,' Andreas said, his tone flat and grimly accepting. 'He will send in more men and I will kill them, too, until I take out so many that Roth has no choice but to face me himself. I welcome that moment. I don't care what it takes to get there.'

Claire shuddered internally at the thought of so much violence and death. She was desperate for answers of her own from Wilhelm, and she wasn't about to stand around and wait to witness more bloodshed and flames. She walked past Andreas and headed toward the road that led off the estate.

'Claire,' he called from behind her, but she kept walking, moving with a new kind of resolve. Andreas's deep voice reached out to her from the stretch of darkness in her wake. 'Claire . . . where the hell do you think you're going?'

She paused, turned a weary look on him. 'You say you mean to locate Wilhelm and take your revenge on him. Now I need the truth from him. Most of his business is conducted from a private office in the city. Maybe if we go there, we'll both find the answers we need.'

⇥ CHAPTER EIGHT ⇤

Reichen wasn't sure which was worse: the persistent pain of his gunshot wound, or the way his gut twisted with the urgency to feed. One thing would take care of both problems.

Blood.

He felt a snarl work its way up his parched throat as his nostrils filled with the mingled odors of dozens of humans in close proximity to him, all of them trapped together in the tight compartment of the train into Hamburg. The temptation to glance up and single out viable prey – the need to quench his burning thirst – was almost overwhelming.

'Keep your head down,' Claire whispered to him, her breath skating warmly against his ear. 'Your eyes, too, Andre.'

Bad enough he was injured and bleeding, and that both he and Claire smelled like a pair of chimney sweeps. It wouldn't be a good idea to let any of the passengers seated around them get a look at his transformed eyes or his rather unusual dental situation.

At least his fury had cooled.

He and Claire had walked for about an hour before the glow of his pyrokinesis had ebbed. They'd had no choice but to travel on foot. Until his metabolism leveled out, anything he touched, anything that got too near him, would incinerate to ashes. Claire seemed to pick up on that fact, and she'd kept a careful distance from him while he struggled to get his internal systems back in line.

Being Breed, and despite being shot, Reichen could have easily walked the entire two-hour distance from Roth's country house to his private office in Hamburg. He could have crossed the miles at a speed human eyes couldn't possibly track, but no way would he have abandoned Claire to the night by herself. Not after everything she'd been through. Or, rather, everything that he had put her through.

She was weary and fatigued, even now, seated next to him on the inbound train. She hadn't put up much of an argument at all when he led her to the rural village station and asked her which line they needed to take. They'd had no money on them, so Reichen had procured their passage with a little Breed-born sleight of hand. At his suggestion, the man collecting tickets fell into a quick but brief trance, giving them the opportunity to slip past the turnstiles and board the train with no one the wiser.

The trick had sapped just about all of his strength, but at least Claire was out of the cold and able to relax. He, on the other hand, was as twitchy and tense as he could be. Reichen tucked his chin down to his chest and hunched his shoulders to help conceal his assorted visible problems from any curious human eyes.

His thirst was another thing.

It gnawed at him, always at its most fevered after the fire. Under ordinary circumstances, he and his kind could go a week or more without feeding, but since the attack on his Darkhaven and the reawakening of the deadly power inside him, his thirst was persistent.

Almost constant.

He'd seen others among his kind fall into blood addiction. It didn't happen often, mostly among those of weaker minds and lesser years, or, on the other end of the spectrum, the earliest generations of the Breed whose bloodlines were less diluted with human genes and closer to the Ancients – the alien fathers of the vampire race on Earth.

Reichen's pyrokinetic curse was bad enough, but the thirst that rose in its wake horrified him every bit as much as the fires he could summon at will. And if he was being honest, with himself at least, he could hardly deny that the fires were becoming less of a response to his fury and more of a ruling part of who he was.

Since he'd begun his mission of vengeance on Roth a few weeks ago, the fires were strengthening. Now they sprang to life with barely a thought, burning deeper and longer, more explosive every time. And once they faded, he was gripped with a blood thirst that could hardly be contained or sated.

He was losing himself to both, and he knew it. If he stayed in Claire's company much longer, she would know it, too.

Even as the gravity of that thought coiled around him, Reichen couldn't help watching in his periphery as a young hipster got up from his seat across the compartment from him and moved to a place that had been vacated at the last stop. Reichen followed the human male with a predator's gaze, noting the young man's lack of awareness of his surroundings as he flopped down onto the seat. White earbuds emitted tinny echoes of the music that was blaring into the human's head. Downcast, sullen eyes peeked out from under a sweep of jagged black bangs, all of the hipster's focus rooted on the touch screen of his iPhone as he busied himself with an intense round of text messaging.

Reichen watched with the same keen interest as a lion observing wildebeests at the watering hole, his hunting instincts prickling to attention, already separating the easiest prey from the pack of other commuters. The train slowed. As it pulled into a station, the human got up. Reichen's muscles tensed in reflex. He started to follow, hunger ruling him, but Claire's hand came down gently on his forearm.

'Not this one. We get off at the next station.'

He sat back down and tried not to let the irritated growl

escape him as the train's doors slid shut and his erstwhile meal ambled obliviously into the crowd newly poured onto the platform.

A few minutes later, he and Claire reached their stop. They got off the train and walked the rest of the way to the Speicherstadt, Hamburg's warehouse district. Rows of tall redbrick buildings divided by canal waterways glowed with incandescent light against the night sky. The mingled aromas of coffee beans and spices rode on the crisp breeze as Claire led him over a sweeping arched bridge, then deeper into the historic district. As the scents would indicate, some of the gothic buildings appeared to still be in use as commodities warehouses; others had been converted to stores housing fine Oriental rugs.

Claire continued on for another couple of blocks before she paused in front of a brick-and-limestone building that looked like any of its neighbors. A trio of concrete steps flanked by delicate wrought-iron railings led up to an unmarked, unnumbered door.

'This place belongs to Roth?' Reichen asked as they reached the top step.

She nodded. 'One of several private offices he keeps in the city. Will you be able to open the locks?'

'If not by will, then by brute force,' he said, moving in front of her to direct a mental command at the double dead bolts on the door. He hit them hard with his mind, careful not to wake the fire that still lurked at the edge of his control, waiting for the excuse to burn again. With a series of metallic *clicks*, the dead bolts twisted free and the door inched open. When Claire started to pass him and walk inside, Reichen held her back with a look. 'Wait here while I look around. It might not be safe.'

He recognized the irony in his protectiveness as he stepped into the dark building and searched for any signs of trouble. Running into more Enforcement Agents would be a definite problem, but he was by far the worst threat to Claire's safety. Especially in his current hungered state.

'All right,' he told her when he was certain the quiet building was empty. He flicked on a light switch for her as she entered.

Roth's tastes in this place were an incongruous mix of Old World and modern minimalist. Slick chrome-and-glass pieces competed with exquisite antiques. The art on the walls were beautiful masterworks, yet every painting depicted a scene of horrific brutality. Death scenes appeared to be a favorite, whether the subject was men, women, or animals. Apparently Roth didn't discriminate when it came to his appreciation for violence.

'How often does he stay here?' Reichen asked, not missing the fact that there was a bedroom loft occupying the entire upper floor.

'Often. At least, from what I understand,' Claire said quietly, but without any bitterness as she walked over to a computer workstation and turned on the machine. As it fired up, she opened one of the desk drawers and began sifting through its contents. 'I do know that his work for the Agency has also taken him to Berlin from time to time.'

Reichen looked up at her, seeing the doubt in her soft brown gaze. She may not want to believe his accusations against her mate, but Claire was wrestling with at least some measure of uncertainty about Wilhelm Roth.

'How is your wound?' she asked, looking remorseful where she had no reason to be.

Reichen shrugged his good shoulder. The bullet had passed through cleanly; once he fed, the healing would speed even faster. 'I'll live,' he said. 'Long enough to do what must be done.'

He could see her throat work as she swallowed. 'When will you stop all of this, Andre? How many more people have to die?'

His answer was grim and resolute. 'Just one.'

She held his hard stare. 'What will you do if your accusations against him turn out to be false?'

'What will you do if they turn out to be true?'

She didn't say anything as he came over to where she stood, just backed away a few paces and gave him access to the computer and the handful of business cards and receipts that she had emptied onto the desk. Reichen brought up Roth's e-mail and started searching his records – looking for precisely what, he wasn't certain. Clues of Roth's activities, his contacts. Leads on his current whereabouts. Anything.

What he needed to do was focus on his reasons for being there in the first place, not the inescapable awareness of Claire standing so near him, a warmth and presence that he felt straight into his marrow. He was working so hard to ignore his visceral response to her that he looked at the mess of business cards on Roth's desk three times before his eye lit on the one made of silver vellum with elegantly simple black type.

He plucked the card out of the collection and read it, despite that he knew the name and address listed on it by heart. Even though it truly came as no surprise that he should find the card among Roth's possessions, he still felt his blood run cold in his veins.

'What did you find?' Claire asked, no doubt sensing his sudden tension. She came closer, peered around him at the scrap of translucent paper in his hand. 'Aphrodite. What is that?'

'A club in Berlin,' Reichen replied. 'It's an exclusive, very expensive brothel.'

He glanced at Claire in time to see her curiosity change to a look of quiet discomfort. 'Wilhelm's never had a shortage of willing female company. He would consider it beneath him to have to pay for it. The fact that he has that card means nothing.'

'It means he was there,' Reichen said. 'I don't need this scrap of paper to prove it. The owner of Aphrodite and I were . . . close. I trusted Helene implicitly.'

Claire glanced away from him for a moment. 'I'd heard a while ago that you'd taken up with a mortal woman. One of many, from what I understand.'

He let the comment go uncountered, but he was surprised to hear that she'd been aware of his personal affairs. And yes, there had been many women in his life over the years, a string of forgettable liaisons he'd taken little pride in, even now. Especially now.

But he had respected Helene more than the other human females he'd taken into his bed or under his fangs. She had become a close confidante, a true friend, though even she had been oblivious to the darker, deadly side of him he'd worked so hard to suppress.

'Helene was a good woman. She knew I was Breed and she kept the secret. She also kept me informed about things going on at the club. Recently I learned that one of her employees had begun dating a wealthy, very important man on the side. This employee had shown up for work more than once with bite marks on her neck. Not long afterward, she vanished without a trace. I asked Helene to look into it, and she came back with a name: Wilhelm Roth.'

Claire's brow creased with her frown. 'Just because this girl might have spent time with him doesn't mean he killed her.'

'He didn't stop there,' Reichen said, his voice tight. 'While I was away on another matter, Helene showed up at my Darkhaven. Someone let her in, not realizing it was an ambush. Helene had been made a Minion since I'd last seen her. Her master sent her to my home with a unit of armed assassins – an Enforcement Agency death squad. They killed everyone inside. They shot all of them in cold blood, Claire. Even the children.'

She gaped up at him aghast, slowly shaking her head. 'No, there was an explosion. A terrible fire –'

'Yes, there was,' Reichen admitted, taking her by the arms as his anger began to roil in remembrance. 'I set the house ablaze, but not until after I arrived and saw the slaughter inside. And not until after I found Helene waiting for me, covered in my family's blood. She told me who made her, Claire . . . just before I ended her misery then burned my home and all the souls in it to the ground.'

Claire's tender brown eyes swam with a sudden rise of tears, but she said nothing. Not a word of denial or disbelief. Not a single syllable in defense of her mate.

'Andre . . .'

She shouldn't have touched him. The warm feel of her palm coming up to rest gently on his cheek sent him over an edge he'd been teetering on since the moment he laid eyes on her again. A hell of a lot longer than that, if he was being honest.

Reichen brought his hand around to the soft arch of her nape and pulled her close. He bent his head and pressed his mouth to hers. There was no tentativeness, no meek beginnings, as their lips came together and meshed in a fevered kiss that was as familiar and righteous as it was forbidden.

Claire.

Ah, Christ.

He'd nearly forgotten what it felt like to hold her, to kiss her. To want her with a need that scorched as hot as lava in his belly. His body remembered all the ways she'd once made him burn. Arousal surged through him, turning his blood to fire and his cock to hard-forged steel. In that instant, he didn't care that he was injured and bleeding and hell-bent on vengeance.

He didn't care that she belonged to another – his most treacherous enemy. All he knew was the heat of Claire's mouth on his. The warm press of her curves against him.

He wanted more.

He wanted all of her, and now the hunger that had been clinging to him so relentlessly was wrapping its tendrils around him even tighter. His stomach twisted, burning. His fangs ripped farther out of his gums, the sharp points throbbing with every moist brush of her lips against his.

He wanted to taste her. God help him, he wanted to drown in her, right here and now.

She should be his. This kiss told him she was his, still, even if Breed law and the blood bond she'd given to another male forbade it.

She would always be his . . .

No.

Reichen growled as he tore his mouth away from hers and set her away from him with rough, unsteady hands. His chest was heaving, breath sawing through his teeth and fangs. The bullet wound in his upper chest screamed with renewed pain, all the worse for the way his veins were pounding with hunger. The room felt too hot, stifling. He needed to cool down before his threadbare restraint got any thinner.

Claire was staring at him with her fingers pressed to her kiss-swollen mouth, as if she didn't know whether to scream or cry.

'I need some air,' he muttered. 'Jesus Christ, this was a fucking mistake coming here with you. I need to get the hell out of here.'

'Andreas.' He pivoted to head for the door, but before he could take more than a couple of steps, Claire was right behind him. 'Where are you going? Talk to me, please.'

He kept walking, hoping like hell she would just let him go. He wanted Roth to pay for what he'd done, but did he really have a right to take Claire down in the process? Some selfish part of him reasoned that it would only be fair if Roth's mate was part of his price. What better vengeance than to ruin the corrupt son of a bitch and claim his woman for his own?

Jesus.

He didn't want to go there.

As tempting as it was, that wasn't what this was about. He'd gone to great lengths decades ago to shield Claire from the deadly monster he had become. He hadn't done that only to come back and destroy her now . . . had he?

'Andreas, please don't walk away from me.' Her voice trailed him as he reached to open the door. She let out a choked, humorless laugh, full of pain and raw contempt. When she finally found her voice again, it was soft with condemnation. 'Goddamn you. How can you still make me feel this way after all these years? Damn you for leaving me! And damn you for coming back like this, just when I thought you were gone forever and I might finally be able to forget you.'

In spite of every instinct that shouted for him to put one foot in front of the other and take his deadly business with Roth far away from Claire, Reichen paused. She didn't know how dangerous he was right now. Or maybe she did, but was too confused and pissed off to care.

She drew in an audible breath, then blew it out on a defeated-sounding sigh. 'Goddamn you, Andre, for standing here and making me doubt every choice I've ever made.'

He turned to face her justifiable outrage. Blood thirst swamped him as he looked at her, his physical need for sustenance warring with the carnal desire that no amount of chill night air would be able to cool. She was so beautiful and strong. So good and honest. And she was furious with him now; the frantic ticking of her pulse at the base of her buttery light brown throat was testament to that.

Reichen couldn't look away from the steady pound of her heartbeat.

The fire had taken its toll on him as much as the hit he took to the chest earlier tonight. He was no longer in control of his thirst; it had overthrown his will now. It was all he knew as he moved toward Claire, everything about him that was Breed and male trained wholly on this woman.

'Why did you leave me?' she asked as he neared her.

He grunted, savoring the vanilla sweet scent of her blood as it raced beneath the surface of her delicate skin. 'To protect you.'

She frowned, dubious. 'From what?'

'From the worst of me.'

She gave a slow shake of her head. 'I was never afraid of you, Andre. I'm still not afraid.'

'You damn well should be . . . *Frau Roth.*'

He bared his fangs and pinned her in the amber glow of his transformed eyes – one brief moment's warning, enough for her to back away from him or hit him or scream. She couldn't know how hard it was for him to give her even that much. He moved closer to her, crowding her with his body, even as he told himself he still had honor, that the fire living inside him hadn't yet burned away all of his humanity.

But that was a lie.

He felt the bleak hollowness of that hope crumble the instant his fangs bit into the tender flesh of Claire's throat.

She gasped. Her hands came up between the hard press of his body against hers, her palms flattened across his sternum. He felt her sudden tension, her jolt of shock and adrenaline as he caged her in his arms and drew the first taste of her warm, rich blood into his mouth.

At first, he fed with mindless hunger. Gulp after gulp, driven by the primal need for nourishment. But through the haze of his blood-fevered mind, as he drank from Claire's vein, he began to feel something . . . else.

Her blood scent swamped him, filling his head like the sweetest intoxication. The rapid beat of her pulse against his tongue now blossomed into a visceral pound that echoed in his own blood. Possession rose within him, dark and dangerous. He held her fast in his bite, savoring the taste of her as his body went rigid with the need to claim her in a more carnal way, as well.

He felt her fingers digging into his back as he drank from

her, breath rasping in soft, shallow pants against his ear. His senses filled with her. A low, humming power flowed into him, power he felt roaring through his cells and into every fiber of his body. Deeper still, into the fabric of his soul, the core of his entire being.

Claire was the first, the only Breedmate he'd ever drunk from, and now there could be no other for him so long as she lived. All that was Breed in him came alive as though he'd been asleep all his life and now overflowed with a profound awareness of this female – now and forever. An eternal stamp, a bond of blood.

A connection to her that he could not undo except by death, hers or his own.

'Andreas.'

Claire's soft cry of distress tore through him like a knife.

Horrified at what he'd just done to her – to both of them – he sealed her wound with a quick sweep of his tongue and reeled back on his heels. Her cheeks were flushed dark rose, her breath sawing through her parted lips as she stared at him in abject shock. Reichen felt her dread like his own. Every intense emotion she felt from now on would be his, as well.

'Andre,' she whispered, lifting her hand up to touch his healing bite. Her face was twisted with a miserable sort of confusion. 'Oh, my God . . . What have you done?'

He took a step backward, leveled by shame.

Claire belonged to another male. Not him. She had given herself to Roth, whether Reichen liked it or not. She was already blood bonded, as Roth was blood bonded to her. Now, with this unconscionable breach of that sacrament, Reichen had imposed himself on that bond.

In drinking from Claire, he had irrevocably linked himself to her.

He would be drawn to her always. Aware of her always. It was the most sacred gift a Breedmate could give one of his kind, and he had taken it from her – stolen it – in an act of pure selfish need.

'Forgive me, Claire,' he murmured. Sick with himself for how deeply he wanted her, with or without the drumming intensity of a blood bond, he drew farther away from her. He drifted backward, inching toward the door. 'Ah, Christ . . . Please, forgive me.'

⤙ CHAPTER NINE ⤚

Andreas, wait.'

He didn't wait. No, he wouldn't even look at her. Spinning around, he was at the door faster than her human eyes could follow the motion. He threw the door open to the cold night. Stepped onto the concrete stoop outside.

'Andre . . .'

The brief glance he cast at her over his shoulder was feral and hot. His fangs gleamed stark white, frighteningly large. Claire could still feel their sharp points at the tender spot on her neck. If she lived a hundred more years, she didn't think she would ever forget the shocking, sensual pain of his bite. Or the pleasure.

God, the searing, wondrous rush of pleasure to feel Andreas suckling from her vein.

It had damned them both in an instant. She knew it, and so did he; the truth of it had been written across the taut lines of his face, and was now, in the tormented glow of his gaze as he paused to stare at her under the light of the streetlamps.

She was not his to claim. Claire had to remind herself of that fact when her legs started to move instinctively toward him. She belonged to another by blood and vow, if not by love.

Another who would have felt the emotional spike in Claire's body as if it were his own. According to Breed law, there was no greater sin than to betray the sacrament of the blood bond.

But as Andreas wheeled around and leapt off the stoop, and Claire ran to the door only in time to see him disappear into the night, she knew a far worse sin. The sin of having given herself to someone as his blood-bonded mate while her heart still yearned for another.

Thirty years ago, she had been a young woman barely into her twenties – naive about so many things, not the least of which was the existence of another race of beings that thrived on blood and darkness, incredible beings that were somehow human . . . yet far from it.

She had been a student abroad on her own for the first time when she was assaulted by a vampire in this very district of Hamburg. She'd been spared from the bite by another like him, not a crude beast who lunged at her from the shadows but a tall, golden, sophisticated gentleman named Wilhelm Roth.

He took her into his home – his Darkhaven, as she would learn it was called – and offered her his protection while she was in the city. Claire had liked Wilhelm Roth and his mate, a timid young woman named Ilsa who bore the same odd birthmark on her ankle as Claire had on the side of her neck. Claire learned a lot in those first few weeks of living among the Breed as Wilhelm Roth's ward, including the fact that it was entirely possible for her to fall in love with one of their kind, which is exactly what happened once she met Andreas Reichen.

After four months together, she'd been devastated when Andreas had abruptly vanished from her life. Wilhelm Roth had given her a strong shoulder to lean on. Not long afterward it had been Claire's turn to offer him support, when he lost Ilsa to a Rogue vampire attack. Claire had known even then that compassion and sympathy were hardly the same thing as love. Wilhelm hadn't seemed to mind that her heart was still broken and bleeding for Andreas when he pressed her to be his mate later that year. Then again, it wasn't even a week after they were blood bonded and mated that Wilhelm moved her out to the country while he remained in Hamburg.

What a terrible, foolish mistake she'd made. She knew that now – a bitter lesson when her head was filled with doubts about Wilhelm and her heart was breaking all over again for Andreas.

Claire was still reeling from that understanding as a black SUV screeched to a halt at the curb below her. Two heavily armed Enforcement Agents climbed out of the vehicle and caught her in the blinding beam of a flashlight.

'Frau Roth?' one of them asked, clearly surprised to find her there. 'We were alerted by silent alarm to a break-in at the office. Are you all right?'

She didn't know if she responded or not. She felt numb, adrift . . . bereft.

'Is anyone else in the building?' the other guard asked her. 'Are you alone here, Frau Roth? How did you manage to escape the madman who's been wreaking bloody havoc the past couple of nights?'

Claire had no answers for them. All she wanted to do was run after Andreas, but the two big, well-armed agents kept her close as they ushered her back inside and began a search of the place.

'Don't worry,' one of them assured her. 'This nightmare is all over now. We, along with Director Roth, are going to get the bastard who attacked your home and put him down like the rabid dog he is.'

'That's right,' agreed the second man, smiling as if to reassure her. 'You'll see. Soon you'll be someplace safe, as if none of the past two nights ever happened.'

Claire excused herself to the bathroom and sat in the darkness, trying not to scream.

*   *   *

In an underground facility hidden below an unspoiled forest in southern New England, a creature that did not belong to this age – or, in fact, this Earth – bared its enormous fangs and let out a bone-jarring roar. Seven feet tall, hairless and naked except for the thick tangle of undulating skin markings that covered it from head to toe, the Ancient was an awesome, terrible sight to behold. All the more so as it paced the cylindrical UV prison that confined it, murder blazing from the thin pupils nestled in pits of fiery amber.

Watching from a safe distance above in the observation room of the high-tech laboratory wing, Wilhelm Roth was distracted by a sudden, simple truth: His Breedmate was betraying him with Andreas Reichen. Roth's senses told him the instant she'd bled for Reichen. The taste of it was acid on his tongue. Like the captive Ancient in the other room, Roth shook with the sudden urge to bellow in wild rage, but he clamped his molars together and bit back his fury.

Even now he could feel Claire's torment, the spike of her emotions – her confusion and despair – reverberating in his own veins. That she still pined for Reichen came as no surprise to him. She'd tried very hard to banish her feelings for him all these years, but her will was weak and her blood had easily given her away. Not that Roth had ever particularly cared about Claire's faithless heart. Love was a fleeting, fickle emotion that he'd never had much use for. Ambition and drive, possessions and winning . . . these were the things he valued.

And he was a damned sore loser.

'The Ancient has been denied feeding for twenty-one days,' said the Breed male who watched with Roth from the windowed observation room above.

His name was Dragos, although he'd gone by another name, one of several aliases, when he first approached Roth about joining his revolution. Or, rather, his *evolution*, as Dragos's plan was intended to elevate the Breed from the shadowy underworld they were forced to inhabit now, to a place of supreme power over mankind. One that would see Dragos and a few of his hand-picked associates at the helm.

'The prolonged lack of sustenance is painful, of course,' Dragos continued, 'but in another few days, his bodily functions will begin to slow to a suitable level. We've been administering regular doses of sedatives to speed the process along, but unfortunately with this type of operation, time is the only proven, most certain method . . . do tell me if I'm boring you, Herr Roth.'

Roth snapped himself out of his distraction. He inclined his head in a nod that was full of careful respect. 'Not at all, sire.'

It was suicide to piss Dragos off, and based on the Breed male's outwardly pleasant tone, he was positively seething.

'You're beginning to concern me, Roth. Is the trouble you've been having lately with that pest back home in Germany diverting your attention away from more important matters?'

Although it grated, he lowered his head even farther. 'No, sire. Not in the least.'

Dragos knew about the destruction of Roth's Darkhaven in Hamburg and the country house. He knew Roth's mate had been caught up in the violence, but he knew nothing of the fact that she and the one perpetrating the assaults had a history together.

Roth had his own history with Reichen, too. A hatred that began months before Claire entered the picture, though he often wondered if Reichen understood the depth of his enmity, or the lengths to which Roth had been willing to go in order to see Reichen suffer for it.

He had to rein in the current situation back home in Hamburg, and that meant making sure that Andreas Reichen met a swift, certain, and preferably painful, demise.

Roth lifted his head to meet the hard stare of his commander. 'You've no cause for concern whatsoever, sire. Our mission is my only priority.'

'Good.' Dragos's shrewd gaze drilled into him. 'See that it is, Herr Roth.'

On the other side of the viewing window, the Ancient let loose with another agonized howl. Dragos watched, unflinching, as the creature who was his father's father clawed at himself and shrieked in pain.

'I've no further need of you at this time,' Dragos murmured without looking at Roth. 'I will look for a report of your current status later this evening.'

'Yes, sire,' Roth hissed through a tightly held smile.

That smile turned to a sneer as he exited the lab and headed out to attend his business for Dragos. When his cell phone rang in his pocket, it was all he could do not to crush the thing in his fist as he stormed through the bunker.

'What is it,' he snapped into the receiver.

He listened, blood boiling in his veins, as an Enforcement Agent from Hamburg informed him that they had his Breedmate safely in custody.

'Is she alone?'

'Yes, Director Roth. And by some miracle, she appears to be unharmed. We have her with us here at your office in the Speicherstadt.'

'Excellent.' Roth turned into an unoccupied supply room and closed the door behind him. 'Put her on the line. I would have a word with her.'

Claire wanted to ignore the Enforcement Agent knocking on the bathroom door, but she couldn't hide in there forever. No more than she could avoid talking to Wilhelm, who was apparently on the phone right now, waiting to speak with her.

'Frau Roth,' called the agent. 'Is everything all right in there?'

She got up from the floor where she'd been sitting and went over to open the door. As she came out of the dark room, the agent thrust his cell phone toward her. She took it. Slowly brought it up to her ear.

As soon as she heard Wilhelm's breath blowing hotly across the receiver, she knew that he was furious with her. Her veins jangled a warning that she had no patience to acknowledge.

'You lied to me,' she said by way of greeting. 'But then, you've lied about many things, haven't you?'

His answering scoff was as sharp as a blade. 'What the hell are you talking about?'

'The men you sent to the house earlier tonight. They had no intention of taking Andreas out of there peacefully. You sent a death squad to kill him.'

'Andreas Reichen is a very dangerous individual,' came the icy reply. 'I was only thinking of your safety, Claire.'

'Really?' Her voice climbed up slightly, enough to draw anxious looks from her Enforcement Agency watchdogs. 'If my safety was anything of an issue to you, then why did you insist that I stay there with him? You practically thrust me at him.'

A low-toned, amused chuckle grated across her nerves. 'Truthfully, I don't see the point of your distress, darling. You did manage to come out of the situation with your pretty neck unscathed, I assume.'

Claire dismissed the obviously weighted comment with a tight shake of her head. She wasn't going to let him shame her when he made her sick with anger and revulsion and not a little fear. 'What about the girl from *Aphrodite*, Wilhelm? Did she walk away from you unscathed?'

Silence stretched on the other end of the line and it gave Claire the courage to keep going, to lay everything out in one rush of breath.

'What do you know about the attack on Andreas's Darkhaven, Wilhelm? Did you have something to do with that?' She practically choked on the awful words. 'Did you send a Minion into his home with a death squad on orders to kill everyone inside? Are you the cold-blooded murderer he says you are?'

'For Christ's sake, Claire. Listen to yourself. You are spewing a lot of paranoid nonsense.'

'Am I?' She heard the hesitancy in his voice. She could practically hear the wheels in his shrewd mind turning, calculating his errors and how to smooth them over. 'What is this thing between you and Andreas? Has he threatened to expose you in some way, or is this personal . . . because of the past?'

'I could care less about the past,' he replied, utterly devoid of emotion. 'And unless I miss my guess, Claire, this thing between Reichen and me became about as personal as it could get just a short time ago. What kind of mate would I be to you if I let him defile the sanctity of our bond and simply walk away uncontested? There's not a male alive in the entire Breed nation who would deny me the right to defend your honor.'

Oh, God. He was right.

If the violence Andreas had orchestrated the past few weeks was not reason enough, in drinking from her, a blood-bonded Breedmate, he had just written his own death warrant.

Claire swallowed the lump of dread that crawled into her throat. 'You've never loved me, Wilhelm. Have you? Why did you want me for your mate? Why do you care what I do now, when I have never truly been a part of your life? Our bond has never been anything but a farce –'

'If you are looking for a way to justify your actions, Claire, you are sorely mistaken. The fact is, you are my mate. If and when I get my hands on Andreas Reichen, I will demand the full rights due me. You may count on that.'

She could hear the danger in his tone and knew from the sharp way he'd cut her off that she would find no mercy in him whatsoever. She had never been one to cower, but the thought of him sending more of his death dealers into the city after Andre made her heart squeeze like it was in a vise. 'Wilhelm, please . . .'

'Don't beg me, Claire. Not for him,' he snapped, full of venom. 'Put the agent back on the phone now. You're going to go with the Enforcement Agents to their headquarters and help them in their pursuit of this . . . animal.'

'Wilhelm, no –'

'Put the agent on the phone, goddamn you!'

She didn't have to get the armed guards' attention. Both of them gaped at her as Wilhelm's furious outburst ricocheted across the room. One of the agents came over to her and extracted the phone from her reluctant grasp. He listened for only a moment before he motioned the other guard over to Claire and instructed him not to let her leave their custody.

Claire's heart banged in her chest as the agent wrapped up the private conversation. She could see the confusion and sympathy in the Breed male's eyes as he hung up and came toward her with the steady calm of a soldier accustomed to handling difficult situations.

'You need to come with us now,' he told her gently but firmly. 'We have orders, Frau Roth. I'm sorry.'

'No.' He reached for her and Claire's panic spiked. 'I won't go with you. Take your hands off me!'

The second agent moved in, his expression grave. 'Let's not make this difficult, all right?'

Claire wrenched her arm out of the bruising grasp. She took two lunging steps away from them, fully prepared to bolt if she could just reach the door. She didn't even come close. One guard was there before she had a chance to blink. The other came up behind her and shoved something hard and cold against the small of her back.

She felt the searing bite of the taser for only an instant before the shock took her legs out from under her. She crashed to the floor on a broken scream, pain rippling through her.

'Pick her up,' she heard one of them say from above her. 'I'll go open the vehicle.'

Claire felt large, hard hands hoist her to her feet. She heard the apartment door open, felt the incoming chill of night air skate across the floor from outside. Then a low grunt and a sick, sodden sound of someone choking, gasping, sputtering for breath.

The agent holding on to Claire let go as he faced whatever it was that now stood on the threshold of the open door. 'What the fuck!'

Claire lifted her head and couldn't hold back her cry of stunned relief.

Andreas.

Oh, God . . . he came back for her.

His big body blocked the doorway, his eyes blazing, fangs glistening white with menace. At his feet lay the bleeding corpse of the agent who'd tasered her, his throat brutally skewered and all but severed by a length of twisted black wrought iron. As the second agent drew his weapon and prepared to fire, Andreas stalked inside and fired on him with his companion's gun, killing him with the swift, deadly aim of a sniper.

Then he was at her side as if nothing else existed.

'Claire . . . Jesus Christ,' he said, his voice gruff, his expression as grave as she'd ever seen it. He smoothed his hands over her face, touching every inch of her as if he feared she was broken. His strong fingers trembled against her skin. For one moment she thought – desperately hoped – he might kiss her again. 'Are you hurt?'

She shook her head, feeling wobbly and unstable until Andreas wrapped his arm around her shoulders and guided her away from the blood and death on the floor. 'We're not safe in the city now,' she told him. 'I just talked to Wilhelm. He knows that I'm with you. He knows that you drank from me tonight.'

Andreas's mouth compressed tightly. Something dark flashed in his eyes. Remorse, perhaps? Was it regret?

'I don't think either one of us is safe from him now,' she said.

He stared at her for a long moment, an intense, searching look. Then he gave her a curt nod. 'You're coming with me, Claire. No matter what happens, I will keep you safe.'

⊰ CHAPTER TEN ⊱

Stripped of their weapons, keys, cell phones, and cash, Reichen left the dead Enforcement Agents where they lay, then motioned for Claire to follow him to the SUV parked on the street outside.

'Where will we go?' she asked him as they leapt into the vehicle and Reichen hauled ass away from the curb. 'It won't take Wilhelm long to have half the Agency on our heels.'

Reichen acknowledged that fact with a grim nod. 'We can't stay in Hamburg. It would probably be wise if we left Germany altogether.'

'And go where? He has contacts all over Europe. We can't trust anyone in the Darkhavens or the Enforcement Agency not to turn us in to him the first chance they get.'

'We can trust the Order.'

In his periphery, Reichen saw Claire's doubtful reaction. 'The Order? From what I've heard about them, they don't exactly have an open-door policy. Why would a dangerous group of vigilantes from the States be willing to help us?'

Reichen resisted the urge to correct her opinion of the Order, one that had been unfairly yet widely accepted among the general Breed population for generations. He slid a glance at her. 'I've been working with Lucan, Tegan, and the other warriors for close to a year now. The night my Darkhaven was attacked, I was away from Berlin, following up on a mission for the Order. We'd been gathering intel concerning a spate of Gen One assassinations and looking into possible links to blood clubs around Europe.'

'You and the Order . . . working together?' She got quiet then, considering him in studied silence as he turned the SUV onto a busy boulevard that led out of Hamburg. 'There's so much I don't know about you anymore, Andre. Everything about you seems so different now.'

Not everything, he thought, recalling all too easily how familiar she'd felt pressed against him, her mouth on his in a heated kiss. He felt possessive around her. Fiercely protective. All the things he'd felt with her in the beginning. Time had diffused none of it, though that hardly gave him cause to celebrate.

The need to hold her close right here and now was nearly overwhelming. He knew she was basically all right, but just the idea of her being shoved around by the agents – tasered by them, for God's sake – made his blood boil with fury. The taste of her fear, her pain, still echoed in his veins.

Here was one thing that was different about him now: the bond he'd stolen from her with his uninvited bite. Even though Claire had yet to condemn him for it, he would carry the guilt of his actions forever. Especially once he left her widowed and alone, after he crushed the life out of Wilhelm Roth.

Some mercenary part of him found the prospect of Roth's imminent death even more attractive when it would free Claire to take another mate. Particularly if that new mate might be him. But regardless of the fact that he had already bound himself to her by blood, Claire deserved something more than what he could ever give her. She always had.

'Are you hungry?' he asked her, eager to turn his mind away from all the things he'd done wrong by her, now and before. 'You haven't eaten all day. You must be starving.'

She gave him a noncommittal shrug. 'If it's not a good idea to stop anywhere yet, I'll understand –'

'You need food,' he said, more sharply than intended. 'We'll stop.'

As a Breedmate, Claire's perfect health and ageless longevity depended on the regular intake of a Breed male's blood, but her body still required food to function. It was a hell of a lot more palatable for Reichen to risk the time it would take to get her a sandwich than it was for him to think about Wilhelm Roth nourishing Claire as only her true mate could do. He wondered how long it had been since she'd fed from Roth's vein. Not long, he was guessing, based on how youthful and strong she looked. He wondered how long it had been since she'd lain with Roth. Had she ever loved him?

The questions were bitter on his tongue, but he choked them back. He didn't want to know all of the ways that Wilhelm Roth had been with Claire, or how recently. She wasn't his, and he had better put all thoughts of her aside to maintain his focus on the thing that truly mattered to him now – upholding his promise to avenge the innocent souls whom Roth destroyed. If he couldn't do that, then he was no good to himself or anyone else.

Reichen drove for a while without speaking, working hard to ignore the fact that only a small space of leather and plastic separated him from Claire. At least he hadn't gone pyro back at Roth's office. Claire's blood was likely to thank for that small blessing. He'd felt the fires leap to life inside him when he sensed her distress a few blocks away from the place, but somehow, by the time he'd returned to face the agents who were hurting her, he'd managed to keep the flames from erupting.

Barely.

For all his reassurances that he would keep her safe, he knew that his destructive power posed a very real danger to her. The more he used it, the more slippery his hold on it became. He didn't know how long it might be before the fire trapped within him burned out of his control completely.

He couldn't care less what happened to him, but if the heat should snap its tether while Claire was nearby . . .

Reichen looked at her pretty profile in the milky light of the dashboard. Her head was tipped down as she tried to smooth a nasty snag in her sweater. She concentrated on the imperfection, worrying the loose thread between her graceful, pianist's fingers, her loose ebony hair stirring in the low draft of the heat blowing out of the vent.

'What is he afraid of?' she murmured. She glanced over, frowning now. 'What is it that Wilhelm feels he needs to protect from you?'

Reichen shook his head. 'I don't know, and frankly, I can't say that it matters to me now. I don't care why he did what he did. All that's left is the fact that he must pay.'

She pivoted in her seat, her dark eyes shining, stubbornly suspicious. 'He's threatened by you, Andreas. Not because of anything that happened these past two nights, but before that. Why else would he take such a drastic step and order an attack on your Darkhaven?'

'I suppose he didn't appreciate me digging around in his affairs. He felt he needed to send a strong message to me.'

Claire nodded grimly. 'And just what did he think you might find? I can't believe it had anything to do with that missing girl from the club. Not to warrant the kind of retaliation you described.'

'So, you believe me now?' he asked.

She gave him a frank, unflinching look. 'I don't want to, but after talking with Wilhelm tonight . . . it's harder for me to doubt you than it is to trust anything he says. You scared him, Andre. He's still afraid of what you might know or what you could do to him. The question is, why? What is he protecting . . . or whom?'

A knot of coldness formed in Reichen's gut as Claire spoke. He'd never asked himself why Roth came after him. He'd assumed it was due to a mix of old animosity and new opportunity when Reichen had unwittingly sent Helene into Roth's crosshairs. The why of it really hadn't seemed important. Not when rage and grief had been the only things Reichen had known in the aftermath of the slaughter.

He'd been blinded by his fury. By the need for vengeance. He'd never stopped to consider the simple truth that Claire had just laid out for him so plainly.

Roth had something very significant to hide. Something that went much deeper than his whispered gangster alliances with the crooks and politicians who tended to gravitate toward the Enforcement Agency. He was protecting a monumental secret. Something worth spilling the lives of more than a dozen people without a moment's hesitation. Worth even more than that, Reichen was certain now.

As he stared ahead at the dark ribbon of road, a name crept into his mind like a serpent: *Dragos.*

Good Christ. Could the two of them be connected in some way? Had he gotten too close to uncovering some kind of alliance between Dragos and Roth?

If he'd had cause to contact the Order in Boston before, now he couldn't reach them fast enough. Reichen leaned on the accelerator, his thoughts flying as black as the night landscape zooming past the windows of the SUV.

A few minutes out of the city, he spotted an Internet café. He turned off the road and headed for the place, praying like hell that his instincts were wrong about Roth and Dragos being in league together.

If his instincts were right?

Ah, fuck.

If they were right, then he had just nailed the lid shut on not only his coffin, but Claire's, as well.

He brought her inside the café, to an empty workstation and table as far away from the rest of the patrons as he could find.

Using some of the euros he'd lifted off the dead agents, Reichen bought Claire a bowl of soup and a sandwich, and purchased himself an hour's time on the computer.

While she went to work on her meal, he opened an Internet browser on his rented workstation and brought up the secured emergency access site address that belonged to the Order. It was a generic-looking page, basic black, with an unlabeled prompt blinking on the screen as it waited for input. Reichen typed in an access code and password that Gideon back in Boston had given him some months ago, when he'd first begun his remote work for the Order. He hit the enter key and waited, uncertain if the unique ID he'd been assigned was still valid, as the prompt disappeared and he was left staring at the empty black screen.

'What's it doing?' Claire asked, leaning close to him.

Reichen shook his head, guessing that the warriors might have written him off as dead in the three months he'd been out of contact since the destruction of his Darkhaven. 'This site links up to the Boston compound. It's fully encrypted and continuously monitored by the Order. Once I'm verified, we should get a response from Gideon.'

No sooner had he said it than the prompt reappeared, asking for method of contact. Reichen typed in one of the numbers from the Agency cell phones, advising that the line was stolen, most likely compromised, and far from secure.

Gideon's response was instantaneous: *Acknowledged, and not a problem. Calling on a scramble right now.*

The cell phone started ringing.

Reichen answered, speaking his name and a string of security words at the computerized request that stated simply: *Identify.*

'Guess it's a damn good thing I got lazy and kept your access data in the system,' Gideon said as the call connected. 'Jesus. Good to hear your voice, Reichen. Word out of Germany was we'd lost you. I see you're calling in from Hamburg. What the hell's been going on over there?'

Reichen tried to condense the past several weeks into a succinct explanation of events, laying it all out, from the attack on his home by Wilhelm Roth to the systematic, often fiery payback he'd been delivering on the vampire and his known associates ever since.

He told him that Roth and his Enforcement Agency cronies were on his tail and that the situation had just gotten even more complicated now that Claire was on the run with him. And he couldn't leave the subject of Claire without confessing to what he'd done to her in Roth's office.

'For crissake, Reichen,' the warrior hissed on the other end of the line. 'She's his blood-bonded mate. You know he'd be within his rights to kill you for that. Hell, he could take your head in front of every Darkhaven leader in the whole vampire nation and no one would condemn him for it.'

'Yes, I know.' He couldn't keep from looking over at Claire and thinking how far south her life had gone in the couple of days since she'd been in his company. 'I don't care what Roth might try to do to me. It's Claire who needs protection right now. Roth is more than upset, and I wouldn't put it past him to take his anger out on her. Just tonight his agents tried to haul her into custody on his orders. One of them hit her with a taser before I had a chance to disable him.'

Gideon blew out a sharp sigh. 'Jesus. This Roth is a real prince, eh?'

'He's about as dirty as they come,' Reichen said. 'And there's more. I'm beginning to suspect he might be involved in something much bigger than his usual shady dealings. There's a possibility he could be mixed up with Dragos.'

'Ah, fuck . . . you got proof, or are you going on your gut?'

'Gut for now, but it sure as hell wouldn't surprise me.'

'Okay,' Gideon said. There was a sudden clack of fingers flying over a keyboard as the warrior in Boston spoke. 'First things first, we have to get both of you out of Hamburg. I'm arranging for your pickup right now, but unfortunately we won't be able to get wings on the ground over there until tomorrow night. You got somewhere you can hole up in the next few hours before sunrise to wait for your ride?'

Reichen considered his options, which were few to nonexistent. 'Nothing solid over here right now, I'm afraid. Roth's got his fingers in the pockets of too many people. Any one of them could turn us in to him.'

'Understood. All right, listen. You're only about three hours by train away from Denmark. If we arrange safe haven for you there with a friend of the Order, do you think you can handle making the trip on your own?'

'We'll make it,' Reichen said, determined that they would. His gunshot wound was mending rapidly now, and his strength was on full power. If he had to make the trip to Denmark on foot, carrying Claire in his arms, by God, he'd do it.

More typing clatter sounded in the background. 'I'm sending the message out to our contact as we speak,' Gideon said. 'Should only take a minute or two to hear back.'

'Gideon,' Reichen broke in. 'I cannot thank you enough.'

'No thanks necessary. You've had our back more than once. We've got yours now.' There was a slight pause on Gideon's end, then a low chuckle. 'Okay, we just got confirmation out of Denmark. Your contact will meet you at the train station in Varde. She knows to watch for you. Look for a statuesque blonde with a toddler son on her hip. Her name is Danika.'

Reichen listened, then gave Claire a reassuring nod. 'All right. We're on our way there now.'

Dragos jolted awake from a nightmare, cold sweat beading on his brow. He sat up in his bed and blinked at his surroundings, relieved to find that he was still in his lavish headquarters. Still lord and master of the hidden, underground domain he'd had carved out of a large tract of Connecticut granite and bedrock more than a century ago. It was all still here.

The nightmare wasn't real.

Not yet, anyway.

And never would be, if he had anything to say about it.

In the several weeks since he'd first glimpsed the vision of his humiliating defeat – a vision that had been revealed to him in the witchy eyes of a young girl presumably now ensconced with the Order – Dragos had been plagued by nightmares. He couldn't shake the sight of his lab lying in smoke-filled shambles, all of his precious equipment shattered and destroyed . . . and the UV light cage empty, its monstrous occupant – Dragos's secret weapon – no longer held inside.

Worst of all was the pitiful vision he'd seen of himself: beaten, begging, on his knees pleading for mercy.

'Never,' he bit off sharply, as though he could banish the child seer's revelation with his fury alone.

He got out of bed and threw a silk charmeuse robe over his naked body as he stalked out of his bedroom to the adjacent study. A large touch-screen computer monitor sat on an antique, ornate desk that had once belonged to a human emperor. Dragos ran his finger over the smooth surface of the screen, bringing up a video feed from his laboratory.

Ah, yes, he thought, disturbed by the depth of his relief. *Everything is still there.*

The glow from the tightly spaced vertical UV bars stung his hypersensitive eyes, but he didn't care. He zoomed in on the lethargic, half-starved creature contained inside the cell – the creature who shared the same bloodline as he. The lethal otherworlder who was, in fact, his grandfather. Not that bloodlines mattered to him personally. The Ancient's powerful blood cells and DNA, on the other hand, had proven instrumental to Dragos's goals.

After decades of work, after centuries of patience spent in

hiding, arranging his pieces just so as he waited for the right time to make his move, Dragos's crowning hour was almost at hand.

He'd be damned if he was going to let the Order snatch it out of his grasp before he had a chance to seize the glory that was meant to be his.

Steps were already under way to prevent the vision he'd witnessed from coming true. He was making a few changes to his operation. Taking expensive and somewhat drastic measures to protect his assets.

And he wasn't at all content to sit by and let the warriors in Boston continue to disrupt his work. The Order was a problem he did not need – one he could not afford to risk when he was so close to knowing victory. They'd invited war when they raided his gathering outside Montreal this past summer, sending him and his private inner circle of high-ranking Breed associates fleeing into the woods like rats off a sinking ship. It had been a public sucker-punch that undermined his authority, not to mention cost him precious time. He would see the warriors pay for that.

But Dragos had another problem, too.

He brought up the teleconferencing program on his computer and dialed Wilhelm Roth's quarters at the other end of the stronghold. The German vampire, a hard-edged director of the Hamburg Enforcement Agency, was doubtless unaccustomed to playing the subordinate, and Dragos took some amusement in the notion that the midmorning wakeup call would grate the male. To his credit, he picked up the call before the second ring, efficient as always. It was one of his saving graces as far as Dragos was concerned. That, and the fact that Roth was ruthless in his ambitions.

'Sire,' he said, his face moving in front of the monitor in his chambers. 'How can I serve?'

'Status,' Dragos demanded, staring hard at his lieutenant.

Roth cleared his throat. 'Everything is arranged. The operation's first strike began last evening. It should not be long before we have engagement.'

Dragos grunted his approval. 'And the other matter?'

There was a moment's hesitation, but that was all. Dragos wondered if Roth knew that his honesty right now was the only thing keeping him alive. Roth cleared his throat. 'I am dealing with something of a . . . a personal situation in Hamburg, sire.'

'Yes,' Dragos said, no need for coyness. He'd heard all about the devastating assault on two of the German's residences from other contacts overseas. He'd also heard that Roth's Breedmate was missing. After a confrontation with Enforcement Agents at Roth's private office in Hamburg, she was presumed to have been abducted by the vampire who evidently had something of a bone to pick with Roth.

A vampire with rumored ties to the Order.

Dragos's jaw went tight with anger as he considered the many ways a scenario like that could land a lot of troubles on his doorstep.

'What do you intend to do, Herr Roth?'

'It will be handled, sire.'

'See that it is,' Dragos hissed. 'I'm sure I don't need to tell you that the female is a liability now. If she's in enemy hands, then she is nothing more than a weapon to be used against you. And against me.'

Roth stared, his shrewd eyes narrowed. 'She has no idea where I am. I've never confided in her about anything of importance. Besides, she knows her place when it comes to my affairs.'

'And how long do you think it will take her captor to find you through your blood bond with her?' Dragos asked. 'If they use her to find you, they find me, as well.'

'That won't happen, sire.'

'I require a permanent solution to this,' Dragos said, knowing what he asked of the male. 'Are you prepared to carry that out, Herr Roth?'

The German smiled coldly. 'Consider it done, sire.'

Dragos nodded. 'Good. Obviously, so long as the female is breathing, your presence is poison to this operation. Remove yourself to Boston until you can assure me that you've eliminated this problem. Be gone by sundown, Herr Roth.'

The vampire inclined his head in a deferential nod. 'Of course, sire. As you wish.'

❧ CHAPTER ELEVEN ❧

A few hours after they left the Internet café in Hamburg to board a train to Denmark, Claire and Andreas were being escorted to a rural village Darkhaven, courtesy of the Order. Their contact, a beautiful blond Breedmate named Danika, had taken them into her living quarters like family of her own – all warmth and hospitality, no questions asked.

'I hope you don't mind cozy,' she said as she walked them into a cheery kitchen located off the back door. 'We've only got one spare bedroom and bath, but you're welcome to it.'

The farmhouse where Danika lived with her baby boy, Connor, and one other mated couple was small by Darkhaven standards. Usually members of the Breed population lived in mansions or large brownstones, sometimes the occasional high-rise apartment building. Darkhavens generally comprised tight-knit communities of a dozen or so individuals, everyone looking out for one another like kin, even if they were unrelated by blood.

But Danika's living arrangements weren't the only unusual thing about her. She was mother to a very young child, a sweet baby boy with her fair coloring and the unmistakably strong genes of a father who was Breed. She hadn't mentioned a mate, and there seemed to be an air of wistfulness about the woman, especially when she was looking at her son.

Like now, when little Connor was leaning out of Danika's arms to point emphatically at Andreas. The boy's big blue eyes were wide and eager, while Andreas's gaze was shadowed by the furrow of his brow.

'I'm sorry,' Danika said to him. 'It's the *dermaglyph* peeking over the top of your collar. Connor has become fascinated by them in the past couple of weeks.'

Andreas grunted and gave a nod to the Breed youngster. 'He recognizes his own kind already. Smart boy.'

Danika beamed. 'Yes, he is.'

Claire watched in quiet surprise as Andreas pushed up his sleeve to reveal more of his Breed skin markings, to Connor's obvious delight. The vampire toddler reached out with his pudgy little hand and patted the beautiful swirls and arcs that ran along Andreas's muscled forearm.

'Da,' he exclaimed. 'Da! Da!'

'Oh!' Danika's milky complected cheeks went instantly bright pink. 'No, sweetheart, this isn't your father. Oh, God . . . I'm sorry. How embarrassing.'

Claire laughed and Andreas chuckled, too. 'It's all right,' he said. 'I assure you, I've been called much worse.'

Danika smiled, but that trace of sorrow was back in her eyes. 'Connor's father, Conlan, was a warrior with the Order. He was killed on a mission in Boston before Connor was born.'

'I'm so sorry,' Claire murmured, realizing how fresh the loss still was, since Danika's son was probably not even two years old.

Danika gave a mild shrug, cleared her throat. 'After I lost Conlan, I went to Scotland – his homeland – to have Connor. I thought I might stay there permanently and raise our son in the highlands Conlan loved so much, but being in his country without him only made me miss him more. I came back home to Denmark last year.'

Andreas smoothed his broad palm over the top of Connor's pale blond head. 'He would be proud of you, Danika, no matter where you choose to raise his son.'

'Thank you for saying so.'

She smiled shyly, charmed, Claire was guessing by the soft look she gave him. And Andreas was charming, particularly as he took the little boy into his big arms to let him closer explore the *glyphs* that so intrigued him. Claire saw a glimmer of the man she remembered from before – the carefree, charismatic man she'd fallen helplessly in love with all those years ago.

Since he'd come storming back into her life two nights ago, Claire thought that man she'd known and adored was long gone. She thought that part of him had been consumed by the flames that had taken his kin and left him the sole survivor, hellbent on revenge.

To think she had actually condemned him once for not being serious enough about life . . . about her. She'd grown to fear his elusive, devil-may-care ways. She'd worried that he might never be content with just one woman, and maybe he hadn't been after all. She'd certainly heard of his numerous female companions over the years, mortal women, all of them.

She knew he had never taken a Breedmate of his own and settled down to have his sons with her, and Claire had long nurtured a secret gladness that he had remained unbonded all this time. As for her own ill-chosen mate, her loveless match with Wilhelm Roth had produced no offspring either – a blessing, now that she was coming to understand more about Wilhelm's treachery.

Despite Andreas's outward recklessness and rakish leanings back when Claire had known him best, he would have made some woman a wonderful mate. She saw that now, in the way he spoke so kindly to Danika and how he took to her son with such ease.

Claire looked at him now and wondered how they'd let so much time – so many mistakes and missteps – get in their way.

She wondered how long it would take for her to forget this vibrant, magnetic side of him again, once the dust and ash settled on the perilous journey they found themselves on together.

How could her life ever go on in light of all she was learning about Wilhelm and all she yearned to have once more with Andreas?

'My goodness, I can't believe it's nearly dawn already,' Danika said, her melodic voice breaking through the heavy weight of Claire's thoughts. 'You must be exhausted. Would you like to see where you'll be sleeping?'

Claire nodded, afraid her feelings had shown all over her face, for the way the other Breedmate was looking at her with such tenderness and sympathy. She schooled her features into a placid, unreadable mask – a skill she'd perfected during her years as Wilhelm Roth's mate. 'What I could really use is a nice hot bath,' she said, feeling Andreas's gaze fix on her, even though it had seemed a perfectly reasonable request.

'Of course,' Danika replied. She glanced to Andreas, who was still holding the delighted Connor. 'Would you mind watching him while I show Claire upstairs?'

'No problem,' he said, his eyes pinning Claire with an intensity that made her blood sizzle in her veins. 'Take whatever time you need. The little guy and I will be fine on our own.'

Claire felt his hot stare following her, as palpable as a lingering caress, as Danika led her out of the kitchen and up the stairs to the second floor of the house.

'The bathroom is here,' the tall blond female said, gesturing to the open door of a full bath at the top of the stairs. 'No one uses this part of the house, so please consider it yours. Here is the bedroom at the end of the hallway.'

Claire could hardly contain her contented sigh as she walked into the inviting chamber with its golden hardwood floors, dark cherry furnishings, and king-size, quilt-covered bed. It had been a long time since she'd been in a room that exuded such homespun, simple warmth.

'I set out a sleep shirt for you, and you'll find plenty of towels in the bathroom. I don't know what you might be used to at home, but I hope you'll be comfortable enough here.'

'It's lovely,' Claire replied. She drifted over to the massive bed and trailed her fingers across the careful needlework on the quilt's beautiful teal, gray, and cream Nordic design. 'This room reminds me of my family's home in Rhode Island.'

Danika smiled. 'Oh, then you're American?' She walked over to a tall, footed armoire and opened the cabinet's burnished-brass-handled doors. 'I didn't think you sounded like a German native. No accent at all.'

'No. I came to Europe many years ago, to study music, actually.' Claire walked over to help the other woman retrieve a couple of extra pillows and a folded wool blanket. 'I suppose I was very idealistic then, like many young people. As for me, I was torn between my love of the piano and my personal need to do something important with my life, like saving the world.'

'I'm not sure the world can be saved,' Danika said, turning a solemn blue gaze on her. 'There's so much corruption and tragedy everywhere you look. Good people die all the time, even the ones whose only faults are striving to do good work and make things better for others.'

Claire nodded. 'My parents were those kind of people. My mother left a very comfortable life in New England to help bring clean water and medical supplies to a small country in Africa. She met my father, a young doctor from Zimbabwe, while she was working overseas. They fell in love almost instantly, but at that time, marriage wasn't an easy thing to obtain for a white American woman and a black man from Africa. When my mother became pregnant with me, she returned to the States until I was born. My father stayed behind to continue his work and wait for us to come back to be a family. A few months later, conflict broke out in the region. My mother couldn't bear to be away from him while the village they'd worked so hard to build up was being threatened by war. She went back to Africa, and within a month of her arrival they were both killed when rebel forces shot up their camp.'

'Oh, Claire.' Danika pulled her into a caring embrace. 'How awful for you and the rest of your family. I'm so sorry.'

It had been a long time since she'd thought about losing her parents – a couple known to her only by pictures and stories her grandmother in Rhode Island had shared with her as she was growing up, parentless and different, yet a child of privilege in Newport's high society. Now all her relatives in the States were gone. The house in Newport was still held in trust for her, cared for by a private staff who looked after the grounds and the basic maintenance of the place, but it had been nearly two decades since Claire had been back. She missed it suddenly, missed the feeling of truly being home.

Danika released her after a moment and attempted a lighter topic. 'So, which of your goals did you end up pursuing?'

'Neither, in fact,' Claire admitted. 'Not long after I arrived in Germany, I had my first run-in with one of the Breed. He was very young – a teenager at most. It was late at night, I was walking home from a concert by myself. I thought he wanted to steal my purse, but he was actually after something else. He was about to bite me when another Breed male stopped him.'

'Andreas?' Danika guessed, smiling.

Claire shook her head. 'No, not him. It was someone . . . else. Someone very important in Hamburg, although I didn't know it at the time. He caught the scent of my blood when the other male knocked me to the ground and I skinned my knees. He realized right away that I was a Breedmate, so he drove the other vampire off and took me in as his ward. I didn't meet Andreas until later.'

And, like her parents' doomed relationship, she and Andre also fell instantly, impossibly, in love. She'd spent the past thirty years trying to forget him. Trying to convince herself that she wasn't still in love with him after all this time.

'Such a long time to be kept apart. I know how difficult it is, being denied of the thing your heart craves the most,' Danika murmured somewhat absently.

Claire swung an astonished look at her. 'What . . . how did you know –'

The other Breedmate sucked in her breath. 'Forgive me. I didn't mean to intrude on your thoughts.' She brought her index finger up to her temple. 'My talent, I'm afraid. I don't like to read thoughts, and to tell you the truth, most of the time I hate that I can. Unfortunately, since Conlan has been gone my talent is becoming unmanageable. I haven't taken another mate, nor do I intend to, and without the regular intake of Conlan's blood, my ability seems to turn on and off at its own whim. I'm sorry, Claire. It was very rude of me.'

'It's all right.'

'I don't know that it will bring you any comfort, but you are not suffering alone. Andreas feels it, as well, you know. He feels the same regret that you carry inside.' Danika smiled gently. 'His thoughts were just as plain to me in the other room as yours are now. He is torn and broken from rage, but he's hurting in another way, too.'

Claire stared at her, unable to speak. Barely able to breathe.

'Life is precious,' Danika continued. 'And it is so very short, even for those like us. Four hundred and two years with Conlan wasn't nearly enough time. We don't often get second chances, not in life or in love. If I had just one more minute with my Conlan, I wouldn't waste a second of it on regret. Let Andreas know how you truly feel.'

'But he isn't mine,' Claire murmured softly. 'Not anymore.'

'Try to tell that to your heart.' Danika gave Claire's hand a light squeeze. 'Try to tell that to his.'

*   *   *

Reichen avoided going upstairs for hours after Danika had returned to collect her son. She and Connor had gone to find their own rest for the day, leaving Reichen to prowl the quiet farmhouse, killing time and trying not to think about the fact that Claire was in bed somewhere above him.

In bed all alone, her sweet body relaxed and languid. Her buttery light brown skin like velvet to the touch, every exquisite inch of her clean and soft and warm . . .

Good Christ.

Since the moment she asked about taking a bath, she'd doomed him to imagining her undressed and fragrant from a long, hot soak. He'd been tempted almost beyond reason to vault up the stairs behind her when she left with Danika, a feeling that had yet to pass. There was nothing he wanted more than to be with her right now, to comfort her and let her know that she was protected from Roth and his cronies. To assure her that no matter what evil was at work around them, he would keep her safe at any cost.

Things he'd failed to provide his kin or Helene.

Spending time around Danika and her young son had brought his attention back to that reality with scathing focus. He wasn't here to smooth over Claire's fears, any more than he was here to slake his own longings for her or to answer the primal call of the blood bond that would draw him to her always. A blood bond he'd imposed on her, he was quick to remind himself.

No. He was here now for one purpose: vengeance.

Everything else – his wants and desires, his future, his right to claim even the thinnest moment of selfish joy – had burned away in the fire that devoured his Darkhaven home.

Longer ago than that, he thought grimly, reflecting back on the night he'd last seen Claire. It had been a night of stupidity and violence that had left him beaten and bloodied, baking in an open field under a harsh morning sun. Until that moment, he'd known nothing of the power he'd been cursed with at birth – a power passed down to him by a Breedmate mother he'd never met, who hadn't lived long enough to warn him of what his fury could do.

He'd learned that lesson in a brutally vivid moment that awful morning outside Hamburg, and the horror of what he'd done had never left him.

So many innocent lives had crumbled to ash around him. His own life was heading swiftly in that same direction, but he still had time to see justice met, at least for those lives that had been lost at Wilhelm Roth's command. He had no doubt that his anger and hatred were only strengthening the fire living inside him. It would destroy him sooner than later, but he'd be damned if he went down without taking Roth with him.

He only prayed that his resolve was firm enough to keep Claire far away from him as he moved ever closer to that inevitable end.

It was the depth of that conviction that finally gave him the strength to climb the stairs and find the room that Danika had given them. He also didn't know if the couple who shared the farmhouse was aware of him and Claire, and he wasn't about to put Danika in the position of having to lie to cover for him should the other residents happen to come down and find a stranger in their midst.

Reichen paused in front of the closed bedroom at the far end of hallway. His pulse kicked with a visceral awareness of Claire on the other side of that painted white door. He prayed she was asleep, figured she had to be after the hours he'd stalled downstairs. As quietly as he could, he turned the worn porcelain knob and peered inside.

'Hello,' she said, barely above a whisper. She was sitting up on one side of the king-size bed, wearing a thin baby blue T-shirt that didn't quite conceal the dark buds of her nipples or the shapely swell of her breasts. A small lamp glowed on the nightstand beside her, golden light playing in her ebony hair and across her lovely face.

He scowled and stepped into the room, shutting the door behind him without a sound. 'You should be sleeping.'

She lifted her shoulder. 'I thought the bath would relax me, but I can't seem to close my eyes.'

He had to work damn hard to ignore the bolt of lust that shot through him with the renewed image of Claire sitting naked in a tub full of steaming water and silky white bubbles.

'Nightfall will come early,' he grumbled. 'We've got to be ready to catch our ride back to the States at sundown. You'd better douse that lamp and try to get some rest.'

She moved on the bed, but only to reach over and gesture to the empty side. 'I took one of the softer pillows, but if you'd rather have it you can.'

He glowered at her, more from the discomfort of his growing erection than her offer of his choice of pillow. Her shift on the mattress had stretched her T-shirt into a second skin. And with the dislodging of the quilt coverlet as she moved, his burning gaze fixated on the tiny scrap of her panties.

Crimson red panties, for the love of God.

He froze where he stood, every nerve ending in his body going nuclear with arousal.

'You might remember that I'm a very sound sleeper,' she said, but he was hardly hearing what she was saying. 'Don't worry about waking me up if you still toss and turn and hog the covers over there. I probably won't even notice.'

He shook himself back to consciousness when he realized she expected him to sleep in the bed with her. Right beside her, when the only thing preventing him from acting on his unholy desire for her was a paltry slip of cotton and a minuscule triangle of red satin.

'The bed is yours,' he said, his voice a rough scrape in his throat. 'This isn't a slumber party, for fuck's sake. You can't actually expect me to sleep with you, Claire.'

Her expression faltered. 'I didn't mean . . .'

'Jesus Christ,' he muttered. His skin prickled with a sudden wash of heat and hunger that made his desire stoke even hotter. 'Getting in bed with you is the bloody last thing I need to do right now.'

He must have sounded even more harsh than he realized, based on how quickly she glanced away from him. She shook her head, then exhaled a sigh. 'The bed is big enough for both of us. That's all I was trying to say.'

He stared at her for a long moment, his muscles twitching with the urge to move, to propel him over to where she was on the mattress and ease her down beneath him.

He wanted that so badly it was all he could see. All he could taste as the points of his emerging fangs pressed into the flesh of his tongue.

'Get some sleep, Claire.'

He tore himself away from the sight of her and took his own place on the floor nearby. The hand-loomed rug that covered the old wood planks was lumpy and smelled vaguely of lemon wax. He tossed onto his side on the hard floor, the only position that didn't make him painfully aware of the hard-on that was jutting between his thighs like a column of stone.

Had he actually tried to caution her a few minutes ago that nightfall would come early?

Like hell.

It was going to be a long fucking wait till sundown.

⇥ CHAPTER TWELVE ⇤

Claire lay on the huge bed, wide awake, staring into the shuttered darkness of the room. She hadn't moved since Andreas took himself to the floor. Time dragged, and for quite a while she was certain he'd been just as awake and alert as she was – and just as determined to lie there in silence and pretend he didn't notice.

But somewhere around an hour ago, his breathing had changed from the controlled inhaling and exhaling she could barely discern, to the deep, rhythmic soughing of sleep.

Claire listened to the slow sounds of his slumber, while Danika's words about the rarity of second chances and not wasting precious time on regrets were playing over and over in her mind like a song she couldn't get out of her head. There was so much she wanted to say to Andreas. Things she needed him to hear.

Not that he would listen. He didn't seem inclined to let her get close enough to reach him at all. And she needed to be close to him now, if only to feel his strength beside her when everything she thought she knew about her world was crumbling at her feet.

She'd felt a wall come up between them tonight. It seemed to grow taller and less scalable the longer they were at the farmhouse Darkhaven. Claire wasn't sure what she'd done to upset him, or maybe it was simply the fact that he'd been forced to look after her now that Wilhelm was likely gunning for them both.

For a moment she wished she'd been gifted with Danika's talent so that Andreas's mind, and his cryptic emotions, wouldn't be such a mystery to her right now.

Her own ability could help her there, too. Everyone was more accessible in the dream realm. Not everything said or seen was truth, of course, but the surreal nature of dreams had a way of peeling back inhibitions.

Claire ventured a look over the expanse of the wide bed to the large bulk of Andreas's body where he slept on the floor. She tucked her arm under her head and curled up on her side, watching him. Wondering where his dreams had taken him. She closed her eyes and thought about him as she let her body relax, willing her mind to calm and prepare for sleep.

She let her talent stretch, tendrils of awareness reaching . . . searching.

It usually took incredible focus to find the dreamer, but with Andreas, she'd no sooner slipped under the veil of consciousness and slumber than there he was. It had always been like that with him, as if their connection had been there from the instant they first met and had never weakened.

There had been times, long after Andreas was gone from her life, that Claire had been tempted to seek him out, if only in the dream realm. But she'd been too afraid of facing more of his rejection, and too ashamed of herself that, try as she might, she could not find for Wilhelm anything close to the love she had been unable to purge for Andreas.

After all that had happened the past couple of nights, what she felt now for Wilhelm and the blood bond that shackled her to him was a cold and biting mistrust. Contempt, if everything she was learning about him was true.

After all she'd been through with Andreas in these harrowing, intense long hours together, she had to admit to some measure of fear for the lethal individual he was now. But along with that fear had come a rush of emotion that terrified her even more for how strongly she still felt for him.

For how deeply she still wanted him, needed him.

How easily she could see herself falling back in love with him . . . if she'd ever truly stopped.

As she walked into his dream now, her breath caught to find him under the starlight of a clear evening, seated shirtless and barefoot in the crisp, cool grass of the parkland sanctuary she had designed for his vacant Darkhaven property. All the details were just as she had them on the architect's model, down to the very last bench and flower bed.

Good lord. He had memorized the entire plan.

'It's beautiful,' he said, his deep voice a vibration she felt all the way into her bones. 'You knew exactly what needed to be here. Somehow, you knew.'

He didn't turn to face her as she cautiously approached him at the edge of his dream, where the land he was imagining in his sleep hugged the glittering lake beyond. Andreas's golden skin was luminescent in the moonlight, made all the more striking by the flourish of twisting, twining *glyphs* that rode his muscular back like the masterwork of an artist's paintbrush. Claire remembered tracing those beautiful marks with her tongue; if she closed her eyes, she could still picture every unique arc and flourish that tracked over his smooth, firm skin.

'You know you shouldn't be here,' he said once her feet stopped moving and she was standing beside him. Now he did look at her, and his expression wasn't what she considered friendly. His irises were throwing off piercing amber light. When he curled his lip back to speak, the tips of his fangs gleamed stark white and razor sharp. 'You don't belong here, Claire. Not with me. Not like this. You shouldn't have come in here when you weren't invited.'

'I had to find you.'

'What for?'

'I needed to see you. I wanted . . . to talk . . .'

'Talk.' He spat the word on a huffed exhalation. Before Claire knew what he was doing, he was up on his feet, towering over her. His eyes were blazing, so hot it was a wonder her T-shirt and panties didn't melt away as his intense gaze roamed over her from the top of her head to her bare toes. 'What do you want to talk about, Frau Roth?'

'Don't do that,' she said, wincing at his biting tone. 'Don't use him to drive a wedge between us.'

'He is the wedge between us, Claire. We both put him there, didn't we? If you're only regretting it now, that's not my problem.'

She frowned at him, not wanting to feel the scrape of his words when she came there out of affection for him, as his friend. 'Why are you doing this, Andre?'

'What am I doing?'

'Pushing me away. Treating me like Wilhelm and I are one and the same, both of us your enemies.'

'What would you have me do instead? Tell you that everything will work out between us in the end? Pretend that Roth doesn't exist so that you and I can pick up where we left off all those years ago?'

Claire glanced down, feeling foolish for having wanted him to say those very things – and more. Words he might never offer her again, even in the flimsy haven of a dream.

He lifted her chin on the tips of his strong fingers. 'We can't change anything that's happened, Claire. I won't stand here and give you lies to make either one of us feel better. And I'm not going to give you promises that I know I can't keep.'

'No,' she said. 'You'd rather run away.'

His mouth flattened and he shook his head, his eyes glittering darkly. 'You think I wanted to leave you.'

Not a question, but a quiet accusation.

'Would it matter if I did?' she tossed back at him. She

scoffed, still stinging from the wound he'd inflicted on her thirty years ago. 'Never mind, don't answer that. I wouldn't want to press you into saying something only to make me feel better.'

Realizing she'd made a mistake in coming there, she pivoted, about to walk off and leave him to sulk alone in his dream. But before she could take a single step away, his fingers wrapped around her arm and he held her in place. He moved in front of her, his face taut and deadly serious.

'Leaving you was the last thing I ever wanted to do.' He scowled, his grip holding her tighter, moving her farther into the heated wall of his body. 'It was the hardest goddamn thing I've ever done. *Ever*, Claire.'

She stared up at him speechless, lost in the dark glimmer of his eyes. In the next moment, he bent his head down and kissed her, their mouths fusing together in a long, breathless joining.

She never wanted to stop. She didn't think she could let go of him now that he was in her arms again, even if only in her dreams.

'God, I want you, Claire,' he moaned against her mouth, the sharp prick of his fangs grazing her lips. 'I want to be with you now . . . Ah, Christ, I have needed to be with you for so long.'

Because it was a dream, wishes often need only be whispered to make them so. In an instant, Claire found herself pressed down on the soft, cool grass, Andreas's magnificent body poised above her.

They were naked now, clothing having fallen away as if it were made of mist. But even in dreams, Andreas's skin was warm and firm to the touch. His broad shoulders and thick arms, his muscular chest and ridged abdomen . . . all of him was real and strong and perfect in its masculinity. Claire couldn't keep her eyes from traveling the length of him. She remembered all too vividly that Andreas's perfection extended farther down, as well.

Because it was a dream, she cast aside the knowledge of all

the reasons they should not be together. She knew only the calling of her heart, and as her palm came to rest on the center of his chest, she knew the calling of his heart, too. His pulse hammered against her fingers. His breath was coming fast, heavy, hot with need. Claire looked up into eyes that burned as bright as any flame, his face a tight, tormented mask.

'Yes,' she hissed, almost incapable of words.

She sucked in her breath as the broad head of his cock nudged her, cleaved her. With a slow push of his hips he was sliding inside her, burying himself in a long, gloriously deep thrust. Claire cried out, arching up to take all of him within her, needing him to fill her. He stretched her tight, his length touching her very core.

'Oh, yes,' she panted as they found a familiar rhythm, fitting together as though they'd never been apart.

He was a ferocious lover; she knew that about him already and reveled in his animalistic intensity. Every hard stroke made her shatter just a little, every low moan and growl sent a shiver coursing through her veins.

He knew just how to move with her, just the right tempo to wring every ounce of pleasure from her body. Claire felt the first tremors of release streak through her like tiny bolts of lightning in her blood. She couldn't contain it, had no strength to resist Andreas's mastery of her senses.

She could only dig her fingers into the thick muscle of his shoulders and hold on as he steered her toward a splintering climax. She didn't know if he followed her there. All she knew was the incredible wave of pleasure that rushed over her . . . then the sudden hollow grief of realizing Andreas was gone.

Claire called out to him in the dream, but he was nowhere to be seen.

And now the garden sanctuary where they'd lain together was gone, as well. She was sitting in the middle of a sun-baked field, daylight blinding her eyes.

'Andre?'

She got up and started walking, holding her arm up to her brow like a visor as she struggled to get her bearings. She didn't know this place. She couldn't make sense of the golden light, or the pungent stink of smoke and something worse, something unidentifiable that filled her nostrils and choked her throat. Coughing, Claire stepped over the scorched vegetation.

She stumbled, her foot catching on a charred black lump that lay on the ground.

Horror washed over her even before her senses processed what she was seeing.

It was a child.

A dead child, burned beyond recognition.

'Oh, my God.' Claire backed away, repulsed. Stricken. 'Andreas!'

She swiveled her head and cried out with relief to see the broad green lawn and the stone-and-timber mansion that had been Andreas's Darkhaven estate seated at the top of a gently sloping incline. Claire ran toward the house. She was naked and cold, terrified and confused by what she'd just seen outside.

'Andre?' she called frantically as she walked along the back of the mansion, seeing no light or movement inside. 'Andreas . . . are you in there?'

She went around to the front, her arms wrapped around her nudity as she climbed the steps to the elegant entry. She knocked on the door. It eased open on silent hinges, but no one waited for her inside.

Claire stepped over the threshold and into a strange mausoleum of white. Everywhere she looked – the floors, the walls, the furnishings – all of it was pristine, snowy white. And quiet as a tomb.

'Andreas, please. I'm frightened. Where are –'

He emerged from one of the rooms off the ghostly foyer. He was naked like she was, his eyes still burning amber, his fangs still filling his mouth. He stalked forward without a word and hauled her into a bruising, unyielding grasp. Kissed her with so much heat and desire, her knees almost buckled beneath her.

Then, just as she was beginning to feel safe again, he drew back from her. He let go so forcefully, thrusting her out of his reach, that she stumbled a bit before catching herself. Something wet and slippery was under her feet. She slid in it . . . an instant before the coppery tang of spilled blood registered in her nose.

'Oh, my God.'

Claire looked down at the floor, which was no longer white but veined marble. Marble that was bloodstained and awful with gore. The walls and furnishings were no longer pristine and colorless either. Now everything was ruined, bullet-riddled, bloodied. Furniture and wall art toppled, broken, all of it in shambles.

'Oh, no . . . Oh, God . . . *no.*'

She didn't know what to make of the burnt field or the tragic child outside, but there could be no mistaking what she was seeing here. Claire looked at him in abject horror and heartsick misery, realizing that he was showing her the destruction of his home. Destruction called for by Wilhelm Roth, just as he'd told her that first night at the country house. She put her hand out to Andreas in support, but he didn't take it. His expression was hard, condemning. When she glanced down, she saw why.

Blood coated her fingers and palms. She was splattered with it all over her front, even her hair was sticky with it. And there, at her feet, was the lifeless body of a little boy – one of Reichen's nephews' sons, murdered by gunfire. Still more bodies lay elsewhere in the mansion, on the first floor, halfway up the staircase, near the door to the cellar down the hall. She was standing in the center of a massacre she wouldn't have been able to imagine in the worst of her nightmares.

When she looked to Andreas again, he was engulfed in

white-hot, deadly heat. Flames leapt off his body to ignite the walls and furniture. In mere seconds, all Claire could see was fire.

The scream ripped out of her throat, raw and despairing.

She jolted herself out of the dream, unable to bear another moment of the ugliness of it.

Sickened and trembling, she sat up in the bed and threw aside the quilt and sheets. No blood on her now. No cinders. Just the cold sweat of true terror and the anguish of having witnessed Andreas's horrific nightmare for herself.

Claire expected him to wake up and offer her some kind of explanation or comfort. He had to know how shaken up she was now. But he kept on sleeping, lying still and breathing unruffled on the floor next to the bed. He let her weather her deep distress alone, as if he'd wanted her to be disturbed – horrified – by what he'd shown her.

Perhaps he'd wanted her to be horrified by him in some way as well.

Claire waited until her pulse leveled out and her body stopped trembling, then she inched down under the covers and counted the hours until dusk.

⫷ CHAPTER THIRTEEN ⫸

'Fucking place is dead tonight,' Chase muttered as he scanned the crowded dance club and apparently found little to his liking. 'Should have hit the north side of the city like I told you, instead of wasting our time in Dorchester.'

Kade shrugged, slanting a grin at Brock, the third member of their patrol. 'You wanna see dead clubs, let me take you to Alaska. It's pathetic, man. We've got more moose per square mile than women.'

'Is that right?' Chase grunted. 'No wonder you jumped at the chance to get out of there and come to Boston last year. How many months of freezing your nuts off before all those moose start looking like prime pieces of ass?'

At Brock's low chuckle, Kade curled his lip back off the points of his fangs and saluted both of the Breed males with double-barreled middle fingers.

'Well, this has been fun, but I'm outta here,' Chase announced. He scrubbed his hand over his stubbled jaw, his blue eyes looking a bit dodgy and unfocused under the edge of his black knit skullcap. 'Got an itch that won't get scratched hanging out in this dive. Good luck with the moose-hunting.'

Kade gave the ex–Enforcement Agent a nod. 'See you back at the compound.'

'Eventually,' Chase replied, already heading for the club's exit.

When he was gone, Brock blew out a low sigh and shook his dark head. 'That son of a bitch has got a serious problem.'

'You mean, other than walking around all the time with that Agency-installed stick shoved up his ass?' Kade drawled, looking at the big warrior who'd been recruited into the Order out of Detroit around the same time he'd come in from Alaska.

It wasn't that Kade didn't like Sterling Chase – or Harvard, as he was sometimes referred to, on account of his fancy Ivy League pedigree. Chase was a competent enough warrior, one of the best, in fact. He was a crack shot and one hell of a man to have at your back in combat, but on the personal side, he was as cold as a glacier.

'I don't know what his deal is,' Brock said. 'But he'd better watch his step, is all I'm saying. He strikes me as the kind who's got one foot in the grave and the other one eager to follow. He just doesn't give a shit about anything, and that is dangerous. Not only to himself, but to anyone who needs to count on him.'

Kade considered that as he glanced out across the bar and dance floor.

A couple of young females were heading over from a table nearby. Brock gave them his knockout grin, the one that never failed to net him the hottest woman in any gathering. The guy had moves, no doubt about it. Not that Kade was any kind of slouch. He eyed the pair of lovelies as they sauntered through the crowd, locked on to the two vampires like laser-guided missiles.

'You can have the blonde,' he murmured, setting his own sights on the brunette with the legs that went on forever under her short red leather miniskirt.

It took all of three seconds for Brock and him to talk the ladies into stepping outside with them. Unfortunately, once they were out in the parking lot, it only took another three for Kade's nose to twitch with the prickling of his Breed senses coming online with a vengeance.

He smelled blood.

Fresh blood, and a lot of it, coming from somewhere around the rear of the club.

A glance to Brock told him that the other vampire hadn't missed the coppery tang of spilled human red cells, either. They broke into a tandem jog, leaving the women complaining in their wake as the two of them hauled ass to the back of the building.

Nothing there.

The lone working security light mounted to the roof of the place shone down on empty concrete and sparse, weed-choked grass. But the scent of blood permeated the air, particularly strong for Kade and any of his kind.

'There,' he said, spotting the dark stain in the dirt a few feet away from him.

Spatters in close proximity to each other soaked the dry earth near a leaning stretch of ragged chain-link fence. The bleeding human took the worst of his damage over there, and the trail of hemoglobin on the ground made it clear that whatever had happened, the victim wasn't going to get too far before he or she bled out completely.

'This isn't only human blood,' Brock said, his deep bass voice grim. 'The attacker was Breed. He spilled some of his own blood in the process.'

Now that the warrior mentioned it, Kade's nose also picked up on something other than basic *Homo sapiens* cells. 'Not a Rogue,' he guessed, detecting none of the foul odor left behind by the addicts of their race. 'Who else would be idiot enough to feed this carelessly and let his Host stagger off like a stuck pig?'

Brock shook his head, but suspicion darkened his steady, obsidian gaze. Although he didn't say it, Kade read the quiet doubt in the big male's eyes.

'Chase?' Kade scoffed. 'No fucking way.'

'Something's not right with him, man.'

'Not this,' Kade said. The ex-agent was no Mr. Rogers, but to bleed out a human and break one of the Breed's most essential laws? When he said he had an itch that needed scratching, he sure as hell couldn't have meant something like this . . .

Brock nodded gravely. 'Maybe we'd better go have a look, just to be sure.'

They took off, following the blood trail across a vacant lot and down a narrow alley. The deeper they went, the more serious the blood spill became. Spatters turned to pools, some of them spread wide and smeared from where the victim had apparently fallen then somehow managed to get up and run some more.

The trail led them to the entrance of a junkyard at the end of an industrial area. The place was gated, but the padlock and heavy chain that secured it had been loosened. There was just enough room for someone to squeeze inside. And someone had; the wet crimson stains on the latch and edge of the gate left no question about that.

'Come on,' Kade said, wrenching the thing open wide enough for Brock and him to slip through.

He heard the rush of movement the instant before the big black dogs came barreling around a pile of scrap and rubbish. Two rottweilers, big as tanks and mean as hell.

'Holy shit!'

Brock's shout was all but drowned out by the savage barks and growls of the oncoming dogs. No animal alive could take a vampire, but that didn't mean the sight of a combined three hundred pounds of seething, furious canine wasn't cause for a little alarm. Kade stood firm, his legs braced wide as the pair of rotties swiftly closed the distance on him.

He stared them down, eye to eye.

They slowed . . . then stopped, both of them dropping into a cower at his feet. The hounds whimpered, shifting on their bellies and keeping their big heads low as their dark eyes searched out his favor.

'Get out of here.'

They loped off, as docile as puppies.

Brock gaped. 'What the hell was that?'

'This way,' Kade said, ignoring the question and the astonished stare that followed him as he stalked deeper into the junkyard. They had bigger things to deal with right now.

It wasn't hard to find the bloodied victim. The young man had collapsed against a rusted metal crate, one jeans-clad leg stretched out in front of him, the other bent at the knee. He looked boneless and weary, like a puppet whose strings had been severed. He held his hand up against his throat where the bleeding was the worst. He couldn't stanch the flow. In just a few more minutes, he would be dead.

'Jesus Christ,' Brock hissed.

The warrior's voice was thick and strained, but whether from revulsion or the simple fact that the sight and smell of so much fresh blood made even the most controlled vampire thirst like he was starving, there was no way to tell.

Kade's own fangs tore farther out of his gums as he looked at the bleeding human. He tried his best to mask the sharp tips as he edged closer. 'What happened to you?' he asked, despite the obvious injuries that could only have come from one of his kind.

'Jumped . . . me,' the human wheezed. 'My neck . . . fucker . . . bit me.'

When the man removed his hand to show him the injury, the copper punch of his blood hit Kade like a fist to the gut. He'd fed only yesterday, but the urge to drink again pulled at him. His vision sharpened, bathing everything in amber.

'Who bit you?' Brock asked the human, smoothly stepping in when Kade had to glance away. 'Can you describe who did this to you?'

The man exhaled a slow, shuddering sigh. He didn't have long now. He looked up, eyes listless and glassy in the dark. He lifted his arm, slowly extending his finger to point somewhere past Brock's thick shoulder. 'Him,' he gasped, the voice thready and airless. 'Behind you . . . that's him . . .'

Kade and Brock swung their heads around in unison – just in time to see a huge Breed male running for the back acre of the junkyard. The vampire wore black fatigues and a long-sleeved black knit shirt. His head was shaved bald, the back of his naked skull covered in an unmistakable pattern of *dermaglyphs*.

'Holy hell,' Kade muttered.

He broke into a run with Brock thundering at his heels. They bolted for the rear of the littered yard, but the Gen One male in front of them was ten times faster. He vaulted up onto a mountain of crushed cars in one swift leap, then he was gone.

It wasn't Chase who'd brutalized the human and left him for dead, but another Breed male who was recently familiar to all of the Order. A Gen One who'd joined them only a few weeks ago.

'Hunter,' Brock growled. 'Son of a bitch.'

⊰ CHAPTER FOURTEEN ⊱

Claire felt a bit queasy from the flight as she and Andreas stepped off the Order's private jet in Boston later that night. It had been a long trip, mostly because of the chasm of uncomfortable silence that seemed to have opened up between Andreas and her. Fortunately, her lack of sleep after the dreamwalking disaster with him had made her plenty tired on the flight from Denmark to the States. She slept most of the way, but he had seemed much too edgy for rest.

Even now, as he guided her across the private hangar toward a sleek black Land Rover that pulled up to greet them, Andreas practically vibrated with broody, dangerous energy.

'Tegan and Elise,' he told her as a big tawny-haired Breed male and his petite blond mate climbed out of the vehicle. At the sight of them, Andreas's demeanor changed from the maddening aloofness he'd been subjecting her to on the flight, to one of warm familiarity. 'My friends,' he said, stepping forward to greet the golden, beautiful couple.

In one of his brief moments of conversation on the flight, Andreas had mentioned that Elise had been mated to a director of the Enforcement Agency here in Boston. She'd lost him a few years past to an altercation with a Rogue while on the job, and had lost her only son more recently than that. Claire wasn't privy to the details of how Elise had found happiness again with Tegan, but it was obvious from the glow of peace they both radiated as they approached that the two of them were deeply in love.

Claire hung back as Andreas took the female's hand to his lips and brushed her fingers with a chaste but friendly kiss. She had no right to feel the least bit possessive of him, but the pang stabbed her a little as the pretty Breedmate took Andreas into a welcoming hug.

Elise's mate looked nearly as affected as Claire felt. The tall, muscular Breed warrior had a hard-edged look about him, from the wild tousle of his golden hair, to the glittering gem-green eyes that watched over his woman with a combination of pride and purely masculine protectiveness. Andreas had said Tegan was Gen One Breed, and seeing him up close, Claire would have guessed it on her own. His studied stillness called to mind the mien of a big cat; all those muscles might seem coiled and at ease, but it would take only a fraction of a second for him to spring into deadly action if he felt his world or the mate he openly adored were threatened in any way.

'Hello, Claire. I'm Elise,' Tegan's Breedmate said, releasing Andreas to come over and greet her with equal kindness. While the two males shook hands, Claire found herself engulfed in a quick, welcoming hug. Elise stepped back, her pale lavender eyes bright with intellect and warmth, her chin-length light blond bob framing her delicate face. 'It's very nice to meet you. Even though our paths never crossed in the Agency, I am familiar with some of your philanthropic work in Hamburg. You've really done a lot for the Darkhaven communities over there.'

Claire shrugged faintly, uncomfortable with the praise, given the purpose of her emergency arrival in the States with Andreas. And although the two males spoke in low voices, she heard Tegan's murmured condolences on the deaths of Andreas's kin and the destruction of his Darkhaven.

'I recall one of your young nephews and his shy Breedmate who'd been with child when I last saw you in Berlin a year ago,' Tegan added, his brows furrowed over those fierce green eyes.

Andreas gave him a sober nod. 'They asked me to be godfather while you were there, I believe.'

'Yes,' the warrior replied, a faint smile in remembrance before his expression darkened with sympathy. 'We were all stunned to hear what happened. The attack won't go unmet, not if the Order has anything to say about it.'

Tegan sent the briefest look in Claire's direction, unspoken acknowledgment of her mate's hand in the tragedy that Andreas alone had managed to survive. Her sense of guilt and awkwardness increased, as did the tense knot in her belly. Her nerves were stretched peculiarly taut, putting an anxious flutter in her chest.

Andreas put his hand on Tegan's shoulder as they continued their quiet conversation. 'I want your word on something, my friend. If it turns out that Dragos is even remotely connected to what happened to my Darkhaven, I'll do whatever I can to help you get the bastard and shut him down. But Roth is mine alone. Can you give me that much?'

The warrior inclined his head in a slow nod. 'I know the kind of hatred you're feeling. I've been there myself. I'm the last one to tell you how to deal with your own demons, but just be careful, yeah? Plenty of bastards out there deserve a good killing, but vengeance will consume you if you don't control it.'

It may be too late for that advice, Claire thought, watching Andreas's rigid stance and haunted, hardened gaze as the four of them made their way toward the waiting SUV. His need to avenge his family and his human lover only seemed to be growing stronger, more volatile, for the fact that the justice he craved had yet to be realized.

After the horrors he showed her in his dream, there was a part of her that understood his rage, even shared it. But from what she'd seen of him these past couple of days, she worried that his own life might mean nothing to him. Would he hold anything sacred if he finally got his chance to destroy the one who'd hurt him?

Wilhelm.

Just thinking about him turned her stomach with contempt. Claire couldn't cling to any reasonable hope that Andreas's accusations against Wilhelm had no basis. But what terrified her the most was that her involvement with Andreas now could bring no good – not to either of them. Her affection for him was something he didn't seem to want or need. He had a single purpose in living now, and she knew him well enough to understand that if it came down to a choice between his own life and getting the justice he felt he needed, he would spend his last breath seeing that purpose through to the end.

The idea of Andreas dying – again, after the miracle of his resurrection and return to her life – was something Claire would be unable to bear. The thought nearly staggered her as she neared the vehicle and felt the cool night air coming in from the city beyond.

The feeling of unease dogged her now, and there was a mounting jangle swelling in her veins. A waking sense of a presence she hadn't quite recognized until now, when it was clanging in her cells like an alarm.

Wilhelm was near.

Oh, God. How had she missed that? She'd been so wrapped up in Andreas and his friends, in her own confusion of emotions, that she hadn't picked up on her body's signals that her blood-bonded mate was somewhere in the area.

Somewhere in the city of Boston, she was certain of it.

What was he doing here?

'Claire, are you okay?' Elise placed her hand on her arm in concern. 'What is it?'

She shook her head, more fervently when Andreas paused with Tegan and turned a questioning, suspicious look on her.

'I feel a little light-headed,' she said, casting for a reasonable excuse that didn't involve telling Andreas that the enemy he intended to kill – who would be equally determined to kill him, as well – was probably only a few miles away from where he stood. Andreas couldn't know that Wilhelm was so close now. She couldn't let him know that, she thought, a sudden dread crawling into her throat.

'What's wrong?' Andreas's deep voice soaked into her, but it wasn't enough to calm the alarm that was rising inside her now.

'Nothing's wrong,' she said, lying only because the truth would send him storming straight into death's hands. 'I'm fine. I haven't flown in a while, so it's probably just a bit of air sickness. I'll be okay. I need a moment to let it pass, that's all. Is there a restroom somewhere?'

'Over there,' Elise said, gesturing toward the annex terminal nearby. 'I'll take you –'

'No,' Claire blurted. 'I can find it on my own. Please . . . wait here. I'll be back in a couple of minutes.'

All that kept her from running was Andreas's dubious look. He knew she was distressed; the blood bond that linked him to her now would tell him that easily enough. But it was her other bond – the one that would shackle her to Wilhelm Roth for as long as he lived – that sent her fleeing in a state of near panic.

She flew into the restroom, breathless and trembling. If she felt in her blood that Wilhelm was near, then he had to know that she was in the city now, too. The odds of him coming to look for her were too awful to consider. Conversely, if Andreas were to force her to help him find Wilhelm through her blood bond? She would never forgive herself, or him.

And there was a larger, more troubling question, as well. What if Wilhelm Roth truly was involved in something bigger than she'd ever guessed – something related to Dragos? How could Andreas stand up to Wilhelm's death squads and the greater evil of someone not even the Order had been able to defeat thus far?

Oh, God. She couldn't let Andreas know that Wilhelm was in the area.

As much as he wanted his revenge, Claire wanted him alive even more. She could not be a party to his destruction, which was exactly what she was right now, so long as she remained in his company.

She had to get out of Boston.

She had to get far away from Andreas . . . before the bond she shared with Wilhelm Roth betrayed her and led him directly to his death.

'You sure that's what you saw? Because this is some serious shit, and I need to be absolutely clear.' Lucan stopped his pacing of the tech lab to look at Kade and Brock, who'd just come in from patrol with one hell of a report. 'There's no doubt in either of your minds that it was Hunter.'

'Yeah,' Kade said, raking his fingers through the thicket of his spiky black hair. His dark-lashed, quicksilver eyes held Lucan's gaze. 'It was him. Hard to mistake those *glyphs*, and it's not as if we run into Gen Ones every night on patrol.'

Lucan grunted. 'And he saw you both – he recognized you, too?'

'Son of a bitch looked right at us before he disappeared into the city,' Brock replied. The black warrior bared his teeth in a scarcely contained snarl. 'It was like he wanted us to see him. Like he wanted us to see what he had done.'

While Lucan absorbed that bit of happy news, the tech lab's doors whisked open and Chase came stalking into the room. He smelled of gunpowder, adrenaline, and the metallic odor of coagulating human blood.

At the interruption, Gideon turned away from his computers as a screen full of hacked data scrolled behind him. 'Jesus, Harvard. What the hell happened to you?'

The ex-agent dropped into a slouch in the nearest chair and swept off his black knit skullcap to toss it on the conference table in front of him. 'I just spent the last hour disposing of a dead gangbanger over on the north side of town. Someone tore the bastard's throat out and practically drained him. Left him lying where he dropped, right out in the open for anyone to find the body.'

Lucan caught Kade's sidelong glance. The description of the injuries and the brazen manner of the attack was too damned similar to be coincidence. 'You see any trace of the vampire who did it?'

Chase looked up and hesitated, as though he wasn't sure he ought to speak his suspicions aloud. 'I saw someone in the area, but he took off before I got a close enough look to positively ID him.'

'Yeah, well, we sure as shit got close enough,' Kade interjected.

Chase's steely blue eyes narrowed. 'What do you mean?'

'After you left the club tonight, Brock and I ran across the same kind of thing in Dorchester. Human with a serious case of shredded larynx, trailing blood for about two blocks and left for dead in a public area. When we tracked the victim, his killer was still hanging close. Big bastard with Gen One *glyphs* and a shaved head.'

'Ah, fuck,' Chase said on a slow exhale. 'So, it really was Hunter. I saw him, too, but my gut was telling me not to condemn him until I got a better look. Damn, I know the guy doesn't have a lot of social skills, given his background, but this shit is psychotic.'

'Guess we don't have to ask him what he likes to do in his spare time,' Gideon put in dryly.

Lucan shot his fellow warriors a dark look. 'If anyone sees him or hears from him, I wanna know ASAP. And if any of you witness another human slaying like the ones tonight and our boy is in the vicinity and refuses to come in peacefully, you've got my permission to take the bastard out.'

'Shit, Lucan. You serious?' Gideon gave a shake of his head. 'There's a little girl living here at the compound who's going to have her heart torn up if anything happens to Hunter. He might not be winning any personality contests, but Mira adores him. Odd as this is going to sound, I think the feeling is mutual. You've seen how careful he is with that kid. He knows that if it wasn't for Mira pleading for his life after the raid on Dragos's gathering, Niko would have put a bullet in his skull. Hunter would do anything for that kid.'

'That doesn't diminish the fact of what he is,' Lucan reminded Gideon and the others. 'I want to believe he's on our side as much as anyone else – hell, the way things are going lately, we need him on our side. But let's not forget that until three months ago he was just another weapon in Dragos's arsenal. A stone-cold, deadly weapon.'

Gideon gave an accepting nod. 'Maybe Tegan ought to have a talk with him, see what kind of a reading he gets off soldier-boy now,' he said, referring to Tegan's ability to discern someone's emotions with a touch. An ability that had given Hunter a green light when he'd pledged his arm in service to the Order the past summer in Montreal.

'Tegan's running a pickup at the airport,' Lucan said. 'Anyone know when Hunter was due back from his patrols tonight?'

At the round of shrugs that circled the room, Lucan blew out a sigh. 'We've got enough on our plates right now without dealing with shit like this. I want it contained, and I want Hunter pulled in ASAP so we can get some fucking answers.'

Kade, Brock, and Chase all murmured their agreement, then headed out of the tech lab together. When they were gone, Lucan turned his attention back to Gideon.

'If you've got any good news out of those missing persons' reports that Dylan and Savannah have been working on with the area Darkhavens, I'll be glad to hear it.'

From the look that Gideon gave him, Lucan got the feeling his night was going to go from grim to worse.

Reichen sat in the Rover with Tegan and Elise, growing more anxious by the minute. Claire had been gone for a while now. Seventeen minutes and counting.

She'd all but run away immediately after he and Tegan had been discussing what to do about Wilhelm Roth. It had been callous of him to speak so insensitively while she was present; he realized that now. Regardless of the hatred he felt for Roth, the male was still Claire's mate of many years, and that did count for something. He owed her an apology, which he would give her as soon as she came back to the vehicle.

He'd sensed Claire's quiet discomfiture during the flight, too, and knew he was also to blame for that. He felt like an ass after what happened when she'd walked into his dream at Danika's place. The sex, while incredible, hadn't been planned. He had wanted her so badly, and once she was standing there in front of him – her dream self or not – he'd been incapable of pushing her away.

It was the other part of the dream that he regretted.

Equally impossible to curb, he'd had no intention of bringing Claire into the center of the carnage at his Darkhaven. Nor had he meant to expose her to the other bit of nightmarish truth that had haunted him for a long time, and always would.

No one needed to witness that kind of horror, least of all her. She wasn't to blame for any of it, but that hadn't stopped his mind from projecting her into the carnage and, worse, into the role of Helene. His guilt over everything that had happened to his kin and to Helene was still a raw ache in his soul.

And yes, perhaps in some paranoid corner of his heart he worried that, like Helene, Claire could be used against him – that her blood bond might betray him in some way to Roth.

There was little more Roth could do to hurt him; he'd already taken everything Reichen had.

But he could hurt Claire.

Reichen had endured and survived more than he'd thought himself capable of. If any harm were to come to Claire, especially because of her unwilling involvement in his search for vengeance, he knew without a doubt that it would send him over the edge. It would kill him, no question.

'She's been gone too long,' he murmured, an odd sense of emptiness beginning to expand in his chest. 'Something's not right.'

Elise pivoted to face him from the front passenger seat. 'It has been a while. I'll go make sure she's okay.'

Tegan's Breedmate got out of the SUV and headed for the terminal where Claire had gone. She came back out not even a minute later, a look of concern tightening her mouth as she hurried back to the car. 'She's not in the bathroom. I checked all the stalls and the area just outside in the terminal. She's not there.'

'Damn. Get in, babe,' Tegan told Elise. 'She can't be far. We'll drive until we find her.'

'No.' Reichen opened the back door and climbed out. 'I'll take care of this. I think I know where she might have gone.'

He grasped for the blood bond that had told him she was moving farther away from him, focusing his senses on her like a beacon. The bond would lead him to her, but even without it, he had a feeling he knew where Claire would run to if she was feeling overwhelmed and confused.

Tegan put his window down and fixed his intense emerald stare on him. 'You sure you don't need a hand?'

Reichen shook his head. 'Go on without me. I have to go after her.'

Tegan gave him a nod, then reached into his jacket pocket and withdrew a cell phone. 'Take this. The last two speed dials will connect you to the compound.'

'Thanks,' Reichen said. 'I'll be in touch as soon as I can.'

⊰ CHAPTER FIFTEEN ⊱

Claire's footsteps echoed hollowly off the bare floors of her grandmother's house. It had been a long time since she'd last been in the grand old Victorian that stood on the rough shore of Narragansett Bay, but it still felt the same. It still smelled the same, like old wood and furniture polish and crisp salt air. Of course, in the time since she was last here, before she'd left as a young woman to begin her studies abroad in Germany, much had changed. Her grandmother had since passed away, and now the estate was held in trust in Claire's name, as she was the sole heir and last of her mother's line. Not even Wilhelm knew about this place. She had kept its existence all to herself, a secret she was glad to have from him now.

The caretakers who'd been hired out of the trust had done a superb job looking after the house and the extensive grounds after her grandmother's passing. As stipulated in the agreement, a spare key was kept behind a loose foundation brick next to the veranda – the same spot that had been used since the time when Claire's mother was a little girl growing up in the grand old house. Claire had been counting on that key's safekeeping when she'd fled the airport in Boston and hopped on the bus that took her down to Newport.

Finding it where it had always been had given her hope that maybe everything would be all right again. Maybe she would still find some peace – find her true home – when all of the dust settled from the upheaval of her life right now.

The trouble with that hope was that she kept picturing Andreas in her future, and that was only setting herself up for disappointment.

She tried to put him out of her mind as she drifted through the ground floor of the house, reacquainting herself with the memories of her distant past. Family portraits and framed art had been taken down and crated to preserve them. The elegant furniture her grandmother had taken such meticulous care of was shrouded in long white dust covers, giving everything a ghostly, forgotten appearance even with all the lights burning. The curtains and blinds were drawn over the windows and the wall of French doors that let out onto the patio that overlooked the ocean.

It was toward those tall French doors that Claire strode now. She pulled them open, all four pairs, and let the briny autumn wind blow in from off the Atlantic. Its call was too strong for her to resist. She stepped outside and crossed the wide bricks of the patio terrace, then walked down onto the grass, breathing deeply of the ocean scent that had always meant home to her.

Farther out was a jut of rocks that had been one of her favorite thinking spots. She went there now, navigating carefully over the bulky black stone in the dark. She found the flat ledge that formed the perfect seat on the rough edge of the outcropping and eased herself down onto it.

For a long while, she simply stared out at the water, watching the waves shimmer under the pale glow of the moon and stars.

She could have stayed in that tranquil spot for hours more, but the incoming tide was creeping ever higher on the rocks and soon the water would drive her away. Regretfully, she turned around and crawled back from the edge. When she stood up, she was startled to find she wasn't alone.

'Andreas,' she said, astonished to see him.

His chest was rising and falling visibly, concern spread across the taut lines of his face.

Claire had to force her feet to remain grounded and not move toward him in reflex. She didn't want him here, despite what her heart seemed to think. 'How did you find me?'

Even as she asked the question she knew the answer. Breed senses were superhumanly acute. As if the blood bond he now had with her wasn't beacon enough, he could have easily tracked her by scent. Not that he seemed inclined to explain himself. He was pissed off and worried, and the fact that he'd come all this way to find her should have been reassuring, even flattering.

It might have been, if not for the fact that with Wilhelm Roth less than a hundred miles away, she needed Andreas gone as far as possible from her. And the sooner, the better.

'You left without a word, Claire.'

She tried not to scoff at the irony in that. 'I would have expected you'd be a bit more accepting, considering your history with good-byes.'

He stared at her, eyes narrowed. 'What's going on with you?'

She shrugged with a casualness she didn't feel. 'Nothing.'

'Why did you leave like that? You didn't think for one minute that I would be concerned if you just vanished without any explanation?' He exhaled a low curse and shook his head, contrite, even though his eyes were still hot with anger. 'I damn well deserved it, I know. But you scared the hell out of me back there. Talk to me. Tell me what's going on.'

She couldn't tell him. Fear for what he would do if he knew Roth was close by froze that part of the truth in her throat. She glanced away from his intense, probing stare. 'I'm afraid, Andreas. I just wanted to be somewhere familiar, somewhere that I belong. After everything that's happened, I suppose I just wanted to be home. I wanted a little peace.'

'Home and peace,' he said, doubt bracketing his mouth in tense lines. 'No, I don't think so. You bolted out of there like it was me you couldn't get away from fast enough. I want to know why. Was it because of what happened . . . in the dream? Because I didn't mean to hurt you. I want you to know that.'

When she only stared at him in mute torment, his hand came up to gently stroke her cheek. 'God, Claire . . . all I have ever wanted was to keep you safe.'

A sob worked its way up her throat. 'Why?' she murmured. 'Why are you showing me all of this tenderness now, Andre? Why not then?'

He swore softly. 'To keep you safe, I had to let you go.'

She shook her head, unwilling to accept that excuse, but he softly caught her chin. The pad of his thumb was a whisper of contact as he brushed it across her lips. 'I left because of what I had become. You've seen it now – the fire that lives inside me. I was horrified when I thought of what it could do to those I loved. Like you, Claire. Christ . . . especially you.'

She swallowed with a dry throat. 'Why didn't you tell me all of this at the time? We could have worked through it –'

'No,' he said. 'There was no working through it, not then. It exploded out of me without any warning. I lived most of my life never knowing what my fury could do. Once it got loose the first time, it owned me. I left Germany because it was the only thing I could do. It took the better part of a year for me to finally bring the fires to heel. By the time I returned, you were already with Roth.'

Claire listened, struggling to put all the pieces in place in her mind. 'So, all your life, you never knew anything about your pyrokinetic ability?'

'Not until the last night I saw you.'

'We argued,' she said, remembering their parting words.

They'd been out most of the evening in Hamburg, enjoying each other's company as they had for the handful of months they'd been together. But then she'd become jealous when another woman started flirting with him. Andreas had always been a magnet for female company, with his good looks and easy charisma, but he swore to her that he was interested only in her. Claire hadn't believed him. She told him she wanted proof – a commitment that his love was true. When he hesitated, she had become upset and scared that he didn't really love her. She called him selfish, irresponsible. Unkind things. She'd been unreasonable and she knew it, even then.

'I regretted my words the minute I said them,' she told him now, an apology some decades too late. 'I was young and stupid, and I was unfairly harsh with you, Andreas.'

He shrugged. 'And I was a pigheaded fool who should have known better. Instead, I had been all too eager to prove you right. After I left you at Roth's Darkhaven, I went into the city looking for a fight. I found a few, actually, and after I had sufficiently bloodied my knuckles and used my face to crack a few others, I found myself in a run-down hotel in the company of two intoxicated women I brought with me from a bar along the way.'

Claire's disappointment to hear this now was couched by her concern for what had apparently happened to him next.

'At some point, there was a knock on the door. Another woman. I let her in, and because I was . . . distracted by my own idiocy, I didn't realize she had a knife in her hand until she'd sliced it across my throat.'

Claire winced, her heart twisting at the thought. 'What did you do?'

'I bled,' he answered simply. 'I bled so much, I thought I would die from it. I nearly did, in fact. I was too weak to struggle when a group of Breed males came into the room and carried me to a truck in the alley outside. They chained me and dumped me in a remote farmer's field to bleed out and then fry to dust with the sunrise.'

'Oh, my God. Andre . . . I saw that field, didn't I? You showed it to me in your dream yesterday.'

His answering look was a grim confirmation. 'Sometime between that awful hour and daybreak, I felt an unnatural heat beginning to burn inside me. It kept growing, until my entire body was bathed in blistering energy. And then it exploded out of me. I don't recall everything – that's one of the least unpleasant aftereffects, as I would learn. The fires burned from within me, but my skin didn't ignite. By the time dawn started to rise, the chains had melted away. I tried to scramble for some shade, but I was weak from blood loss. I didn't see the young girl until she was standing right next to me.'

A knot of dread tightened behind Claire's breastbone. 'A girl?'

He nodded, only the slightest movement of his head. His mouth was drawn tight, his face rigid with regret. 'She only could have been about ten or twelve years old, out in the field that morning calling for a missing cat. She came upon me struggling in the dirt and asked what she could do to help me. Because of the injury to my throat, I had no voice. I couldn't have warned her away, even if I had any idea of what would happen to her if she got too close to me while my body was still deadly with heat.'

Claire closed her eyes, understanding now. She placed her hand against his cheek, having no words to express the pain she knew he must have felt for what he'd done to the child. Pain it was clear that he felt even now, all this time later.

'I crawled away from the field like an animal, which is what I felt I was. Worse than an animal, to have destroyed someone so innocent and pure. I found shelter in a cave so I could heal. Once I was recovered, I fled. I couldn't stay . . . not after what I'd done. And in the time since, even though many years passed without the fires returning, I still lived with the fear that I might hurt the people I cared about the most.' His fingers were light in her hair, tender as they brushed her brow. 'Leaving you had never been in my plans. After I came back and heard you'd been mated to Roth, I stayed in Berlin and told myself you were better off with him. That way I could be sure you would always be safe from the death inside me.'

'I've seen your power, Andre. I've seen what it can do. But it hasn't hurt me – *you* haven't hurt me.'

'Not yet,' he replied, his tone dark. 'But now it's stronger than it ever was before. It was reckless of me to summon the fires the night my Darkhaven was attacked. It's more deadly than before, and each time the fury comes alive in me, it burns hotter than the last time.'

Claire saw his torment, but instead of rousing her sympathy, it stirred a biting anger. 'Is your vengeance worth all of that? Is anything worth killing yourself in order to have it? That's what you're doing, Andre. You're killing yourself with this awful power of yours, and you know it.'

He scoffed sharply, a wordless denial. 'I'm doing what needs to be done. I don't care what happens to me in the end.'

'I do,' she said. 'Damn it, I care what happens to you. I'm looking at you now and I see a man who is destroying himself with fury. How many more times can you come out of the flames without losing yourself to them? How long before the fire consumes your humanity?'

He stared at her for a long moment, his square jaw held tight. He shook his head. 'What would you have me do?'

'Stop,' she said. 'Stop all of this, before you no longer have the ability to end it.'

The logic was so clear to her. He had an obvious choice here: Let go of his rage and live, or continue his pursuit of vengeance and perish – either by the power that she could see was destroying him, or by the war he was purposely stoking with Wilhelm Roth.

'There is no stopping it, Claire. I've come too far to turn back now and you know it. I've pushed Roth too far these past few nights and weeks that I've been hunting him down.' He exhaled a clipped sigh and his mouth curved into a humorless smile. 'Ironic, isn't it? That what drove me away from you then is now the thing that's brought us back together, such as it is. But what you said earlier is right. You do deserve peace now . . . and I should leave you to it.'

He moved close and pressed his lips against her forehead, then dropped a tender kiss on her mouth. He drew back, then turned and started to walk away.

Claire watched him start up the lawn. Her heart broke a little with every step he took. She couldn't let him go – not like this. Not when every fiber of her being was crying out for him to stay.

'Andreas, wait.'

He kept going, long strides carrying him farther and farther away from her.

She couldn't have held back from him if she herself were chained and dumped and forgotten behind him. Claire ran up the grass and caught his hand. She turned him around to face her, so many words and regrets clogging her throat.

'Don't go' was all she managed to say. It was threadbare, a plea.

His dark eyes glittered with sparks of amber. His golden skin seemed tighter in the moonlight, his mouth a stern, determined line that didn't quite conceal the swell of fangs behind his lips.

'Andre, please . . . don't go.'

Claire lifted up onto her toes and curved her fingers around his strong nape, dragging him down to meet her lips. She kissed him with all the passion she'd always held for him – all the desperate, impossible yearnings that had lived in her heart all these long years.

He kissed her back with even greater ardor. His arms went around her, crushing her to him so that she could feel the hard heat of his chest and thighs against her and the harder, hotter part of him that pressed like a length of thick steel at her hip.

Claire reveled in his arousal, in the warm, rough moan that vibrated in her bones as he broke their kiss to bury his face in the curve of her neck and shoulder. He wanted her, as much or more than she wanted – needed – him.

This was no dream now. This was real and raw and so, so right.

'God, Claire,' he rasped, the tips of his fangs abrading the tender skin of her collarbone. 'Why couldn't you have just let me go?'

She shook her head, too lost for words or reason. All she knew was the desire she had for this man, this incredible, honorable Breed male who should have been hers. Who might never be hers again, once his search for the justice that consumed him finally did take him away from her.

Claire stroked her hands over the muscled ridges of his body, tipping her head back to let his mouth roam wherever it wanted on her skin. She was panting with hunger, her legs melting beneath her from the heat that was detonating in her core.

Andreas drew back to gaze down into her face. He looked so beautiful, so wild and powerful, it made her heart ache. She saw the naked passion in his crackling amber eyes and knew that he saw the same need in her. She couldn't deny it. She wasn't nearly strong enough to try.

Too much time had kept them apart. Too many obstacles that now seemed impossible to surpass. But they had desire. Claire trembled with it, and felt a similar vibration coursing through Andreas as she clung to him.

'Please,' she whispered, needing to feel his weight against her.

She needed to feel his body merged with hers, not in a dream or memory, but flesh to flesh. Naked and carnal.

'Oh, God, Andre . . . please be with me again now.'

He growled against her throat, a rough profanity that only made her pulse throb harder.

With a sure, fluid grace of movement, he swept her up, lifting her feet off the ground and cradling her in the muscled strength of his arms. He carried her across the lawn, to the open French doors of the house. Inside, he slowly set her down amid the shrouded, ghostly furniture. He kissed her tenderly, sweetly, as he grabbed the edge of a white sheet that draped an antique, cushioned chaise and cast it aside.

Claire let him guide her down onto the elegant seat, lying back as he loomed over her like some kind of immense, otherworldly god. He kissed her some more, while his fingers began unfastening the buttons of her prim sweater.

Unlike their encounter in his dream, this time clothing did not simply dissolve away. Andreas took his time undressing her, his mouth skimming worshipfully over every inch of her skin as he unveiled her. He suckled her breasts and teased the curve of her belly and hip. When he painstakingly peeled away her slacks and panties, he dipped his head into the juncture of her thighs and nipped maddeningly at the tender skin, his tongue cleaving the wet petals of her core.

Claire threw her head back and moaned in pleasure as he loved her with his mouth and teased her with the sharp white points of his fangs.

Her first orgasm took her by total surprise. It rushed up on her and swept her high, pleasure she could not contain any more than the broken cry she sent up to the ceiling as her climax overcame her. Andreas lapped at her lovingly, patiently, even though his hands trembled as they skated over her bare flesh, kneading and caressing her heated skin.

'You taste so good,' he murmured against her wetness. 'Even sweeter than I remembered. Better than any dream.'

Claire put her palms on his shoulders, pushing him back as she drew herself up. She eased him down, then crawled up over him, straddling his legs with her bare thighs. She ran her hands under his loose shirt, baring him for her mouth to explore.

When she had worked her way up to his throat, she stripped the shirt off completely and let her eyes take in the unique beauty of his *dermaglyph* patterns. Right now, with desire etched in Andreas's every taut muscle and expression, his *glyphs* were flooded with indigo, burgundy, and darkest autumn gold. Claire traced them with her fingertip, then bent her head and followed the intricate swirls and flourishes with her tongue as she'd been dying to do since she saw him sitting on the moonlit lakeshore of his dream.

Some of those *glyphs* tracked farther down his body, as she vividly recalled. Not wanting to neglect any part of him, Claire unfastened the button of his pants and loosened the zipper. He sucked in his breath as she nuzzled the soft skin of his groin and nipped at his tender flesh. When she tugged his pants down lower, past the smooth, jutting head of his penis, then lower still, he exhaled a pleading oath.

Claire kissed her way around his thick cock, admiring the breadth and length and power of him before she dipped her head and caught the blunt tip of him in her mouth. She only teased for now, loving the silky, salty taste of him. She didn't want to rush. She wanted to prolong this moment, this stolen night that she'd dreamed of for so long.

When she spoke, her voice was husky from passion and a fresh, kindling need. 'Do you have any idea how many times I wanted to seek you out when I was sleeping? There were days, sometimes weeks at a time, when it was all I thought of . . . all I wanted to do was run away to find you. To know this pleasure again with you. You were the only one, Andre. It's always been you.'

He growled, a sound of total, unabashed possessiveness. His hands were rough in her hair, hard against the back of her skull as she bent over him once more and took him fully into her mouth. He arched up, hissing a wordless cry as she sucked him deeper.

'Ah, God,' he gasped. 'That feels so damn good. Claire, if you don't stop . . .'

She didn't stop. She couldn't get enough of him, not even when his body gave a hard shudder and his release roared out of him. She stroked him with her tongue and throat, greedy for everything he would give her after so many years of wanting him.

Of loving him.

She couldn't deny that it was love she felt for him as he drew out of her grasp and plundered her mouth with a fevered, demanding kiss. It was love that filled her heart as he filled her body with his own.

Love that made her scream his name as he brought her to the height of another devastating climax, before he began to seduce her all over again.

The bitch was sorely trying his patience.

Wilhelm Roth fisted his hand and drove it through the clouded window of the Boston warehouse he'd been forced to relocate to recently. Pain ripped through him as he brought his hand out of the shattered glass, the flesh over his knuckles shredded and bloodied. He knew Claire would feel it, too, if distantly, just as he was feeling the proof of her current infidelity with Andreas Reichen.

Her pleasure made acid boil in his gut.

That it was pleasure shared with Reichen made him want to kill them both.

Savagely.

He'd been more than a little surprised to detect Claire's presence near Boston earlier tonight. The awareness of her had since faded, but he was certain she was in New England somewhere. She and Reichen both, apparently.

The only thing keeping him from hunting the pair down was the fact that his hands were full with the current mission for Dragos in the city. His priorities had been made crystal clear by Dragos when he'd exiled him to Boston, and Roth wasn't about to let him down.

He would have his chance to make Claire and her damnable lover pay. He was certain he'd have ample opportunity to inflict great pain on both of them soon enough.

And he could hardly wait.

He'd been chewing on the fact that Dragos had intimated that Reichen was involved with the Order. It wouldn't be surprising if it were true. Despite the male's arrogance and insubordination, there had long been an air of self-righteousness about him.

Roth supposed the male had subscribed to a certain code of honor, even then, in the past, when he had come sniffing around Claire's skirts after Roth had already decided she would belong to him alone. Never mind that he already had a mate; he and Ilsa had been a poor match, one he'd made hastily in a moment of passion and grown bored of not long afterward. He should have gotten rid of her sooner than he had, but then Claire came along and gave him all the excuse he needed.

Or, rather, Andreas Reichen had provided the excuse, just a short time before either man had even met the beautiful Claire Samuels.

Roth had often wondered if Reichen realized the seething contempt he'd inspired when he'd shown weak little Ilsa a gesture of kindness at a Darkhaven reception. It had been a small thing, really, a dry jacket to cover her after Roth had sent her weeping to a rain-drenched balcony when she dared to contradict him in front of his peers. He'd meant to punish her privately, but Reichen had strolled by and discovered her sitting outside by herself in the cold. Incredibly, he'd had the gall to insist she take his coat and then arranged for his driver to send her home without Roth's permission.

Roth fumed even now just to think on it.

He'd fumed then, too, and waited for a chance to put Reichen firmly in his place. He found that chance once Claire arrived in Hamburg and caught the eye of nearly every available Breed male in the region. Reichen included. So Roth had waited and watched, and when the time was right, he'd had his men deal with Reichen. Then he threw himself into the task of helping poor, devastated Claire pick up the pieces of her shattered heart. Taking her as his mate was merely icing on an already delectable cake.

Oh, he'd had to kill Ilsa to clear the way, but it was a small inconvenience to have the satisfaction of knowing he'd made his point with Reichen and stolen the female he loved.

He couldn't have been more stunned to learn that Reichen had reappeared in Berlin later that year. To the younger male's credit, after what was likely a very bitter lesson learned, he stayed well away from Hamburg, and from Claire. Until the past summer, when the human whore who'd been Reichen's latest lover began snooping around in Roth's affairs.

He'd had no patience to deal with Reichen again, and so he'd sent a very swift, clear message to the Berlin Darkhaven where Reichen and his kin lived. Swift and clear, but not quite thorough enough, as the attack had left Reichen alive.

Not again, Roth vowed.

When he next got Andreas Reichen in his sights, the son of a bitch was going down. So much the better if he could send Claire to her death alongside him.

Pleasantly sadistic musings of just how he might accomplish those two goals were swirling in his head when the cell phone in his coat pocket went off.

'Yes, sire.'

'I trust your operation is proceeding as planned,' Dragos said, his tone practically daring Roth to disappoint him.

'The diversion is perfectly under control, sire. As I promised you it would be.'

Dragos grunted. 'Keep it that way. I am nearly finished with the preparations here. Soon the new objective will be under way.'

'Very good, sire,' Roth said. 'I will continue with the plan we discussed and await your further command.'

❧ CHAPTER SIXTEEN ☙

The next morning, while Reichen stayed behind and tried not to be paranoid about danger lurking on every street corner or alleyway, Claire left the house with their remaining euros and drove into town to exchange the money and pick up some food for herself and fresh clothing for both of them. Reichen had attempted to persuade her into waiting until evening when he could go with her – just in case she ran into trouble – but she brushed him off with a look and left him sitting in the big empty house by himself. He had forgotten how independent she was, and a part of him admired the fact that several decades under Roth's thumb hadn't stolen any of her spirit.

Still, he worried.

He knew she was safe from Roth or Dragos or any other members of the Breed so long as it was daytime and the sun would keep all of his kind locked indoors. But the protective part of him – the part of him that had yet to accept that he wasn't still the leader of a Darkhaven, responsible for keeping his home and family safe from harm – balked at the idea of Claire walking around out there without him looking out for her. She was too precious, too vulnerable in a world filled with hidden dangers. She was a treasure worth preserving at any cost.

And she was . . . *not his.*

Damn, but it took some effort to remember that, especially after last night. They'd spent an incredible evening together, making love in the living room overlooking the Atlantic, then again upstairs, on the four-poster bed in the palatial room that had been Claire's when she was a young woman living in her grandmother's house. And yet another time before daybreak this morning, after she'd gotten up to ensure that all the blinds and curtains were drawn tight to protect him from the sun.

He'd have liked to have followed her into the shower before she left to run her errands, but she'd gently chided him to pace himself, that they would have plenty of time together. But they didn't have that luxury, and he knew it. It was easy to imagine that their reunion – this respite in an idyllic setting, without the constant reminders of the darkness they'd left behind in Germany – could go on forever.

It couldn't.

As good as it felt to be with Claire again, they couldn't stay in Newport together for long. Until Roth was found and eliminated, she needed to be somewhere protected and well out of his reach. She wasn't going to like it, but so long as Roth was alive and able to get his hands on her, she needed to be placed under the guard of the Order. The sooner the better.

As for Reichen, each minute he wasn't looking for Roth was an opportunity for the bastard to dig in deeper wherever he was and continue his presumed machinations alongside Dragos. Reichen knew he should be spending every breathing moment and exhausting every effort to hunt Roth down. Vengeance still burned in his belly, and his issue with Wilhelm Roth would not be forgiven simply because he had Claire to warm his heart and his bed.

Roth could not be permitted to continue breathing when he was evil to his core. Nor so long as he might decide to punish Claire for letting herself be pulled back into Reichen's life again.

With that grave thought fueling him, he took out the cell phone Tegan had given him and pressed the last number in the speed dial queue. The number rang twice before Gideon's British-tinged accent came on the line.

'Talk to me,' he said, chipper despite the intrusion on his morning.

'It's Reichen. I apologize for not phoning last night.'

'No worries. Where are you?'

Naked from his recent shower, he leaned back on a shrouded chair. 'Newport, Rhode Island.'

'You find your female?'

'Yes,' Reichen answered, not bothering to clarify that she wasn't, in fact, his at all. 'Everything is fine. Claire is safe, and so am I. Have you found anything yet on Roth?'

'Nothing yet, but we're working on it. I'm running down a couple of international leads right now. Trust me, we want to get this bastard as badly as you do. He may be our most solid link to Dragos at the moment, so we're hitting hard on every bit of intel we can gather on him.'

As Gideon spoke, Reichen considered the fact that he should be there with the warriors, digging into every clue on Roth's whereabouts and helping them flush the son of a bitch out. He was eager to do just that, his palms itching with the need to choke the life out of Roth for all he'd done.

'So, what's the story over there in Newport?' Gideon asked. 'You gonna be delayed there for a while yet?'

'No,' he said, even though he'd been torn between what his heart wanted him to say and what his duty demanded. 'No more delaying. I need to smooth a few things out on this end, but Claire and I can be ready for pickup later tonight if that can be arranged.'

'No problem. I can have one of the guys there about an hour after sundown.'

Reichen scowled, calculating the short span of hours that

would leave him for breaking the news to Claire that he was going to be yanking her out of her home. Again. 'I may need a bit more time than that, Gideon. Claire doesn't know I've called you, or that she's going to be leaving Newport tonight. She's just left one gilded cage; I have a feeling she won't be eager to be put into another one.'

'Ah.' The warrior blew out a shallow sigh. 'Hence the smoothing out of a few things, eh? Well, good luck with that.'

'Right,' Reichen replied, knowing it was a conversation he had to have with Claire eventually, but dreading it all the same. 'I'll be in touch later about scheduling that pickup.'

As he disconnected the call, the front door lock slid open. Claire came in, cautiously peering inside the house to make sure he wouldn't be in the path of the light that spilled in around her.

'Hi,' she said, smiling as she closed the door and he stood to greet her. 'You're naked.'

'And you should be,' he said, struck by how rapidly his body responded to just the sight of her. 'How was the shopping?'

'Successful.' She lifted two filled grocery bags in one hand and an armful of department store bags in the other. 'One of these bags is for you,' she said, holding up the one bearing a men's clothing store logo. 'One is a set of sheets and pillows, and the rest is for me. I can't wait to put on something fresher than these stale old things from home.'

Reichen walked toward her, his intentions blatantly clear. 'I think I should help you.'

Her answering smile was quicksilver and playful. It killed him that he was going to have to take that away from her. 'You'll have to catch me first.'

She dropped the groceries in the foyer and bolted for the stairs with the clothing bags rustling at her side. Reichen lunged after her, taking one step to every three of hers. He caught her halfway up to the second floor. Her startled shriek dissolved into laughter . . . then, before long, the breathless moans and sighs of a woman well pleasured and fully sated.

That evening, as Claire toweled off from a long, hot shower, her body was still humming from the hours of lovemaking she'd spent with Andreas. She walked out of the en suite bathroom and found him lounging like a negligent king on the bed. One long, muscular leg was stretched out to the end of the mattress, the other bent casually at the knee. He was propped up on the pillows, his right arm tucked behind his head. The *glyphs* on his torso, arms, and thighs were still alive with color, but slowly muting toward the golden hue of his skin.

And even at rest, his sex was impressive.

She couldn't get used to seeing him naked; it always stopped her dead in her tracks so she could pause to admire him. The slow curve of his lips said he knew precisely what the sight of him did to her, and his male ego – not to mention other parts – were proud to be noticed so regularly and appreciatively.

Claire broke the spell his naked body seemed to cast over her and walked to pick up the fresh clothes she'd set out for herself. She slanted him a wry look as she pulled the tags off the pair of jeans and the pale gray sweater. 'You're bad for me, you know that?'

'Undoubtedly,' he replied, but while she was joking, he seemed grimly sober. He seemed preoccupied somehow, as though dark thoughts weighed him down. She was about to ask him what was wrong when he got up off the bed and walked toward her, bringing a clingy black wool skirt with him. 'Wear this tonight instead of the jeans. The tall boots with the heels, too.'

She looked up at him, uncertain.

'I want to take you out. You can show me around your old hometown.'

'A date?' she asked, undeniably thrilled by the idea.

Part of her wondered about the fact that the whole day had

passed without Andreas mentioning Wilhelm Roth or the business with the Order that still awaited him in Boston. Not that Claire wanted any of those things to intrude on their time together, but she wasn't naive enough to think that a few hours of sex – really amazing sex – would make him forget the vengeance that was driving him.

As she looked at him, she knew a moment of worry that this was perhaps a pleasant lull before a storm. That she might wake up and find this brief escape with Andreas had just been a dream. She waited for this perfect slice of time to shatter and fall to pieces around her feet.

But Andreas's smile now was just as charming as ever, even more so, when her body was still warm and buzzing in the afterglow of his lovemaking. 'It's been a long time since I asked you out on a proper date, Claire. Will you accept?'

'Yes.' She nodded enthusiastically. 'I'd love to.'

'Get dressed,' he said. 'I'll shower and meet you downstairs.'

Giddy as a schoolgirl with a new crush, she put on the skirt and sweater, then zipped into the sexy black boots and floated down to the living room to wait for him. When he came down a few minutes later, freshly showered, shaved, and dressed, his brown hair damp and tousled around his face, Claire's heart did a little flip in her chest. He looked amazing in the charcoal gray trousers and black silk shirt she bought him. So amazing, all she wanted to do was strip him naked and have her wicked way with him all over again.

'Ready?' he asked.

She nodded and took his outstretched hand. It was a pleasant night outside, crisp but clear as they walked the short distance into Newport's historic downtown. Much had changed since the last time Claire had been home some twenty years ago. Quaint boutiques, mom-and-pop stores, and greasy-spoon restaurants had been crowded out by hotels and timeshares, retail clothing chains, and swanky fine dining.

But pockets of the old hometown still remained, even down by the wharfs, Claire's favorite part of Newport. The town docks were a magical place, especially at night. Bobbing gently on the dark, incoming tide was an eclectic mix of millionaire yachts and sailboats tied alongside weathered commercial fishers and the ubiquitous harbor tour boats. Galleries, shops, and restaurants lined the bricked pedestrian alleys that led to the wharfs, everything aglow with soft yellow lights and vibrant with the sounds of laughter and conversation as crowds of late-autumn tourists strolled and perused, just as Claire and Andreas were doing.

Out there, among this vast, anonymous humanity and so very far away from the trauma and violence of the life she'd left behind just a couple nights past, Claire could almost close her eyes and imagine a peaceful future. So much the better with her hand caught gently in Andreas's strong grasp. With him beside her like this, she could almost pretend that they were still a couple, still in love as they had been before, with nothing but adventure and happiness ahead of them.

Claire tried not to think about Wilhelm Roth. She could no longer think of him as her mate, if he'd ever truly filled that role. She knew he was dangerous – all the more so now that he was aware she'd lain with Andreas. He'd made his displeasure known last night, when he sent her a stab of physical pain through the blood connection she shared with him. His message couldn't have been more clear if he'd carved it into her flesh. Mate or not, Wilhelm Roth was now her enemy as much as he was Andreas's.

That troubling thought clung to her as she and Andreas stepped into a gourmet chocolate shop adjacent to the wharf.

'Come here,' he said, leading her to the gleaming glass cases that contained a mouthwatering assortment of confections.

Claire looked at him quizzically, knowing the Breed's digestive systems could not process human foods except in the most

minuscule quantities and generally only to effect the appearance
of being human themselves. Which was a terrible pity, she
thought, looking at the collection of chocolates that dazzled
the eye and tempted the tastebuds.

'Which one would you like to try first?'

She bit her lip, hard-pressed to decide. 'The glossy one with
the red stripes looks good. Ooh, so does the little square with
the flecks of gold on it. And the one with the coconut on top.'

While she was vascillating between her choices, a balding,
middle-aged man came out of the back of the store carrying
a supply of empty gift boxes. He gave them a polite smile and
a nod of greeting as he set down his things behind the counter.

'Another fine Indian summer evening,' he said. 'Could I help
you folks with something?'

'The lady would like to try some of your chocolates,' Andreas
said.

'Of course. Which ones are you interested in, my dear?'

Claire glanced up and met the kindly gaze of the shopkeeper.
'May I try the little chocolate square?'

He nodded and reached into the case to retrieve one for her.
'An excellent choice. It's our signature piece.'

Claire took a small bite and savored the sweet-tart taste of
dark, high-percentage cocoa. It melted like butter on her tongue.
'Oh, my God,' she murmured around the bliss exploding in
her mouth. 'It's wonderful.'

The shopkeeper smiled at her, his eyes seeming to linger on
her face for a long moment before he glanced to Andreas. 'For
you, sir?'

'No, thank you. But please give her whatever she likes.'

The man chuckled. 'A wise philosophy.'

Claire pointed to the puffy chocolate painted with dark red
stripes. 'What's this one?'

'Dark chocolate with raspberry puree. Would you like one?'
There was that studying glance again. And as Claire looked at

him now, she felt the tiniest flicker of recognition. 'I'm sorry,' he said, frowning. 'Have we met?'

'No, I don't think so.'

He chuckled, scratching his grizzled chin. 'You just look like someone I knew a long time ago. The spitting image, in fact.'

'Is that right?' Claire asked, her attention drifting down to the brass-plated name tag that bore the store's logo and the shopkeeper's name: Robert Vincent. 'I don't believe I know you.'

'It's the darnedest thing. You look exactly like a classmate of mine from high school. Does the name Claire Samuels mean anything to you?'

Beside her now, Andreas had gone stock still and deadly silent. Claire blinked, startled to hear her maiden name come out of the man's mouth. Of course she could have been classmates with him. She'd left the States to study abroad when she was twenty. If not for Wilhelm Roth's blood and the unusual chemical makeup of her own body, she would show similar outward signs of middle age. Instead, she looked essentially the same as she had thirty years ago.

'M-my mother,' she stammered. 'You must be thinking of my mother.'

'Ah!' His smile went even wider now. 'Your mother, of course. Good Lord, you could be her twin.'

Claire smiled. 'I hear that from time to time.'

'We should be on our way,' Andreas interjected, a dark tone in his voice.

'How is your mother?' the shopkeeper asked.

'Good,' Claire replied. 'She's been living overseas for many years.'

'I used to have such a thing for her back in school. She was the prettiest girl in our class – one of the kindest, too. And brother, did she know how to play the piano. That's where I first met her, you see. I was the conductor's assistant in our high school symphony.'

'Buddy Vincent,' Claire blurted, remembering the endearing but awkward boy as she stared into the time-worn face of an aging, mortal man.

'She's mentioned me to you, then?' He beamed.

Andreas cleared his throat impatiently, but Claire ignored it.

'You were always very sweet,' she told Buddy, recalling how he'd often tried to make her feel welcome and special at a time when being different wasn't always the easiest thing. 'It meant a lot to her that you were her friend.'

'Well,' he said, his thin chest puffing out a bit now. He walked over to pick up one of the small gift boxes and began filling it with several pieces of the two chocolates that had caught Claire's eye. 'It was never a chore being nice to a beautiful young lady. When you speak to her next, please tell your mother I send my best.'

'I will,' Claire said.

He came back and handed her the filled box. 'Enjoy these, with my compliments.'

'Are you sure?'

'We'll pay for them,' Andreas said at the same time. 'How much are they?'

Buddy only shook his head. 'I wouldn't dream of taking your money. Please. They're a gift.'

Claire reached out and gave his hand a gentle squeeze. 'Thank you, Buddy. It was a pleasure seeing you.'

'You take care now. You and your beautiful mother both.'

Claire said a polite good-bye to her former classmate, and Andreas ushered her outside in an oddly brooding silence. More than that, he seemed downright irritated about something.

'Are you . . . jealous?'

He snorted. 'Please.'

'You are!' Claire threw her head back and laughed. 'Oh, I don't believe this. You walk through a crowd and every head turns, female and male alike. I happen to catch the eye of a harmless old man –'

'No man is harmless, Claire.'

'Buddy Vincent is easily fifty years old and as sweet as a kitten,' she pointed out, still smiling and thoroughly amused.

'He's still male,' Andreas all but growled. 'And he is still watching us.'

'Yeah?' Claire grabbed the front of his shirt to get his attention. 'Then why don't you stop looking at him and kiss me instead.'

With a dark gaze that promised more than kisses, Andreas did exactly what she asked.

✈ CHAPTER SEVENTEEN ☙

Kade caught the scent of freshly spilled human blood only a couple hours into the night's patrol.

'Down that alley,' he said to Brock and Chase, who both nodded their agreement in silence.

The three warriors headed off together, stealthy, weapons drawn and ready to fire, as they started down the lightless stretch of asphalt that separated two old brick buildings in the seedier part of town. The narrow strip of pavement was foul with the stench of human waste and rotting garbage. But none of that could disguise the coppery tang that emanated from the other side of a dilapidated Dumpster.

Kade reached the dead human first. It was a young female this time, savaged just as brutally as the male he and Brock had found last night. Unfortunately for her, the vampire who'd butchered her throat had also had a taste for something else. Her short skirt was shredded down the front and gory with blood. Her bright pink painted fingernails were broken, her knees scraped, as if she had tried unsuccessfully to get away from her killer.

'Jesus,' Brock muttered under his breath. 'This girl is somebody's daughter. Maybe somebody's sister. What kind of fucking animal would do –'

Chase's fist went up in a signal to cut the chatter. He pointed to the rooftops above their heads. Someone was up there. The crunch of a footstep traveled down to the alley on the quiet of the clear autumn night.

Was it Hunter?

This new corpse sure seemed to fit his apparent pastime.

'I'm going up,' Chase mouthed.

'Not without backup,' Kade replied, but the ex-agent was already in motion. He holstered his weapon and leapt up onto the Dumpster in silence before jumping from there to grab the bottom of a black fire escape on the building. With hardly a sound, he scaled the rickety iron steps, then vaulted up and onto the roof.

Gunfire erupted the instant Chase disappeared from view.

'Ah, shit,' Brock hissed. 'That crazy motherfucker. You take the stairwell inside; I'm going up the escape after him.'

They took off via separate routes to the roof, both of them arriving within seconds to find Chase lying in a pool of his own blood, bleeding from a ferocious chest wound. He was badly hit, but breathing.

'Son of a bitch,' Kade said as he raced to the fallen warrior's side.

'Not . . . him,' Chase groaned, grimacing with the effort. 'Wasn't Hunter . . .'

'What do you mean, it's not Hunter?' Kade said. 'Then who the hell –'

Another hail of incoming rounds ripped through the darkness from a point unseen. Metal *ping*ed. Aged brick shattered.

Kade and Brock returned fire, shooting toward the source of the assault but seeing nothing solid to aim for. More bullets flew at them.

Brock shouted in sudden pain. 'Fuck! I'm hit.'

'Goddamn it,' Kade snarled, glancing over in time to see that the big black warrior had taken a bullet to the upper biceps. It was an impairing wound, but nothing fatal. Chase, on the other hand . . . shit, the guy was in real bad shape.

Fury over his wounded brethren roared through Kade's veins as he squeezed off a hellish volley of rounds. He caught a flash of movement – dark against the darkness – and saw their assailant leap to the rooftop of the adjacent building.

'Fucker's on the move. I'm going after him.'

He left Brock to cover Chase and hauled ass after the huge vampire who was jumping from building to building like a cat. Not being Gen One, as his quarry obviously was, Kade didn't have that kind of speed, but he had determination. He kept up, navigating the assorted clutter of ventilation systems, access doors, loose pipes and tools, and other items that had somehow found their way up to the rooftops above Boston.

Just as he was gaining ground on the son of a bitch, he got a glimpse of more trouble heading his way. On a distant rooftop, another Gen One dressed in black emerged. This one had an automatic weapon, too. If both of the vampires came after him with guns blazing, he was more than screwed.

But the second Gen One didn't open fire on him. He opened fire on Kade's fleeing quarry.

There was an awful racket as both guns lit up the night. Kade stood on the nearest rooftop and watched in amazement as the fight across the way turned from firearms to hand to hand.

The struggle was savage. Bones were cracked, flesh was torn, and sounds that were nothing close to human split the air as the battle intensified.

Kade held his own weapon aimed and prepared to open fire, but amid the scuffle he couldn't be sure which of the vampires to take out. Finally one gained control over the other. He slammed his opponent's head down into the concrete of the roof, then grabbed what looked to be a length of pipe and raised it high over his head. The Gen One who held it let out a furious roar, then brought the pipe crashing down like hell's own hammer.

A sharp, metallic *clank* sounded in the instant before a blinding flash of pure white light shot out against the darkness.

Kade hit the deck. Instinct took him down on his belly and kept him there until the piercing ray went out a moment later. When it was dark again, he sat up on his haunches. On the other rooftop, the victorious Gen One was also starting to get up. Despite most of his muscles and nearly all of his good sense telling him to keep his ass planted, Kade grabbed his weapon and leapt across the distance to confront him.

He cautiously approached, finger poised to load the bastard with a lot of lead. As he moved closer, he got a look at the dead Gen One. His head was separated from his body, burns still sizzling in a perfect circle around his neck and those familiar *dermaglyphs* Kade had spotted on the vampire he'd run into last night.

On the ground next to the smoking corpse lay a black, dented collar rigged with some kind of electronic device. A small LED was blinking red, then faded out.

Kade peered down at the face of the dead vampire and cursed under his breath. Chase was right. It wasn't Hunter. It looked close enough to be blood related – brothers, even – but it wasn't the Gen One assassin who'd come on board with the Order a few weeks ago.

No, Hunter stood and walked up beside Kade now. He cast a dispassionate eye on the grisly death he'd just dealt to someone obviously very close to him genetically. He moved forward, then bent to retrieve the strange collar from its nest of gore.

'The last time I saw Dragos, he said there were others like me,' Hunter said flatly. 'I've been tracking this one in the city for the past three nights. He is not alone. And more will be coming. Soon.'

Kade raked a hand over his scalp. 'Well, aren't you just a lovely ray of sunshine.'

Hunter pivoted his head and stared at him without replying.

'Come on,' Kade said. 'Let's go take care of the others and report back to the compound.'

He didn't want their evening together to end. The stroll around Newport had been pleasant enough, if only for watching the way Claire lit up as she showed him all the places she recalled as a young woman, the places that still seemed to matter to her. This was her home, not Germany. She belonged here, with the salty breezes and the crisp New England autumn flushing her cheeks a deep, ruddy red.

Reichen couldn't see her returning to Germany. He didn't know what was to transpire in the coming days or weeks, however long it took him to find Wilhelm Roth and remove him from existence. He didn't even know if he himself would be alive once all of the smoke cleared. But he knew this: The time he had with Claire, right now, this unlikely – and far too brief – reunion they were experiencing would prove to be the most precious hours of his life.

In truth, if he did not survive his confrontation with Roth, his death would be worth it, just to have known Claire again like this and to have the certainty that Roth could never do anything to harm her.

'It's really too bad you can't share any of this chocolate with me,' she said, biting into a piece as she sailed past him into the house. Closing the door behind them, he flicked on the lights for her and watched the fluid sway of her hips in the form-hugging black skirt. That view had been tempting him most of the night. 'You sure I can't convince you to try even just a little taste?'

He closed the space between them in about the time it took for her to blink. He kissed her, sweeping his tongue past her soft lips and into the delectable warmth of her mouth. The chocolate was bittersweet on her tongue, but nowhere near as tempting as the feel of her in his arms. 'Delicious,' he murmured against her mouth. 'I think I might just have to eat you.'

She laughed and gave him a teasing push, but her eyes were bright with interest as she looked up at him. 'Let's go take a short walk along the shore.'

He shook his head. 'I have a better idea.'

'Oh, yeah, I'll just bet you do.'

He smiled, gave her flushed cheek a gentle stroke. 'Will you do something for me instead?' At her quizzical look, he took her hand and walked her over to the grand piano that was shrouded with a drape of fabric. 'Play for me, Claire.'

'Oh, I don't know . . .' she hedged, frowning as he removed the large square of cloth and unveiled the gleaming black Steinway. 'It's been so long since I've played anything. I'm sure I'll be terrible. Besides, it's probably been years since this piano has been tuned.'

'Please,' he said, refusing to be deterred. They would be leaving Newport in a matter of a couple of hours – as soon as he broke the news to her and called the Order to send a car – and he didn't know if this might be one of their last times together. Selfish or not, he wanted to wring out every last moment of this special night together. 'Play whatever you wish. I'm not interested in perfection. I just want to hear your music again. For me.'

'For you,' she replied, giving him a slow smile as she pulled out the little bench and sat down. 'All right, but don't blame me when your ears start to bleed.'

He chuckled. 'I have no concern whatsoever. Play, Claire.'

She lifted the lid that protected the keys, then sighed thoughtfully as she brought her hands up to hover over them.

From the very first notes, she mesmerized him. He didn't know the piece she played, but it was beautiful – haunting and sad, powerful. There was a heart breaking in every note, lyrical movement so deep and emotional, he could only stand there and let the music wash over him . . . through him.

As he watched her play the piece from memory, he felt the

profundity of her own reaction to the music. She was living it as she played it, every stanza full of meaning. It was her own creation, he realized.

The beautiful composition had come from Claire's own heart . . . her own soul.

'You wrote that,' he said softly as the final note trailed off.

She looked up at him with shining eyes. 'After you left, music was all I had for a while. I wrote several pieces, including this one. It just seemed to . . . I don't know . . . pour out of me in the first few weeks after you were gone.'

Reichen drifted closer to her, moved by the power of everything he was hearing and feeling when he was in this woman's presence. 'It's incredible, Claire. You are incredible.'

He sat down beside her on the little bench. He gazed into her dark eyes, his fingers softly caressing the smooth perfection of her beautiful dusky brown skin.

When he kissed her this time, it was not with searing hunger but with infinite care and reverence. He held her as if she were made of glass, worshipped her mouth as though it were the rarest delicacy.

He loved her.

If he had longed to deny it – even to himself – the truth was staring him full in the face now. He loved this woman, even though she wasn't his. Even though he was not good enough for her, and never had been. If nothing else, Roth had been right about that all those years ago.

'He knows about us,' Claire blurted quietly as Reichen held her in his arms. 'He knows we've been together – that I am with you now.'

It didn't shock him to hear it. Roth's blood bond with Claire would have betrayed her to him. But the little tremor of fear in her voice made Reichen's own blood seethe. 'What happened? Did he do something to you?'

'Last night, while we were making love, he let me know that

he was aware of my infidelity to him. I don't know what he might have done, but his message of pain came through loud and clear to me.'

'You didn't tell me.' Reichen drew her away from him and stared hard into her eyes. 'Why did you keep that from me?'

'Because there is nothing to be done about it, Andre.'

'Like hell there isn't,' he gritted. 'As soon as I know where that bastard is hiding, I will damned well do something about him.'

Claire winced, slowly shook her head. 'I'm afraid of what he will do to you. He will kill you if he can. You have to know that. It's no stretch to assume that it was him who tried to kill you back in Hamburg all those years ago. He was there at the Darkhaven after you and I argued. I was crying when I went inside. I told him what happened, how I wished more than anything that you wanted me for your mate. I told him everything, Andre. And the next thing I knew, you had disappeared. I didn't think about the fact that I went to him about you then, but now . . .'

Reichen pulled her close and placed a kiss to the top of her head. 'You didn't do anything wrong. I've felt all along that the assault on me was too personal and violent to be random. It might not even be centered entirely on us being together. But whether or not Roth had a hand in it doesn't matter, because the end result – the change that came over me in that field – is the thing that drove me away from you. It's the only thing that could have kept me away.'

She wrapped her arms around him and buried her face in his chest. 'I'm so sorry. I'm sorry for everything he's done to you. Your family, your female friend in Berlin that he turned Minion . . . Oh, God, Andre. I'm so very sorry for all the pain you've endured.'

Reichen hushed her, holding her close. 'This is between Roth and me. None of the blame rests with you. What happened to me is insignificant. But my family deserves justice. So does Helene.'

Claire was silent for a long moment, then she asked gently, 'Did you love her very much?'

He thought about Helene and the strong bond of trust and understanding they'd shared. She was a remarkable woman who had been something more than just another of his long line of casual, noncommittal dalliances. It had nearly killed him to see her drained of her humanity, but no more than it had devastated him to have to be the one to finish her after Roth had left her an empty shell, her mind enslaved to carry out his evil bidding.

'I cared for Helene deeply,' he admitted. 'I loved her as best as I was capable. But I wasn't able to give her my heart, because it was already lost to another.'

Claire drew out of his arms then and gazed up at him.

'It's always been you, you know.' He cupped her face in his palms. 'I have been in love with you all along.'

She closed her eyes for a long moment. When she opened them again, they were welling with tears. 'Oh, Andreas. I still love you. I never stopped.'

With a growl he could not contain, Reichen captured her mouth in a possessive kiss. When they were both panting with desire, he pushed the piano bench back and stood her up in front of him. The keys let out a burst of discordant noise as Claire leaned against them. He threw her long skirt up over her thighs.

'Ah, Jesus,' he hissed through his huge fangs. 'You're not wearing panties.'

She gave him a saucy smile. 'Surprise.'

If he'd known that, they never would have made it out of the house in the first place. Ravenous for the taste of her, he buried his head between her legs and plundered her sweetness. She held on to him, fingers twisting in his hair. He kissed her ruthlessly, needing to feel her come apart against his mouth. When she was writhing, moaning and sighing with the rush of a ferocious orgasm, he reached down to unzip his trousers and free his raging erection.

He rose from the bench and wedged himself between her gorgeous thighs. All he wanted to do was drive his cock home, but she looked too enticing to rush, her sex flushed deep red and juicy, her dark curls like wet silk. He took himself in hand and played the head of his penis along the slick cleft of her body, delighting in her breathless mewls of pleasure.

It was a torture that broke him before it did her.

On the knife's edge of coming just from the feel of her, he shifted his hips and pushed inside. She was molten heat around him, her plush sheath swallowing him from tip to balls. He began to pump, slowly at first, still delusioned enough to think that he had any patience where loving Claire was concerned. Her body milked him, the hot, wet friction driving him toward a more urgent tempo. He couldn't stop. He couldn't hold it, not for another second.

He gritted his teeth and let out a sharp roar as his seed exploded out of him and deep into her. She climaxed with him, her fingernails scoring his shoulders as she cried out with her own release. He murmured her name over and over, his cock as hard as marble even as the last tremors of his orgasm racked him.

He stared down at her, moved as always by her exquisite, delicate beauty. He loved the way they looked together, the contrast of their skin, the perfect fit of them when they were joined. And he loved her spicy warm blood scent, especially when it mixed with the musky perfume of her arousal.

'I don't want to let go of this night,' he murmured, gazing into the absorbing color of her eyes. 'I don't want to let go of you.'

'Then don't let go.' She wrapped her arms around him a bit tighter. 'This time, I won't let you go.'

He smiled, regret and duty tearing at him from inside. He had intended to explain to her at least half a dozen times already this evening that their time in Newport was over. He had intended to explain it now, too, but instead he found himself lost in her eyes. Lost in the intoxicating pleasure of her body.

'For now,' he said, kissing her as he spoke, 'let's neither one of us let go.'

'Yes,' she said, moving her hips in a provocative way against him. She stared up at him then, her eyes intense and imploring. 'Will you do something else for me tonight, Andre?'

He grunted, bending his head to taste the soft skin below her ear. 'Anything.'

'Make love to me again, the way you would if we were truly mated.'

He came up to regard her with a frown.

'Drink from me,' she said, stroking his face with a lovingly tender touch. 'Let me pretend that we're together as blood-bonded mates. Just for tonight.'

God, the very notion lit through his veins like a flash fire. He could feel his *glyphs* surging with hungered colors, and his fangs stretched even longer in his mouth.

'I want you to do it,' she said, a soft demand. 'Drink from me as though I were really yours.'

The sound that left his lips was raw, profane. He reared back, fighting the need that shot through him. But then Claire tilted her head to the side and moved her hair away from her neck, and he was lost.

He bore down on her in a primal surge of motion, fangs seeking out her vein as he plunged deep into her welcoming heat once more.

The taste of her sweet, warm blood slammed into his senses in a flood of roaring power. He couldn't curb his possessive growl as he suckled hard at her throat. Nor could he get close enough as he held Claire tight against him and buried himself to the hilt. He pumped hard and fast, unable to be gentle when her blood was spurring him like the most potent, intoxicating drug.

He had never known this kind of primal, visceral union.

It staggered him.

It humbled him.

It shamed him too, when he wanted more than anything to give himself to Claire in the same way, but could not because she was already bonded to another male. Reichen could offer her his vein, but no matter how much of him she drank, her bond would remain to Wilhelm Roth.

A flicker of aggression and fury began to twist and kindle in Reichen's gut when he thought of any male having a claim on Claire. That it was Roth only gave more fuel to the anger threatening to ignite inside him.

No, he thought fiercely, denying the heat that was so eager to leap to life, just waiting for his summons.

Reichen centered all of his focus on Claire, ignoring everything but the strong beat of her pulse against his tongue, and the gentle squeeze of her sex around his. He reveled in her soft cries as she came, memorizing every flush and quiver that traveled her body as he pleasured her time and again, loath to let the night – and their fleeting time together – come to its end.

◄ CHAPTER EIGHTEEN ►

'How's Harvard doing?' Lucan asked as Gideon came out of the compound's infirmary.

'Still unconscious, which is probably for the best right now. Fortunately, the bullet passed clean through, but the holes it left behind in his chest and back are going to need some time to heal. He's going to be okay, but he'll be hurting for a while, and he's down for a week, minimum.'

'Shit,' Lucan muttered. 'The last thing we need is to lose any of our numbers while Dragos is apparently ramping up his operation.'

The altercation earlier that night in the city had proven to be one hell of a revelation. The Order had been aware of the fact that Dragos had other highly skilled assassins like Hunter at his beck and call, all of them presumably kept loyal by unremovable UV collars, programmed to detonate and sever the head of any who tampered with the device or disobeyed his command. But what Lucan and the Order hadn't known for a fact – and, frankly, had dreaded to imagine – was that one or more of those assassins might be first-generation Breed, like Hunter.

And to take that disturbing thought one step further, it was easily feasible to assume that if Dragos had other Gen One assassins in his service, Gen Ones who looked remarkably like Hunter himself and with similar *glyphs*, then the son of a bitch had to be breeding them from scratch off one of the original, otherworldly fathers of the vampire race on this planet.

An Ancient.

Like the one that the Order recently discovered had been kept in hibernation deep within the rock of the Bohemian mountains for probably centuries. The one that Dragos had awakened and removed God only knew how long ago.

If that creature was in fact alive, being used to produce new sons with first-generation strength and abilities – if a breeding process like that had been going on for decades or longer – then it wasn't only the Order and the vampire nation that had cause for concern, but all of humankind. Bred in great numbers, a force that brutal, that bloodthirsty and powerful, would be virtually unstoppable.

The dark thoughts followed Lucan as he and Gideon left the infirmary wing and walked the twisting corridors to the tech lab. The entire compound was gathered there, the warriors in from patrol, and all of the Breedmates. Hunter was also in attendance, the big Gen One looming at the back of the room, while the rest of the group had taken seats around the large table in the center.

Lucan gave the male a brief nod of greeting, silent acknowledgment of Hunter's assistance tonight – assistance that had probably saved more than one warrior's ass and also netted the Order an up-close look at the technological wonder of the dead assassin's UV collar. Although it was smashed and detonated, Gideon had been playing with the device ever since it arrived, trying to get a handle on how the thing worked and how it could potentially be used against its wearer.

'How's the arm?' Lucan asked, turning his attention to Brock, who sat between Kade and Nikolai at the table.

The bulky black warrior shrugged his wounded shoulder and cracked a broad grin. 'It'll feel a helluva lot better when I get a chance to smoke one of these Gen One freaks of nature.' He glanced over at Hunter. 'No offense.'

The vampire's golden gaze was as flat as slate. 'None taken.'

Lucan took his place next to Gabrielle at the head of the table and addressed the assembled team. 'Obviously, after what we learned a few hours ago, our mission to disable Dragos and his operation has acquired a new, immediate objective. I don't need to tell any of you that the last thing we need is a Gen One killer loose in the city, slaughtering humans at will and wreaking general havoc. Now, we can hope that it was just the one individual, an isolated incident, but I'm not the kind to rely on hope. I need answers. Solid intel on just what we might be dealing with here – before Dragos sends it to our doorstep.'

There were a few nods around the table, and more than one of the mated warriors shot Lucan a look that communicated the same dread he felt whenever he thought of the potential of their war with Dragos coming home to the compound.

'Tomorrow night I want a sweep of the entire city,' he said. 'We'll divide up: Tegan, Hunter, and myself each accompanying one group in case we run into more Gen Ones. This is an extermination mission. If one of Dragos's assassins is spotted, we take him out. I want to send a very clear message to that son of a bitch and drive him back. Hard.'

'That could be exactly what he wants us to do,' Tegan replied. 'Have you considered that what happened these past two nights might have been Dragos's way of baiting us? Trying to pull us into street combat with his underlings so we're not going after him?'

Lucan nodded. 'It could be. But if he's sent assassins into the city, can we really afford to take that chance and not confront the threat head-on?'

Very subtly, tenderly, Tegan slid his hand over to cover Elise's. 'No, we can't.'

'Okay,' Lucan said. 'Let's go over the map and divvy up territories for tonight's patrol.'

Reichen closed the cell phone and raked his hand over the top of his head. 'Jesus Christ.'

'Is it bad news?' Claire came out of the bathroom wrapped in a towel, her body still glistening with droplets of water from her shower.

'It's not good,' he said, glancing up from where he sat on the edge of the bed. It was close to midnight, and he'd been waiting for Claire to get cleaned up and dressed before he broached the subject of leaving Newport, when the disturbing call came in from the Order. 'Two of the warriors were shot earlier tonight in a confrontation with one of Dragos's henchmen.'

'Good lord,' she whispered. 'I'm sorry to hear that, Andre. How terrible.'

Reichen nodded gravely. 'They're down one man now, and planning to run intensive sweeps of the city tomorrow night to rout out any other potential threats.'

Claire inched over to join him where he sat, but instead of touching him, she wrapped her arms around herself. He could feel her unease in both the tentative way she moved and the sudden spike of her adrenaline, which echoed in his own veins. 'Do they believe Dragos is in Boston, then?'

'I don't know. Bad enough he's sent his Gen One assassins in to stir up problems.'

'He has assassins who are also first-generation Breed?' Claire's expression fell a little more. 'I had no idea. Dragos must be a very dangerous enemy to have.'

'Yes,' Reichen agreed. 'But Gen One assassins are only part of what makes him so dangerous. He has other things, too . . . the Order believes he controls one of the Ancients, hidden somewhere in a location we've yet to uncover.'

Claire frowned. 'But all of the Ancients were killed during the Middle Ages. It was the Order that declared war on them and carried out the slayings. Even I know that part of Breed history.'

Reichen slowly shook his head. 'One escaped the war with the Order. He was secreted away in a crypt in Bohemia for a very long time – until Dragos had him removed. I saw the empty crypt myself, last year, when I climbed the mountain outside Prague with some of the warriors. We'd been hoping the Ancient was dead and dust by now, but he's not. Apparently Dragos has been keeping the creature alive for centuries, using him to create a new generation of the most powerful vampires in existence. With enough time and resources, Dragos could craft his own personal army of Gen One assassins bred to do his bidding.'

'Not if the Order can stop him,' Claire said hopefully.

'We *have* to stop him,' Reichen corrected. 'We have to strike at him wherever and however we can.'

Claire watched him with cautious eyes. 'We? But you aren't –'

'I owe them,' he said solemnly. 'The Order has been there for me when I needed them in the past, and I have pledged to them that I am here when they need me. I meant that. I can't go back on it.'

'What are you saying?'

'They're down one man in Boston now. I need to step in and help them.'

'You're going to Boston?' He didn't know why that should make her pulse lurch the way it did, but he felt her alarm echo in his own veins. 'But you're not one of them, Andreas. You're not a warrior, so how could they ask that of you?'

'They've asked nothing of me. I've offered them my assistance because they are my friends.'

She glanced away from him, seeming to struggle with her words. 'But I thought we were . . . I thought, after last night, after everything we said to each other . . .'

He laid his hand gently on the side of her face. 'It doesn't change a thing about what we've shared here, or how I feel about you. I love you, Claire. But this isn't a choice between you and them. It's simply my duty. My honor. And if teaming with the Order to move against Dragos brings me closer to finding Roth, so much the better.'

Claire got up and paced away from him, across the room. Her shoulders were held in a tense line. Even if he hadn't been linked to her by blood, he would have known without question that she was troubled by something deeper than anything she had said so far. 'I don't want you to go, Andre. You can't go to Boston. Not now.'

'You had to know that neither one of us could stay here like this for long.' He moved toward her, gently turned her around to face him. 'The Order is sending a vehicle. It will be here within the hour.'

'You'll be killed,' she said, her voice cracking. 'Andreas, you will die if you go to Boston. I can feel it in my heart. If this vengeance of yours doesn't kill you, then your fury surely will.'

He lifted her chin so that she was forced to look into his eyes. 'I have more reason to live than ever. I'm not looking for death, but I can't pretend I'll have a moment's peace until Roth and his ilk are wiped from existence. Neither will you.'

'You can't go,' she murmured, stubbornly refusing to hear him. When he started to shake his head in denial, she spoke with even more determination. 'What if I asked you to let go of your hatred of Wilhelm Roth? What if I were to ask you to choose –'

'Don't,' he whispered. 'There is no choice for me to make here.' He smoothed her hair out of her face, feeling as though something precious were slipping through his fingers. 'If I stayed now – even if I set aside my hatred of Roth – what will we do when he comes looking for us? Because he will, Claire. You know that as well as I do.'

'Then we will face him together. When and if that time comes, we'll defeat him together.'

Reichen shook his head slowly. 'This is my battle, not yours. I wouldn't want you anywhere near when I finally get my hands on Roth. It's far too great a risk. What do you think would happen to you if the fires inside me ignite and won't ebb?'

God, he'd thought about that awful scenario a hundred times, beginning on that day in the farmer's field outside Hamburg. He'd been thinking about it as recently as last night, and today, as well, when he could still feel the heated embers glowing in his belly.

How would he ever forgive himself if he brought any harm to Claire?

'I can't risk it,' he said again, more forcefully now. 'And I won't let you risk it, either. I want you to come with me tonight to the Order's headquarters. You'll be protected in their compound, and you can stay there until –'

'Until when?' She closed her eyes for a long moment, as if absorbing the weight of his words. 'Until you are either dead or very near to it? You want me to stand by and watch you pursue your own destruction, Andre? Now you are the one asking too much.'

He wanted to tell her that her fears were unfounded. More than anything, he wanted to promise her that he had no doubts about how this thing with Roth was going to work out. He wished he could assure her that somehow they would come through all of this in the end, that they could have a future together – the future Wilhelm Roth had denied them so many years ago.

But he couldn't deceive her.

Taking down Roth might demand the last of his thin control. If he had to unleash his power to its hellish maximum in order to destroy the bastard, he would. And if the situation called for that, he knew the odds of him emerging from it with any shred of his humanity intact was virtually nil.

He gazed down at her lovely face and tenderly smoothed a damp tendril from her brow. 'Get dressed now, all right? We can talk more, but it won't be long before our ride arrives to pick us up. And you are going with me, Claire. That much is not open to debate.'

She looked at him for a long moment, saying nothing. Then she pressed her lips together and gave a faint shake of her head. 'I know where Roth is, Andre.'

Reichen couldn't speak as those words spilled out of her mouth. He stood there, dumbstruck and confused, a building sense of rage forming swiftly from deep inside him.

'I felt his presence through my blood bond to him last night, when we first arrived in Boston.'

Her admission was calmly voiced and steady, filled with certainty. It made him pause, even while his pulse slammed into a violent tempo. 'He's here in the United States?'

She nodded faintly. 'In Boston.'

Reichen's blood began to sizzle. 'You knew this? You knew this, but you didn't tell me.'

He didn't mean for it to come out as an accusation, but the heat flickering to life within him made it hard to form words. His head was buzzing, and it was hard to do anything but fight to keep control of the kindling fire that was already starting to spread through his body.

Roth was a mere hour away.

All this time, so close to his grasp.

'I couldn't tell you, Andre. I didn't want to give you information that might only get you killed. That's why I left the airport without telling you. But then you followed me here, and I thought maybe if we spent some time together, the way we used to, then I could convince you to give up your need for vengeance.'

Reichen could barely breathe. His nostrils filled with the acrid tang of smoke and heat. All along his limbs, electricity crackled, growing hotter by the second. 'For fuck's sake, Claire. You should have told me about this. I needed to know. Goddamn it, the Order needed to know also.'

'I didn't want my blood bond to Roth putting you or anyone else in danger.'

His vision beginning to bleed red with rage, he stalked away from her, fuming.

'Claire, you have been the one in danger all this time. With Roth so close, he had to know you were here, too. He could have shown up on this doorstep at any time.'

'But he didn't,' she said quietly from behind him. 'I couldn't tell you that I knew where he was, or you would have gone after him. You can't tell me that you wouldn't have insisted I help you locate him, Andreas. You're so determined to claim your justice, how long would it have taken you before you asked me to use my blood bond to lead you to him?'

'Never,' he said, appalled. He spun around to face her then, his body teeming with heat. 'I never would have used you. Never. God, don't you know that?'

'I suppose I wasn't willing to find out,' she replied. 'Andreas, please, don't be angry with me –'

'I'm fucking furious with you!' he roared, unable to bite back the fear that had such a firm hold on his heart. His chest heaved with every breath he pulled into his lungs. He shook from a place deep within, a pit of dread so black and endless, it might have swallowed him whole. And the heat of his destructive power continued to rise, burning through his reason and self-control. 'I can't be near you right now. I have to get the hell out of here.'

When he moved to walk past her, Claire's hand shot out to him.

Too late to warn her away, he felt her fingers close around his hand. She yelped in sudden pain and pulled back, cradling her palm to her chest.

Oh, God. He'd burned her.

He had stomped on her heart and now he was hurting her in still another way. Just as he feared he would do eventually.

He stepped past her and, with a few brisk strides, chewed up the distance to the door.

'Andreas,' she called out behind him.

He didn't look back.

His body lethal with the heat of his fury, he stormed out of the room and leapt off the second-floor balcony to the foyer below. He heard her cry his name again, but he didn't so much as pause for a second.

Glowing now, his pyrokinetic curse screaming through his veins and limbs, mind and soul, he threw open the front door with a sharp mental command. Then he stalked out into the crisp, cool night air without looking back.

⊰ CHAPTER NINETEEN ⊱

It took him the better part of an hour before he was able to rein in the worst of his pyrokinetic heat. He was still angry with Claire by the time he returned to the house, but at least he couldn't hurt her further. Not that she wasn't still feeling some pain, he acknowledged as he walked up the driveway and found her standing outside with the warrior who'd been sent from Boston to pick them up.

'Ah, you see?' Rio said when he spotted Reichen. 'I told you he would come back.'

The Breed male's rich voice rolled with his Spanish accent, and when he flashed a welcoming grin and thrust out his hand to Reichen in greeting, the scars that marred the left side of his face practically vanished. 'Good to see you, my friend.'

'And you, as well,' Reichen said as he briefly clasped the warrior's hand.

Rio's pretty auburn-haired Breedmate, Dylan, was with him tonight. She strode up and gave Reichen a casual kiss on the cheek. 'You had us all a bit worried here.'

'My apologies,' he murmured, slanting a look at Claire.

She would hardly look at him, and he could see that she was cradling her singed fingers close to her chest. Reichen felt sick that his curse had wounded her, even a little. He wanted to tell her as much, but it was a conversation best done privately.

She didn't seem eager to talk to him anyway.

Nor did she seem inclined to argue anymore about going with him to the Order's headquarters. She followed Dylan to the vehicle and started to climb into the backseat.

'Everything good?' Rio asked when the females were out of earshot. 'You don't look so well, amigo.'

'I'll feel better once she's safe in the compound,' he said.

In truth, he'd feel better once he had a chance to hunt and slake the thirst that was still riding him from the pyro. The last thing he needed was to be cooped up with Claire for the next hour or more on the drive back to Boston. Bad enough he craved blood to cool the final few embers that still burned inside him. It would be pure torture having to curb his need if he was seated mere inches away from the woman he thirsted for above all others.

Rio seemed to clue in on that as they walked together toward the SUV. 'Dylan won't mind if you ride shotgun,' he said. 'She and Claire can ride together in back and get acquainted. Dylan's far better company than either one of us.'

Reichen wasn't about to argue. He took the front passenger side and sat back as Rio wheeled the Rover down the driveway and headed for the road that would take them to the interstate.

He was right about the trip being one long exercise in patience and control. While Claire and Dylan chatted softly behind him about the things they loved most about New England, and where they'd each grown up, and a hundred other harmless pleasantries, Reichen stared out the dark-tinted glass of the window and tried not to think about his hunger.

It was a losing battle.

By the time they exited the tollway and reached the inner city limits of Boston, his feverish hunger was demanding to be fed.

'I need to walk for a while,' he told Rio as the warrior came to a stop at a traffic light. He didn't wait for permission, just opened the door and jumped out. 'I'll meet up with you at the compound shortly. I know how to find you.'

From the backseat, he caught Claire's look of concern. He felt her worry rattle in his own blood, too. She thought he might be going after Roth on his own.

He might have been tempted, if not for the clamoring of his thirst. Instead, once the SUV rolled away into the darkness, Reichen skulked through the thickly settled, working-class neighborhoods. He was careful to keep to the back-alley shadows, where it was easier to conceal his presence and his dark intentions. It was a blustery, rainy night in Boston, which meant far fewer loiterers on the sidewalks or standing outside the pubs sucking on cigarettes. Only a handful of the roughest and most desperate individuals had any reason to be outdoors tonight – Reichen among them.

He searched the city's offerings with a cool eye, knowing that when he was like this, riding the far outer edge of his power, he was a predator in the meanest sense of the word. His mouth was parched, his fangs digging into his tongue. Like this, he was as deadly as the Ancient in Dragos's hidden lair. A thirsting, savage monster.

As Reichen prowled the back of a narrow neighborhood street, the bang of a storm door drew his head sharply up. A human male in a ball cap and baggy sweats stomped down a rickety wooden porch, screaming obscenities at the older woman who appeared backlit by lights from inside the house.

'Getcha ass back here, Daniel! Do you hear me?' she shouted, loud enough for the surrounding four blocks to hear.

The young male flipped her off and kept walking while he hollered back at her. 'Yeah, yeah, fuck you too, Ma! Go back to ya bottle and stay the hell outta my weed, why don't ya! You owe me twenty bucks for the shit you stole from me!'

Reichen cocked his head, watching the human cut down a dark side road. With his head down and his mouth working absently on all the things he still wanted to say to the drunk who spawned him, the kid didn't even notice that he wasn't alone in the narrow alley.

He didn't see Reichen moving in from behind; probably only sensed him as a rush of cold air at the back of his tattooed neck. Before the human had a chance to utter a single startled gasp, Reichen sprang on him.

He swiftly took him down to the cracked asphalt. Pushed the human's chin up and to the side, baring the hammering pulse at the side of his neck. He bit in deep, and sucked in a mouthful of warm, nourishing blood. He fed hungrily, greedily, ignoring the feeble struggles of his Host. Every gulp was bitter on his tongue, and did little to quench the desert dryness of his throat.

His hunger persisted, even when the human's resistance had ended. Reichen kept feeding. He couldn't stop. He wasn't even sure he knew how – one of the terrible consequences of summoning his talent.

He might have killed the man if not for the sudden awareness of cold hard steel pressing tight against the side of his head.

'The buffet is closed, asshole.'

Reichen grunted, only the dimmest flicker of recognition burning into his brain. He kept drinking, starving for more.

The hammer on the large pistol cocked with a loud metallic warning. 'Back the fuck off, or you're gonna be eating lead.'

He growled now, pissed off by the interruption and still too fevered to let up on his Host. Blood gushed over his tongue and down his throat, but the fire in his gut still burned, impossible to extinguish. He slid a feral gaze to the side to gauge the Breed male with the gun locked and loaded at his head.

'Holy hell,' the huge vampire muttered. The icy nose of the pistol fell away from his temple. 'Reichen? What the fuck.'

Reichen knew this immense male with the wild tawny hair and stark green eyes. Instinct called him warrior – friend, even though his stance and tone a moment ago had conveyed deadly serious murder. It was that instinctive awareness that kept Reichen from turning on the vampire as a strong hand came down on his shoulder and physically peeled him off his prey. He was shoved back hard, and the other male grabbed the human to seal the punctures with an efficient sweep of his tongue.

Reichen watched, ass planted on the concrete, as the big Breed male palmed the human's forehead and erased his memory of the attack. 'Now get the hell out of here.'

The stunned man stood up and wandered dazedly toward the other end of the alley.

'Tegan,' Reichen murmured thickly, voicing the name that finally sprang into his consciousness.

The warrior stalked over to him. 'What are you doing down here? Last I heard, Lucan had sent Rio out to Newport to chauffeur your sorry ass into the compound.'

Reichen shrugged. 'I had the sudden urge for takeout along the way.'

Tegan didn't laugh. He kept that fierce gaze trained on Reichen, watching him as he might an armed grenade. 'You look like shit.'

'I'm better now,' Reichen replied, feeling the new blood quenching his organs and cells. But it hadn't been enough. His thirst was still gnawing at him, greedy for more. 'I am fine.'

Tegan scoffed. 'You've got the shakes and you can't keep your eyes focused on a damn thing.'

'It will pass.'

This time a raw curse. 'Give me your hand. Doesn't look like you can get up on your own motor.'

Reichen took the offered help, clasping Tegan's hand and letting himself be pulled to his feet. No sooner had he risen than Tegan drew in a sharp hiss. His fangs punched into view behind his lip, and the green of his eyes was suddenly shot with flecks of glowing amber. Reichen recalled the warrior's ability to read emotion with a touch, and he could only guess at the torrent of disturbing things he'd just picked up from that brief contact.

'What the fuck is going on with you, man?' he demanded.

'It's the pyro . . . does this to me afterward. No big deal.' Even as he said it, Reichen wondered if it was true. Summoning his power was getting easier all the time; coming out of its wake was another thing.

Maybe Claire was right when she challenged him about his fury. How many more times could he do this and hope to emerge from it in one piece? How soon before he reached the tipping point and the fires ate away the very last scrap of his humanity?

And if the fires didn't do it, he had the sickening feeling that the nearly insatiable thirst left in their wake surely would.

'Shit,' Tegan exhaled, holding him in a narrowed, assessing look. He pulled a cell phone out of his jacket pocket and pressed a key. 'Yeah, it's me. I'm down in Jamaica Plain. I've got Reichen here with me, I'm bringing him in to the compound.'

The women of the Order made Claire feel as welcome as she ever had by her contemporaries in the Darkhavens. Three of the warriors' Breedmates, Savannah, Gabrielle, and Elise, had prepared her a lovely dinner of creamy soup and homemade biscuits, and Dylan had shown her to a private apartment down the maze of marbled corridors that Claire was offered for her own while she was at the compound.

They had told her to make herself at home, and she couldn't resist spending a few minutes nosing around the massive headquarters that spread out seemingly endlessly. It was fascinating – and a bit unsettling – to realize that an organization like the Order not only existed but *needed* to exist. She felt so naive, reflecting on how Wilhelm Roth and his Enforcement Agency cronies strutted around, professing to be the protectors of the Breed, when they had been as corrupt as a cancer, slowly chewing away at the foundation of what was truly good and just. Wilhelm Roth had been a villain all along, and Claire had been too blind to see it.

But what hurt much worse than that was the fact that she'd been in love with Andreas Reichen for most of her life, and now that she had been given a miraculous second chance with him, it might be Wilhelm Roth who tore them apart once more. She could only hope that good would win out over evil like him and Dragos. She could only pray that once the worst was over, she and Andreas could begin to smooth over the fear and anger that stood between them now.

The drive from Newport to Boston seemed to take years instead of an hour. She'd hated that she and Andreas hadn't been able to talk before Rio and Dylan had arrived to bring them to the compound. And she still weathered the knot of cold anxiety that had settled in her heart in that instant when he'd leapt out of the vehicle once they reached the city.

She didn't know where he'd gone, but she'd taken some small comfort in the fact that Elise had informed her that he was with Tegan now, both of them presumably on their way back to the compound.

At least he was safe.

At least she would still have the opportunity to try to make things right between them.

Claire turned down one of the winding white hallways and followed the pattern of black *glyphs* inlaid in the floor. The marks were mesmerizing, especially when she was already lost in her thoughts. She caught a faint whiff of chlorine an instant before a door swung open in front of her in the corridor.

A young girl with wet blond hair came to an abrupt stop directly in her path. She had a towel wrapped around her tiny frame, the straps of a pink swimsuit tank peeking over the top of the white terry cloth.

'Oh!' Claire exclaimed, startled and surprised to see the child in the compound. 'I'm sorry. I didn't see you coming out of . . .'

Her voice trailed off as she found herself staring into a pair of wide, luminescent eyes the color of polished silver. They were the oddest color – not really a color at all, but nearly white. Smooth as glass . . . hypnotic.

'I was just . . .' Claire murmured, uncertain what she meant to say next because in that instant the girl's eyes began to change.

The surface of her irises warbled, like a pond suddenly sent quaking by the drop of a pebble into the water. Her pupils began to shrink to tiny pinpoints, drawing Claire deeper into the peculiar spell of the girl's eyes. Then she saw something move within the mirrorlike depths.

It was an image taking shape swiftly, coming into focus as Claire peered in total rapt fascination. It was a woman, running in darkness. Screaming, grief-stricken.

It was herself.

Claire watched as the vision played out like a clip from a movie. But this was no movie; it was her life. Her personal anguish. She knew it instinctively, as she watched herself tearing through a thicket of trees and bramble, desperate to reach something – or someone – yet knowing from the ache in her soul that what she sought was lost to her already. There was a blinding glow of fire ahead of her, a deep pit of rubble that roared with flames and smoke, throwing off heat so intense it seared her like she was walking into a furnace.

Someone shouted for her to get back.

Still, she ran toward it.

She couldn't turn away from it.

Even though she knew in her heart that he was gone, she couldn't turn away from *him*.

'Andre,' she murmured aloud.

The door swung open again and a woman came out this time. 'Oh, God . . . Mira,' she exclaimed, and hastily turned the little girl away from Claire, burying the child's face in the generous swell of her pregnant belly.

Claire came out of her daze as if she'd been slapped. 'What just happened?'

The other woman was kneeling down in front of the child now, smoothing a gentle palm over her cheeks and murmuring reassuring words to her. She offered Claire an apologetic look. 'Hi, I'm Tess. You must be Claire. This is Mira. We were just having a swim. Are you all right?'

Claire nodded. 'Her eyes . . .'

'Yes,' Tess said. 'Mira is a seer. She usually wears special contact lenses to mute her talent, but she took them out because she was afraid to lose them in the pool.'

'Hi, Claire,' Mira said, careful to keep her gaze down now. 'I didn't mean to scare you.'

'That's okay.' Claire smiled and ran her hand over the top of the girl's damp head, even though she was still very rattled by what she'd witnessed.

Tess seemed to pick up on her unease. The pregnant Breedmate's aquamarine eyes were tender, compassionate. 'Mira, why don't you run along now. I'll be right there to read you a story while we wait for Renata and Niko to come in from their patrol.'

'Okay.' The little girl pivoted toward Claire and murmured to her feet, 'Nice to meet you.'

'You, too, Mira.'

After she was gone, Tess gave Claire a sympathetic smile. 'Was it awful, the thing she showed you?'

'Yes,' she answered, too stricken to explain what she saw.

Tess winced. 'I'm sorry. I wish I could tell you that Mira's visions don't always come true. Her gift is mercilessly honest. She can't help it. She can't even control it, which is why she has the special lenses now. Each time she uses her talent, she loses some of her own sight.'

'How awful.' And now Claire felt worse for having inadvertently taken something away from her. 'I had no idea –'

'You couldn't have, so please don't feel bad,' Tess said, kindly absolving her of her guilt. 'The vampire who had Mira before she came here to the compound used her talent constantly. Niko and Renata took her out of that bad situation just a few weeks ago. It's our hope that her sight can be restored in time.'

'I hope so, too,' Claire murmured, feeling sorry for the girl, but her own thoughts were miles away.

She had to tell Andreas what she'd seen.

She didn't kid herself that he would listen to anything more she had to say, or even that he would want to see her after the way they'd left things between them in Newport. But she had to try to get through to him, if only so that he had the knowledge and could decide on his own what to do about it.

Claire felt the other Breedmate watching her closely, as if she understood the weight of her thoughts. 'When I walked past the weapons room a short while ago, he was in there with Tegan and Rio. I believe they'd just come in. Would you like me to walk you down there?'

'Thank you,' Claire said, then fell in step beside Tess, her heart squeezed tightly in her chest.

CHAPTER TWENTY

In the few short minutes it took Claire and Tess to reach the Order's weapons room, Andreas was no longer there. Tegan and Rio were standing near the firing range with Gideon, reviewing a cache of ammunition and firearms laid out on a table near a large cabinet filled with more of the same. Tegan looked up as Tess led Claire into the room.

'Have you seen Andreas?' Claire asked the formidable Gen One male.

He nodded gravely. 'I've seen him. And I sure as hell wouldn't recommend it. At least not for a few more hours. He's not exactly fit for company.'

'I need to talk to him, Tegan. It's important.'

When the warrior looked like he was going to shut her down flat, Tess chimed in. 'I was swimming with Mira at the pool. She didn't have her lenses in, and . . . Claire saw something.'

'Ah, fuck.' Tegan wasn't the only vampire in the room to mutter a dark curse. He ran a hand over his jaw, then followed it through with a gesture toward the corridor outside. 'His quarters are up that hallway. Fifth door after the first turn.'

Claire nodded her thanks to both Tess and Tegan, then pivoted around and hurried out to the corridor. She found the curve in the marbled walkway and glanced ahead to count the closed doors as she walked quickly toward the fifth one.

Before she even reached the halfway point, she felt the fine hairs at the back of her neck begin to stir. The sensation traveled her skin like a low-current electrical charge. She would know the feeling anywhere.

Andreas.

She paused in front of an arched open entryway on her right. The chamber was dark, lit only by the flicker of a single pillar candle deep inside the room. It was a sanctuary of some sort. A chapel, with carved stone walls and twin rows of benches that faced a simple, unadorned pedestal altar.

Andreas was on his knees before that altar, his dark head bowed low.

Tiny pulses of light skated all over his body. It wasn't the full-scale heat and fire that she'd witnessed before, but a smaller kind of energy. Less volatile by far, but yet strong enough to make her limbs and neck prickle in reaction. As she watched, the pulses began to slow and lessen in strength. Before long, they had faded completely.

Andreas was so still and meditative, Claire was loath to disturb him.

Too late, however. He swiveled his head and opened his eyes, piercing her with a blast of amber that swamped his irises.

'You shouldn't be here,' he said, his voice deadly low and thickened by the presence of his fangs. 'Go, Claire. I don't want you to see me like this.'

She didn't have to ask him what he meant by that because even though his body was released from the hold of his pyrokinesis, misery was pouring off him in palpable waves. He was caught in the grip of a deep blood thirst. His extended fangs and transformed eyes were evidence enough of that, but it was his *dermaglyphs* that truly gave him away. The skin markings that were visible from within the open front of his shirt were livid with the colors of hunger.

Claire drifted farther into the chapel sanctuary. 'Are you all right?'

He growled, animalistic and threatening, as she neared him. Claire thought he might stand up and draw away from her, but he remained on his knees as she moved to the bench nearest him and slowly sat down.

The vision she'd seen in Mira's eyes was still very much on her mind, but as she looked at Andreas, her worry for him was more immediate. She wanted to reach out to him, to brush the tangle of his rain-tousled hair out of his face, but she held her hands close, uncertain whether he would welcome her kindness after the way things had been left between them in Newport.

'Where did you go tonight, Andre?'

'You mean Tegan didn't tell you how he had to peel me off a human before I drained the poor bastard? He didn't tell you that it took the press of cold steel against my temple and the threat of a bullet in my skull to bring me to my senses?'

Claire swallowed. 'No. I didn't know any of that.'

At her denial, he glanced away from her, shaking his head as he stared into the wobbling flame of the crimson altar candle. 'Unless you have a pistol concealed on your person somewhere, I'd advise you to turn around and get the hell away from me while you can.'

She heard the danger in his oddly restrained tone, but she stayed right where she was. 'I'm here because I was concerned about you tonight. And because something happened a short while ago that terrified me.'

He swung a hard look at her, his brows lowered over the bright amber intensity of his gaze. 'What happened? Does it have something to do with Roth? Did he do something to hurt you again?'

'Nothing like that, no. But I saw something that I'm certain pertains to him.' At his questioning scowl, she went on. 'There is a child here in the compound with the gift of premonition –'

'Mira,' he said, having been told of the girl by the warriors.

'Yes, Mira. I saw something terrible in her eyes just a few

minutes ago. I saw your death, Andreas.' Claire exhaled softly and closed her eyes for a moment, pained just to say the words. 'I saw a pit of fire and rubble, and you were inside it. I tried to save you, but I couldn't reach you in time. And the fire was so hot . . .'

He cursed softly and stood up. His dark expression said he was ready to deny what he was hearing, but Claire cut him off before he had a chance to speak.

'I *felt* your death, Andre. I was there, in the vision. It was real. If you don't let go of this need to destroy Wilhelm Roth, I believe you're going to die.'

He listened, his jaw set in what seemed to be a grim acceptance. As if he'd known for a while that his death would come amid flames and ruin, but saw no need to run from it.

'My God,' she said, furious that she was only just understanding now. 'Every time you let the fires rise within you, you're staring your own death full in the face. You know that, don't you? You've known it all along, and yet you continue to use the very power that can only destroy you in the end.'

He listened unfazed, his expression unreadable and infuriatingly unemotional. 'I'm not afraid to die, Claire.'

'No,' she said, forcing the word past her tongue on a miserable laugh. 'You're not afraid of it, Andre. I see that now, finally. You're running toward it as fast as you can. Am I that easy to walk away from? I must be, since you keep doing it.'

'What would you have me do?' he murmured.

'Give up your revenge on Wilhelm Roth, here and now. Let the Order take him down when they go after Dragos, but not you. I want you to stay away from him. Can't you do that . . . for me?'

His hand came up tenderly, his fingers curving around the quivering line of her jaw. 'You're asking me to turn my back on those who've been willing to risk their lives for me in the past. You're asking me to forget everything Roth has done to me and my kin – what he has done to numerous innocent lives. You're asking me to look the other way on a criminal who would not hesitate to take his fury out on you, Claire.'

She looked into his amber-soaked eyes – a vampire's hungering eyes – and saw a flood of raw emotion swelling up inside him. 'There are a thousand things I want to say to you, Claire. Promises I wish I could make you. But I've taken this too far with Roth now. I've ignited a war with him that's not going to be extinguished until one or the other of us goes down in flames. I don't want it to be me, but I'm not about to shrink away from any conflagration still to come.'

God help her, she didn't want to forgive him right now – not for coming back into her life, not for reminding her so vividly that she'd never stopped loving him, and most certainly not for the prospect of losing him again after having been given such an extraordinary taste of happiness.

But when he carried her fingers to his lips with tender care and total reverence, Claire's anger and fear melted beneath his touch.

And when he kissed the heart of her palm, then lavished the same soft worship on her mouth, she was lost to him completely.

She didn't even try to resist as he drew back, panting and wild, before stripping them both of their clothing in the middle of the compound's sacred chapel. His kisses grew more demanding, more savage. She reveled in his passion, her breath catching as he lifted her legs around his waist and kissed her ever deeper. He impaled her on him in a long, hard thrust, capturing her sharp gasp of pleasure with his mouth.

Then he was moving with her, flesh on flesh, as he carried her with the swift speed and strength that marked him as something more than human. Claire felt the chill of firm, carved stone come up against her naked back. And riding at the spread juncture of her thighs, she felt the warmth of rigid, hot flesh filling her so deeply, so deliciously.

Andreas held her in a tight grasp as he drove into her, his tempo aggressive and unapologetic. Claire understood his need. She felt it, too. She welcomed every crushing thrust, every furious pound and cruel withdrawal.

She wanted to hear him shout his release, even if it betrayed their passion to the entire compound. She didn't care about anything else but him, and the shattering pleasure of their bodies joined together for what she prayed would not be the last time.

'Fuck me,' she whispered against his ear as he rocked his hips against her in a more urgent rhythm. 'Oh, God, Andre . . . I need to feel this. Please, don't stop.'

With a snarl, he rode her harder, taking her to a level of climax she didn't know existed. Claire broke apart with a muffled cry, burying her face in his shoulder as her body contracted around him in a great, shuddering rush of sensation. He came along with her, huffing a dark curse as he bucked his pelvis tight against her and held her close, swamping her core with the hot, exploding rush of his release.

Reichen released Claire's thighs and gently placed her feet back down on solid ground. He was shaking with the aftershocks of his release, but even more so from the pounding need to bury his fangs in her tender neck.

He'd never felt more alive than when he was with Claire. Being with her only amplified what a farce he'd been living all the years they'd been apart. After the curse of his pyrokinesis made itself known to him, he had been so careful to hold everyone at a distance. He'd bricked up his heart behind fortress-thick walls.

But not with Claire. She had somehow worked her way into the fiber of who he was and who he one day hoped he could be. He was her mate in all the ways that mattered.

But not in the one way that she needed.

He shouldn't have done this with her – for a dozen reasons and then some.

Not the least of which being that it wasn't going to change his mind about going after Roth.

She knew that, too.

He could see it in her eyes, as she stood before him with flushed cheeks and dark brown eyes gone even duskier for the velvety blackness of her passion-drenched pupils. 'Have you already spoken with them about how you mean to help the Order?'

No sense in trying to shield her from the truth when it was plain that she still knew him better than anyone else ever had. Or ever would. 'Tegan and I discussed a few things on the way back in tonight. Starting tomorrow evening, I'll be joining the patrols in place of the warrior that was injured. Since we now know Roth is in Boston, we'll be sweeping the city with an eye on locating him, as well.'

She nodded briefly, then moved past him to collect her clothes. She dressed expediently, hastily, as if she couldn't get away from him fast enough now.

Reichen gave a feeble shake of his head, lost for the right words. 'I'm sorry, Claire.'

'I know,' she replied quietly. 'I'm sorry, too.'

He didn't try to stop her as she walked out of the chapel and disappeared down the winding corridor. As hard as it was to keep his feet rooted to the floor, he stood there as still as a statue, until he was certain she was gone.

Then he dropped back down onto his knees and continued to pray for the strength he would need to see his vengeance through to its necessary end.

⌐ CHAPTER TWENTY-ONE ⌐

It was sometime after daybreak when Claire stood outside the shower in her compound quarters and reached in to turn on the water. She stared, unseeing, into the warm mist that began to rise on the other side of the glass.

She was losing him again.

Again, because of Wilhelm Roth.

Cold all over when she thought of everything Roth had already taken from Andreas, and from her, she stepped under the steaming spray and stood there, trembling from the chill that permeated down into her bones. In just a few hours, the sun would be setting again and Andreas would be joining the Order on their combat patrols – heading right into the very city where Roth was now. Heading potentially into death.

He'd made it very clear that nothing she said would keep him from lending his help to the Order. Just as nothing would stop him from pursuing the justice he felt he needed, no matter the cost to him. Or the cost to the love they were rediscovering after being kept so long apart.

At least this time he wasn't walking away without any explanation at all. He had his reasons. Good, noble reasons. None of which made the truth any easier to accept.

Some desperate, selfish part of her had wanted to run back immediately to the Order's chapel and beg him to reconsider. She would offer him anything. Say anything.

But she knew he couldn't, or wouldn't, change his mind.

He was too honorable a man.

And she loved him too much to try to make him bend his integrity just to satisfy her breaking heart. But God, it hurt to think of letting him go. Of possibly losing him forever.

Grief and anger swamped her.

She felt so confused and afraid . . . so alone already.

Claire sank down onto the tile floor of the shower and let the hot water and steam engulf her. She closed her eyes and thought about how difficult it was going to be when he left with the warriors that night. Being at the compound to await his return would assuage some of the ache in her heart, but only until she considered that he would also be out there looking to have his battle with Roth. And if she added Dragos to that equation, too?

She could hardly bear to imagine the outcome of a confrontation of that magnitude.

But what could she do to prevent it?

A small, desperate voice in the corner of her mind whispered that there was something. Something she hadn't yet considered. Something so distasteful that it caused bile to rise in the back of her throat.

She could go directly to Roth himself.

Not for mercy, because she knew he had none, particularly not now. Not where she or Andreas were concerned. But as certain as she was of that fact, she was also certain of just how deeply Wilhelm Roth despised losing.

He had always been consumed with winning, even the most trivial of contests.

Would he be willing to accept the only thing she had left to offer him?

Claire couldn't be sure unless she tried.

Repulsed by what she was about to do, but feeling it was her last hope where Andreas was concerned, she leaned her head back and slowed her breathing. She was adept at putting herself into a swift sleep, but finding Roth – hoping that he might be sleeping too – was not quite as easy. She rode the tide away from consciousness and drifted toward the dream realm, searching, praying she would find Roth there.

It took her several long minutes before she felt the edge of his dreaming mind through the veil of slumber. Ice formed in her stomach as she moved toward him, ignoring every instinct inside her that screamed for her to flee in the other direction as fast as she could.

She saw him in front of her now. He had his back to her, hastily making his way through what appeared to be some kind of earthen vault. Claire followed him in silence, formulating her desperate appeal. Ahead of him, a heavy door opened to let him pass. Claire slipped in behind him just as the thick stone panel swung closed.

Roth was grumbling to himself low under his breath, unintelligible words filled with venom and frustration. Inside another room, this one more clinical than the primitive-looking anterior chamber, he stormed past a counter lined with microscopes, dishes, and beakers. As he neared the end of the long surface, he shot his hand out and swept a bunch of the equipment to the floor. Claire gasped as glass crashed and shattered in front of her.

'What the fuck –' Roth wheeled around. When he saw her there, his cruel eyes narrowed and he laughed, a brittle, dangerous rumble in the back of his throat. 'Well, well. If it isn't my faithless bitch of a Breedmate.'

She didn't let his verbal slap hurt her. 'We need to talk, Wilhelm. You and I need to come to some kind of agreement before things go any further between you and Andreas.'

Now he chortled in true amusement. 'Let me guess. He sent you here to appeal to my mercy? My sense of honor?'

'He didn't send me, no. He doesn't even know I'm here.'

When his brow quirked with curiosity, she forged on. 'I've come to ask you to stay away from Andreas. Drop your animosity for him – and for me – and let Andreas move on with his life.'

Roth scoffed. 'You can't be serious.'

'I am,' Claire said. 'And I'm willing to offer you everything I have to secure your word right here and now. I will come back to you, Wilhelm. Do whatever you want to me – take your hatred for him out on me, I don't care anymore. Just leave him alone. Please.'

His eyes went narrow as blades, cutting her with their malice. 'Are you truly so naive, Claire? I could care less about him,' he said, utterly devoid of emotion. 'You either, for that matter.'

Hope kindled, dim but promising. But then Wilhelm Roth let loose with a terrible laugh that made the hairs on the back of her neck rise.

'It's never been about you, Claire. Didn't you know that? Didn't you ever suspect? You were just a prize I wanted because it would mean taking something precious away from him. Destroying his Darkhaven and the people closest to him was a pleasure I hadn't anticipated. One I relished, nevertheless.'

'You're sick, Wilhelm.' Her stomach twisted with contempt. 'My God. You really are a monster.'

'And you, Claire, are already dead to me,' he whispered, his voice an airless growl that chilled her to the bone. 'You and Andreas are both already dead. You just don't know it yet. You are obstacles standing in the way of greatness, and you *will* be removed. You and the Order, as well.'

'Is that your promise to Dragos?' she asked woodenly. 'How long have you been doing his evil for him?'

Roth smiled maliciously at her disgust. 'Our revolution began even before I made the misjudgment of taking you as my mate. I should never have bothered wasting time on you, no matter how much it pleased me to know what I had taken from you and Reichen both. It might have been just as gratifying to me had I farmed you off to Dragos with the other females I sent to him over the years.'

Claire struggled to make sense of what he was saying. *Other females*. Roth was sending females – did he mean Breedmate females? – to Dragos. For what purpose, she wondered, but only needed to guess for another moment.

From out of the ether of the dream, a wall of barred cells appeared. Dank, lightless, terrible prisons. And within them were captive women. Breedmates. Claire could see the teardrop-and-crescent-moon birthmark on a few of them even from where she stood.

The same birthmark she bore. The same birthmark that denoted a human female capable of bonding with a Breed male and bearing his young.

Good lord, there were upward of twenty women caged in those cells. Her stomach roiled even more miserably to see that some of them were pregnant.

'What's going on here?' she asked, appalled and sickened. 'What the hell are you and Dragos doing?'

As she said it, her voice rising in outrage, she caught the low howl of an animal emanating from somewhere deep within the place where she and Roth stood. The howl rose to a roar – a pained, keening cry that vibrated through the soles of her feet and straight into her marrow.

It was unlike anything she'd ever heard before . . . an utterly alien noise that put a knot of terror in her lungs.

God, what was this place? What horrors were Dragos and Roth conducting in here?

The terrible cry kept going, so loud it rattled the floor beneath her feet. Roth threw his head back and howled along with the unseen creature, mocking and sadistic.

Then he smiled a murderous smile. 'You're dead, Claire. Just like those Breedmates over there. He's going to tear you limb from tender limb. Unless I have the pleasure first. You think about that the next time you let Reichen touch you. The next time you let him fuck you, know that this is waiting for you. I'm going to kill you both and relish doing it.'

Then just like that, Roth and the chamber of horrors were gone. He severed the web that connected them in sleep, and Claire woke up shaking, panting under the warm spray of the shower.

'Oh, God,' she gasped, putting her face into her wet palms. Bile rose in her throat. 'Oh, God . . . what have I done?'

It wasn't until a few minutes after he woke that Wilhelm Roth realized the depth of the mistake he'd just made with Claire.

At first he'd been shocked to see her in his dream – he hadn't expected the female to have that kind of guts, putting herself in close proximity to him, even in the realm of sleep, after having knowingly stoked his anger with her whoring for Andreas Reichen. After the surprise of her sneaking up on him had worn off, Roth had let himself indulge in provoking her, baiting her fear with a good hard look at what he and Dragos were capable of.

He'd delighted in letting her hear the savage roars of the Ancient in his cage. Her horror over seeing the captive Breedmates that Dragos had been using in all manner of experiments had given him a deliciously sadistic thrill.

Now that he was awake, he had time to consider the price of his little game.

He had shown her the laboratory and underground bunker where Dragos kept all of his secrets.

Would she understand what she'd seen? He hoped not.

Claire had an inquisitive mind, but what could she do with this knowledge? Tell the Order, of course, but the saving grace there was that Dragos was already anticipating a move by the warriors in Boston. He'd been banking on the Order eventually finding him out, ever since the gathering they had disrupted near Montreal. Dragos had been making plans, moving pieces on the chessboard of his master design.

Still, Roth knew he could not let this slip go untold. If he did, he knew without question that Dragos would somehow unearth the truth in no time. He had to own up to the error and let the chips fall where they may. With luck, his head would not be made to fall along with them.

Formulating his excuses, Roth called Dragos's private line.

'Sire,' he said as the other vampire picked up with a snarled greeting. 'Forgive the interruption, but I have news that, unfortunately, could not wait.'

'Speak.'

Roth told him about the encounter with Claire in his dream. He was careful to gloss over most of his self-blame for the slip, pinning the fault on the weasly stealth of his Breedmate's talent. 'She spied on me without my knowledge, sire. When I discovered her there in the dream with me, it was too late to prevent her from seeing the lab.'

'Hmm,' Dragos grunted, listening in a maddening silence. 'I'm growing very tired of knowing that this female and her companion are still breathing, Herr Roth. Now that you have things under way in Boston, perhaps it's time you dealt with her as we discussed.'

'Yes, sire. And I will.' He cleared his throat, feeling the aggression pouring over the phone line despite Dragos's outward calm. 'It will be my personal pleasure to choke the life out of the bitch – after I let her watch me kill Andreas Reichen.'

'I have a better idea,' Dragos said, his voice soft and venomous. 'I want you to come to the headquarters at sundown.'

'Sire?' Roth was confused. 'What about the blood bond?'

'What about it?'

'If she tells the Order what she saw today, what's to say that the warriors won't use her blood bond to find me and the lab?'

There was only the briefest hesitation on the other end. 'Be here at sundown, Herr Roth. Your instructions will be waiting for you.'

⪦ CHAPTER TWENTY-TWO ⪧

The Order's compound in Boston was an architectural and technological marvel. Even in spite of the gravity of Claire's reasons for being there, she couldn't help but be impressed by the subterranean network of sprawling corridors and chambers hidden beneath the grand limestone mansion at street level.

The Order lived in unquestionable comfort, but it was clear that this was a tactical location. Their headquarters' primary function – the neurological center of the entire location – was the tech lab, with its banks of computers, surveillance equipment, wall charts, and strategical maps of key cities in the United States and abroad. She had entered a war room, and even though she had been welcomed there as a guest by everyone she'd met so far, as she sat at the large conference table, she was acutely aware of the fact that she was still Wilhelm Roth's mate and the closest link to an individual in alliance with the Order's most treacherous enemy.

'Everyone's on the way,' Gideon said as he ended a call to summon the rest of the warriors and their mates to hear what Claire had to tell them.

One of the compound's female residents, a regal-looking, auburn-haired young woman, placed her hand over Claire's in a show of feminine support. Her name was Gabrielle, and she was the Breedmate of the Order's leader, Lucan, who had been the first to learn of the disturbing news Claire had reported after her dreamwalk to Wilhelm Roth earlier today. The big Gen One vampire began a pace of the room, his long legs carrying him across the width of the place in no more than half a dozen strides while Rio and Dylan watched from the other side of the table.

Claire hadn't known what to expect of the Order, and frankly had been more than a little apprehensive when she'd first arrived at their Boston headquarters last night. It surprised her to see that they were not the crude lot their reputation among the general Breed population painted them to be, but rather a professional, close-knit cadre of brothers in arms.

With their Breedmates, who lived in the compound with them, the Order was a community not unlike any of the Darkhavens Claire had known. The warriors and their mates obviously looked out for one another, cared for one another.

They were a family.

Claire registered a small pang of envy for that, but even more guilt when she considered the fact that Wilhelm Roth might have anything to do with the danger threatening the warriors now. After the horror of what she'd seen in her dream a short time ago, she was suddenly, unwaveringly, committed to the Order's cause. Whatever she could do to prevent Roth – or Dragos – from inflicting more harm, she would.

Unfortunately, since sundown today, her blood-bond link to Roth seemed to be progressively diminishing. He was on the move; she was certain of it. He might have been in Boston a couple of nights ago when she'd first arrived with Reichen from Europe, and even as recently as last night, when they'd been driving up from Newport, but her senses told her that he wasn't in the city anymore. She'd been explaining that very fact to Gideon and the others who were gathered in the tech lab before the start of the night's patrols.

'Do you have any idea where Roth might go?' Savannah,

Gideon's mate, sat beside him near the computer workstations. The tall black female was a calming presence in the room, a source of serene strength that seemed a good counterpoint to Gideon's frenetic energy. 'Were there any recognizable landmarks in the dream?'

Claire shook her head. 'Nothing that I could point to, unfortunately. I wish there were.'

'Do you think he's aware that you knew he was in Boston?' Rio asked, his voice rolling with a rich Spanish accent, his dark brows lowered over smoky topaz eyes.

'It's possible that he might have suspected I was,' Claire guessed. 'And if I sensed him, I have to assume he sensed my presence in the city as well.'

Gideon nodded. 'That could be reason enough for him to leave town, if he also thinks you might be persuaded to turn over that information to us.'

'And if he's carrying out orders for Dragos,' Dylan piped in from next to Rio, 'then it could be that he's moved himself somewhere near Dragos's lair. Maybe if we find out where he is now, we'll find Dragos, too.'

Gideon scowled pensively, then glanced to Claire. 'Let's go over again what you saw in your dream. Maybe Roth left us some further clues to help us find him.'

Claire started to rehash her dreamwalk from the beginning. As she recounted the details of her confrontation with Roth, the glass doors of the tech lab slid open and in walked Tegan with a few other warriors, all of them dressed for combat in head-to-toe black. And behind them was Andreas, dressed similarly and looking every bit as lethal as his heavily armed companions.

Claire's heart stuttered at the sight of him. She'd considered going to him directly after her dreamwalk with Roth, but she didn't think she could bear to be near him after the way they'd parted in the chapel. And a more cowardly part of her knew

that he would be furious to find out what she'd done. The look
he gave her as he entered the room with Tegan could hardly
be described as friendly. Evidently he'd already been informed
of the purpose behind this impromptu meeting of the Order.

'What else do you recall, Claire?' Gideon asked her now.
'You said you saw chemistry equipment and tables lined with
laboratory supplies.'

She nodded. 'Yes, there were microscopes, computers and
beakers, and lots of chemical vials. It all seemed very state of
the art, but I couldn't tell you what kind of experiments were
being conducted there.'

'And past the lab there were the barred cells,' Gideon
prompted.

'Yes. Rows of cells containing captive women. Breedmates.
Some of them were pregnant.' Claire felt Andreas's gaze fixed
on her as she spoke. It burned, the way he stared at her in
simmering silence from across the room. 'To hear Roth speak,
I got the distinct impression that the Breedmates were being
given to the creature.'

'For mating purposes,' Gideon said, sending a grim look in
Tegan's direction. 'A new generation of Breed males, spawned
off an Ancient.'

Claire relived the sick feeling she'd had after seeing them
and hearing what Roth had told her. 'He said he'd been supplying
Dragos with Breedmates since well before I met him, which
was thirty years ago.'

'Jesus,' Tegan hissed. 'How many Gen Ones could he create
over the course of a few decades?'

'If he had a continuous supply of Breedmates?' Gideon
replied. 'I shudder to imagine.'

'And who's to say Roth was the only one supplying him?'
Rio added gravely. He glanced over to Dylan. 'How many
missing persons' reports on Breedmates have you collected from
the Darkhavens' records, babe?'

'Going how far back?' she replied, her expression sober. 'Although the numbers have increased significantly in recent times, we've found reports stretching back to the turn of the last century. That doesn't even count the number of women who vanish out of the human populations every year who might be Breedmates, as well.'

She turned to Claire to explain. 'A few months ago, when Rio and I met, I discovered that my special talent is seeing dead people. Well, dead people who happen to be Breedmates, that is. I saw several at the shelter where my mom used to work. They asked me to help their captive sisters – to save them before he killed them all. They told me there were more, still alive, being kept underground, in darkness. They gave me the name of their captor, too: Dragos.'

'Oh, my God,' Claire whispered, astonished.

'Finding them has become a bit of an obsession for me. Ever since then, we've been searching missing persons' records, trying to follow up on leads to see where some of these women might have last been seen, where they might have gone. Maybe we can find them. If we can save just one life, it will be worth it.'

'I will help you however I can,' Claire said. 'If I have to cover the entire length and breadth of the United States and Germany combined to find Wilhelm Roth and force him to give up Dragos, then I'll do it.'

Dylan smiled. 'I like you already.'

'That's not a bad idea, you know.' Gideon launched out of his swivel chair and jogged over to one of the large New England maps that hung on the wall. He pointed to a red pin stuck into a location near the New York and Connecticut border. 'We know where Dragos has been seen recently. We know that he once had a residence in New York under one of his aliases. If we start searching in this region and sweep out toward the coast, maybe we'll find something.' He looked at Claire. 'It's too close to dawn to do anything tonight yet, but would you be willing to come along on a recon sweep and use your blood bond to see if you can get a reading on Roth's whereabouts?'

'Of course.' She pretended she couldn't hear the low, barely audible growl that emanated from Andreas's direction. He could try to dissuade her, but her mind was made up. She was in this battle now, too, no matter if he liked it or not. 'I can be ready anytime.'

⤳ CHAPTER TWENTY-THREE ⤳

Reichen caught up to Claire as the meeting in the tech lab dispersed. He hung back while the rest of the warriors filed out of the room to prepare for the night's last mission in the city, his gaze locked on to Claire in a volatile mix of outrage and absolute fear.

'What the hell was that all about?' he demanded as she and Gabrielle and Savannah exited the lab together. 'When Tegan told me a few minutes ago that you had made contact with Roth, I didn't believe him. What the fuck were you thinking, Claire? More to the point, were you thinking at all?'

She swallowed hard under the verbal assault, but she didn't flinch. 'It's all right,' she told the two Breedmates accompanying her. 'Andreas and I should talk alone.'

Reichen's fury simmered as Lucan and Gideon's mates departed and left him standing in the corridor with a very defiant, very unfazed Claire.

'My God,' he said, feeling as though the wind had been knocked out of him. The same feeling he'd had when Tegan broke the news of Claire's dreamwalk visit to her mate after the encounter that had ended so clumsily in the compound's chapel. 'What did you think to accomplish by approaching Roth like you did?'

'I had my reasons,' she answered evenly.

'Such as?'

'It doesn't matter. He wasn't interested in negotiating. I'm sure that comes as little surprise to you.'

Reichen scoffed. 'Roth never negotiates. He takes. And where he can't simply take, he steals. He kills, Claire. What the hell did you possibly think you could gain by seeking him out, even in a dream?'

She started to move past him, as if she intended to leave him standing in the hallway without an answer. Before she could take two steps, he grabbed her by the arm and drew her back to him.

'What did you ask him for, Claire? Your freedom? His mercy?' He scowled, as furious at her recklessness as he was relieved that she was alive and warm in his tightly gripped hand. 'Did you think he would simply release you if you asked him to let you go?'

'No,' she said, her proud chin hiking up with her reply. 'I didn't ask him to let me go, Andre. I asked him to take me back . . . but only on the condition that he would agree to let you live.'

She might as well have punched him in the sternum with a lead fist. 'You what?'

Good Christ, the thought of her going back to Roth – under any conditions – was enough to make his blood boil. That she would offer herself up to Roth in exchange for him? He wanted to roar his outrage to the rafters.

'He doesn't want me. He never did.' She shook her head as she extricated herself from his grasp. 'He said he only took me as his mate because he knew it would hurt you. He has been trying to hurt you for a long time, Andreas.'

That Roth's hatred spanned many years was no shock to him, but he could hardly process any of that when the gravity of what Claire had done – what she'd been willing to subject herself to, for him – was still settling like hot oil in his heart. 'Do you have any idea how it would have hurt me if he'd agreed to your offer?'

'Probably not as much as it will hurt me when you go to your death trying to destroy him.'

Reichen deserved that; he knew he did. But it didn't prevent him from blocking her path as she tried to dodge around him again. 'You're not going anywhere near him, Claire. Not with the Order, not with an entire goddamn army at your side. I heard what you said in there, and I know you want to help take him down, but you're not leaving the compound so long as Roth is out there somewhere. I forbid it.'

She gaped at him. 'You what? You forbid –'

'I won't let you do it.'

'And I don't recall asking for your permission,' she said, anger spiking in her pulse now, so sharp he could feel it echo in his own. 'After what I saw in Roth's dream today, I have to help the Order take him down. By whatever means I can. I would think you of all people could understand that.'

Reichen shook his head, refusing to so much as consider the idea. 'You're not doing it, Claire. I can't let you.'

She stared at him for a long moment, then something caught her eye past his shoulder, at the other end of the corridor. 'Your comrades are waiting for you.'

He turned to look and found Tegan, Rio, and a couple of the other warriors standing near the elevator that would take them topside. He nodded to them, indicating that he needed another minute. When he looked back to Claire, she was no longer standing in front of him but walking at a determined pace down the corridor.

'Damn it,' he whispered low under his breath.

Then he pivoted back to the warriors and fell into a jog to join up with them for the night's patrols.

Wilhelm Roth felt the cold, emotionless eyes of five Gen One assassins staring at him as he performed yet another systems check of Dragos's underground laboratory. Everything was in place precisely as he'd been instructed, and now all he could do was wait. Wait and hope that Claire was with the Order right now, wailing over his mistreatment of her and Andreas Reichen, and telling the warriors everything she saw in her damnable dreamwalk.

As difficult as it may be to find the hidden location of Dragos's lair, the Order was resourceful and determined. Those were the very qualities Dragos was counting on to get them halfway into the trap that he and Roth had set for them.

Claire's blood bond to Roth and her ridiculous sense of honor would do the rest.

Roth had no misconceptions that his future was riding on the success of this pending offensive strike against the warriors. If none of the assassins charged with aiding him didn't finish him off should he fail, then Dragos certainly would. As he made his final inspection of the detonators and pounds of explosives, he wondered if he hadn't been handed a suicide mission.

But he had no intention of dying here.

The warriors, however . . .

Once they were led into his trap, there would be no chance of any one of them getting out alive. He could only hope that the Order sent their entire membership after him. It would be such a pleasure to watch the group of them perish in one fell swoop.

So much the better if that number included Claire and her reunited lover.

Satisfied that all was in readiness in the lab, Roth headed into the UV-light prison area to check the settings one final time. He wanted everything to be perfect for the Order's imminent arrival . . . and their resulting demise.

It was too damned quiet.

Lucan and the rest of the Order had spent the better part

of the night combing the city, looking for any signs of Dragos or the Gen One assassins he'd apparently loosed on the streets to bring the Order out. Several hours of searching every deserted lot, warehouse, back alley, and rooftop, and Lucan was coming up empty.

So were the rest of the teams on patrol tonight. He'd just hung up with Niko and Renata, who'd been jointly sweeping the area down by the Mystic River with Dante and Hunter. Not a trace of trouble, other than the usual bullshit perpetrated by mankind against its brothers.

Frankly, the relative peace he was finding tonight didn't sit well with him.

Something seemed . . . off.

Lucan could still feel it in his marrow that some serious trouble had been ramping up in the city the other night. Those human killings were significant in their brutality and their brazenness. The Order was being lured out to play in a very blatant manner, so why would Dragos pull back his strikes now that he had their attention?

As Lucan made one more visual sweep of his area in the final hour before dawn, he couldn't help feeling that he and the rest of the Order were standing in the way of a pending tsunami. The tide and wind had sucked back hard, leaving an eerie, false state of calm.

It was quiet now, but at any minute that mother of a wave was going to come pouring over them and consume everything in its path.

~§ CHAPTER TWENTY-FOUR §~

I still say we're wasting precious time and opportunity if we don't at least consider a daytime reconnaissance.' Nikolai's mate, Renata, hopped down off the counter in the weapons room and started pacing in her combat boots and black fatigues. Her chin-length black hair was loosened from the band that had held it back during her patrols and now swung freely around her face as she argued her point for the second time. 'I mean, come on, you guys. If the he-man resistance being thrown around here right now is only about keeping us safe, it's a nonissue. The worst we can run into during daylight hours are Minions, and I dare any one of you to tell me I can't take out a human mind slave in my sleep. With one hand tied behind my back.'

Niko grinned at his woman. 'She's got a good point, Lucan. We're not talking about a combat situation, just sending them in to gather intel and report back so we can move in.'

Lucan grunted, looking up from beneath his dark brows. 'I don't like it.'

'I don't like it, either,' Rio put in. 'But I know Dylan will be safe with Renata. If the women are open to doing this, then maybe we should let them help. You've said it yourself, Lucan: Right now we need all hands on deck.'

Reichen sat off to the side and listened in silence, biting back his own opinion, which was basically that whatever the Order decided was fine with him so long as they left Claire out of the picture entirely.

Unfortunately for him and his opinions, Claire seemed to have other plans.

He felt her in the doorway of the room before he actually saw her, the pull of his bond to her turning his head in her direction as if the core of him were connected to her by a wire. She came in with Dante's mate, both of them moving to the back of the room as the debate continued between Lucan and Renata.

'Think about it, Lucan. If we work the daylight, that gives us an eight- to ten-hour advantage,' she said. 'Eight to ten more hours closer to Roth could be a crucial advantage to actually getting close to Dragos. If the pullback we saw tonight in Boston is an indicator that they're scared and running, then we don't have any time to waste.'

Several heads nodded in agreement with Renata.

'And if the pullback is an indicator of something else?' Lucan asked grimly. 'If they've abruptly pulled out of Boston not because they're worried about being found, but because they're working on something bigger?'

'Actually, I think we need to assume that it's not fear so much as strategy.' Claire's voice drew everyone's attention to the back of the weapons room. She glanced around at the group, lingering the longest on Reichen. Her gaze was troubled, and he could feel the distress that had her heart pounding uncomfortably in her breast. 'I don't know Dragos, but I know Wilhelm Roth well enough. He never operates from a position of fear. He believes himself invincible, smarter than everyone else. Wherever he is, he's got an alternative plan to strike even harder than he has before.'

'All the better reason to use any advantage we can to find him,' Rio added.

Lucan's gaze traveled from Claire to Renata to Dylan, the

trio of Breedmates who would be carrying out the daytime mission. 'You're all in agreement, then? You want to do this?'

'Yes,' they answered in unison.

He considered it for a long moment, then gave a solemn nod. 'All right, then. Gideon will grid the best area for you to start searching. Let's plan on meeting for one final review in the tech lab before you roll out.'

With a round of assenting comments, the meeting began to disperse. Reichen started to move toward Claire, but before he could reach her and offer the dozen different apologies he'd been rehearsing in his mind since they'd last parted, Renata and Dylan swept her along in a rush of conversation.

She gave him only the briefest look as she passed, the message in her gaze unmistakably clear. He had nothing to say about what she was doing. He had refused to give her promises he couldn't keep, and now she was dealing it back to him in spades. The taste of his comeuppance was bitter as hell.

Claire turned away from him, then continued on with her two female companions to discuss the daytime mission that had put a lump of icy dread in Reichen's gut.

By the time the sun rose, Claire's frustration with Andreas had long dried up. She understood his concern, and his anger. She had been foolish to think she could negotiate with Roth. Even more foolish to think that she could ever endure a return as his mate. She would have done it, though. She would have done anything to ensure Andreas's well-being. Especially after the vision she'd seen of his fiery demise.

All she'd known was the need to hold on tightly to him. That was why she'd asked him to give up his quest to avenge his family and all but begged him to let the Order fight the battle with Roth and Dragos on the front lines. It had been a moment of keen and selfish desperation, one that had made her blind to anything else but her love for him. All she had known was her need to keep him near so that nothing and no one could take him away from her again.

But as Claire prepared to leave the compound with Dylan and Renata that morning, she had come to realize that she had been asking too much of him. In the compound's tech lab with the others, she watched from the periphery as the two females' mates, Rio and Nikolai, spent a last few quiet moments murmuring tender words to them and holding them close.

Witnessing the soft good-byes and lingering embraces of the two couples parting for the day, Claire felt a sting of shame for what she'd expected of Andreas. Their love was no more sacred than what she was seeing here. The safety of either of them was no more important than that of any of the warriors or their Breedmates.

Andreas had been right to reject what she had asked of him.

Claire might have told him as much, but he hadn't come to see her off with the rest of the Order. Instead it was Tess and Savannah who pulled her into quick, warm hugs as she and Dylan and Renata began gathering their gear for the day's mission. Lucan and Gabrielle came over a moment later, the Order's leader giving her a somber nod as his Breedmate briefly embraced Claire.

'My thanks for your willingness in helping us try to track Roth,' he said in his deep, commanding voice. 'I don't expect it's easy for you. There is still time for you to change your mind, if you'd rather not –'

'No,' Claire interrupted. She gave a mild shake of her head. 'I want to do this. After all I know about him now, I need to do this.'

A grim nod was Lucan's only reply as Gideon summoned everyone's attention for a final run-through of the grid he'd mapped out for the females to follow. Claire listened to the instructions that would take them south of Boston and into Connecticut, beginning a sweep of the area near the New York

State line, where she'd learned that Dragos had once been confronted by Dylan's mate, Rio, but managed to escape. From there, the recon mission would cover as much ground as possible during daylight hours, hoping that somewhere along the way, Claire's blood bond to Roth would pick up a solid trail that the Order could follow up on after dark.

'I'm giving you each a phone equipped with GPS,' Gideon was saying now, walking away from the map he'd charted on the wall to retrieve three cell phones from the table. He handed them out to Claire, Dylan, and Renata. 'Keep them turned on and secured on your person at all times. We're going to be monitoring your location and progress from here, but we want hourly check-ins, minimum. You get a beat on Roth, you phone in ASAP. Anything looks or feels off to any of you while you're on this mission, you phone in. If you have any reason to stop the vehicle, even for a two minute bathroom run, you phone in. Understood?'

The three of them nodded their agreement, although Renata did so while rolling her eyes at Claire and Dylan. Underneath her calf-length black trench coat, the ebony-haired Breedmate wore lug-soled boots, dark denim jeans, and a black turtleneck – passable enough as street clothes, if one didn't look too closely at the lumpiness that ringed her slender hips. A small arsenal of blades and pistols were sheathed and holstered on the leather belts that wrapped her waist.

To this impressive collection of weaponry, Nikolai added one more: a nasty-looking, long-barreled gun roughly the length of Claire's arm. He handed it to Renata, then placed a clip of ammunition in her open palm.

'Your special titanium hollowpoints?' she murmured, then beamed up at him as if he'd given her a bouquet of prize-winning roses.

Niko grinned, twin dimples framing his broad smile. 'Nothing says I love you like custom-made rounds.'

Renata kissed him and laughed, pocketing the clip and carefully slinging the gun's strap over her shoulder. 'Unnecessary, but sweet. Thanks, babe.'

'Those Rogue-smoking rounds aren't just for killing vampires,' Lucan said. 'They'll take down a Minion just as well. Don't hesitate to shoot if you feel the situation warrants it at any time.'

Renata nodded. 'Trust me, no worries there.' She sent a look at Claire and Dylan. 'Ready to hit the road, girls? Let's rock and roll.'

Claire slipped the cell phone into the pocket of her loose jeans, then moved along with the other two women as they made their way to the automatic glass door of the tech lab. She couldn't keep her eyes from searching the corridor outside, looking for Andreas. But he wasn't there, and he wasn't coming either. She didn't know if she had driven him away or if she had already lost him before their fruitless confrontation a few hours earlier.

Not that it mattered.

He wasn't there.

He wasn't hers, and possibly never would be.

Claire supposed that now was as good a time as any to start getting used to that fact all over again.

⇥ CHAPTER TWENTY-FIVE ⇤

Reichen had been prowling the compound's corridors for the better part of the morning, trying unsuccessfully to walk off the spasms and tremors that were racking his body. He padded barefoot down one of the long, twisting spokes of white marble hallway, forced to pause every twenty paces or so when the shakes and dry heaves got too bad for him to keep moving.

His chest was clammy, the cool air of the compound hitting his skin like an arctic gust. The jeans he wore felt like heavy weights on his legs, the fabric damp with sweat. He shuddered and reached for the wall to stabilize himself as his head started buzzing and another wave of nausea gripped him. When he opened his eyes, his vision bled amber-bright through the slits of his lids. He tasted blood on his tongue and realized with some alarm that his fangs were fully extended, sharp points digging into the flesh of his lower lip. His *dermaglyphs* pulsed all over his body, the skin markings flooded dark with the colors of intense hunger.

'Shit,' he hissed tightly, as fresh pain slammed his gut and he dropped to his knees on the hard, polished floor.

Doubled over and panting, he crossed his arms over his shredding stomach and bit back the groan that curled deep in his throat. His ears rang with the sound of his own blood racing through his veins, the pound of it practically driving him mad.

He leaned forward to plant his cheek and brow against the cold stone beneath him until the agony passed, simply concentrating on breathing in and out, in and out . . .

God help him, but his blood thirst was back again, worse than ever. It had been pecking at him like a raven on carrion for the better part of the morning, the only thing that had kept him away from Claire when she and the other two Breedmates had been leaving to begin their daytime intel-gathering trip for the Order.

Fortunately for him, most of the warriors and their mates were in the tech lab now or in their private quarters – a small mercy, as it would have only added insult to an already unbearable injury should anyone happen to see him in such pitiful condition.

Summoning every ounce of his will, Reichen forced himself to his feet and began an unsteady shuffle out of the corridor. He was near the weapons room, as it turned out, the darkness of the empty facility welcome as he dragged himself inside and collapsed against the nearest wall. He slumped there, exhausted and wretched, his breath rasping through his bared teeth and fangs.

He might have slept for a few seconds or even an hour; he had no idea how much time had passed before the soft *whisk* of the opening door jolted him awake and the lights of the firing range lit up all around him. Reflections bounced off the mirrored glass of the training area, and through the bleariness of his vision, he saw that Tegan was standing near the door, his hand just now coming away from the light switch.

The warrior muttered a ripe curse and something about déjà vu, but Reichen's brain was too beleaguered to try to comprehend his meaning. He sat there in misery, growling a warning for the other male to leave him alone.

Tegan scoffed and took a couple of long strides toward him instead. Piercing green eyes bore into Reichen with a cold brand of understanding. 'Feeling about as shitty as you look, I take it.'

Reichen swallowed, his throat too parched for words. He glared up at the Gen One he considered a friend, his vision swimming from the steady pound filling his head. He caught the downward flick of Tegan's gaze, knew that the warrior could read his agony in the churning colors of his exposed *glyphs*.

'That blood you took in the city a couple of nights ago should have held you long past now,' he said, his deep voice flat as hammered steel. Tegan's jaw went tight, nostrils flaring slightly with his indrawn breath as he crouched down on his haunches in front of Reichen. 'How long has the thirst been dogging you?'

He managed a vague shrug of one shoulder. 'All day . . . it never really let up, even after I fed.'

'Fuck.' Tegan ran a hand through his loose tawny hair. 'You know what this is, don't you?'

Reichen grunted, let his eyes fall shut when his lids got too heavy to keep open. 'It's because of the pyro,' he murmured thickly. 'The fires ease up . . . then the blood hunger sets in. Happens every time.'

'And every time it happens, the hunger gets worse,' Tegan said, not even close to a question. 'Shit, Reichen. It might be the pyro bringing it on, but what you're feeling is the first whiffs of Bloodlust, my man. You haven't fallen over the steepest ledge yet, but you're heading there fast. And you know damn well that's what's going on, don't you?'

Reichen attempted to deny it with a shake of his head, but Tegan was no fool. When Reichen looked up into the warrior's face, he saw bleak understanding there. Hell, he saw a male who'd tasted this same blinding thirst himself. A male who, from the grave look of him now, was still haunted by the memory of an even deeper blood addiction than the one Reichen battled each time his pyro overtook him.

He wanted to ask him how he'd fought it – how he'd won against the fierce thirst that could turn even the strongest members of the Breed into savage killers – but just then his gut gave another violent twist. He snarled with the spasming pain, his limbs contracting in on his body.

'Breathe through it,' Tegan commanded him. 'You gotta be stronger than the thirst. Don't let it own you.'

Reichen did as he was told, willing to grasp at any advice if it would help alleviate some of his agony. It took several minutes before the worst of it passed. Once it had, he nodded weakly, relieved by the sliver of peace that followed the pain.

'Tell me about the pyrokinesis,' Tegan said when Reichen huffed out a breath and dragged himself up to a sitting position. 'How have you managed it so well until now? Hell, we've known each other off and on for the better part of a couple centuries, and I had no clue about your ability.'

'I'm not proud of it,' Reichen murmured, an understatement if ever he'd uttered one.

Tegan's expression was sober but not condemning. 'You think I haven't done things that I regret? It's hard to walk through even a year of life without hurting someone or something when you didn't intend it. If I started telling you about all the shit I've done wrong or wish I could take back . . . trust me, we don't have that kind of time. So, why don't you go first. Tell me about the pyro.'

It might only have been the warrior's way of distracting him, enticing him to talk instead of anticipating the next round of agony, but whatever Tegan's motives, Reichen found himself explaining how he'd lived most of his life with no knowledge of the curse that lurked inside him. He told Tegan how he'd first come to discover the fires through Roth's treachery some scant thirty years ago . . . and how abhorred he'd been to realize for that first, godawful time what his pyrokinetic heat would do to anyone careless enough to get near him.

'I killed an innocent young girl, Tegan. In mere seconds, she was so charred I couldn't even recognize her as human.' He felt sickened all over again – not from blood hunger but from a profound self-loathing that hadn't dampened and likely never would. 'After that, I was determined to never let my power surface again. And I worked damned hard to make sure it didn't. Then Roth sent his death squad to my Darkhaven and there was nothing I could do to hold the fires back. He took away everything and everyone who mattered to me.'

'Almost everyone,' Tegan said, those shrewd gem-green eyes unflinching. 'How long have you been in love with Claire?'

Reichen expelled a deep sigh. 'So long, I don't even recall what it was like not to be in love with her.'

'You've drunk from her, yeah?'

He nodded, seeing no point in denying it.

'How about after the pyro? You drink from her then?'

'Yes,' Reichen said, recalling that first time he'd put his fangs into her throat, the night in Roth's office in Hamburg. It seemed like a lifetime ago to him now. 'I drank from her the night after I went to Roth's Darkhaven.'

'How'd you feel after you drank from Claire? How bad was the thirst after you had her blood inside you?'

Reichen considered it for a moment. 'Better, I guess. Not as severe.'

He hadn't noticed it then, but now he was certain that drinking from Claire had lessened his need to overload on blood. He craved her always, but in a much different way than the post-pyro urge that turned him into something close to an animal.

Reichen nodded. 'I would do anything for her, Tegan. Including walk away from her, which I did a long time ago.'

'And now?' Tegan prompted.

'Now . . .'

Reichen frowned, thinking of the way he'd left things with her. She'd asked him only to be with her – the one thing he wanted more than anything else – but in his heart he knew he couldn't give her that. Not when his power was so close to ruling him. Closer than he wanted to admit, even to himself. And then there was the fact that Wilhelm Roth and Dragos were still breathing, still walking free and able to carry out their evil designs.

Reichen's power was terrible, but perhaps a necessary weapon in this worsening war. At least then it might serve a purpose – a noble one. *He* might then serve a purpose, something more than just his own wants and desires.

'One more fire and I really don't know if I will be able to come out of it, Tegan. Each time my power rises, it becomes stronger. Less controllable. The blood thirst afterward is hellish enough, but the fire itself is death to anyone who gets near it. I don't care what happens to me, but Claire –' He broke off abruptly, refusing to consider the thought. 'She doesn't deserve to be caught up in my personal hell.'

Tegan arched a tawny brow. 'You really think she's not already caught up in it? Just because you push her away doesn't mean she'll be any safer without you.'

'She saw my death, Tegan.'

'What?'

'The little girl, Mira, showed her a vision of my death earlier today. Claire told me she saw the flames and the smoke. Saw herself running toward the fire, into the heat, to try to save me.'

'Jesus.'

Reichen nodded grimly. 'You understand, of course, I can't let her do that. She can't be anywhere near me, not when the fire is in control. Harming her is the one thing I could not bear. I want her safe from Roth, as well. I don't care how long it takes me to hunt down the bastard, I will find him, and I will see him dead.'

'Yeah, about that,' Tegan said. 'You might get your chance

sooner than later. It's actually the reason I came looking for you. We got an update from Claire and the others a few minutes ago.'

Alarm spiked through Reichen's blood, even stronger than the thirst that was still stabbing at him. 'What happened? Is she all right?'

'Claire's fine. Nothing's wrong, but she did pick up on Roth's presence a couple hours south of here. It was getting stronger the farther they drove into Connecticut, so they're chasing it down, hoping to triangulate a location on him before sundown.'

'Roth is in Connecticut now? Where, exactly?' Reichen swallowed hard, every muscle tense. He felt the kindling flickers of his fury begin to awaken. He recognized the need to tamp them down, but his concern for Claire overrode all other rational thought. 'Damn it, I don't want her getting close to that son of a bitch!'

'Relax,' Tegan said evenly, taking quick, obvious note of the heat that had started to crackle under the surface of Reichen's skin. 'Claire is in no danger on this op, I promise you. They're only mapping things out from the road, and they'll be heading back for Boston in a few hours with whatever intel they find.'

Reichen simmered down, letting himself sag back against the wall. He cursed roundly and dropped his head between his updrawn knees. He could feel Claire in his blood, his bond to her giving him the assurance he needed that she was, in fact, okay. She was a calmness beneath the torrent raging in his own veins, cool water soothing the dry heat of the fire waiting for the opportunity to devour him.

'What if this has gone too far, Tegan?' His voice sounded wooden and hollow, even to his own ears. 'What if after everything we've been through, after everything I've tried to do to protect her, it's not enough? What if the vision she saw proves to be right? The one thing I can't protect her from is me. What if Claire gets too close one day, and the heat destroys her?'

'And what if you're wrong?' Tegan said. 'What if she's the only thing that might save you from yourself?'

Reichen stared at the hardened Gen One warrior who'd once struck down sixteen Rogue vampires in a feat of legendary, single-handed efficiency. Tegan had never been the warmest of individuals, but there was a tranquil wisdom in his eyes now – a soulful knowledge that hadn't been present even when Reichen had seen him last, almost a year ago in Berlin. Love for his Breedmate, Elise, had transformed him somehow, made him stronger while at the same time it had smoothed away some of his roughest edges.

But Tegan and Elise had different obstacles they'd had to overcome. Reichen's relationship with Claire had been complicated nearly from the beginning. Now it had become one impossibility after another.

'I can't risk it,' Reichen said. 'I won't risk it. If I go down, damn it, I go down alone.'

Tegan exhaled sharply and bared his teeth in a smile that wasn't quite friendly. 'Blaze of glory, eh?'

'Something like that,' Reichen replied.

The warrior abruptly stood up and cast an assessing look on him. 'You may think you're keeping Claire out of harm's way by shoving her aside right now, but the only one you're protecting is yourself. If you go down, whether it's the pyro or the Bloodlust that gets you, it's going to kill that female, and you know it. You just want to make sure you're not around to see it.'

Reichen didn't try to deny the accusation. Not that Tegan gave him the chance. He backed away from where Reichen sat, then strode out of the weapons room, hitting the light switch on his way out and plunging the place back into darkness.

Wilhelm Roth was on a phone call with Dragos when his veins came alive with awareness of his erstwhile Breedmate. Remarkably, it seemed Claire was not far. In fact, by the way his pulse was stirring from his blood bond to her, he was damn well certain that Claire was within some twenty miles of where he stood . . . and moving closer all the time.

What the hell was she up to?

He checked the clock in Dragos's lab and scowled to see that it was just past one in the afternoon. Broad daylight.

Had she and Reichen not turned to the Order for help, after all? Or had the warriors for some reason denied them sanctuary at their compound?

Roth could think of no reason Claire would be in the area in the middle of the day – presumably without the protection of Reichen or any of the warriors from Boston.

Could she actually be foolish enough to seek him out again on her own?

Roth might have laughed at such idiocy if not for the fact that his current objective for Dragos depended on Claire leading the Order straight into his hands. If she was coming alone, she would be fucking up the entire plan.

'You're suddenly very quiet, Herr Roth. Anything amiss?' Dragos asked. His voice had to compete with a din of noise in the background on the other end of the line, a metallic roar that didn't quite mask the fury that rode just below the surface of the vampire's outward calm. 'You were telling me how everything is in place, just as we arranged.'

'Yes, sire,' Roth replied. 'But there is . . . something odd.'

'Oh?' The tone was as level as a blade poised above a head soon to roll. 'Do tell.'

'It's Claire. I sense her on the move, sire. I believe she may be getting close to the lab's location. I'm certain she must sense me, the same as I am aware of her. It's my guess that she has decided to come looking for me.'

'What time is it?' Dragos asked, his question pierced by the sudden blast of a horn and a muffled voice squawking unintelligibly over some manner of warehouse loudspeaker.

'It's early afternoon, sire. A few minutes past one.'

Dragos grunted, contemplating in silence for a long moment. 'If your lovely Breedmate is coming to find you, by all means, let's help her get there. Give the Minions on ground-level security a description of the female. Tell them I want them to go out and find her, bring her into the facility.'

'But the plan,' Roth interjected. 'I thought we needed her to lead the Order to us.'

'Yes,' Dragos hissed. 'And she will. Her pain will draw the male who's bonded to her, and he will ensure that the Order comes along.'

'Torture?' Roth suggested, torn between delight at Claire's imminent pain and his own shared agony, since his blood bond to her would absorb everything that she was subjected to, as well.

Dragos chuckled on the other end of the line. 'I'll leave the specifics of her treatment up to you, Herr Roth. Contact me as soon as you learn anything more.'

'Yes, sire,' Roth answered.

He flipped the phone closed and began to imagine the many slow, sadistic ways he could make Claire scream.

⊰ CHAPTER TWENTY-SIX ⊱

Claire dried her hands on a brown paper towel as she came out of the public restroom of a small gas station situated on a rural stretch of two-lane blacktop somewhere near the northwestern border of Connecticut. At midafternoon, the sun was already beginning its descent toward the tops of the brushy pines and the leafless oaks that covered the hilly, forested region of the state. She squinted, shielding her eyes from the blinding orange rays and wishing they had a few more hours to continue their search.

They were so close now; she could feel it all the way to her marrow. For the past couple of hours, she and Renata and Dylan had been circumnavigating the area where the blood bond Claire had now grown to hate beat the strongest. They were tightening the noose on Wilhelm Roth mile by mile, systematically narrowing down the range of locations where the Order was likely to find him. Another couple of hours combing the area and Claire was certain they'd have his location nailed to within an easy square mile.

If only the late-autumn day could stretch a bit longer, she thought, impatient as she tossed the used paper towel in a trash can and walked the short distance back to the Order's black Range Rover parked at the gas pumps. Renata was filling the tank for the return trip to Boston, her stance cautiously casual as she leaned against the vehicle and watched the digital gauges clock on the pump's display. Claire didn't miss the fact that the female's right hand was crossed over the front of her body and hidden beneath the folds of her dark trench coat, no doubt either resting on the butt of a pistol or wrapped around the hilt of one of her blades. She was as vigilant as any of the warriors, and, Claire imagined, just as deadly when the situation warranted lethal force.

Nodding to Renata as she approached, Claire climbed into the SUV and gently closed the passenger door behind her, careful not to wake Dylan, who was taking a quick doze in the backseat. It had been a long day, made even longer by the fact that none of them had gotten much sleep before they'd left the compound that morning. Claire was exhausted, but she couldn't stand the idea of giving up before they'd gotten a solid lock on Roth. She reached around the seat to pick up the map that they'd been working from, which was now highlighted in color-block patches of yellow, green, and orange, to indicate the range of areas where her sense of Roth had been the strongest.

'Where the hell are you?' she whispered low under her breath, tuning out the *ding* of the station bell as a car pulled into the full-service pump next to her. She put all her concentration into that beat of dark, visceral awareness that ticked in her pulse, trying not to think about the fact that Roth must be sensing her in much the same way.

Did he know how close she was to finding him right now? He must, surely. Only the simple fact that the sun had yet to set gave her any kind of comfort when she thought about the fury she would face if she ever fell into his hands again. He would kill her, she was certain. But not before he took his anger out on her and made her wish she was dead.

Rattled by the thought of him, Claire pivoted in her seat again to stow the map.

It was then she noticed the two men getting out of the car beside her. They were big men, both dressed in black from their zipped-up leather jackets to the fatigues tucked into the tops of their combat boots. They looked her way as she watched them, and a chill settled deep in Claire's bones. Their eyes were cruel, strangely vacant.

And this wasn't the first time she'd seen the pair of human males today.

Claire had noticed them just a couple of hours earlier, when she and Renata and Dylan had paused at a greasy-spoon diner for lunch in a neighboring town. Hard to miss all that dark clothing and barely concealed menace. Hard to miss the way the two men studied her now, then exchanged a wordless look with each other before one of them went around back to get something out of the trunk.

She jumped when Renata opened the driver's-side door. 'We've got a tail.'

'I know,' Claire said as Renata dropped into the seat, closing the door with one hand and turning the key in the ignition with the other. 'I saw them earlier. They were staring at us then, too. There's something wrong with them – with their eyes. It's making my skin crawl.'

'That's because they're Minions,' Renata said matter-of-factly as she threw the SUV into gear.

From the backseat, Dylan sat up and sucked in a quick breath. 'Oh, shit. You guys, we've got company.'

'Yeah, we're on it,' Renata replied, glancing in the rearview mirror. 'Buckle up.'

Dylan started to say something more, but then Renata stomped on the gas and the Range Rover's tires peeled rubber on the pavement. They screamed out of the gas station and onto the tree-lined, curvy two-laner.

In seconds, the Minions were right behind them.

Claire pivoted around to gauge their distance. 'They're coming up fast. Oh, my God, they're going to ram –'

The sudden jolt of impact made the Rover jump and jostle

on the road. To Renata's credit, she held the wheel steady, correcting the vehicle when it started to veer sharply into the other lane. She sped up, gaining a couple of car lengths before the sedan came roaring up on them again, trying to force them off the road.

'There's a small access lane up ahead on the right,' Dylan said, her voice raised to be heard over the whine of the engine and the pounding air of urgency that filled the cabin. 'Turn in there, Renata. It's just past that dead tree stump. Do you see it?'

'I see it,' Renata said, 'but I don't want to risk turning off and getting us trapped in the middle of the forest. Hang on. I think I can outrun these bastards.'

'We won't be trapped,' Dylan insisted. 'You have to do it now!'

Claire glanced back at the auburn-haired Breedmate and saw the certainty in her gaze. 'How can you be sure of that?'

'Because the ghost of the dead Breedmate sitting back here next to me is telling me it's our best chance of surviving.'

Claire felt her eyes go wide.

'Good enough for me in that case,' Renata said, and eased up on the gas only enough for her to make the turn off the road and onto the bumpy woodland path that Dylan had indicated.

'Keep going,' Dylan instructed. 'Just follow this thing until I tell you to stop.'

'All right.' Renata gunned it, throwing up dust and pebbles in their wake.

Behind them, the Minions in the sedan had to hit their brakes hard as they skidded sideways to make the turn. They managed it, the car lurching forward like a bullet, still fast on their tail. Through the cloud of debris between the two vehicles, Claire could just make out the bared teeth and dark, sharklike eyes of the two human mind slaves.

Were they Roth's Minions, or did they belong to someone even more dangerous than him – Dragos? She didn't want to know. She only hoped that Renata's driving skills and Dylan's Breedmate talent would be enough to spare them. If not . . .

If not, then this stretch of thicket-choked forest might be the last thing any of them saw.

'Faster, Renata!' Dylan urged. 'Keep going – as fast as you can!'

The Range Rover rocked and bounced, branches scraping its sides and slapping at the windshield and windows like spiny tentacles.

And still the Minions kept coming.

'Cut left,' Dylan shouted. 'As sharply as you can, Renata. Cut left then punch the gas!'

Claire gripped the dashboard as the vehicle made a sudden, swinging pivot on its front wheels. The rear of the SUV arced out behind them in what felt like a slow-motion turn, as graceful as a ballerina. Claire glanced out her window just in time to see that they were riding the very edge of a sharp drop. Below them a couple of steep yards, a river raced and tumbled past boulders the size of a small car.

She couldn't bite back her scream. Nor could she do anything but watch in stricken wonder as the Minions' sedan came barreling toward them in that same instant. It smashed into their back bumper in a sickening *crunch* of protesting metal and kept going, shoving them forward out of the way as the car catapulted over the edge and plunged down, the hood crashing into the water.

'Holy shit!' Dylan cried. 'It worked! Did you see that?'

Renata looked far from celebratory. The Range Rover was out of control, coming to an abrupt halt as the front bumper wrapped around the trunk of a small tree. Airbags exploded out of the dashboard with the impact, throwing off an airy whine and a puff of electronic smoke as they deployed. Dazed and shaken, it took a few seconds for Claire to get her bearings as the restraints slowly deflated.

Renata, meanwhile, calmly batted the obstacle out of her way and climbed out of the vehicle. She stalked around to the back of the SUV and grabbed the nasty-looking weapon that Nikolai had given her. Then she walked swiftly but steadily over to the edge of the embankment.

Claire and Dylan got out of the smashed Rover and followed, jogging to her side just as the Breedmate readied her aim on the Minions, who were scrambling to get out of their car before the river swept them downstream. Renata took just two shots – each hitting its target with unerring accuracy.

The Minions, both bleeding from gaping holes in their heads, drifted lifelessly into the swift-moving current.

'Everybody okay?' she asked, glancing over with a steady, unnerving calm.

'We're fine,' Claire answered, still astonished by everything she'd just witnessed – not the least of which being Renata's coolly efficient manner as she'd killed the two deadly assailants.

As the women turned away from the ledge, Dylan froze in her tracks. 'Um . . . you guys? You know how we were hoping that if we found Roth we might also be able to use him to find solid intel on Dragos's location?' She looked at Claire and Renata. 'I think we're getting close.'

'Is that what the dead Breedmate is telling you now?' Claire asked.

'Uh-huh.' Dylan slowly lifted her hand to indicate the wooded area all around them. 'She and about twenty others like her. They're coming out of the trees one after the other and standing right in front of us.'

Claire swallowed hard as she stared into the empty forest, the last few rays of daylight burnishing everything in a deep russet glow. She couldn't see what Dylan was reporting, but the fine hairs began to rise on the back of her neck.

'We'd better call the compound,' Renata said.

'Uh-huh,' Dylan murmured. 'Good idea. Because I think we may be standing almost on top of Dragos's lair right now.'

⤜ CHAPTER TWENTY-SEVEN ⤛

Reichen had slept off most of the day, but he'd still awoken twitchy with the need to feed. After his confrontation with Tegan, he'd somehow managed to get himself from the weapons room to his temporary quarters in the compound, where he'd crashed on the bed and swiftly fallen into a state of unconscious oblivion.

Now, showered and dressed, finally able to remain upright on his own motor, he was swamped with the urge to hunt. He knew enough about Bloodlust to realize that the hunger would only worsen if he fed it now, but that didn't slow his pace as he made his way along the corridor to the bank of elevators that would carry him up to street level and the city that pulsed with humanity just beyond the gates of the Order's headquarters. His mouth watered at the thought, his gums aching with the swell of his fangs.

Aboveground it could only barely be sunset, but Reichen wasn't worried about a few minutes of ultraviolet sizzle. He stalked to the elevators and pushed the button to call the car.

As he waited, impatient as a cat, he heard heavy bootfalls coming up from the other direction. Warriors Kade and Brock rounded a curve in the corridor, both of them garbed in full combat gear and hard-core weaponry. They looked as though they were suited up for war.

'Hey,' Kade said, his wolfish quicksilver eyes grim and

narrowed as he greeted Reichen with a slight lift of his square jaw. His spiky jet hair was covered by a black knit skullcap, the same thing that stretched over Brock's dark-skinned, close-shaved head. The two big males paused when Reichen turned to face them.

'What's going on?' he asked the warriors, hoping they weren't about to ask him the same thing.

'Heading out in a few minutes for Connecticut, my man,' Brock said, his deep voice a thunderous roll of bass and battle readiness. 'With any luck, we're gonna be handing Dragos his own ass on a platter before the night is through.'

'Dragos,' Reichen echoed. 'We've got a lead on him?'

'Best one so far,' Kade put in. 'Gideon's getting the coordinates from Renata as we speak.'

'When did the women return?'

Brock gave a slow shake of his head. 'They haven't. The Rover is toast, so we'll be picking them up tonight when we get there.'

Alarms kicked up a sudden racket in Reichen's whole body. 'What do you mean – the vehicle broke down on them?'

'Crashed into a tree,' Kade said. 'Could have been a hell of a lot worse, if the Minions trying to run them off the road had actually gotten ahold of them. Everyone's okay, and the mind slaves are dead. Renata gave them both a fatal case of lead poisoning.'

'Good Christ.' Reichen's blood ran ice cold.

Minions.

A car crash and gunfire.

Claire . . .

'Gideon is on the phone with the women now?' he demanded. Kade nodded.

'Where?'

'The tech lab.'

Reichen took off at a dead run, feet and heart pounding

with the need to hear Claire's voice, to hear from her own lips that she truly was unharmed.

Gideon was inside with most of the Order, everyone gathered and reviewing the map and coordinates that hung on the far wall of the lab. Tegan, Nikolai, Rio, and the former Gen One assassin named Hunter were all dressed like Kade and Brock, all dripping weapons and lethal purpose.

Reichen entered the room and walked straight over to Gideon, just in time to hear the warrior end his conversation with Renata and disconnect the call. 'I need to talk to Claire.'

'She's fine,' Gideon said. 'The situation is totally under control.'

'Like hell it is,' he roared, practically shaking with concern. 'They were attacked by Minions and now they're stranded out there? What the fuck happened?'

'We knew the mission was not entirely without risk,' Lucan said soberly. When Reichen pivoted to face him, the Order's leader went on. 'The women knew the risks, too. They accepted it, and they handled it. Quite well, in fact.'

Reichen simmered down, but only slightly. 'Tell me what happened.'

Gideon gave him a quick rundown of the facts Renata had reported: Claire's certainty that they were within mere miles of Roth; the double sightings of the Minions who'd apparently been following them since early afternoon; the high-speed pursuit that ended in an undeveloped stretch of woodlands some three hours away; and the astonishing news that Dylan's psychic gift had not only delivered the women to safety but also, apparently, had led them right into the vicinity of what could only be Dragos's hidden lair.

As stunned as he was to hear the day's extraordinary events – as relieved as he was to know that neither Claire nor the other two women had been injured – another part of him was awash in confusion . . . and guilt.

Claire must have been terrified when she and her companions had come under attack by the Minions. At the very least, her adrenaline should have kicked into high gear, and yet Reichen's blood bond to her had told him nothing.

'You didn't know?' Tegan said, his gaze seeming to read right through him.

Reichen gave a curt shake of his head. He'd been laid flat while Claire was in serious danger. The knowledge of how badly he might have failed her hit him like a stab to the chest.

And now she was out there in the open, vulnerable, near enough to Roth that she could feel him, and possibly within Dragos's reach, as well.

Reichen bristled with the thought. He felt the first crackling trace of heat begin to bloom in his gut while the Order went back to reviewing the night's operation. Pushing the fire down deep, all his focus centered on Claire, he listened in to the warriors' plan to search the wooded area the females had mapped out, with the goal of uncovering Dragos's apparent base of operations. From the information Claire's blood bond had given them, they were confident they'd find Roth, but the ideal goal remained to locate Dragos himself, flush the bastard out of hiding and into the Order's hands.

The warriors began to disperse, those in combat fatigues heading for the corridor while Lucan, Dante, and Gideon would be monitoring the mission from the compound. When Reichen moved to join Tegan and the others on their way to the hallway, Lucan stopped him with a look.

'This is the Order's mission, and we can't afford any weak links in the chain.' At Reichen's disapproving scowl, Lucan went on. 'Listen, you've been a hell of an ally thus far, Reichen, but Tegan's filled me in on a few things – what you're going through with the pyro and the aftereffects. I also heard about the vision that Roth's Breedmate saw in Mira's eyes. Those are no small things, and we can't afford any liabilities right now.'

Reichen held the Gen One warrior's keen gray eyes. 'I'm bonded to her, Lucan. I love her. If you want to keep me out of this, you're going to have to kill me right here and now.'

A silence fell over the lab and the group of warriors standing around them.

'I've given the Order my full support,' Reichen said. 'It's cost me dearly, but I am dealing with that. Now I'm asking you to give me this one thing: I want Roth dead. I need Roth dead, and so does the Order. Let me take the son of a bitch down, if it's the last thing I do.'

'And if it *is* the last thing you do?' Lucan pressed.

Reichen gave a slow shake of his head, feeling determination light up his veins in far greater measure than even the worst of his pyro. 'I don't intend to lose this battle, Lucan. I don't intend to lose Claire, either.'

The Gen One vampire stared at him for a long moment, his gray eyes weighing him in unflinching scrutiny. 'Very well,' he said at last. 'Suit up and get the hell out of here. Godspeed, Reichen. I have a feeling you might need it.'

The last ray of sunlight dipped behind the westerly tree line just as Claire, Renata, and Dylan left the Range Rover behind them near the river and started walking up the dirt lane toward the road. They had collected everything of importance from the disabled SUV – maps, notes, weapons, and ammunition – and were taking up a post near the main road as the warriors had instructed Renata when she'd phoned in their situation a short time ago.

As they walked up the narrow path in the gathering dusk, Claire couldn't keep from looking over her shoulder or jumping at every unexpected noise that came out of the ever-darkening forest that flanked both sides of them. The day had been unsettling enough as it was, but it was the buzzing in her veins – the dreadful certainty that Wilhelm Roth was near – that had her skin feeling too tight on her body, all of her senses on edge.

She kept revisiting her last dreamwalk with Roth, chilled to remember how he'd seethed with his promise to make Andreas and her suffer. And she also recalled, all too vividly, the numerous women being held in Dragos's cages – prison cells that might be located not far from where she and her two companions had been standing not long ago. It sickened her to think of the horrors those captive Breedmates might have been through. Horrors that had ended in death for many of them, as evidenced by the group of specters that had shown themselves to Dylan back in those remote woods.

Dragos had to be stopped. Wilhelm Roth, as well, and any other members of the Breed who would condone the kind of torment and terror that she'd witnessed through Roth's subconscious mind.

Claire knew men like that needed to be removed from existence, but it didn't dampen her fear for the ones who had made it their life's mission to see that kind of evil destroyed. It didn't dampen her worry about Andreas, and the harrowing vision of fire and death that she prayed would never come true.

As she and her two companions sought shelter to wait for the warriors to come and meet them, Claire couldn't help thinking that the night ahead of her might be only the beginning of an even greater darkness yet to come.

CHAPTER TWENTY-EIGHT

Reichen sat beside Tegan in the backseat of a black Range Rover for what seemed an interminable drive to the northwestern corner of Connecticut. Rio was at the wheel, Nikolai riding shotgun, maintaining constant cell phone contact with Renata since the warriors left Boston some three hours past. Behind them in another SUV was the rest of the team accompanying them on the mission: Kade, Brock, and Hunter.

About forty-five minutes ago, they'd turned off the interstate and begun a meandering jog along one rural route after another, following both the coordinates the women had provided and the strength of the blood bonds that would have led Niko and Rio to their mates even without the use of maps and GPS systems. Likewise, Reichen's sensory pull toward Claire was intensifying the farther they drove along the winding stretch of moonlit, two-lane blacktop.

'We just passed the mom-and-pop gas station you mentioned,' Niko said into his cell phone as the closed establishment fell behind them in the darkness. 'We're coming around the bend now. You should see the Rover's headlights any second. We'll blink them so you know it's us.'

Up ahead of the vehicle, the road flared brighter as Rio flashed the high beams a couple of times.

'Yep, we see you,' Niko said when a dark-clothed figure came out of the woods up ahead some hundred yards and waved a signal of her location.

Watching from behind Nikolai, Reichen hardly drew breath until Rio had navigated the Rover off the road and onto the wooded access lane where the three Breedmates waited. His gaze searched out and settled hard on Claire. She looked so vulnerable and out of place surrounded by so much night and dark forest, to say nothing of the fact that Wilhelm Roth could not be far from the very spot where she now stood.

But Reichen read only the faintest bit of fear in her. Claire's pulse beat steady and strong in his heart, and her gait was sure as she and her two companions came to meet the vehicle.

No sooner had Rio parked the SUV did he and Niko both jump out to pull their mates into relieved, unhurried embraces. Reichen and Tegan climbed out, as well. Tegan walking around back to greet the second vehicle as it rolled to stop behind them on the wooded dirt lane. Conversations buzzed quietly, talk of tactics and strategy, and quick reviews of the established plans for combing the area where Dylan had seen the ghostly Breedmates in the hopes of launching an offensive attack on Dragos's possible hideout.

Reichen, meanwhile, couldn't take his eyes off Claire. He drifted over to her, crossing his arms when the urge to wrap them around her felt too strong to deny. He wasn't sure she'd welcome his concern after the way they'd left things at the compound.

'Are you all right?' he asked, noticing that she, too, had kept her hands close to herself as he approached. 'My God, Claire. I heard what happened today. You have no idea how worried I've been . . .'

She gave him an unreadable look, taking in his black combat gear and the many weapons supplied him by the Order and holstered on the belt around his hips. Then she met his eyes once more and nodded her head. 'I'm fine,' she said tonelessly. 'Thank you for the concern.'

God, he hated this forced politeness, just as he hated the fact that the scant arm's length that separated them now might as well be a mile. Claire gave him that perfected expression of placidity that had once belonged to Wilhelm Roth – the shuttered, pleasant mask from the photographs Reichen had seen of her. Now she was turning that look on him. Shutting him out with the same kind of cordial distance she'd once reserved for strangers and other individuals she didn't quite trust.

The realization cut deep, despite the fact that he'd earned her cold shoulder. Hell, he'd earned much more than that where Claire was concerned. He'd upended her whole world, put her in the crosshairs of a deadly personal war. Worse by far was the fact that he'd come back into her life only to drag her into the center of his conflict with Roth.

'Claire,' he said softly, words intended for her ears alone. 'There is so much I want to apologize to you for –'

'Please, don't.' She glanced up at him in the darkness, gave him a faint shake of her head. There was no condemnation in her voice, no raw hurt. Only quiet resignation. 'Do you really think I'm looking for you to tell me you're sorry? I'm not, Andreas, not anymore. Especially not right now. When this is all over tonight, then you can say whatever you need to say to me.'

She worried that he was walking into his death, and maybe he was. He blew out a slow breath, amazed as always by the strength that she carried inside her. He caressed her for only the briefest second, memorizing the velvet texture of her warm, honeyed skin. 'I've always loved you, Claire. You know that, don't you?'

She pressed her fingers tenderly against his lips. 'Don't you dare pretend this is good-bye,' she whispered fiercely. 'Damn you, Andre, don't you dare.'

Reichen kissed the soft pads of her fingertips, then hooked his arm around the small of her spine and brought her up against him. Hunger seared him, blood and desire inflamed together, twin needs that centered on the woman who felt so right in his embrace.

'You're mine, Claire,' he growled into her mouth as he kissed her, long and deep. All around them, the warriors were preparing to fan out and begin their search of the outlying forest. Reichen took a step away from Claire, feeling the gap of space like a sudden gust of chill air. 'I have to go now.'

'I know,' she said softly. 'But you'll come back to me, right? This time, promise me, Andre . . . you will come back to me.'

He cast a quick glance into the dark woods, his senses prickling with the knowledge of a hard battle soon to come. He looked back to Claire and drank in the sight of her. His beautiful, extraordinary Claire. After tonight, she would be free of Roth for good. Reichen would make certain of that. After tonight, Claire would be safe, no matter what he had to do to ensure it.

'I have to go,' he said again.

Her gaze was imploring, a blade twisting below his sternum. 'Andre . . . promise me?'

'Stay safe, Claire. I love you.'

He fell in beside Tegan and the other warriors and didn't look back.

Claire stood there for a long moment, watching numbly as the forest swallowed up Andreas and the other warriors. She'd kept up her brave front longer than she thought she could, but now that he was gone, her spine felt less solid, her legs a bit unsteady beneath her. She started when a hand touched down lightly on her shoulder.

'Hey.' It was Dylan, her expression soft, sympathetic. 'Come on back to the Rover, Claire. It's warmer inside. Rio and I will keep you company until this is over.'

She let herself be led around to the waiting vehicle, realizing belatedly that Renata had joined the warriors as well. Inside the Range Rover, Rio was on two-way tactical communication with each member of the mission, including Andreas. The connection to him, even electronically, gave her a small degree of comfort. At least she could hear his voice from time to time, and know that he was still with her. Still alive.

She refused to consider the many terrible ways this night could end. Instead she clung to the remembered warmth of Andreas's embrace, his passionate kiss, his loving words.

He had to come back to her.

He had to survive.

As she held those thoughts close to her like a shield, Tegan's deep voice came over the receiver mounted to the Rover's dashboard.

'Fuck, I think we've got something out here.' There was a rustle of movement in the background, the sound of boots traipsing carefully over dried leaves. The warrior dropped his voice to a low whisper. 'Oh, hell yeah . . . we got something, all right. Dilapidated barn roughly four hundred and fifty yards northeast of the Rover.'

'Copy,' came Brock's bass growl. 'Moving in now.'

Claire exchanged an anxious look with Dylan as more warriors reported that they were circling over to the location Tegan had given.

'Couple of Minions posted outside of it armed with semiautos,' Tegan added. 'Reichen and I are moving in on them. Everyone else bring up the rear.'

Not a few seconds later, gunfire exploded from out of the distant woods.

CHAPTER TWENTY-NINE

Wilhelm Roth turned away from the old barn's hidden closed-circuit cameras after the Order had mowed down the handful of Minions posted as guards at the ground-level entrance of the lab. The Minions were expendable, nothing more than an obstacle for appearance sake. After all, the Order might be suspicious if he and Dragos had rolled out a red carpet to welcome them. Let them think they had to expend some effort for their prize. Lull them into believing they were actually the ones in control, when their arrival had been anticipated – indeed, encouraged – all along.

Now that they had all gained entrance to the underground facility, it would be only minutes before the group of warriors and Andreas Reichen found their way down the bunker's earthen catacombs to the heart of Dragos's headquarters. A few minutes more than that before they realized the trap they'd entered and understood there could be no escape.

Just a matter of minutes before Roth had the distinct pleasure of killing them all in one fell swoop.

He smiled with genuine glee as he motioned to the half-dozen Gen One assassins gathered with him in the control room.

'Two of you come with me,' he said, not caring which of Dragos's homegrown, highly trained killers accompanied him since they were all born and bred to deal in death. 'The rest of you head up to guard the entrance. Make sure no one gets in or out.'

As four of them moved to carry out his command, Wilhelm Roth walked out of the control room to await his moment of triumph over Andreas Reichen and his doomed companions.

Tegan and Nikolai were the first ones down the dank, dark tunnel that had been carved deep into the earth and fortified by concrete and carbide steel supports. A few seconds after they'd descended, Niko came back up and signaled an all-clear to Brock, Kade, and Reichen. Hunter and Renata stayed on watch outside, covering the search party's exit.

Once they'd removed the Minion guards from the entrance, Reichen and the others had moved into the old barn, which, they soon realized, wasn't so old after all. Nothing about the hidden bunker was as it seemed on the outside.

At the other end of the sloping tunnel, easily some several hundred feet below, the bunker expanded and spread out as wide and long as a gymnasium. Fluorescent lights washed the place out in a pale white glow, illuminating cafeteria-style tables and chairs that had been stacked neatly against one wall. A hinged door with a round window at eye level appeared to open into some sort of kitchen and service area, also empty and evidently closed for business although the odors of recently cooked food still hung cloyingly in the air.

'Guess who's coming to dinner,' Kade drawled under his breath.

Brock scowled as he nodded. 'Humans.'

'Minions,' Tegan corrected with a snarl as he sniffed derisively. 'Helluva lot of them, too. Dragos keeps plenty of staff down here.'

Nikolai grunted. 'Yeah, but for what?'

'Let's find out,' Tegan said, motioning the group forward

with him as he moved through the empty space to the corridor that let out on the other side.

They crept soundlessly past multiple spoking hallways and door after door of vacant dormitory-type rooms with basic twin cots, shared toilets, and a decided lack of personal touches.

'Jesus,' Kade whispered. 'How many Minions does one twisted bastard need at his beck and call, anyway?'

'Enough to man a very expansive clinical endeavor,' Reichen said, pausing in front of a pair of steel doors that he'd pushed open a crack in order to peer inside.

Beyond the doors was a massive laboratory with half-emptied cabinets and gaping file drawers, clumsily cleared work spaces, and a polished floor littered with pieces of equipment broken in what appeared to have been a hasty evacuation. The warriors entered cautiously, taking note of what little assets remained. There were a handful of toppled microscopes and cracked slides, and sundry other items that looked like they'd once starred in a chemist's wet dream.

'Check this out,' Kade called from the far side of the lab. He indicated a lidded stainless steel drum that looked like a giant pressure cooker. 'Now, what the hell do you suppose this thing does?'

Reichen and Tegan walked over with Brock and Nikolai, glancing inside the large cylinder as Kade popped the seals on the top and opened the lid. It was no longer plugged in, so the temperature inside had warmed considerably from the deep freeze maintained while the unit was operable, and the contents had all been removed. Still, there was no mistaking the machine's purpose.

'It's a cryo container,' Reichen said.

Tegan nodded grimly. He jerked his chin toward another nearby room, where a skewed fleet of clear Plexiglas boxes like one might expect to see in the maternity wing of a human hospital had been parked haphazardly along the far wall.

'Incubators. Jesus Christ. Dragos is running a fucking breeding factory down here.'

'Or was,' Nikolai said. 'He obviously cleared out in a hurry.'

'Maybe he knew we were coming,' Brock suggested. 'Can't speak for anyone else, but I'm starting to get a real bad vibe.'

Kade gave his buddy an affirming look. 'I don't like it, either. Getting in was too easy. This could be some kind of trap.'

'All the rats do seem to have fled this ship,' Nikolai added. 'Maybe they were on to something. Dragos wouldn't leave a facility like this vulnerable to attack unless it was deliberate. I'd bet my left nut that he's long gone from here, and took everything of value with him.'

'Dragos may be gone,' Reichen said, 'but Wilhelm Roth is in here somewhere, and I mean to find the son of a bitch.' Anger spiked as he dismissed his own sense of unease to focus on a more immediate, crucial goal. 'Turn back, if you want. I won't begrudge any of you for it. But I'm going to push on.'

Tegan's green eyes glittered dangerously. 'Too many unanswered questions down here to turn back without covering every square inch of this hellhole. Fuck you very much, if you think we're gonna let you do this on your own, Reichen.'

Reichen held that verdant stare and knew a deep appreciation for the kinship he'd formed with this warrior. With all of the Order, in fact. The rest of the warriors didn't hesitate to nod their agreement with Tegan, or to fall in beside Reichen and him as they headed deeper into the empty facility.

Just when Dragos's secret operation seemed it couldn't get any more disturbing, Reichen caught his first glimpse of a long wing of prison cells, just as Claire had described from her dreamwalk with Roth. Except none of them contained captive Breedmates, a fact that gave little comfort when it was obvious from the condition of the cells that they'd only recently been evacuated.

'Holy hell,' Niko murmured as the group of them strode

into the area to see them up close. 'There's got to be fifty cages here. If these were occupied with imprisoned females, what has Dragos done with them all?'

'Moved them, no doubt,' Tegan said. 'Possibly to the same place he relocated all of his staff and equipment, although he might be splitting up his assets now that he's been forced to leave this location in a hurry.'

'That is one sick fuck,' Brock remarked as he peered inside one of the cells and ran his big hand over his skull-trimmed head.

'You ain't seen nothing yet.' Kade had walked over to a heavily bolted door perhaps a bit too conveniently unlocked now. He stepped into the room on the other side and blew out a low whistle. 'What. The. Fuck.'

Reichen and the others followed him inside. A shocked and prolonged silence fell over each of the Breed males, from the youngest of the group to the centuries-old Gen One whom Reichen had never once seen rattled beyond words.

For within the space on the other side of that door was a broad platform raised slightly off the floor. And on that platform was a large, pivotable chair rigged with heavy restraints built for an individual of immense size and strength. Ankle braces as thick as a woman's thigh. Shackles for powerful wrists that must have supported hands big enough to crack an average human's skull like a walnut.

'This is where he's been keeping the Ancient,' Tegan said, the first of them able to form words. 'Holy shit. He's had the Ancient under his control all this time.'

'How?' Nikolai asked, then glanced down near their feet and exhaled a sober curse. 'Ultraviolet light bars. Check the floor. The ceiling, too. The entire perimeter of this platform is circled by an array of UV light fixtures. When they're activated, the UV bars would contain the Ancient inside better than the strongest, thickest kind of metal.'

The words were barely out of Niko's mouth before a sudden, odd hum rent the air around them. Intense light exploded from all directions, so bright and hot, Reichen and the others had no choice but to cover their eyes with updrawn arms. He smelled the acrid taint of singed skin. At first, he worried that his pyro had awakened from out of nowhere. Then he realized this was something even worse.

Reichen squinted beyond the piercing blast of light, upward, toward a glassed-in viewing area he hadn't noticed above the Ancient's holding cell until that very moment.

Inside that viewing area stood Wilhelm Roth, grinning with smug satisfaction as Reichen, Tegan, and the rest of the warriors who'd come with them were hemmed in tight by the lethal vertical beams of ultraviolet light that surrounded them on all sides. Roth motioned to a pair of big males – black-clad, hard-eyed, and bristling with automatic weapons. Both males bore thick black polymer collars around their necks, their shaved heads and bare throats covered in Gen One *glyphs*, every massive, muscled inch of them seething deadly purpose. The two assassins exited both sides of the viewing area to twin landings at the top of a double flight of stairs.

They took aim on Reichen and the others trapped inside the UV light cage, then opened fire.

❧ CHAPTER THIRTY ❧

Claire's heart slammed against her sternum at the sudden cacophony of gunfire that erupted over the comm device on the Rover's dashboard. She'd been tensely monitoring the team's progress inside Dragos's lair along with Dylan and Rio, fear twisting like a serpent in her stomach with each step Andreas and the others took deeper into the horrible place.

Now her fear shot up her throat, exploding out of her in a scream as the sounds of ripping bullets, shouts, and chaos filled the vehicle.

'Oh, my God!' she cried, her blood freezing in her veins. 'Oh, my God! No!'

She made a frantic lunge for the door handle beside her in the backseat, but Rio pivoted around from in front of her and clamped his hand down on her shoulder, keeping her in place.

'Stay, Claire. You can't do anything to help them,' he said, his Spanish accent rolling, dark-fringed eyes grave. He hissed a curse as more gunfire cracked over the receiver.

Then, another disaster, this time from the ground level post near the barn's entrance, where Renata and the male called Hunter were stationed.

Renata's voice came into the vehicle in a breathless rush. 'Ah, shit. We've got company. Four guards coming into view right now outside the old barn . . . Fuck, I think they're Gen Ones –'

Blam! Blam! Blam!

More bullets began to fly, the racket cutting Renata off and echoing from out of the forest like thunderclaps.

'Oh, Jesus,' Dylan whispered from her seat beside her mate in the front of the SUV as the Order came under attack both inside Dragos's lair and outside on ground level. 'Rio . . . what should we do?'

'Stay here, both of you,' he ordered them grimly, pulling a nasty-looking pistol out of its holster on his belt and loading the chamber. He threw open the driver-side door and leapt out. 'Stay in the Rover and keep it running in case things go any further south and you need to haul ass out of here. I'm going in.'

The Gen One assassins rained down a hail of bullets on Reichen and the warriors caught within the UV prison below. Returning their fire wasn't easy. The light bars were blinding and searingly hot, offering little room to dodge the incoming rounds while the warriors volleyed back shots with their own weapons.

From his periphery, Reichen saw Tegan take a bullet to the shoulder. Another grazed Nikolai in the thigh, knocking him on his ass for a second before he locked and loaded a second pistol and squeezed off several semiautomatic rounds. And up above, secure behind the bulletproof Plexiglas that shielded him from the fray, Wilhelm Roth was still watching, still gloating. Smiling, as though it were all merely entertainment and he'd already won this war.

Reichen's fury churned on a swift, hard boil.

Already the pyro was rising up inside him; he felt the living heat ripple over his skin, watched with nonchalant acceptance as the bullets that should have punctured his body instead fell away the instant they met the field of psychic energy that enveloped him.

'Get behind me!' he shouted to Tegan and the others,

spreading his arms wide to create an even wider field of protection. 'Not too close,' he warned. 'The heat will deflect the bullets, but it also kills.'

The warriors moved in as tight as was prudent, using Reichen's body like a shield as they continued to strike back at their attackers, who had the advantage of unrestricted movement and seemingly endless firepower.

Reichen's vision began to warp before his eyes. His pyro was building faster now, burning hotter than ever as he glared up at Roth. He let his rage expand, coaxed the flames to swell even bigger from within him. He summoned every ounce of fire at his command, letting it tumble and roil in his gut, willing it to strengthen as he held it down well past the point of pain. Past even the point of sanity.

Some threadbare shred of instinct told him that he was courting disaster, but he shoved reason aside and stoked the flames brighter. Tasting the need for vengeance – for a final, bloody justice – like potent liquor on his tongue.

'Wilhelm Roth,' he bellowed darkly, centering all of his hatred, all of his white-hot energy, on the male who had taken so much from him, even before he'd called for the slaughter of Reichen's Darkhaven kin. 'Tonight you die, Roth!'

Focusing his talent, Reichen fisted his hand and punched it through the ultraviolet light bars of the cell. He felt no burn, other than the heat coursing through him already. He glanced up and took great satisfaction in the sudden, slack-jawed astonishment written across Roth's face. Grinning himself now in a smile full of hatred and laser-sighted purpose, Reichen stepped out of the Ancient's cage with a roar of mingled triumph and murderous rage.

The two Gen One assassins blasted at him with their useless weapons. Reichen glanced up at them, heat rippling outward from his body with nuclear intensity. He summoned power to his raised and fisted hands, then turned it loose on the pair.

Twin fireballs rocketed out of his palms. The spinning white-hot orbs struck their targets in an instant, incinerating the vampires on impact, bodies and weapons reduced to a flurry of drifting ash and molten bits of metal showering down from the top of the double staircases.

'Holy shit!' one of the warriors crowed from behind him, but Reichen had no time to relish the small victory.

Not when Roth was staring wide-eyed in panic, backing away from the window as if he was preparing to bolt.

Reichen crouched low, then sprang into the air. In one fluid motion, fire engulfing him, he leapt off the floor and sailed up to the broad sheet of Plexiglas that separated him from his quarry. He locked eyes with Roth, curling his lip off his teeth and fangs as he smashed into the window and watched the barrier shatter inward in a million melting pebbles.

Wilhelm Roth gaped at the towering pillar of hellish fire that had transformed Andreas Reichen into something too incredible for words. He'd understood the male's unique Breed-born talent was pyrokinesis, but this . . . this was beyond reckoning.

It was awesome in its power, and Roth could not keep himself from staring, struck dumb with wonder and fear, as Reichen stalked toward him. The concrete floor scorched black beneath Reichen's boots. The fluorescent lights overhead popped and smoked as he passed under them, moving inch by inch across the viewing room. Roth retreated, feeling his hair and skin singe from the intensity of the heat rolling off Reichen.

'You think you can accomplish anything by killing me?' he asked the glowing form that stalked him with obvious deadly intent. 'You've seen this place, Reichen. You can figure out what it's been used for all these years. Dragos has bred his own army down here. He's done much more than that, and he cannot be stopped now. Do you actually think my death will make a difference in the grand scheme of things?'

'It will make a difference to Claire,' came the deep, heat-warped reply. 'It will make a difference to me.'

Roth kept moving backward, until the gauges and switches of the UV cage's control panel behind him bit into his spine. 'Let me go, and maybe your friends down there in that cell will live.'

'You can't harm anyone. Not anymore.'

Reichen's glance bounced from point to point on the control panel. Circuits crackled, shooting off sparks and bitter, electronic smoke. Roth had to duck out of the way of the small explosions, the fallout of Reichen's searing gaze driving him deep into the corner of the room in a cower. Roth snarled, infuriated to have been sent to his knees, particularly by this male, whose death he had craved and sought for far too long.

As Reichen stepped closer, murder blazing from every pore of his body, Roth made an abrupt lunge for one of the gauges on the control panel. He understood the fact that he wasn't going to walk away from this fight now, but damn if he would accept defeat alone.

With a grunt of determination, Roth smashed his fist onto the panic switch that would activate the lab's emergency detonation sequence. Sirens immediately began to wail overhead. The alarms sounded from every direction, signaling the start of an irreversible countdown.

Roth chuckled. 'My God. It's almost worth it – knowing that I am about to die down here alongside you and the bulk of the Order. Seeing that look on your face right now . . . your defeat is palpable, Reichen. So is the horror and outrage – the raw, emotional pain – it's all there, in your eyes.' He sighed, knowingly dramatic. 'I only wish I could take Claire along with us when this whole goddamned place blows to kingdom come in the next five – ah, make that four minutes and forty-nine seconds.'

✐ CHAPTER THIRTY-ONE ✐

Claire wanted it to all be a dream. A terrible nightmare that she could simply wake from and the world would go back to normal. She wanted to go back to three nights ago, when she and Andreas had been alone at the house in Newport, making love, walking along the wharfs, embracing under the moonlight.

But the sound of Wilhelm Roth's cruelly animated voice – the realization of what he had just done to Andreas, to the warriors inside the abandoned lair with him . . . to the women who would be mourning their mates in mere minutes – sank into Claire's soul like a poison.

'I can't stay in here another second,' she murmured, meeting Dylan's ashen look.

'We can't leave, Claire. Can't you hear the gunfire out there by the entrance?'

Claire heard it. Rio had been gone for only a few minutes. He and Renata and Hunter were still engaged with the Gen One assassins who'd come up to ground level. It was dangerous outside the vehicle; Claire knew that. But as she stared anxiously out the tinted windshield at the forest that surrounded her, she knew a deeper sense of dread.

'Oh, my God . . . no. This cannot be Mira's vision.'

She opened the door and slid out of the Rover, realizing just now that the premonition she'd seen in the little girl's eyes was about to come true. Right here, within the next five awful minutes.

Dylan came out of the vehicle and circled around to grab her by the arms. 'Claire, please, get back inside. You can't –'

'This is the same woods I saw in Mira's eyes,' she cried, sick with certainty. The same location where she'd felt the anguish of losing Andreas in that pile of smoking rubble and ash. 'The explosion, Dylan. This is exactly what Mira showed me. It's really going to happen. Oh, my God . . . no!'

Tearing loose of the other Breedmate's hold, Claire raced into the darkened woods, her heart breaking, about to burst from her chest, and Andreas's name a desperate prayer on her lips.

Every cell in Reichen's body screamed for him to unleash the full power of his fury on Wilhelm Roth. It would be the matter of an instant to render the bastard nothing but ashes to be trampled under his boots.

But incinerating Roth with a single blast of rage was far too merciful. Evil like him deserved to suffer, especially after the cowardice he'd just shown in activating explosives that none of the warriors trapped in the UV cage below had any hope of escaping. His friends should not have to die as part of this bad blood between Roth and himself.

It was that thought, more than any other, that gave Reichen the ability to ignore his hatred of Roth and loose his rage on the control panel that encompassed the entire back wall of the viewing room. He threw one bolt of flame after another at the gauges and monitoring devices, until finally there was a loud *pop* and the entire space went dark.

He didn't see Roth moving until the son of a bitch had managed to scramble through a side door. Reichen pivoted to the blown-out window and glanced down at the warriors leaping off the cell's deactivated platform.

'Reichen!' It was Tegan's deep voice calling up to him, although Reichen's vision was swamped with amber and rippling with the heat that was escalating ever hotter inside him. 'Reichen, come on! Leave the son of a bitch. He's dead if he stays in here.'

True enough, Reichen thought. But the way his body felt now, the way his veins were seething lava and his mind fixed on one thing – destruction – he realized that the moment he'd dreaded for so long had finally arrived.

He was too far gone. The fires were intensifying within him, no longer his to control.

'Reichen, goddamn it!' Tegan shouted, hesitating when the rest of the warriors were wisely rushing to evacuate. 'Forget Roth and let's haul ass out of this place before it fucking blows!'

'Take care of her for me,' he somehow managed to say, his throat feeling as dry as kindling, scraping with each syllable. 'Get her somewhere safe . . . do that for me, Tegan.'

He didn't wait to hear the dark curse that shot up from the room below. Reichen took off after Wilhelm Roth, trusting the warrior – his friend – to carry out his request. If he could be certain of Claire's safety, he didn't need anything else.

Nothing but the knowledge that Wilhelm Roth was dead.

He stalked through the anterior hallway where Roth had run, hearing the bow of metal bending, the steel and concrete reinforcements of the underground bunker protesting his presence. Empty metal supply carts sagged as he passed them, glass windows in doors and offices shattering from the sheer intensity of the white-hot flames that ringed his limbs and torso like an impenetrable, living cocoon of energy.

'Wilhelm Roth!' he roared, coming up on the vampire from a few dozen yards away.

Roth had been running like the vermin he was, but now he slowed, then stopped. No doubt he sensed the futility in trying to escape the death that was coming to him, either by Reichen's hand or his own, when he'd smashed that detonator switch some three minutes ago.

Roth slowly turned around to face him. 'You surprise me, Reichen. I would have thought your love for my faithless mate was stronger than your hatred of me.'

Reichen grunted. He wasn't about to discuss Claire or his feelings for her with this offal. Roth had to know that with less than three minutes on the detonator, neither one of them was getting out of the bunker before it blew.

Reichen stalked forward, using all his focus to keep from ashing Roth on the spot. He wanted to make the next two minutes of his life count, and he could think of no greater purpose than killing Roth second by second, burning away his existence inch by inch. As he approached, Roth had no choice but to retreat backward, edging nearer to the end of the corridor.

He saw Roth's skin start to go red. He moved closer, driving him farther back. Beads of sweat erupted from Roth's brow and upper lip, then his entire face and throat sheened with moisture. And still Reichen advanced. Roth hissed as his exposed skin began to blister and burn. A stench rose up from his fair hair as it, too, started to singe under the heat of Reichen's merciless talent.

Roth cried out when his clothes began to smoke. 'Go ahead and do your worst,' he sputtered, gasping in agony yet finding the ability to peel back his splitting, scorched lips into a sadistic smile. 'Have you forgotten? My blood bond to Claire . . . so long as I'm alive, she feels my pain. Torture me, and you torture her, too.'

Claire screamed and dropped to the ground on her knees. Up ahead of her in the dark, she saw Renata, Hunter, and Rio taking on the last of the Gen One assassins at the old barn. Through the black maw of the entrance, Claire watched as Kade and Nikolai, then Brock and Tegan came up from the depths of Dragos's lair. What about Andreas? She was about to call out to the warriors, but the searing pain that racked her so suddenly had stolen her breath.

It had taken her down swiftly, heat running over her body as if she were standing in the heart of the devil's own furnace. Or, rather, Wilhelm Roth was standing in that hellish inferno. It was his agony that rocked her, his pain echoing in her blood.

Andre.

He was the source of Roth's pain. Which meant he was still alive. Still breathing somewhere in that underground bunker, which meant he still had a chance to get out before the worst could happen. He still had a chance to come back to her.

Claire dragged herself up to her feet, buoyed by hope.

She pushed through the painful psychic link to Roth and started running once more. If Tegan and the rest of the warriors had made it out all right, then she was certain that Andreas couldn't be far behind them.

CHAPTER THIRTY-TWO

Reichen staggered back on his heels at the realization that he was hurting Claire as he took his hatred out on Roth. Like the heavy, Bloodlust-induced sleep that had muted his own bond to her earlier that day, his pyro now had obliterated nearly all his senses. It had stripped him of nearly everything but his fury, and the fire that rose along with it.

'Why did you do it?' Reichen demanded roughly. 'Why did you need to have Claire?'

Roth's smile stretched tight behind the cracking skin of his scorched lips. 'Because you wanted her. And because she couldn't see that I was a far better man. You were nothing compared to me. You never were. I even removed the one obstacle that prevented me from pursuing Claire in earnest —'

'The female you'd already taken as your mate,' Reichen growled.

'The female you had the audacity to coddle after I'd put her in her rightful place.'

Roth was staring at Reichen as though he should remember the event he spoke of. Reichen thought back to his dealings with Roth . . . and suddenly recalled a timid Breedmate sitting outside a Darkhaven party on a rain-soaked balcony. 'I brought her inside and gave her my jacket,' he said, picturing her stricken face as he'd shown her that small kindness. 'She was freezing and crying, so I sent her home with my driver.'

'You humiliated me in front of my peers. Even worse, in front of my subordinates. You and Ilsa both humiliated me that evening.'

'So you had her killed?' Reichen snarled, incredulous.

'Attacked by a Rogue vampire,' Roth said lightly. He shrugged. 'No one questioned me about the incident, since it was my close associates who took the report.'

'Out of spite, you killed an innocent woman who trusted you above all others. Then you took Claire as your mate to get back at me.'

'I did more than that.' Roth sneered. 'I arranged to get rid of you, as well. You vanished for a year without a word of excuse. Everyone wondered if you were dead. And yet Claire still wanted *you*.'

He practically spat the word.

Jealousy and pride, Reichen thought, sickened that something so petty had caused so much pain.

Roth's stare was sharp, cuttingly so. 'I suppose after I realized that, my hate for Claire exceeded even the hate I had for you. I would have enjoyed killing her, Reichen. Just as I enjoyed ordering the deaths of your Darkhaven kin and turning that human whore of yours into my Minion.'

Reichen roared with fresh anguish and outrage. He was through with Roth now. Sick to death of the bastard's ugly words. He brought his hands out before him and felt the fires travel from his core through his limbs. Out to his fingertips that stretched toward Wilhelm Roth.

'Die, you sick fuck,' he snarled.

And then he released a double-barreled blast of flame and heat at the face of his most treacherous enemy. Roth's death was instant, a mercy Reichen granted only because of Claire.

Reichen was still screaming with animal fury, still torching the empty floor where Roth's ashes had piled up, when he felt the first rumblings of the explosion building under the soles of his feet.

The walls around him trembled.

Then the earth heaved violently with the force of the lab's detonation.

Claire knew the precise moment that Wilhelm Roth took his last breath. It came to her as a sudden flood of peace – an impossible sense of freedom that lit up her veins and gave her limbs a renewed strength to carry her forward as she raced the few remaining yards toward the old barn where the warriors had just spilled out.

Roth was dead.

Andreas was alive.

God . . . could the hell of the past several days, of the past several decades that she and Andreas had been separated by Roth's machinations, actually be coming to an end?

She wanted to believe it. Needed to believe it.

Claire clutched hope close, even as the ground beneath her feet gave a prolonged, bone-rattling shudder.

'Jesus Christ!' shouted a low male voice up ahead of her in the dark. 'Did you feel that? This son of a bitch is about to blow!'

Claire kept running, denying what she was hearing. It couldn't be true. It could not be happening. Not when Andreas hadn't yet come out to safety.

'Get back, get back!' Rio's rolling accent sounded from somewhere close. The big warrior came crashing through the trees with Renata, Hunter, and a couple of others from the mission. Rio reached for Claire, tried to pull her along with them, but she dodged his grasp and kept on running.

There were more shouted warnings, more urgent movement in the night-dark woods, as the shudder deep within the earth rumbled louder.

There was a violent jolt, then a deep, thunderous *boom!*

Strong arms and a warm, hard body wrapped itself around

Claire, twisting her around to cushion her fall as the percussion blasted her backward, off her feet. She screamed but could hardly hear her own voice as the forest shook and roared with the force of a seemingly endless, ungodly explosion.

'Stay down, Claire.' Tegan's voice blew hot against her ear. 'I promised him I'd get you out of here in one piece.'

'Noo!' she cried, beyond caring if she lived or died, watching in horror as the derelict barn blasted skyward in a blinding mass of flames and heat and thick, roiling smoke. The plumes of fire shot out in all directions, showering large chunks of splintered wood and burning embers down onto the forest. More heat erupted from out of the hole bored into the earth beneath the barn, the entrance to the bunker from which Andreas had yet to escape. 'Oh, my God . . . no! He's still down there! Andreas, no!'

She vaulted to her feet. Tegan's hold was firm on her arm, but she shook him off with a desperate cry. 'Let me go, damn you!'

Adrenaline and despair sent her flying over the debris-strewn ground, through the thick growth of trees that was illuminated with unearthly orange light from the fire that seethed where the old barn had stood not a minute ago. She felt Tegan following behind her. The other warriors were moving in, too, silent and cautious. One of the Breedmates murmured a soft prayer for Andreas, tender words that Claire could hardly bear to hear.

She walked closer to the roaring heat. It was overwhelming, hitting her like a furnace thrown open in her face. Still, she kept moving toward it, transfixed by the earthen crater of rubble and smoldering ash that had collapsed inward with the blast.

'Andreas,' she called softly. Then louder, hoping he could hear her. Hoping for a miracle. 'Andreas!'

When she would have gone even closer, close enough that the flames would have touched her, Tegan's hands came down gently on her shoulders. 'Come on, Claire. Don't do this to yourself.'

'André!' she cried, stubbornly refusing to give up.

A new plume of sparks belched upward from within the molten core of the crater, making the rubble shift and groan. She felt the warrior's grasp on her tighten, and she knew he was prepared to carry her out of there if she delayed another second. But Claire didn't budge. She called to Andreas again, her voice hitching on a sob as another deep rumble sounded from belowground.

Then she noticed something odd about the smoldering pit of cinders and churning flames . . .

Deep within its core, something was moving.

'Holy hell,' Tegan said, obviously spotting the same thing she had. 'Holy fucking hell. It can't be –'

'Andreas,' Claire gasped, awestruck and incredulous, and so very, very relieved.

She watched the rubble give way and melt around him as he climbed out of the center of the inferno and rose to stand on the edge of the crater, his body aglow with the white-hot power of his extraordinary, terrifying gift. Smoke billowed above him in great black clouds. Flames roared and undulated from behind him like a seething volcano, yet he stood there unscathed.

'Thank God,' she whispered, her heart soaring.

But then she realized something about him was terribly wrong. The heat that enveloped him – the same heat that had proven impervious to bullets that first night she'd seen him like this – might have been the only thing that spared him from the killing force of the explosion, but the glow that surrounded him was brighter than ever. Hotter than the fires that roared all around him from the blast.

His gaze was vacant as it traveled from Claire to the others gathered there. Light poured out of his eye sockets, searing and inhuman. Merciless.

Claire took a step toward him, hesitant now. 'Andreas? Andre . . . can you hear me?'

That flat, burning gaze swung back to her now. Heat blasted her, pushing her several paces in retreat. He wasn't looking at her, she realized, but through her. He didn't see her there, no more than he saw the rest of the warriors – his friends – standing before him in stunned silence. Claire recognized the danger he posed like this, even if he was too far gone to recognize it for himself now.

She had to break through to him. 'Andre, it's me, Claire. Talk to me. Tell me you know me. That you're all right.'

He snarled, low and deadly, in the back of his throat. She didn't let it scare her. Keeping her eyes locked on his, she took a step toward him.

'Jesus Christ,' Tegan hissed from nearby. He moved to block her path. 'Claire, I don't think you should –'

A fireball sailed through the air, crashing into the ground at Tegan's feet.

'Andre, no!'

Tegan leapt out of the way of the assault, taking Claire with him. Andreas roared then, and let fly a sudden hail of flaming orbs. Chunks of dark earth ripped loose as the baseball-size blasts hit the ground, driving everyone back. Claire screamed for him to stop, and for a moment she thought he would. He looked at her, then suddenly lifted his hands to the sides of his head and staggered unsteadily on his feet. The glow around him dimmed as he pressed his palms hard against his temples, his face contorting in a grimace of pain.

When Claire glanced beside her, she saw the reason why.

Renata held him in a fixed, unblinking stare. As the Breedmate had done to the Gen One assassins a short time ago, now she blasted Andreas with the power of her mind. He went down on one knee, the rippling heat that traveled his body flickering like a strobe.

When she let up, Andreas was panting and shuddering. But the glow still enveloped him. And as he lifted his head, the roar that ripped out of his mouth shook the entire forest with feral, deadly fury.

⪤ CHAPTER THIRTY-THREE ⪥

The fire owned him.

He knew this, knew it from the moment the bunker had exploded all around him but didn't take him down with it. He knew he was too far gone, even as he'd crawled out of the ashes and rubble intact, his body protected by the furious heat that only seemed to grow stronger, brighter, more uncontrollable by the second. He had lost the battle with his terrible ability, with himself, just as he'd feared would happen.

The others gaping at him in the flame-drenched darkness of the woods knew it, too. Especially her, the female whose welling, dark brown eyes tore at something deep within him. *He loved her.* Not even the madness of the unrelenting heat could burn away that fact.

She lived in his heart, this female.

His female.

His mate, something primal and anguished howled from inside him.

He loved her deeply, completely, but knew he could not have her. Not now.

Not ever again.

He threw his head back and roared at the thought, and his voice turned loose a ball of white flames. The orb pitched high, then smashed into the ground a half-dozen feet from him, showering the area in sparks and clumps of upheaved loam.

'Andreas, please,' his woman cried. 'Let us help you.'

Fire danced all around her. Tears filled her eyes, her hands trembling as she held them out to him through the smoke and pale, floating ash that was raining down like snowflakes from the canopy of trees above.

'Andre, look at me. Hear me. I know you can.' She stepped toward him, ignoring the sober warnings of more than one of the males in her company. 'I'm not ready to let you go,' she said fiercely, words that seemed to echo back at him like a memory.

Had he heard them in this very spot earlier tonight? Had he been the one to say them to her?

It didn't matter. He couldn't let it matter. She and the others with her – friends, his instinct called them – were not safe around him now. They had to go.

Except she wasn't about to leave him there. He could see that plainly enough in the stubborn tilt of her jaw. He growled with fury, and felt the swell of another ball of heat building in his gut.

Incredibly, she moved even closer to him.

A vision flashed through his mind as he watched her take yet another step toward him. He saw a little girl with sandy pigtails and a gentle smile holding her hand out to him in a gesture of kindness. He saw a bright, innocent face offering him help and compassion . . . just before the fire that lived within him leapt out to consume her.

He'd killed something precious and pure once before. He would not do it again.

Bellowing his self-contempt, he sent a small volley of fireballs at the ground in front of him. A low barrier of flames twisted and crackled, driving her back. It wasn't enough. He needed her gone – needed to know that she was far away from his destructive power.

He needed all of them gone now.

He threw more fire, forcing the entire group to pull back. As they gradually retreated, he saw the tear-streaked, beautiful face of the woman – *his woman* – fixed on him through the climbing wall of flames that separated them.

'No, Andre,' she mouthed. 'No. I'm not going to let you do this.'

Heat gusted from the dancing flames in front of Claire and the others. Behind the wall of undulating fire, she watched Andreas's face. His eyes were filled with torment and pain. With madness, too. Heartbreaking, bleak resolve smoldered in his gaze.

He was giving up.

He was trying to drive her away from him, so he could deal with his suffering – most likely his death as well – alone.

No, Claire thought, firmly rejecting the idea. No goddamn way was she going to accept that. Not after all they'd been through. Not when she'd been waiting for him, had never stopped loving him, all this time.

There had to be some way to break through to him. There had to be some way to help him.

'Renata,' she said, turning to look at the other Breedmate. 'You did something to him a few minutes ago with your mind. It dimmed some of the heat surrounding him –'

'Yes,' Renata agreed. 'I saw it, too.'

'I need you to do it again now.'

Nikolai stepped over, his expression grave. 'Renata's talent is lethal, Claire. It's not something you want to mess around with, trust me. If she turns it loose on Reichen again, it might –'

'Might what? Kill him?' Claire felt hysteria bubble up inside her. 'Look at him. He's already dying. If we don't do something fast, then the pyro will kill him.'

She looked at Renata, desperate for even the slimmest chance of saving Andreas. 'Please . . . please, try.'

Renata gave a curt nod, then looked away to fix her attention on the formidable tower of heat and flames that was Andreas. She stared unblinking, focused like a laser. Claire felt the air beside her shift almost imperceptibly as an unseen current leapt outward from Renata's mind and seized on its target.

He reared back the instant it hit him.

Claire's heart lurched as he threw his head back and howled, all of his muscles going taut as cables. He grabbed both sides of his head and doubled over as Renata held him in the debilitating psychic grasp of her strong mind. Andreas shuddered and roared . . . and as he struggled, the glow that swamped him began to fade.

'Keep going, Renata! Oh, my God, I think it's working.'

Claire heard more than one of the warriors curse from nearby, where they all stood watching, everyone as transfixed as Claire was as the mental blast Renata delivered continued to douse Andreas's heat. He dropped to his knees, buckled over, still holding his head in his hands. He looked to be in complete agony, but the heat traveling his limbs and torso had lessened even more.

'Please, Andre . . . hang on,' she whispered, her heart shredding to see him suffer so. Her nerve faltered. Just when she was about to tell Renata to stop, Andreas pitched forward and collapsed in a heavy, boneless sprawl.

'Claire, stay back!' someone shouted, but she was already running toward him.

She dodged the flames that still burned in places on the ground and raced to Andreas's side. Energy crackled over his skin, raising goose bumps on her arms, but the glow was gone. The heat was cooled.

'Andre,' she sobbed, folding her legs and dropping down beside him on the ground.

She lifted his head onto her lap and stroked his bloodless cheek and brow. He was cold. Unmoving.

Oh, God.

'Andre, can you hear me?' She cradled his broad shoulders and bent to press her face against his. 'Andreas, please don't die. Please . . . come back to me.'

She kissed him all over, holding him tight. Praying she'd done the right thing. Hoping he was still in there somewhere, and that the gamble she'd taken with his life hadn't been the worst mistake she would ever make.

'Andre, I love you,' she murmured, dimly aware that Renata and Dylan and the warriors had all gathered around them now. 'You can't leave me. You can't.'

Tegan knelt down beside her and put his hand on the side of Andreas's neck. 'He's alive. He's breathing, but he's out cold. Got a strong pulse, at least . . .'

'Thank God,' Renata whispered, clutching Niko in a tight embrace as she looked down at Claire in kinship and shared concern.

'We have to get him out of here,' Tegan said. He glanced up at Renata. 'Will you be able to keep him under control if he comes to on the ride back to Boston?'

She nodded. 'Whatever it takes, yeah. I'll cover him.'

'Come on, Claire.' The warrior nudged her gently as he crouched to heft Andreas's heavy bulk onto his shoulder as he would care for any one of his fallen brothers in arms. 'I'll carry him back to the Rover. Everything's going to be okay now.'

Claire nodded numbly and fell in alongside him as they all made the short trek from the smoldering forest and obliterated bunker to the waiting vehicles.

She wanted to believe Tegan, but when she looked at Andreas's unresponsive, ashen face, she couldn't help feeling that where Andreas was concerned, everything was still a long way from okay.

⇥ CHAPTER THIRTY-FOUR ⇤

Dragos snapped his cell phone closed and jammed it into the pocket of his cashmere dress coat. He stared up at the starlit sky above an industrial park off I-90 in Albany, New York, and hissed a violent oath. Wilhelm Roth wasn't answering his calls.

Which meant that Wilhelm Roth was dead.

The fact that Dragos's cameras and communication systems at his Connecticut headquarters had all gone off-line and ceased working meant that the bunker had been detonated as planned. He could only hope that Roth had managed to ensure that a number of the Order's members had been blown to pieces along with the hastily abandoned lab.

As for Roth himself, Dragos hadn't actually cared if his German lieutenant survived the lab's destruction; it was the matter of a moment to find another right arm to carry out his mission.

And so he had.

Dragos moved away from his Minion-chauffeured sedan to inspect the work of Roth's replacement. The second-generation Breed male who'd been recruited from the West Coast was overseeing the movement of Dragos's assets – a diversification made necessary by the aggravating and persistent interference of the Order.

But Dragos hadn't come this far without anticipating a few

speed bumps in his operation. Alternatives had been explored and provided for years ago, and now it was merely a matter of rearranging the pieces that he already had in play. The Order had cost him only a few days – a couple of weeks at most – then he would be right back in business once again.

Stronger than before.

Unstoppable, no matter what disturbing things he had seen in the witchy eyes of the child seer all those weeks ago in Montreal.

'Are we ready to move out yet?' he asked his lieutenant.

The big vampire nodded curtly where he stood behind one of several semi-trailer trucks that had been loaded and were waiting to roll out of the industrial park to their appointed destinations. The double doors of the one nearest his lieutenant were partially open yet, revealing the anxious faces of the Breedmates who'd been removed from their cells in the lab for transportation elsewhere. They knew better than to scream or try to escape. The industrial park was owned by Dragos, manned by his Minions.

Besides, the chains and shackles that bound the women to one another would prevent any of them from getting very far, even if they were foolish enough to attempt it.

'Seal them up and get them out of here,' Dragos said, watching in satisfaction as his lieutenant swung the doors closed and set the heavy steel bolt and locks. A quick *thump* of the vampire's fist on the back of the truck sent the thing rolling with one of Dragos's Minions at the wheel.

Farther on in the yard, several more trucks awaited their departure orders. Dragos walked past the ones containing his many millions of dollars' worth of state-of-the-art laboratory equipment, his gaze fixed on the large white trailer at the far end of the line.

It was a refrigerated container, specially equipped for preserving the fragile cargo that was locked and sedated inside.

Two Gen One assassins had been stationed within the trailer to stand guard over the contents; another pair would ride up front with the Minion driver and Dragos's West Coast associate to ensure the shipment encountered no problems en route to the rail yard, where the next leg of the container's long journey would begin.

'Everything is ready, sire.'

'Excellent,' Dragos said. 'Contact me as soon as you arrive in Seattle to make the last connection.'

'Yes, sire.'

Dragos watched as the fleet of trucks lurched into motion and exited the yard.

The Order may have disrupted his operation, but he was far from defeated.

With a confident smile tugging at the corner of his lips, Dragos walked back to his waiting car. He climbed into the backseat and waited in boredom as the driver closed the door behind him then hurried back around to get behind the wheel.

Tonight the lair he'd gone to great pains and expense to construct was gone, but Dragos preferred to think of it as a necessary step in the evolution of his plans. Now he would begin a new phase in his operation, and he could hardly wait to get started.

Dragos leaned his head back against the soft leather seat and watched through the rear window as a thread of pale clouds skittered across the milky moon overhead.

Andreas didn't wake up once during the three-plus hours it took to drive back to the Order's headquarters.

Nor the entire next day.

Claire heard Tess use the word 'coma' in conversation with Gabrielle and Savannah when the three women had been preparing the private apartment for him in the compound early that morning. She couldn't pretend it didn't worry her, and the longer he stayed unconscious, the deeper her dread became.

This slow, helpless waiting was even worse than watching him rail and struggle against his pyrokinesis. Claire held his hand as he lay unmoving on the bed. She knew he was in there. She could feel his blood moving beneath his skin, could see the occasional flicker of his closed eyelids when she spoke to him.

'Is there anything else you need?' Tess asked gently, drying her hands on a paper towel from the bathroom. Dante's mate was trained in veterinary medicine and had possessed an even greater psychic gift for healing with her touch before her current pregnancy had inhibited her talent. Now she laid her hand softly on Claire's and offered a kind, compassionate smile. 'You really should eat, you know. And get some rest.'

'I know,' Claire said, glancing to the tray of uneaten food on the rollaway table brought up from the infirmary and now sitting beside the bed. 'I'm fine. I'll have something in a little while. I'm not really hungry. I just want to sit with him for a bit longer.'

Tess didn't look convinced. 'I'm going to come back and check on you in a couple of hours. Promise me that sandwich won't still be sitting on that plate.'

Claire just smiled with an assurance she only wished she felt. 'Please, don't worry about me. I'm fine.'

Tess gave her a faint nod. 'Let someone know if there is any change in him, okay? You both are in everyone's thoughts and prayers right now, Claire.'

'Thank you,' she murmured, touched by the kindness everyone in the compound had shown her. They loved Andreas like one of their own, treated him like kin, and because of that, she loved them all, as well.

'I'll see you in a couple of hours,' Tess said as she slowly closed the door behind her.

Claire turned back to Andreas and smoothed her hand over

his forehead, brushing his tousled brown hair back from his face. She watched him, wondering where he was in his deep, trauma-induced sleep.

Wondering when – and if – he would ever find the strength to return to her.

'Oh, Andre,' she whispered, gazing at the proud, handsome face she had loved for so long. She brought her lips to his and kissed him, unable to stem the tear that rolled down her cheek when his mouth pressed soft and warm, but unresponsive, against hers.

Claire moved up on the bed beside him, needing to be closer. Stretched alongside him, she laid her head against his shoulder and placed the palm of her hand over the steady beat of his heart pounding beneath his sternum. She closed her eyes and let that hardy pulse buoy her thoughts.

Andreas was alive. So long as she could touch him, breathe him, she would not give up hope that he would be with her once again.

And if he wasn't ready to come back to her, then she would go to him.

'Forever this time,' she murmured.

Letting her eyes drift closed, she sought him out in the dream realm.

He wasn't hard to find. Claire walked into a bleak, black void, drawn to the glow of a fire burning hotly in the distance. She was alone and naked, her bare feet walking over a length of cold, dark stone that seemed to stretch out for interminable miles . . . terminating at the place where the flames danced like orange streamers far ahead.

Andreas was up there, too.

Claire could just make out the bulk of a large male form, lying on the ground in front of the roaring wall of fire. He was naked, as well, sprawled brokenly on his side as he had been on the forest floor after Renata had blasted him into unconsciousness.

Claire walked closer, realizing only now that the length of black stone beneath her feet was merely a narrow strip of solid surface, a treacherous promenade that allowed no more than a couple of feet on either side of her. The black stone path floated over a sea of darkness, an abyss, which, at its core burned like the deepest pits of hell.

And Andreas lay at the very end of the long stretch of cold stone.

'Oh, God,' she whispered as she drew nearer, realizing just how precarious his position truly was. One careless movement – one unconscious slip – and he would tumble off the edge and plummet into the inferno raging below.

Claire approached him carefully and inched down next to him on the sheer precipice of stone. Tenderly, terrified of waking him suddenly, she stroked her fingers over his cheek. He didn't stir. His skin was too cold, his breathing unrushed, slumberous.

He slept on, didn't even know she was there.

'That's okay, Andre,' she told him softly as she moved down onto the cold black surface of the ledge. She curled herself behind him, wrapping her arm around him to keep him from falling and molding her body against his to give him her warmth. 'We'll sleep here together for a while. I'll wait with you until you're ready to come back to me.'

❧ CHAPTER THIRTY-FIVE ❧

It's been five days, Lucan. We have some decisions that will need to be made, and made quickly.'

Lucan nodded solemnly and glanced over to the worried gaze of Dante's mate, Tess. She had been the one to discover Claire unconscious at Reichen's side the day after the explosion at Dragos's bunker. In the time since, Tess had been keeping a close watch on both Reichen and Claire, ensuring that they were kept warm and comfortable in the bed the couple shared, and looking for some way to help bring one or both of them around. So far, nothing had worked.

'Andreas's Breed metabolism is stronger than Claire's human one,' she said. 'He can probably survive another few weeks or more without sustenance, but Claire is dehydrating quickly. Unless we get some fluids into her, vital organs are going to start failing soon.'

Lucan stared down at the woman sleeping in the bed. Her petite frame was nestled tightly against Reichen's body, her arms wrapped lovingly around him, holding him in what looked to be a fiercely protective embrace. Her sleep seemed vastly different from Reichen's. Where he lay motionless, unresponsive, Claire's eyes flickered rapidly behind her closed lids. Her fine muscles twitched now and again, as though she were caught in a brief doze, not dead to the world for the past several days.

'You've tried everything to attempt to wake her?' he asked Tess.

'Everything, Lucan. It's as if her body – as well as her heart and mind – simply refuses to come back to consciousness. She's willing herself to remain asleep, I'm certain of it.'

He scowled, watching Claire's eyelids twitch with the movement of her eyes beneath them. 'She's been dreaming this whole time?'

'Yes, since the moment I found her like this. I have to believe she's using her talent to be with Andreas.'

Lucan huffed out a heavy sigh. 'Even if it kills her in the process?'

'You saw them together, didn't you?' Tess's voice was gentle with sympathy and not a little awe. 'I suppose I can understand the depth of devotion – of pure, unshakable love – that would inspire this kind of sacrifice. If it were Dante on that bed and I thought I could reach him in some way – in any way – I'd be right in there, too. For however long it might take. I know if it were Gabrielle, you would do the same for her.'

He was hardly going to stand there and deny it. But neither could he stand by and knowingly allow Claire, or Reichen, to waste away while he watched.

He glanced back to Tess and gave the Breedmate a tight nod. 'Gather whatever you need from the infirmary to get her hydrated. I'll go inform everyone of the situation.'

Several thousand miles away from Boston, on a remote stretch of railroad track that led into the frozen heart of Alaska's interior, the wrecked remains of a large, refrigerated cargo container lay open and abandoned to the elements.

It had made the journey from the industrial yard in Albany, New York, to the rail station that sent it westward across the country, arriving as planned four days ago at the port of Seattle. From there, it had been loaded without incident onto a barge and shipped north, where it was scheduled to reach its final destination just a mere eighteen hours later.

By the time the first inklings of trouble had been detected by Dragos's lieutenant and the cadre of Gen One guards escorting the dangerous cargo, it was already far too late to stop what was about to occur.

Now that dangerous cargo was gone.

The container was empty, aside from the savaged, bloodied bodies that littered its floor and the snow-covered ground outside.

And leading away from the moonlit tracks, into the tree-choked, frozen wilderness beyond, was a trail of huge footprints made by a feral, deadly creature not of this world.

A creature that had been biding its time through weeks of starvation and drugging, feigning lethargy and compliance, while waiting for its chance to escape.

≈ CHAPTER THIRTY-SIX ≈

The endless dark refused to release him. Reichen's lungs expanded and drew in air as if he'd been underwater and just broke through the surface after half a year of drowning in the tide. He gasped in sharply, then immediately began to choke on the acrid taste of sulfur and smoke.

He felt a light weight draped around him in the pitch blackness of his surroundings.

Claire's arms, holding him close.

Her soft, tender body curved along the length of him from behind.

Amid the bleak void that engulfed him, he'd never felt anything so perfect and right.

He knew he was dreaming, but for how long? He couldn't dismiss the feeling that he'd been lost in the darkness of this other realm for a good long time. And Claire was with him.

Good Christ . . . had she been here with him the whole time?

He smoothed his palm over the velvety length of her arm. Her skin was cool to the touch, alarmingly so. She didn't stir at all as he gently stroked her. What troubled him more was the shallow panting of her breath beside his ear, the notable limpness of her cold fingers as he grasped them in his own and tried to rouse her.

'Claire,' he murmured, his tongue thick, his voice sluggish and rusty in the heavy pall of this smoke-clogged dream. 'Claire?'

She wouldn't respond.

Panic clutched him, snapping his eyes open. It was then he noticed the glow of flames rising up from far below the cold hard perch where he and Claire had been lying together. As he sat up, the flames shot higher, as if they, too, had been merely resting but were now stirring with renewed life. Beyond the steep, narrow ledge was a great abyss. A pit of fire and roiling lava churned at the bottom of that hellish drop.

The flames surged violently upward, twisting and tumbling, nearly blinding him with the intensity of their heat.

Like a beast breaking loose of its shackles, the fire lunged for him. Bright white-hot tendrils made a sudden grab across the stone ledge, stretching greedy fingers of flame toward the place where he and Claire sat.

Reichen quickly covered Claire's body with his own, twisting himself over her as the heat roared all around them. The burn licked at his naked skin, searing and relentless. But it couldn't touch her. He wouldn't permit it.

No goddamn way would he let the fires get near her.

He bellowed with fury as the force of his pyro rolled over him and around him. This hellish heat was his – it was *him*, the terrible curse of his birthright.

The very power that had protected him from the explosion in Dragos's underground lair.

Memory of that moment slammed into him in an instant. He recalled how he'd had to conjure every measure of his fury in order to shield himself from the inferno that had erupted all around him. The pyro had spared him from death in the blast, but it wasn't through with him yet. It was still burning inside him. Ready to consume him, just as Claire had tried to warn him.

Just as he himself had known it would, from the moment the very first spark had lit within him in that godforsaken field in Hamburg.

If he let go now – if he gave one fraction of his will to keep Claire safe from the heat – the curse that had plagued him for so long would own him. And it would destroy Claire in the process. He felt the fires searching for her, flames hissing and flicking like serpents' tongues, hungry for a taste of the treasure he was denying them.

'No,' he heard himself growl. *'Goddamn it. No.'*

With his arms and body wrapped around her to shield her, Reichen turned all of his rage inward. He focused on the heat that lived in the deepest core of his being. He reached for it with his mind, with every measure of his will, feeling the pyro try to slither out of his grasp as he seized on it and yanked it tight in the fist of his determination.

He couldn't let it win.

He had to finally take control of the beast.

He had to master it, here and now.

Forever.

He strengthened his mental chokehold on the twisting coil of fire inside him. All around him, he heard the hiss of flames, the sputter of struggling heat that was slowly being beaten down, extinguished. In the periphery of his gaze, he saw the writhing columns of flame drawing back from the stone ledge, back into the deep abyss that had borne them.

And still he didn't let go.

He turned his face toward the rolling, gnashing fires that were still seeking to leap out of the pit, his teeth and fangs bared in a tight sneer as he roared with power and furious intent.

'No!' he bellowed. 'I own you. You will bow to me now!'

It was his love for Claire that gave him the resolve he needed in this moment. His need to protect her, to keep her safe above all else, was the driving force that made him certain he could defeat the curse of his destructive power.

It was the love she'd given him in return – the love he could feel beating inside him, in his veins, in the blood bond that linked him to her now and always – that made him reach for the hope that one day he might not only master his hellish ability but maybe even come to view it as something more than a curse. He knew a sudden certainty that the curse he had dreaded for so long might one day become a talent that would serve him, instead of destroying him.

Reichen clung to hope, and to his love for Claire, as he commanded the fires to quell. He sent them back down into the abyss below, not out of fear or self-contempt but out of strength. Out of a burgeoning sense of unshakable control.

A triumphant cry broke out of him as the last bright flame began to gasp its death.

The fires went dark in the pit.

The choking ash and smoke cleared away.

His eyes blinking open, Reichen lifted his head and found himself no longer isolated on the narrow bridge of cold black stone, but in the center of a large bed. He was curled over the small form of Claire's body, still shielding her, even though the dark dream had finally released them.

He stroked her cheek. 'Claire, are you all right? Open your eyes for me, sweetheart.'

No response.

Panic twisted in his gut. He said her name again, more choked this time for the alarming look of her as she lay motionless across his lap, her silky black hair falling loosely over her cold, sallow brow. He took her slender shoulders in his hands and gave her listless body a firm shake.

'Claire. Wake up now.'

An icy pain stabbed him as he leaned down and pressed his mouth to her parched, cracked lips. She was so weak . . . starving. The piercing jab he was feeling now belonged to her. He felt the severity of her hunger echoing in his blood, keening in his veins.

He thought back to the endless dream, and the swamping, unrelenting weight of it. How long had it been since he was last awake? He remembered storming Dragos's vacated lair with the Order. He remembered killing Wilhelm Roth. He remembered the explosion in the underground headquarters, and the look of fear and horror on Claire's face as he strode out of the rubble engulfed in hellish fire. He remembered her courage as she railed at him in stubborn determination, refusing to let him die.

Then he remembered . . . endless nothing.

It might have been days since he'd lost consciousness. Maybe a week or more.

How long had Claire been with him in the dream realm, neglecting her own well-being to comfort him through the darkness?

'Claire, please. Open your eyes. Tell me you can hear me.' He smoothed his hand over her face and hair, feeling his heart cracking open as he held her weakened body against him. 'Let me know that you are still with me, that I haven't lost you.'

God help him, but she did not respond at all. She was cold and unmoving, her breathing far too thready and shallow.

Reichen vaguely registered the sound of approaching footfalls outside the open door of the room, but all of his focus was rooted on bringing Claire around. Someone gasped from within the corridor, followed by more voices as a small crowd of warriors and their mates gathered outside the door.

'Holy hell,' Tegan muttered, a curse that was echoed by more than one person.

Reichen didn't know if their stunned reaction was meant for the fact that he was awake and absent of the pyro or for the disturbing condition of Claire lying limply in his arms. He swung his head toward Lucan, Tegan, and several other members of the Order who stood outside the room with Tess and the rest of the Breedmates who lived in the compound. Tess and

Savannah were holding IV tubes and bags of clear liquid. Behind them, Gideon had rolled up a gurney from the infirmary.

'Something is wrong with Claire,' he murmured, his throat dry. A cold gust seemed to blow through his body, settling behind his sternum.

'Let us help her,' Tess said gently, lifting the medical supplies she'd brought.

'No. It's too late for that,' he murmured, knowing instinctively that she was beyond the need of any mortal intervention.

She needed blood.

As much as he had once feared that he would only bring her harm, that his love would not be strong enough to keep her safe from what the pyro had made him become, Reichen felt beyond any shadow of doubt that he was the only one who could save her now. He snarled when a couple of the warriors began to enter the room, as if they meant to pull Claire away from him.

She was his – now and always.

'Come back to me,' he whispered, then lifted his wrist to his mouth and sank his fangs deep into his flesh.

Blood surged from his veins as he carried the wound to her slack lips and pressed the punctures against her tongue.

'Drink, Claire,' he whispered softly, holding her head up and willing her to live. He didn't care if he had to beg her. Didn't care that they had an audience watching in solemn, uncertain silence just a few feet away. 'Drink for me now. Please, Claire . . .'

The first sweep of her tongue against his skin made Reichen suck in a sharp breath. Then she began to swallow, fixing her lips more firmly to the source of warm, life-giving blood. His blood, which would flow within her and give her prolonged strength and life.

His blood, which would bind her to him as his mate, now and forever.

'Andre,' she murmured drowsily, lifting her dark-fringed gaze up to him. 'I've been so afraid. I thought I'd lost you.'

'Never,' he replied. 'Never again.'

Her mouth curved into a weak smile as she went back to suckling at his wrist.

'Take all that you need of me, love,' he encouraged her tenderly, his throat clogged with emotion. He didn't care that his voice and hands shook as he brought her closer. He was thoroughly unashamed of the depth of his feeling for this woman.

His woman.

His mate.

His beloved, finally, and for all the rest of their lives.

When he glanced over to where his friends had been gathered, he was surprised to see that they were gone. The door to the room was closed, leaving Claire and him to the intimacy of their reunion alone.

Reichen didn't rush her so much as a second. He let her drink for a long time, content simply to hold her in his arms and watch as his blood brought a glow to her cheeks and renewed life to her body.

And some long while later, after she was finally sated and strong, he settled back on the bed with her and wrapped her in his protective embrace, giving her a hundred solemn promises that he was very eager to keep, and loving her with all the reverence and worship of a blood-bonded male who had stared hell in the face and now understood that he was holding heaven in his arms.

⇥ EPILOGUE ⇥

NEWPORT, RHODE ISLAND
ONE WEEK LATER

Reichen stood alone at the moonlit shore of Narragansett Bay, deep in a private meditation that had become his nightly ritual after he and Claire had left Boston. Behind him, the sounds of her soft piano music drifted down from the house. He let the soothing notes wash over him as he focused all of his mental energy on the bright orb of fire that he held suspended in the foot of space between his palms.

The ball spun faster as he slowly brought his hands into a closer span. The light grew hotter, turning from the orange glow of flame to an intense whitish blue. And still Reichen squeezed it tighter, compressing the fire's power into a smaller and smaller area that was completely under his control.

The pyrokinesis that had once coursed through his entire body like a savage brush fire was slowly coming to heel. Finally bending to his will, obeying his command.

The exercise was exhausting, but each time he worked the fire he got better at it. Tonight he had held it for ten minutes straight – twice as long as he had only the night before. He was determined to shape his ability into a true talent, and he had Claire to thank for getting him this far.

She was his grounding strength. Her blood kept him steady,

and her love kept him whole. He was finally coming to accept himself as he was – all that he was, including this part of him, which he'd tried for so long to deny. He'd gone three decades living a shallow existence, closing himself off from true emotion for fear that it would make him weak. Now he felt everything in exponentially greater measure. With Claire at his side, he was finally coming to embrace all that it meant to truly be alive.

Distantly, as he honed the orb of fire into a smaller, brighter sphere, he registered that the music from inside the house had stopped. It took all of his focus to keep the ball spinning between his palms. So much so that he didn't hear anyone approaching until a deep male voice muttered a vivid curse behind him.

'It's all right, Tegan,' Claire said, as Reichen slowly pivoted to face them. Her smile was amused, and not a little proud as she met her mate's gaze. 'You're getting better at this. Last time you did it, the orb only got as small as an orange.'

Reichen quirked a brow at her as he crushed his hands together and extinguished the flames completely. His body was tired from the exertion it took to manage his talent, but his heart soared to see Claire's confidence in him. And he was glad to see his friend from Boston, too.

'Tegan,' he said, extending his hand to the warrior in greeting.

The Gen One gave him a cautious nod as he clasped the hand that had just been lit with preternatural heat. 'Impressive,' he said, grinning now. 'Someone's obviously been eating his Wheaties.'

Reichen laughed. 'I have something far better than that, my friend.'

Claire came over and wrapped her arm around him, nestling into his side. He would never tire of feeling her pressed close to him, and the past week they'd spent together in Newport had been the best rehabilitation he could have asked for. He was content beyond his wildest imaginings, but seeing Tegan now, he had to admit a growing itch to get back into the thick of the action with his friends in the Order.

'Have there been any further leads on Dragos since we spoke a couple of days ago?' he asked, figuring the warrior hadn't come all the way down to Rhode Island just on a house call.

'We're following up on a few things, but the son of a bitch seems to have cleared out of the area. He clearly knew we would be closing in on his location in Connecticut, and we're not discounting the fact that he might have established alternative locations long before now. Our best bet for the time being is to chase down his network of associates in the Enforcement Agency.'

'Anything I can do to help,' Reichen said. 'Tell me where I am needed. You know I'm available to the Order.'

'You've been invaluable already, my man. Without you and Claire both, we might not have found Dragos's lab at all. Now many of our suspicions about his operation are confirmed. It's more critical than ever that we find Dragos, but we also need to find the Ancient he's been imprisoning all this time. No telling where he might have moved the creature, but the fact that it's out there somewhere is a disaster just waiting to happen.'

Reichen nodded soberly. 'Sounds like the Order has its hands full, even more so now than before.'

'Yeah, we do,' Tegan agreed. 'Actually, Lucan and the rest of us in Boston agree that we could use an envoy to help us gather support among the European population. Your reputation has been gold among the Darkhavens over there, as well as with the Enforcement Agency. We're going to need someone with a cool head and good instincts to help us gather our own alliances, and at the same time root out any possible alliances of Dragos's among those groups. Any chance you might be willing to leave your nice little love nest here in Newport to do some diplomatic work for us from time to time?'

Reichen glanced down to meet Claire's gaze. They had agreed

to make the house in Newport their home, maybe even start a family of their own before too long. He was eager for the life they were planning together, but duty and loyalty to the Order tugged at him, as well.

She understood that fact; he saw the acceptance in her eyes. She smiled and gave him a small nod. 'At the rate you're going, by next week you'll have grown bored of juggling fire. You'll be looking for new challenges. Maybe we both will be. Maybe there is work enough for both of us with the Order,' she said, turning a questioning look on Tegan.

The warrior smiled. 'We would be honored to count on you both.'

'I didn't exactly leave Germany on the best terms,' Reichen murmured. 'The Agency over there may view me as a fugitive, not a friend.'

'Actually,' Tegan said, 'for all intents and purposes, you're a dead man. You died last summer, in the fire that destroyed your Darkhaven. Now Roth and everyone in his circle are dead, too. To anyone else, you're a ghost, Reichen. Which will give you even greater opportunity to get close to our targets over there and shore up covert alliances.'

'A spy for the Order?' Reichen said, liking the idea already.

'I'm not saying it's going to be easy. It's going to be damned hard work at times. And it's going to be deadly dangerous, too.' Tegan asked, 'You think you can handle that?'

Reichen looked to Claire again, feeling stronger than ever when he saw the faith and admiration shining back at him in her soft brown eyes. 'Yes,' he said. 'I think I can handle that.'

With Claire beside him, loving him – believing in him – he could handle anything at all.

Read on for a preview of the first chapter of the first book
in the heart-stopping *Midnight Breed* series.

PROLOGUE

TWENTY-SEVEN YEARS AGO

Her baby wouldn't stop crying. She'd started fussing at the last station, when the Greyhound bus out of Bangor stopped in Portland to pick up more passengers. Now, at a little after 1 A.M., they were almost to the Boston terminal, and the two-plus hours of trying to soothe her infant daughter were, as her friends back in school would say, getting on her last nerve.

The man beside her in the next seat probably wasn't thrilled, either.

'I'm real sorry about this,' she said, turning to speak to him for the first time since he'd gotten on. 'She's usually not this cranky. It's our first trip together. I guess she's just ready to get where we're going.'

The man blinked at her slowly, smiled without showing his teeth. 'Where you headed?'

'New York City.'

'Ah. The Big Apple,' he murmured. His voice was dry, airless. 'You got family there or something?'

She shook her head. The only family she had was in a back-woods town near Rangeley, and they'd made it clear that she was on her own now. 'I'm going there for a job. I mean, I hope to find a job. I want to be a dancer. On Broadway maybe, or one of them Rockettes.'

'Well, you sure are pretty enough.' The man was staring at her now. It was dark in the bus, but she thought there was something kind of weird about his eyes. Again the tight smile. 'With a body like yours, you ought to be a big star.'

Blushing, she glanced down at her complaining baby. Her boyfriend back in Maine used to say stuff like that, too. He used to say a lot of things to get her into the backseat of his car. And he wasn't her boyfriend anymore, either. Not since her junior year of high school when she started swelling up with his kid.

If she hadn't quit to have the baby, she would have graduated this summer.

'Have you had anything to eat yet today?' the man asked, as the bus slowed down and turned into the Boston station.

'Not really.' She gently bounced her baby girl in her arms, for all the good it did. She was red in the face, her tiny fists pumping, still crying like there was no tomorrow.

'What a coincidence,' the stranger said. 'I haven't eaten, either. I could do with a bite, if you're game to join me?'

'Nah. I'm okay. I've got some saltines in my bag. And anyway, I think this is the last bus to New York tonight, so I won't have time to do much more than change the baby and get right back on. Thanks, though.'

He didn't say anything else, just watched her gather her few things once the bus was parked in its bay, then moved out of his seat to let her pass on her way to the station's facilities.

When she came out of the restroom, the man was waiting for her.

A niggle of unease shot through her to see him standing there. He hadn't seemed so big when he was sitting next to her. And now that she was looking at him again, she could see that there was definitely something freaky about his eyes. Was he some kind of stoner?

'What's going on?'

He chuckled under his breath. 'I told you. I need to feed.'

That was an odd way of putting it.

She couldn't help noticing that there were only a few other people around in the station at this late hour. A light rain had begun, wetting the pavement, sending stragglers in for cover. Her bus was idling in its bay, already reloading. But in order to get to it, she first had to get past him.

She shrugged, too tired and anxious to deal with this crap. 'So, if you're hungry, go tell it to McDonald's. I'm late for my bus –'

'Listen, bitch –' He moved so fast, she didn't know what hit her. One second he was standing three feet away from her, the next he had his hand around her throat, cutting off her air. He pushed her back into the shadows near the terminal building. Back where nobody was going to notice if she got mugged. Or worse. His mouth was so close to her face, she could smell his foul breath. She saw his sharp teeth as he curled his lips back and hissed a terrible threat. 'Say another word, move another muscle, and you'll be watching me eat your brat's juicy little heart.'

Her baby was wailing in her arms now, but she didn't say a word.

She didn't so much as think about moving.

All that mattered was her baby. Keeping her safe. And so she didn't dare do a thing, not even when those sharp teeth lunged toward her and bit down hard into her neck.

She stood utterly frozen with terror, clutching her baby close while her attacker drew hard at the bleeding gash he'd made in her throat. His fingers elongated where he gripped her head and shoulder, the tips cutting into her like a demon's claws. He grunted and pulled deeper at her with his mouth and sharp teeth. Although her eyes were wide open in horror, her vision was going dark, her thoughts beginning to tumble, splintering into pieces. Everything around her was growing murky.

He was killing her. The monster was killing her. And then he would kill her baby, too.

'No.' She gulped in air, but tasted only blood. 'Goddamn you – No!'

With a desperate burst of will, she snapped her head into his, cracking the side of her skull into her attacker's face. When he snarled and reared back in surprise, she tore out of his grasp. She stumbled, nearly falling to her knees before she righted herself. One arm wrapped around her howling child, the other coming up to feel the slick, burning wound at her neck, she edged backward, away from the creature that lifted his head and sneered at her with glowing yellow eyes and bloodstained lips.

'Oh, God,' she moaned, sick at the sight.

She took another step back. Pivoted, prepared to bolt, even if it was pointless.

And that's when she saw the other one.

Fierce amber eyes looked right through her, but the hiss that sounded from between his huge, gleaming fangs promised death. She thought he would lace into her and finish what the first one had started, but he didn't. Guttural words were spat between the two of them, then the newcomer strode past her, a long silver blade in his hand.

Take the child, and go.

The command seemed to come out of nowhere, cutting through the fog of her mind. It came again, sharper now, spurring her into action. She ran.

Blind with panic, her mind numb with fear and confusion, she ran away from the terminal and down a nearby street. Deeper and deeper, she fled into the unfamiliar city, into the night. Hysteria clawed at her, making every noise – even the sound of her own running feet – seem monstrous and deadly.

And her baby wouldn't stop crying.

They were going to be found out if she didn't get the baby to quiet down. She had to put her to bed, nice and warm in her crib. Then her little girl would be happy. Then she'd be safe. Yes, that's what she had to do. Put the baby to bed, where the monsters couldn't find her.

She was tired herself, but she couldn't rest. Too dangerous. She had to get home before her mom realized she had missed curfew again. She was numb, disoriented, but she had to run. And so she did. She ran until she dropped, exhausted and unable to take another step.

When she woke sometime later, it was to feel her mind coming unhinged, cracking apart like an eggshell. Sanity was peeling away from her, reality warping into something black and slippery, something that was dancing farther and farther out of her reach.

She heard muffled crying somewhere in the distance. Such a tiny sound. She put her hands up to cover her ears, but she could still hear that helpless little mewl.

'Hush,' she murmured to no one in particular, rocking back and forth. 'Be quiet now, the baby's sleeping. Be quiet be quiet be quiet. . . .'

But the crying kept on. It didn't stop, and didn't stop. It tore at her heart as she sat in the filthy street and stared, unseeing, into the coming dawn.

CHAPTER ONE

PRESENT DAY

R emarkable. Just look at the use of light and shadow. . . .'
'You see how this image hints at the sorrow of the place,
yet manages to convey a promise of hope?'

'. . . one of the youngest photographers to be included in
the museum's new modern art collection.'

Gabrielle Maxwell stood back from the group of exhibit
attendees, nursing a flute of warm champagne as yet another
crowd of faceless, nameless, Very Important People enthused
over the two dozen black-and-white photographs displayed on
the gallery walls. She glanced at the images from across the
room, somewhat bemused. They were good photographs – a
bit edgy, their subject matter being abandoned mills and deso-
late dockyards outside Boston – but she didn't quite get what
everyone else was seeing in them.

Then again, she never did. Gabrielle merely took the photographs; she left their interpretation, and ultimately, their appreciation, up to others. An introvert by nature, it made her
uncomfortable to be on the receiving end of this much praise
and attention . . . but it did pay the bills. Quite nicely, at that.
Tonight, it was also paying the bills for her friend Jamie, the
owner of the funky little art gallery on Newbury Street, which,
at ten minutes to closing, was still packed with prospective buyers.

Numb with the whole process of meeting and greeting, of smiling politely as everyone from moneyed Back Bay wives to multipierced, tattooed Goths tried to impress one another – and her – with analyses of her work, Gabrielle couldn't wait for the exhibit to end. She had been hiding in the shadows for the past hour, contemplating a stealth escape to the comfort of a warm shower and a soft pillow, both waiting at her apartment on the city's east side.

But she had promised a few of her friends – Jamie, Kendra, and Megan – that she would join them for dinner and drinks after the showing. As the last couple of stragglers made their purchases and left, Gabrielle found herself gathered up and swept into a cab before she had a chance to so much as think of begging off.

'What an awesome night!' Jamie's androgynous blond hair swung around his face as he leaned across the other two women to clutch Gabrielle's hand. 'I've never had so much weekend traffic in the gallery – and tonight's sales receipts were amazing! Thank you so much for letting me host you.'

Gabrielle smiled at her friend's excitement. 'Of course. No need to thank me.'

'You weren't too miserable, were you?'

'How could she be, with half of Boston falling at her feet?' gushed Kendra, before Gabrielle could answer for herself. 'Was that the governor I saw you talking with over the canapés?'

Gabrielle nodded. 'He's offered to commission some original works for his cottage on the Vineyard.'

'Sweet!'

'Yeah,' Gabrielle replied without much enthusiasm. She had a stack of business cards in her pocketbook – at least a year of steady work, if she wanted it – so why was she tempted to open the taxi window and scatter them all to the wind?

She let her gaze drift to the night outside the car, watching in queer detachment as lights and lives flickered past. The streets teemed with people: couples strolling hand in hand, groups of friends laughing and talking, all of them having a great time. They dined at café tables outside trendy bistros and paused to browse store window displays. Everywhere she looked, the city pulsed with color and life. Gabrielle absorbed it all with her artist's eye and, yet, felt nothing. This bustle of life – her life as well – seemed to be speeding by without her. More and more lately, she felt as if she were caught on a wheel that wouldn't stop spinning her around, trapping her in an endless cycle of passing time and little purpose.

'Is anything wrong, Gab?' Megan asked from beside her on the taxi's bench seat. 'You seem quiet.'

Gabrielle shrugged. 'I'm sorry. I'm just . . . I don't know. Tired, I guess.'

'Somebody get this woman a drink – stat!' Kendra, the dark-haired nurse, joked.

'Nah,' Jamie countered, sly and catlike. 'What our Gab really needs is a man. You're too serious, sweetie. It's not healthy to let your work consume you like you do. Have some fun! When's the last time you got laid, anyway?'

Too long ago but Gabrielle wasn't really keeping track. She'd never suffered from a shortage of dates when she wanted them, and sex – on those rare occasions she had it – wasn't something she obsessed over like some of her friends. As out of practice as she was right now in that department, she didn't think an orgasm was going to cure whatever was causing her current state of restlessness.

'Jamie is right, you know,' Kendra was saying. 'You need to loosen up, get a little wild.'

'No time like the present,' Jamie added.

'Oh, I don't think so,' Gabrielle said, shaking her head. 'I'm really not up for a late night, you guys. Gallery showings always take a lot out of me and I –'

'Driver?' Ignoring her, Jamie slid to the edge of the seat and rapped on the Plexiglas that separated the cabbie from his passengers. 'Change of plans. We decided we're in the mood for celebrating, so ixnay on the restaurant. We wanna go where all the hot people are.'

'If you like dance clubs, there's a new one just opened in the north end,' the cabbie said, his spearmint chewing gum cracking as he spoke. 'I been takin' fares over there all week. Fact, took two already tonight – fancy after-hours place called La Notte.'

'Ooh, La No-tay,' Jamie purred, tossing a playful look over his shoulder and arching an elegant brow. 'Sounds perfectly wicked to me, girls. Let's go!'

The club, La Notte, was housed in a High Victorian Gothic building that had long been known as St. John's Trinity Parish church, until recent Archdiocese of Boston payouts on priest sex scandals forced the closings of dozens of such places around the city. Now, as Gabrielle and her friends made their way inside the crowded club, synthesized trance and techno music rang in the rafters, blasting out of enormous speakers that framed the DJ pit in the balcony above the altar. Strobe lights flashed against a trio of arched stained-glass windows. The pulsing beams cut through the thin cloud of smoke that hung in the air, pounding to the frenetic beat of a seemingly endless song. On the dance floor – and in nearly every square foot of La Notte's main floor and the gallery above – people moved against one another in writhing, mindless sensuality.

'Holy shit,' Kendra shouted over the music, raising her arms and dancing her way through the thick crowd. 'What a place, huh? This is crazy!'

They hadn't even cleared the first knot of clubbers before a tall, lean guy swooped in on the spunky brunette and bent to say something in her ear. Kendra gave a throaty laugh and nodded enthusiastically at him.

'Boy wants to dance,' she giggled, passing her handbag to Gabrielle. 'Who am I to refuse!'

'This way,' Jamie said, pointing to a small, empty table near the bar as their friend trotted off with her partner.

The three of them got seated and Jamie ordered a round of drinks. Gabrielle scanned the dance floor for Kendra, but she'd been devoured in the midst of the crowded space. Despite the crush of people all around, Gabrielle could not dismiss the sudden sensation that she and her friends were sitting in a spotlight. Like they were somehow under scrutiny simply for being in the club. It was nuts to think it. Maybe she had been working too much, spending too much time alone at home, if being out in public could make her feel so self-conscious. So paranoid.

'Here's to Gab!' Jamie exclaimed over the roar of the music, raising his martini glass in salute.

Megan lifted hers, too, and clinked it against Gabrielle's. 'Congratulations on a great exhibit tonight!'

'Thanks, you guys.'

As she sipped the neon yellow concoction, Gabrielle's feeling of being observed returned. Or rather, increased. She felt a stare reach out to her from across the darkened distance. Over the rim of her martini glass, she glanced up and caught the glint of a strobe light nicking off a pair of dark sunglasses.

Sunglasses hiding a gaze that was unmistakably fixed on her through the crowd.

The quick flashes from the strobes cast his stark features in hard shadow, but Gabrielle's eyes took him in at once. Spiky black hair falling loosely around a broad, intelligent brow and lean, angular cheeks. A strong, stern jaw. And his mouth . . . his mouth was generous and sensual, even when quirked in that cynical, almost cruel line.

Gabrielle looked away, unnerved, a rush of warmth skittering along her limbs. His face lingered in her head, burned there in an instant, like an image set to film. She put down her drink and braved another quick glance to where he stood. But he was gone.

A loud crash sounded at the other end of the bar, jerking Gabrielle's attention over her shoulder. At one of the crowded tables, liquor seeped onto the floor, spilled from several broken glasses that littered the black-lacquered surface. Five guys in dark leather and shades were having words with another guy wearing a Dead Kennedys wife-beater tank and torn, faded blue jeans. One of the thugs in leather had his arm slung around a drunk-looking platinum blond, who seemed to know the punker. Boyfriend, apparently. He made a grab for the girl's arm, but she slapped him away and bent her head to let one of the thugs put his mouth on her neck. She stared defiantly at her furious boyfriend, all the while playing with the long brown hair of the guy fastened to her throat.

'That's messed up,' Megan said, turning back around as the situation escalated.

'Sure is,' Jamie added as he finished off his martini and flagged a server to bring another round. 'Evidently that chick's mama forgot to tell her it's bad news not to leave with the guy who brought you.'

Gabrielle watched for another moment, long enough to see a second biker move in on the girl and descend on her slackened mouth. She accepted both of them together, her hands coming up to caress the dark head at her neck and the pale one that was sucking her face like he meant to eat her alive. The punker boyfriend shouted a string of obscenities at the girl, then turned around and shoved his way into the spectating crowd.

'This place is creeping me out,' Gabrielle confided, just now noticing some clubbers openly doing lines of cocaine off the far end of the long marble bar.

Her friends didn't seem to hear her over the driving pound of the music. They also didn't seem to share Gabrielle's unease.

Something wasn't quite right here and Gabrielle could not shake the feeling that eventually the night was going to get ugly. Jamie and Megan began talking between themselves about local bands, leaving Gabrielle to sip what was left of her martini and wait on the other side of the small table for an opportunity to break in and make her excuses to leave.

Essentially alone at the moment, her gaze drifted over the sea of bobbing heads and swaying bodies, as she surreptitiously searched for the sunglass-shaded eyes that had been watching her before. Was he with the other thugs – one of that gang of bikers still stirring up trouble? He was dressed like them, certainly carried the same dark air of danger about him.

Whoever he was, Gabrielle saw no trace of him now.

She leaned back in her chair, then nearly jumped out of her skin when a pair of hands came to rest on her shoulders from behind.

'Here you are! I've been looking all over for you guys!' Kendra said, sounding breathless and animated at the same time, as she leaned over the table. 'Come on. I've got a table for us on the other side of the club. Brent and some of his friends want to party with us!'

'Cool!'

Jamie was already on his feet, ready to go. Megan took her fresh martini in one hand, Kendra's and her pocketbooks in the other. When Gabrielle didn't rush to join them, Megan paused.

'You coming?'

'No.' Gabrielle stood up and looped the strap of her handbag over her shoulder. 'You go on, have fun. I'm beat. I think I'm just going to catch a cab and head back home.'

Kendra gave her a little-girl pout. 'Gab, you can't go!'

'You want some company for the ride home?' Megan offered, even though Gabrielle could tell she wanted to stay with the others.

'I'll be fine. Enjoy yourselves, but be careful, right?'

'You're sure you won't stay? Just one more drink?'

'Nah. I really need to take off and get some air.'

'Suit yourself, then,' Kendra chided with mock venom. She stepped in and planted a quick peck on Gabrielle's cheek. As she withdrew, Gabrielle caught a whiff of vodka, and, beneath that, something less obvious. Something musky, queerly metallic. 'You're a buzzkill, Gab, but I still love you.'

With a wink, Kendra looped her arms with Jamie's and Megan's, then playfully tugged them toward the churning mass of people.

'Call me tomorrow,' Jamie mouthed over his shoulder as the trio were slowly engulfed by the crowd.

Gabrielle immediately started her trek for the door, anxious to be out of the club. The longer she had stayed, the louder the music seemed to get, drumming in her head, making it hard to think. Hard to focus on her surroundings. People pushed at her from all sides as she tried to pass through them, squeezing her into the press of dancing, flailing, gyrating bodies. She was jostled and nudged, pawed at and groped by unseen hands in the dark, until, finally, she stumbled into the vestibule near the club's entrance, then out the heavy double doors.

The night was cool and dark. She drew in a deep breath, clearing her head of the noise and smoke and the unsettling atmosphere of La Notte. The music still throbbed out here, the strobe lights still flashed like small explosions behind the tall stained-glass windows above, but Gabrielle relaxed a bit now that she was free.

No one paid her any mind as she hurried down to the curb and waited to hail a ride home. Only a few people were outside, some passing by on the sidewalk below, others filing up the concrete steps and into the club. She spotted a yellow cab coming her way, and thrust out her hand to call it over.

'Taxi!'

As the empty cab navigated across the lanes of nighttime traffic and roared up beside her, the doors of the nightclub burst open with the force of a hurricane.

'Hey, man! What the fuck!' Behind Gabrielle on the steps, a male voice rose to an octave just north of fear. 'Touch me again, and I'll fuckin' –'

'You'll fuckin' what?' taunted another voice, this one low and deadly, and flanked by several others that were chuckling in amusement.

'Yeah, tell us, you little asswipe punker piece of shit. What're ya gonna do?'

Her fingers gripping the door handle of the cab, Gabrielle swiveled her head, half in alarm, half in knowing dread of what she would see. It was the gang from the bar, the bikers or whatever they were, in black leather and shades. The six of them circled the punker boyfriend like a pack of wolves, taking turns jabbing at him, toying with him like prey.

The kid threw a swing at one of them – missed – and the situation went from bad to worse in the blink of an eye.

All at once, the scuffle came crashing toward Gabrielle. The gang of thugs threw the punker up against the hood of the cab, slamming their fists into the kid's face. Blood splattered like raindrops from his nose and mouth, some of it hitting Gabrielle. She took a step back, stunned and horrified. The kid scrabbled to get away but his attackers stayed on him, beating him with a fury Gabrielle could hardly fathom.

'Get off my goddamn car!' the cabbie shouted out his open window. 'Jesus Christ! Take it somewhere else, you hear me!'

One of the assailants turned his head toward the cabbie, smiled a terrible smile, then brought his large fist down on the windshield, shattering the glass into a spiderweb of cracks. Gabrielle saw the cabbie cross himself, his mouth working soundlessly within the car. There was a grinding of gears, then a piercing screech of tires as the taxi jerked into reverse, dislodging the burden from its hood.

'Wait!' Gabrielle screamed, too late.

Her ride home – her escape from this brutal scene – was gone. With a cold lump of fear lodged in her throat, she watched the cab speed off, careering into the street and its tail-lights disappearing into the dark.

And on the curb, the six bikers were showing their victim no mercy, too preoccupied with beating the punker senseless to give Gabrielle more than a passing thought.

She turned and bolted up the steps to La Notte's entrance, all the while fishing in her pocketbook for her cell phone. She found the slim device, flipped it open. Punched in 911 as she threw open the doors of the club and skidded into the vestibule, panic rising in her breast. Above the din of music and voices, and the thundering pulse of her own heart, Gabrielle heard only static on the other end of her cell. She pulled the phone away from her ear –

Signal faded.

'Shit!'

She tried 911 again. No luck.

Gabrielle ran for the main area of the club, shouting into the noise in desperation.

'Someone, please help! I need help!'

No one seemed to hear her. She tapped people's shoulders, tugged on sleeves, practically shook the arm of a tattooed military-looking guy, but no one paid any attention. They didn't even look at her, merely continued dancing and talking as if she wasn't even there.

Was this a dream? Some twisted nightmare where only she was aware of the violence taking place outside?

Gabrielle gave up on strangers and decided to search out her friends. As she wended through the dark club, she kept hitting *Redial*, praying for a decent signal. She couldn't get one, and she soon realized she would never find Jamie and the others in the thick crowd.

Frustrated and confused, she ran back to the club's exit. Maybe she could flag down a motorist, find a cop, anything!

Frigid night air hit her face as she pushed open the heavy doors and stepped outside. She dashed down the first set of concrete steps, panting now, uncertain what she was walking into, a woman alone against six, probably drugged-out gang members. But she didn't see them.

They were gone.

A group of young clubbers came strolling up the steps, one of them playing air guitar while his friends talked about hitting a rave later that night.

'Hey,' Gabrielle said, half expecting them to walk right past her. They paused, smiling at her, even though at twenty-eight she was likely a decade older than any of them.

The one in the lead nodded his head at her. ' 'Sup?'

'Did any of you –' She hesitated, not certain she should be relieved that this was not, evidently, a dream after all. 'Did you happen to see the fight that was going on out here a few minutes ago?'

'There was a fight? Awesome!' said the headbanger of the group.

'Nah, man,' answered another. 'We just got here. We ain't seen nothin'.'

They passed by, climbing the rest of the steps while Gabrielle could only watch, wondering if she was losing her mind. She walked down to the curb. There was blood on the pavement, but the punker and his attackers had vanished.

Gabrielle stood under a streetlamp and rubbed a chill from her arms. She pivoted to look down both sides of the street, searching for any sign of the violence she had witnessed a few minutes before.

Nothing.

But then . . . she heard it.

The sound drifted from a narrow alley to her right. Flanked by a concrete shoulder-high wall that acted as an acoustic aid, the almost lightless walkway betrayed its occupants whose faint animal-like grunts carried out to the street. Gabrielle could not place the sick, wet sounds that froze her blood in her veins and tripped off instinctual alarms in every nerve in her body.

Her feet were moving. Not away from the source of those disturbing sounds, but toward it. Her cell phone was like a brick in her hand. She was holding her breath. She didn't realize she wasn't breathing until she had walked a couple of paces into the alleyway and her gaze had settled on a group of figures up ahead.

The thugs in leather and sunglasses.

They were crouched down on their hands and knees, pawing at something, tearing at it. In the scant light from the street, Gabrielle glimpsed a tattered scrap of fabric lying near the carnage. It was the punker's tank top, shredded and stained.

Gabrielle's finger, poised over the *Redial* button of her cell phone, came down silently onto the tiny key. There was a quiet trill on the other end, then the police dispatcher's voice shattered the night like cannon fire.

'911. What is your emergency?'

One of the bikers swung his head around at the sudden disturbance. Feral, hate-filled eyes pinned Gabrielle like daggers where she stood. His face was bloody, slick with gore. And his teeth! They were sharp like an animal's – not teeth at all, but fangs that he bared to her as he opened his mouth and hissed a terrible-sounding foreign word.

'911,' said the dispatcher once again. 'Please state your emergency.'

Gabrielle couldn't speak. She was so shaken, she could hardly breathe. She brought the cell phone up to her mouth, but could not make her throat form words.

Her call for help was wasted.

Knowing this with a certain, bone-deep dread, Gabrielle did the only logical thing that came to her. With trembling fingers, she turned the device toward the gang of sadistic bikers and clicked the image-capture button. A small flash lit up the alley.

They all turned toward her now, raising their hands to shield their sunglass-shaded eyes.

Oh, God. Maybe she still had a chance of escaping this hellish night. Gabrielle clicked the picture button again and again and again, all the while making her retreat back up the alley to the street. She heard murmured voices, snarled curses, the movement of feet on pavement, but she didn't dare look back. Not even when a sharp hiss of steel rang out behind her, followed by unearthly shrieks of agony and rage.

Gabrielle raced into the night on adrenaline and fear, not stopping until she reached a standing taxi on Commercial Street. She jumped in and slammed the door. She was panting, out of her mind with fear.

'Take me to the nearest police station!'

The cabbie slung his arm over the back of the seat and turned around to stare at her, frowning. 'You okay, lady?'

'Yeah,' she replied automatically. Then, 'No. I need to report a –'

Jesus. What *did* she intend to report? A cannibalistic feeding frenzy by a pack of rabid bikers? Or the only other possible explanation, which wasn't any more believable?

Gabrielle met the cabbie's anxious eyes. 'Please hurry. I just witnessed a murder.'

Reality shifts to a dark and deadly realm when Gabrielle Maxwell witnesses a murder outside a night-club; in a shattering instance she is thrust into a world where vampires stalk the shadows and a blood war is set to ignite. Her future bound to a black-haired stranger who stirs her deepest fantasies, she must confront a destiny of danger, seductions and the darkest pleasures of all...

Robinson
978-1-84901-106-8
£6.99

www.constablerobinson.com

To order any of the **Lara Adrian** titles simply contact The Book Service (TBS) by phone, email or by post.
Alternatively visit our website at www.constablerobinson.com.

No. of copies	Title	RRP	Total
	Kiss of Midnight	£6.99	
	Kiss of Crimson	£6.99	
	Midnight Awakening	£6.99	
	Midnight Rising	£6.99	
	Veil of Midnight	£6.99	
	Shades of Midnight	£6.99	
		Grand total	

FREEPOST RLUL-SJGC-SGKJ, Cash Sales Direct Mail Dept.,
The Book Service, Colchester Road, Frating, Colchester, CO7 7DW

Tel: +44 (0) 1206 255 800
Fax: +44 (0) 1206 255 930
Email: sales@tbs-ltd.co.uk

UK customers: please allow £1.00 p&p for the first book, plus 50p for the second, and an additional 30p for each book thereafter, up to a maximum charge of £3.00.

Overseas customers (incl. Ireland): please allow £2.00 p&p for the first book, plus £1.00 for the second, plus 50p for each additional book.

NAME (block letters): _____

ADDRESS: _____

_____

_____ POSTCODE: _____

I enclose a cheque/PO (payable to 'TBS Direct') for the amount of £ _

I wish to pay by Switch/Credit Card

Card number: _____

Expiry date: _____Switch issue number: _____